The Cajun Cowboy

Sandra Hill

NEW YORK   BOSTON

Warner Forever is a registered trademark of Warner Books Inc.

Cover art and design by Shasti O'Leary Soudant
Book design by Giorgetta Bell McRee

Warner Books

Time Warner Book Group
1271 Avenue of the Americas
New York, NY 10020
Visit our Web site at www.twbookmark.com

Printed in the United States of America

First Paperback Printing: June 2004

10 9 8 7 6 5 4 3 2 1

ACCLAIM FOR AWARD-WINNING AUTHOR SANDRA HILL AND HER PREVIOUS (USA TODAY) BESTSELLER TALL, DARK, AND CAJUN

"Fast-moving . . . the bayou setting filled with humor . . . The love scenes had me running for a tall glass of iced tea. This is one of those books I wanted to devour in one sitting."
—TheWordonRomance. com

"Get ready for hours of laughter, page-turning intrigue, passion, sexy hunks, and danger . . . *Tall, Dark, and Cajun* is even better than I dreamed it would be."
—RoadtoRomance.dhs.org

"A funny, sexy sizzler that's smokin' hot and spicy enough to flame roast a reader's sensibilities . . . zesty, witty, outrageous, and very, very enjoyable."
—Heartstrings (RomanticFiction.tripod.com)

"If you like your romances hot and spicy and your men the same way, then you will like *Tall, Dark, and Cajun* . . . eccentric characters, witty dialogue, humorous situations . . . and hot romance . . . [Hill] perfectly captures the bayou's mystique and makes it come to life."
—RomRevToday.com

"Downright laugh-out-loud funny. You'll need to splash water on yourself between giggle fits. The novel has everything . . . to keep you interested from beginning to end."
—BookHaunts.net

"A great story with lots of laughs, emotions, and sizzling scenes."
—WritersUnlimited.com

Effervescent . . . readers are advised not to miss this story."
—Bookloons.com

ALSO BY SANDRA HILL

Tall, Dark, and Cajun

This book is dedicated with much gratitude to Elisa Chauvin, a southern Louisiana lady, who was a godsend to this Yankee writer.

Elisa wrote to me one time with great excitement on hearing that I was going to be writing a book called *The Cajun Cowboy*. She wanted me to know that there really are Cajun cowboys today; in fact, she is married to one.

With much poignancy she told me that Cajun cowboys, and her husband in particular, work hard at their jobs, but then they enjoy a rip-roaring good time, which usually involves Cajun music and food. They can wink and grin with the best of them, but in the end they are strong family men who know how to take care of their women. Does that sound like the hero of a romance novel?

Elisa also shared her grandmother's Cajun recipe book with me, and she vetted the early stages of this novel for Louisiana and ranch details. She sent me tons of photos of the Brown Saddle Club to which her husband belongs. I posted one of those photos on my Web site, and more than a few single ladies wanted to know if any of these handsome cowboys were eligible.

Thank you, Elisa.

The
Cajun Cowboy

Chapter 1

Give me a buzz, baby . . .

"I'm a born-again virgin."

Charmaine LeDeux made that pronouncement with a faint feminine belch after downing three of the six oyster shooters sitting on the table before her at The Swamp Tavern. She was halfway to meeting her goal of getting knee-walking buzzed.

The jukebox played a soft Jimmy Newman rendition of "Louisiana, The Key to My Soul." The jambalaya cooking in the kitchen filled the air with pungent spices. Gater, the bald-headed, longtime bartender, washed glasses behind the bar.

Louise Rivard—better known as Tante Lulu—sat on the opposite side of the booth from Charmaine. She arched a brow at the potent drinks in front of Charmaine compared to her single glass of plain RC cola and looked pointedly at Charmaine's stretchy red T-shirt with its hairdresser logo I CAN BLOW YOU AWAY. Only then did the old lady declare, "And I'm Salome about to lose a few veils." In fact, Tante Lulu, who had to be close to eighty, *was* wearing a harem-style outfit because of a belly dance class she planned to attend on the other side of Houma that afternoon. In the basement of Our Lady of the Bayou Church, no less! But first, she'd agreed to be Charmaine's designated driver.

"I'm sher . . . I mean, serious." Charmaine felt a little woozy already. "My life is a disaster. Twenty-nine years old, and I've been married and divorced four times. Haven't had a date in six months. And I've got a loan shark on my tail."

"A fish? Whass a fish have to do with anything?" Tante Lulu sputtered.

Sometimes Charmaine suspected that Tante Lulu was deliberately dense. But she was precious to Charmaine, who teared up just thinking about all the times the old lady's cottage had been a refuge to her whenever she'd run away from unbearable home conditions. Being the illegitimate daughter of a stripper and the notorious womanizer Valcour LeDeux had made for a rocky childhood, with Tante Lulu being a little girl's only anchor. She wasn't even Charmaine's blood relative; she was blood aunt only to Charmaine's half brothers, Luc, René, and Remy.

So, it was with loving patience that Charmaine explained, "Not just any fish. A shark. Bobby Doucet wants fifty thousand dollars by next Friday or he's gonna put a Mafia hit on me; I didn't even know they had a Mafia in southern Loo-zee-anna. Or maybe they'll just break my knees. Jeesh! Yep, I'd say it's time for some new beginnings. I'm gonna be a born-again virgin."

"What? You doan think the Sopranos kill virgins?" Tante Lulu remarked drolly. "And, yeah, there's a Mafia in Louisiana. Ain't you never heard of the Dixie Mafia?"

"The born-again-virgin thingee is a personal change. The loan-shark thingee would require a different kind of change . . . like fifty thousand dollars, and it's going up a thousand dollars a day in interest. I gotta get out of Dodge fast."

Tante Lulu did a few quick calculations in her head. "Charmaine! Thass 10 percent per day. What were you thinkin'?" Tante Lulu might talk a little dumb sometimes, but she was no dummy.

Charmaine shrugged. "I thought I'd be able to pay it off in a few days. It started out at twenty thousand, by the way."

"Tsk-tsk-tsk!"

"I don't suppose you could lend me the money?"

"Me, I ain't got that kind of money. I thought yer biz-ness was goin' good. What happened?"

"The business is great." Charmaine owned two beauty shops, one in Lafayette and the other a spa here in Houma. Both of them prospered, even in a slow economy, or at least broke even. Apparently, women didn't consider personal appearance a luxury. Nope, her spas were not the problem. "I made a lot of money in the stock market a few years back. That's when I bought my second shop. But I got careless this year and bought some technology stocks on margin. I lost more money than I put in. It was a temporary problem, which spiraled out of control when I borrowed money from Bucks 'r Us. Who knew it was a loan-shark operation?"

"Well, it sure as shootin' doan sound like a bank. Have you gone to the police?"

"Hell's bells, no! I'd be deader'n a Dorchat duck within the hour if I did that."

"How 'bout Luc?" Lucien LeDeux was Charmaine's half brother and a well-known local lawyer.

She nodded. "He's working on it. In the meantime, he suggested, maybe facetiously, that I hire a bodyguard."

Tante Lulu brightened. "I could be yer bodyguard. Me, I got a rifle in the trunk of my T-bird outside. You want I should off Bobby Doucet? Bam-bam! I could do it. I think."

Off? Where does she get this stuff? Charmaine groaned. *That's all I need . . . a senior-citizen, one-woman posse.* "Uh, no thanks." With those words, Charmaine tossed back another shot glass filled with a raw oyster drowning in Tabasco sauce, better known with good reason as Cajun Lightning, then followed it immediately with a chaser of pure one-hundred-proof bourbon. "Whoo-ee!" she said, accompanied by a full-body shiver.

"Back to that other thing," Tante Lulu said. "Charmaine, honey, you caint jist decide to be a virgin again. It's like tryin' to put the egg back together once the shell's been cracked. Like Humpty Dumpty."

Hump me, dump me. That oughta be my slogan. Oughta have it branded on my forehead.

A more upbeat song, "Cajun Born," came on the jukebox, and Charmaine jerked upright. Shaking her fifty-pound head slowly from side to side, she licked her lips, which were starting to get numb. "Can so," she argued irrationally. Or was that rationally? Whatever. "Be a virgin again, I mean. It's a big trend. Some lady even wrote a book about it. There's Web sites all over the Internet where girls promise to be celibate till their wedding day. Born-again virgins."

"Hmpfh!" was Tante Lulu's only response as she sipped on her straw.

"Besides, I might even have my hymen surgically replaced."

Tante Lulu was a noted *traiteur*, or healer, all along the bayou, and she was outrageous beyond belief in her antics and attire. For once, Charmaine had managed to shock her. "Is hey-man what I think it is?"

"It's hi-man, and yes, it is what you think."

"Hey, hi . . . big difference! You are goin' off the deep end, girlie, iffen yer thinkin' of havin' some quack sew you up *there*."

Deep end is right. "I didn't say I was going to do it, for sure. Just considering it. But born-again virgin, that I am gonna do, for sure."

"Hmmm. I really do doubt that, sweetie," Tante Lulu said, peering off toward the front of the tavern, which was mostly empty in the middle of the afternoon on a weekday.

Frankly, I shouldn't be here, either, Charmaine thought. She should be at one of her shops, but she was afraid Mafia thugs would catch up with her in advance of the deadline.

"Seems to me that all yer resolutions are 'bout to melt," Tante Lulu chortled.

Charmaine turned to see what Tante Lulu was gawking at with that strange little smirk on her face. Then Charmaine did a double take.

It was Raoul Lanier, her first ex-husband. Some people called him Rusty, a nickname he'd gained as an adolescent when his changing voice had sounded like a creaking, rusty door. She'd preferred his real name in the past. He always said he liked the way it sounded on her tongue, slow and sexy, especially when . . .

She'd been a nineteen-year-old student at LSU and former Miss Louisiana when she'd married Rusty. He'd been twenty-one and a hotshot football player and premed student at the same school. As good as he'd been at football, which earned him a scholarship, his dream had always been to be a veterinarian. His last words to her before they'd parted had been, "Once a bimbo, always a bimbo." She would never forgive or forget those words. Never.

Charmaine had been avoiding Rusty for weeks, ever since he got released from prison. And, yes, she was bound and determined to think of him as Rusty now. She thought about ducking under the table, but he'd already seen her. And he had a look in his dark Cajun eyes, unusually grim today, that said, "Here I come, baby. Batten down the hatches."

Man-oh-man, her hatches had always been weak where Rusty was concerned. All he had to do was wink at her, and she melted. He wore faded Wrangler jeans with battered, low-heeled boots, a long-sleeved denim shirt, and a cowboy hat. He was six-foot-three of gorgeous, dark-skinned, dark-haired Cajun testosterone. Temptation on the hoof.

Good thing she was a born-again virgin.

Women are the root of all trouble, guar-an-teed!

Finally, after a month of off-and-on bird-dogging Charmaine, Raoul had finally caught up with her. She wasn't going to escape.

"Ladies." He took off his hat and nodded a greeting, first at Charmaine, then at Tante Lulu, who together made an odd couple, with Charmaine being so tall at five feet nine and the old lady such an itty-bitty thing at barely five feet. And Tante Lulu was wearing the most outlandish outfit. Looked like a belly dancer suit or something. But then, Charmaine wasn't any better. She wore her usual suggestive attire designed to tease, which didn't bear close scrutiny in his present mood. Not that he wasn't teasable, especially after two years in the state pen.

But, no, he couldn't blame his reaction to Charmaine on his two years of forced celibacy. She'd always had that hair-trigger arousal effect on him. When she'd dumped him ten years ago, he'd about died. Quit school for a semester. Lost his football scholarship. A nightmare. Every time he'd heard about her remarrying, he'd relived the pain. He couldn't go through that again, especially not with all the current problems in his life.

Steel yourself, buddy. She's only a woman, the logical side of his brain said.

Hah! the perverse side said.

He pulled up a chair and sat down, propping his long legs, and crossing them at the ankles on the edge of Charmaine's side of the booth, barring any hasty departure on her part. He was no fool. He recognized the panic in her wide whiskey eyes.

After taking a swallow from the long neck he'd purchased at the bar, he set the bottle down, noticing for the first time the line of oyster shooters in front of Charmaine. Holy shit! Had she really drunk four of them already? In the middle of the afternoon?

"What are we celebrating, *chère*?" he asked.

"*We* aren't celebrating anything," Charmaine answered churlishly.

Hey, I'm the one who should be churlish here, Ms. Snotty.

"We're celebrating Charmaine's virginity," Tante Lulu announced.

"Is that a fact?" Raoul said with a grin.

Charmaine groaned at Tante Lulu's announcement and downed another oyster shooter, first the oyster, then the bourbon. Gulp-gulp! He watched with fascination the shiver that rippled over her body from her throat, across her mighty-fine breasts, her belly, and all her extremities, including her legs encased in skintight black jeans. Then his eyes moved back to her breasts, and her nipples bloomed under her sizzling red hooker T-shirt. Charmaine watched him watching her and groaned again.

Was it possible he still affected her the way she affected him? *Don't go there, Raoul*, he advised himself.

Tante Lulu chuckled. "Yep, Charmaine's a born-again virgin. She's joinin' a club and everything. Might even have her doo-hickey sewed back up."

Raoul wasn't about to ask Tante Lulu what doo-hickey she referred to. Instead, he commented to Charmaine, "Hot damn, you always manage to surprise me, darlin'."

He immediately regretted his words when Charmaine batted her eyelashes at him and drawled, "That's my goal in life, *darlin'*."

He gritted his teeth. He was so damn mad at her, not because she was being sarcastic now, but because she'd made his life miserable the past few weeks . . . in fact, the past ten years.

Tante Lulu giggled. He glanced toward the old lady, not wanting to rehash old—or new—business in front of her. "Charmaine and I shouldn't be squabbling in front of you."

Tante Lulu just waved a hand in front of her face, and said, "Doan you nevermind me, boy. Squabble all you want. Jist pretend I'm not here."

Right. Like everything we say isn't going to be broadcast on the bayou grapevine by nightfall.

"Was you framed?" Tante Lulu asked him all of a sudden.

He hesitated. Getting sent to Angola for drug dealing was a sore subject with him and not one he was ready to discuss. "Yes," was all he disclosed in the end.

"I knew it!" Tante Lulu whooped, slapping her knee with a hand, which set her bells to jingling. "This is yer lucky day, boy, 'cause I been thinkin' 'bout becomin' a dick."

That pronouncement boggled his mind till he realized that the old lady meant private eye and that she was offering to help clear his name.

He heard Charmaine giggle at his discomfort.

"Uh, thanks for the offer, but no thanks."

"Are you still an animal doctor?"

Raoul's heart wrenched with pain, and he couldn't breathe for a second. This was definitely a subject he did not want to discuss. Finally, after unclenching his fists, he said tersely, "I lost my veterinary license when I went to prison."

"Oh, Raoul." That was Charmaine speaking. Her eyes were filled with sympathy.

Yep, that's what I want from you, babe. Pity. And now you call me Raoul. Talk about bad timing!

"Being a vet was always the most important thing in the world to you."

Not the most important thing. "I'll get it back."

"I hope so," she replied softly.

Before Tante Lulu had a chance to voice her opinion, he steered the conversation in another direction. "What's the reason for the binge, Charmaine?"

"None of your business." She licked her flame red lips, which were probably desensitized from all the booze.

He'd like a shot at sensitizing them up.

No, no, no! I would not. That would be a bad idea. I am not going to fall for Charmaine again. No way!

Still, if she doesn't stop licking those kiss-me-quick lips, I might just leap over the table and do it for her.

Back at the beginning of time—probably post-Garden of Eden since Adam was a dunce, for sure, when it came to Eve—men had learned an important lesson that even today hadn't sunk in with women. The female of the species should never lick anything in front of the male. Licking gave men ideas. Raoul would bet his boots good ol' Eve had licked that apple first before offering it to Adam. *So, keep on lickin', Charmaine, and you might just see what's tickin'.*

"The Mafia is after her," Tante Lulu said. "And her life's in the outhouse."

"The toilet," Charmaine corrected her aunt, with another lick.

"Huh?" Raoul had lost his train of thought somewhere between Charmaine's new virginity and her licking exercise.

"You asked why Charmaine's on a binge. And I said the Mafia is after her," Tante Lulu explained. "You thick or sumpin', boy?"

Raoul should have been insulted, but it was hard to get angry with the old lady, who didn't really mean any offense. Tante Lulu just smiled at him. Every time she moved, the bells on her belly dancer outfit chimed.

"Great outfit, by the way," he remarked. It was always smart to stay on Tante Lulu's good side.

"It's a *bedleh*," she informed him.

He said, "How interesting!" Then he addressed Charmaine. "What's this about the Mafia, darlin'?"

"Don't call me darlin'. I am not your darlin'." How like Charmaine to home in on the most irrelevant thing he'd said.

"They's gonna kill her, or break her knees," Tante Lulu interjected.

"How about her doo-hickey?" he teased.

But Tante Lulu took him seriously. "They doan know 'bout that yet."

"Tante Lulu! I can speak for myself," Charmaine said. She turned to him, slowly, as if aware she might topple over—which seemed a real possibility. "I just have a little money problem to settle with Bucks 'r Us."

Her words were slurred a bit, but he got the message. "A loan shark? You borrowed money from a loan shark?"

"Doan s'pose you have fifty thousand dollars to spare?" Tante Lulu inquired of him.

"Fifty thou?" he mouthed to Charmaine, who just nodded. "No, I can't say that I do."

Charmaine probably hadn't expected him to help her, and the question hadn't even come from her. Still, her shoulders drooped with disappointment.

In that moment, despite everything the flaky Charmaine had ever done to him, he wished he could help.

"So, you can see why Charmaine's a bit depressed," Tante Lulu said. "That, on top of her pushin' thirty, not havin' a date fer six months, and being married and divorced four times. Who wouldn't be depressed by that?" Tante Lulu stood then, her bells ting-a-linging, and said, "I'm outta here. Gotta go to belly dance class. Will you take Charmaine home, Rusty?"

"No!" Charmaine said.

"Yes," he said.

After the old lady left, he moved beside Charmaine in the booth, which required a little forceful pushing of his hips against hers. He put one arm over the back of the booth, just above her shoulders, and relished just for a brief moment the memory of how good Charmaine felt against him. Same perfume. Same big "Texas" hair as her beauty pageant days. Same sleek brunette color. Same soft-as-sin curves. "So, you haven't had a date in six months, huh? Poor baby!"

She lifted her chin with that stubborn pride of hers. "It's not because I haven't been asked."

"I don't doubt that for a minute, *chère*. And, hey, I haven't had a date in two years, so we're sort of even."

"Go away, Rusty. I want to get plastered in private."

He didn't mind people calling him Rusty, except for Charmaine. He wanted her to call him Raoul, in that slow, breathy way she had of saying Raaa-oool. No, it was better that she called him Rusty. Besides, it was an apt description of his equipment these days—out of use and rusty as hell.

"I have a bit of good news for you, baby." He could tell she didn't like his calling her baby by the way her body stiffened up like a steer on branding day. That was probably why he added, "Real good news, *baby*."

Her upper lip curled with disgust. She probably would have belted him one if she weren't half-drunk. "There isn't any news you could impart that I would be interested in hearing."

Wanna bet? "You know how Tante Lulu said you were depressed over being married and divorced four times?"

"Yeah?" she said hesitantly.

"Well, no need to be depressed over that anymore. Guess what? You're not."

She blinked several times with confusion. "Not what?"

"Divorced four times." He took a long swallow of his beer and waited.

It didn't take Charmaine long to figure it out, even in her fuzzy state. Her big brown eyes went wider, and her flushed face got redder. "You mean . . . ?"

He nodded. "You're not even a one-time divorcée, darlin'. You've never been divorced." *How do you like them apples, Mrs. Lanier?*

She sat up straighter, turned slowly in her seat to look at him directly, and asked with unflattering horror, "Rusty, are you saying that you and I are still married?"

"Yep, and you can start callin' me Raoul again anytime you want." *Dumb, dumb, dumb.*

That was when Charmaine leaned against his chest and swooned. Okay, she passed out, but he was taking it as a good sign.

Charmaine Lanier was still his wife, and it was gonna be payback time at the Triple L Ranch. Guar-an-teed!

Chapter 2

Waking from the dead . . .

Charmaine awakened slowly.

She felt as if her body were cemented to the mattress, and her head pounded mercilessly, but she was in the bedroom of her own little house out on Bayou Black. Good news, that.

But then she glanced downward and saw that she was wearing the same red T-shirt over black thong panties. And that was all.

Uh-oh! She turned her head slowly on the pillow, noticing the bright explosion of orange, yellow, and blue outside her window—the light show of a bayou dawn— meaning she must have slept a full twelve hours since the previous afternoon when she'd started out at Swampy's. She moaned then in remembrance. It all came back to her, even before the current bane of her existence walked in carrying a tray of strong-smelling Cajun coffee and whistling. Whistling when her head was about to explode!

"Hi, wifey," he said with way too much cheeriness. "Did you know you snore?"

I do not snore. Do I? Well, maybe when I'm sleeping

off a drunk, but I can't remember the last time I did that.
"Go away," she groaned, pulling the sheet over her head.
Under the linens, she swiped a hand across her mouth,
just to make sure she hadn't been drooling.

"Not till we talk," he insisted, "and you sign some
papers."

That sounded reasonable. He must want her to sign the
divorce papers, though she had done just that ten years
ago when his father, the late Charlie Lanier, had brought
them to her. She'd assumed that the divorce was formal-
ized after that. She could swear she'd received docu-
ments to that effect, but maybe not. She had not been in
a logical frame of mind, more like brain-splintering
devastated.

She sat up straighter and let the sheet fall to her waist.
Taking the mug of black coffee from him, she sipped
slowly, eyeing him warily as he walked about the bedroom checking out photographs and knick-knacks,
including a few St. Jude statues that Tante Lulu had gifted
her. St. Jude was the patron saint of hopeless causes, and
if ever there was a hopeless cause, she was it, apparently.
At the foot of her bed rested the "Good Luck" quilt Tante
Lulu had given her after her marriage to Rusty. Lot of
good it had done her. She saw the look Rusty gave the
hand-crafted heirloom; he probably recognized it since it
had been in their apartment. He must also recognize it as
a mark of her failure—well, *their* failure—and of hopes
dashed.

There were no pictures of Rusty in her room, if that
was what he was searching for. Too painful a reminder
of a short, blissful period in her life. They'd been married for only six months . . . or so she'd thought till
yesterday.

Are we really still married?

How awful! the logical side of her brain exclaimed.

How interesting! another part of her brain countered.

Charmaine was honest, if nothing else, and she had to admit to being a tiny bit thrilled at the prospect of Rusty Lanier still being her husband. Not that she was going to hop in the sack with him. *Uh-uh!*

Still . . .

And there was definitely exhilaration in knowing that she was no longer a four-time divorcée. Maybe she wasn't so inadequate, after all.

Rusty seemed to fill the room as he prowled about, poking in her stuff, but not just because of his six-foot-three height and her low ceilings. There had always been something compelling about him. People's heads turned when he walked down the street. Men, as well as women. No wonder she'd been sucked in before. Well, never again!

Still . . .

"I have to go to the bathroom," she said, once her head stopped spinning and her stomach settled down and she'd pulled her ogling eyes off Rusty's tantalizing figure. Cowboy charisma, that's all it was. There was something about women and cowboys, sort of like women and men in military uniforms. *That's all it is*, she told herself.

"So, go," he replied, settling his tight butt—which she was not noticing—into a low rocking chair. Rock, rock, rock, he went, just watching her in a most infuriating way.

"I'm not dressed and I'm not parading my bare behind in front of you."

He grinned. "Who do you think undressed you, *chère*?

Besides, there ain't nothin' you've got that I haven't seen a hundred times . . . maybe a thousand."

She bared her teeth at him. The schmuck! Flipping the sheet aside, she stood and walked past him, pretending not to care that she presented a full-monty posterior. No doubt he was comparing her twenty-nine-year-old butt to her nineteen-year-old one and finding her lacking or, worse, exceeding what she'd had before. She wasn't about to look and see his reaction, but she thought she heard him mutter, "Mercy!"

Once she was done in the bathroom, she brushed her teeth and hair, skinning the whole mess back into a high ponytail. She scrubbed her face clean, and considered putting makeup on—she never went out in public without makeup—but Rusty would probably think she did it for him; so she put that aside. Then, after pulling on a pair of capri pants, she went into the kitchen and turned on the radio. BeauSoleil was singing *"C'est un Péché de Dire un Menterie,"* their own rendition of that 1930s Fats Waller song "It's a Sin to Tell a Lie."

Rusty soon followed after her, leaning against the doorframe with a casualness belied by the grim expression on his face. He wore the same boots and jeans as yesterday, but somewhere he'd come up with a black T-shirt. And he'd shaved . . . probably with her razor and, yep—she sniffed the air—with her lilac shaving gel. He looked good enough to eat, and Charmaine was hungry.

"You look about nineteen and innocent as a kitten," he remarked, taking in her hairdo, scrubbed face, capri pants . . . in fact, all of her.

Rusty is hungry, too, she realized. But any pathetic notions Charmaine entertained in the feed-the-Cajun category, and she didn't mean food, soon evaporated with his next words.

"Charmaine, exactly how close were you to my father over the years?"

Her head shot up with surprise. There were some things about his father he didn't know . . . that his father hadn't wanted him to know. She hadn't lied to him during the time they'd been together or since, not exactly, but it had been a sin of omission. Like the song. "I visited your father occasionally, and I went to his funeral last year. I liked Charlie. I never got a chance to offer my sympathies to you on your father's death, but I *am* sorry."

He nodded his acceptance of her condolences.

"Charlie was saddened over our divorce, you know?"

"Our nondivorce," he reminded her. "And, no, I didn't know that he was saddened, or gladdened, by anything involving me. He never once came to see me in prison. At my insistence. My old man did not need to see me in that hellhole." He shook his head to clear it of unpleasant images. "But then, you didn't, either."

"Me?" *Why would he have expected me to visit him? Would he have even approved me for his visitor list? Does he still care? Does he think I do?* All that was beside the point. Charlie and his son had never been close. Although his parents had never married, paternity had never been an issue. Despite that, through no fault of Charlie's, the only time the father and son had been permitted to see each other were occasional weekends and summer visits. In Charmaine's opinion, his mother had been a world-class bitch, using her illegitimate son to get back at his father, just because he was an uneducated rancher. "Why did you ask about my relationship with your father?"

"Because he left you half the ranch."

Stunned, Charmaine just gaped at Rusty.

The hostility he leveled at her was palpable in the air. "Why do you suppose he did that, Charmaine?" Hard to believe that these same eyes, which were hard as black ice now, could ever have danced with mischief or gone smoky with passion.

"I . . . I don't know." But in the back of Charmaine's mind, hope bloomed. *I own half of a freakin' ranch? Maybe I'll be able to pay off my loan, after all.* "How could this have happened? I mean, Charlie's been dead for a year. Why am I just now finding out I was in his will?"

Rusty shrugged. "Dad's lawyer told me at the time of his death that I was in the will, but details weren't to be disclosed till after my release. I didn't know you were in the will, too, until I walked out of Angola several weeks ago. That was also at Dad's instructions. Thank God, there was a foreman in place when he died. Clarence has been a lifesaver. But, like I said . . . a mess!"

"Unbelievable!"

He slammed some papers and a pen on the table.

"What are they?"

"Just sign them, dammit."

"What are they?" she repeated. He might think she was a ditzy bimbo, but Charmaine was an astute businesswoman, despite her recent loan fiasco. She did not sign legal papers without reading them first. Besides, these would have to be notarized, wouldn't they?

Briefly scanning the papers, she noted that the first set was a petition for divorce. Okay, there was a tiny pang in the region of her heart. *Only one day after finding out I'm still married, and the brute is this eager to get rid of me.*

The other papers were even more ominous. "You want me to sign over my half of the Triple L Ranch for a token one dollar. Do you think I'm stupid? No, don't answer that."

"Charmaine, you have no use for a ranch. Sign the papers, and I'll be out of here."

"I deserve fair compensation."

"Really?" He gave her an insulting once-over, as if she'd asked about her personal worth, not that of the ranch. "How much?"

"Fifty thousand dollars."

He laughed. "Darlin', you haven't been to the ranch lately if you think that. The property is run-down, the fences are broken in so many places I can't count, and the cattle are emaciated and hardly worth keeping. If you must know, you own half of a helluva lot of debt."

Something peculiar is going on here. She tilted her head in confusion. "How did that happen?"

"I don't know. You tell me since you and dear ol' Dad were so chummy."

Chummy? I swear, you are going to pay for that insult. If I were a man, you'd be flattened by now. "That's not fair."

He shrugged. "Life's not fair."

"Well, I'm not *giving* you my half of the ranch."

"Then I'm not *giving* you a divorce."

She went wide-eyed at that announcement. "Is that a punishment? Of course it is. Torture by marriage. Hey, I'm kinda liking not being a divorcée. Maybe I won't *give* you a divorce. So there."

Clearly not amused by her rebellion, he came up way

too close to her, backing her into the sink. She felt his breath on her mouth. He deliberately invaded her space, trying to intimidate her.

She wasn't scared of him. She was more scared of herself and the effect he still had on her. And he knew it, too. Dammit.

"Be reasonable," she said, trying to move away.

He put an arm on either side of her on the sink, bracketing her in. "Reasonable? I'll give you reasonable. If you want to be half owner of the Triple L, you are going to do half the work. And that means shoveling cow manure, castrating bull calves and all the other necessary jobs that might interfere with your perfect manicure. You are not sitting your pretty little ass out on the veranda while I do all the work."

This is just great! You couldn't turn me into a cowgirl if you tried. And broken nails are a killin' offense, honey. Ha, ha, ha. "Stop being a jerk."

"I've heard you like jerks. Four of them, to be specific."

She made a conscious effort to restrain herself from belting him. *He is just baiting me. He wants me to lose my temper. But, really, he's been through a lot. Going to prison. Losing his vet license. Losing his dad.* Still, Charmaine thought about slapping the louse. Or shaking him silly. Or giving him a talking-to in the blue language she excelled at. But, instead, she did something better. She took him by the ears, pulled on him hard, then kissed him with all the pent-up stress of the past weeks and the hunger of ten long years. She bit his lip, she thrust her tongue inside his mouth, she ground herself against him. They were both moaning. She undulated her hips against him; he pressed his erection against her belly. She'd meant to teach the weasel a lesson, but somehow she was the one learning something.

He finally raised his head and stared at her, dazed for a moment. Then he gave her a little salute and said, "This is war, Charmaine."

Home on the range . . .

Two days later, Charmaine was tooling along scenic Highway 90, about to hit Interstate 10. She leaned back in the leather seat of Tante Lulu's classic blue T-bird convertible, singing "Knock, Knock, Knock" along with Joel Sonnier on the radio.

The raucous tune related the woes of a guy who'd landed in the doghouse again. That was Charmaine. She was in the doghouse of life, so to speak, but she wasn't going to let that get her down. No way! She was a survivor. *Woof, woof!*

She'd given her much prized BMW to Luc to sell, hopefully for twenty thousand dollars, which he would use to negotiate a deal with Bucks 'r Us. She wasn't foolish enough to think that Bobby Doucet—the slimeball—would settle for that amount, but Luc planned to negotiate and threaten him into a plan that would stop her interest clock from ticking away and allow her to pay off her loan in a reasonable period of time without any legs being broken or lives lost.

She should have sold the BMW right at the beginning, when she'd first needed the money to cover the stock loss. Or she should have gone to a regular bank and mortgaged her house. But she'd expected to receive a large check from a convention bureau for an event at which she and all her employees had worked. Unfortunately, the convention bureau promoters skipped town without paying any bills. After that, everything went downhill fast. The bayou region was a gossip mill, and Charmaine's infernal pride had gotten in the way. She hadn't wanted anyone to be able to say, "That Charmaine! Guess what dumb thing the bimbo did now."

Well, that was water over the dam now. Luc had advised her to leave it all in his hands, and in the meantime to stay out of sight for several weeks. So, she had put responsibility for her two beauty shops in her managers' hands with orders to contact her, via Luc, only in the direst emergency. Then she had hightailed it out of Houma, heading for the Triple L Ranch. Not that Rusty had invited her, or knew that she was coming. Their last meeting had ended on a slightly sour note. But she didn't need an invitation. She owned half the ranch, after all. That matter had been placed in Luc's expert legal hands, as well. He also was checking on the status of her marriage, or nonmarriage, to Rusty. *If I'm not careful, the bill from my lawyer will exceed the bill from my loan shark*, she joked to herself.

Charmaine planned a short visit, which was not evident in her overflowing vehicle. The hard top was on the convertible, it being November and the temperature in the low sixties, but still she had managed to pack the other bucket seat, the back storage area and the trunk of the little coupe with everything from designer jeans to blow-dryer to vast amounts of fresh foods, the latter pushed on her by Tante Lulu, whose philosophy was "always be prepared." In other words, overcook, overpack, overclean, overshop, and overdress.

She slowed down eventually as she entered Calcasieu

Parish, which was in the southwestern portion of the state. Soon there would be a turnoff for the *vacherie*, Cajun French for cattle ranch.

Lots of people thought Louisiana was nothing but a semitropical network of bayous and marshes, but prairie grasslands formed a large portion of the southwestern sector. It wasn't one single prairie like parts of Texas, but rather a series of prairies separated by forests and large streams. The largest of these prairies had such colorful names as Faquetique, Mamou, Calcasieu, Sabine, Vermilion, Mermentau, Plaquemine, Opelousas, and Grand.

Even more surprising to many people were the ranches in Louisiana. They'd heard about Texas cowboys, but not about Louisiana cowboys. Little did they know that southwest Louisiana had been known as the "Meadowlands of America" in the 1800s. Some even said that the West had begun there. In fact, the folklorist Alan Lomax suggested that the popular cowboy yell "Hippy Ti Yo!" derived from the Cajun French expression and song, *"Hip et Taïaut."*

Charmaine, like many of the Pelican State's natives, loved Louisiana *because* of its colorful diversity.

Overall, Charmaine was in a surprisingly good mood for the first time in weeks. The worst wasn't over, but she was hopeful that things would get better soon.

Her good mood came crashing down as she drove slowly along the single lane leading to the ranch house. The Triple L was relatively small, only a thousand acres with more than five hundred head of Black Angus cattle, and it had never boasted a big *Dynasty*-style mansion or anything remotely like that, but it had been well kept and profitable. *What happened?* Tears misted her eyes as she got out of her car and gazed about her. The one-story, rambling clapboard house with its wide front and back porches had lost its whitewash years ago. Not a single flower or decorative plant offset the starkness of the setting, except for wisteria vines and bougainvillea bushes, which had gone wild, and a tupelo tree near the front porch and several oaks in the back near a small bayou about a hundred yards from the house. A fenced-in vegetable garden beside the house had gone to seed, overgrown with weeds. The barn door hung on one hinge. Corral fences were broken here and there. Pieces of rusted machinery lay about like a junkyard. Several roosters—escapees from a dilapidated chicken coop—pecked at the hard dirt of the front yard searching for feed. The Triple L was a sad, neglected mirror of its old self. *What happened?*

"Well, well, well! Looks like Rusty's little filly done come home," she heard a crotchety voice say behind her. She turned to see Clarence Guidry, the longtime Triple L foreman, who spat out a wad of tobacco and wiped his mouth with a bandanna before reaching out a hand to her in welcome. Charmaine engulfed the old man in a hug. She would have thought Clarence retired a long time ago, being in his late sixties. The last time she'd seen Clarence was at the funeral home after Charlie Lanier's death.

"I'm not Rusty's filly, and he sure as hell isn't my stallion."

"He usta be."

"Not anymore. I'm only here for a visit," she said, ruffling his gray hair.

"Iffen you say so," he remarked with a grin.

"What happened here?" She indicated with a sweep of her hand the ranch's deplorable condition.

"Thass not fer me to say."

"Where's Rusty?"

"He and a couple of the hands 're out mendin' fences. 'Spect they'll be gone most of the afternoon."

"I'll get moved in then." Noticing that he was grinning again, she added, "For my visit."

"Whatever you say, girlie. I'm goin' inta town. Gotta go ta the feed store and buy some supplies. Might stop off fer a beer or two. Prob'ly won't see you till tomorrow."

She nodded.

"Need some help unloadin' that little bug?" he asked, glancing at the T-bird.

"No, thanks. I'll just bring in a little at a time, as I need it."

"It's good to see you here," he said just before he hopped into a beat-up pickup truck that she'd thought was part of the yard junk. As he bent to ease himself into the driver's seat, she noticed two clear marks in the back pockets of his jeans—a circular one outlining his can of loose-cut tobacco and a rectangular one outlining his much-played harmonica. "Both you *and* Rusty," he emphasized. "Yer both a welcome sight." With those words, he revved up the engine, which took some loud gunning of the gas pedal and shaking of the metal frame, before he took off with a wave out the window.

Charmaine went inside and found conditions just as bad there. A thick layer of dust covered everything. The large great room with its stone fireplace and handcrafted folk furniture made of bent twigs, deer antlers and steer skins. The rustic dining alcove off the kitchen with its built-in corner cupboard and a pedestal table and benches that could seat twenty, easily. The pantry that was half-filled with canned goods, many of which probably had exceeded their expiration dates. The foggy windows that hadn't been cleaned in years.

The only reasonably clean rooms were one of the three bedrooms, the single bathroom, and the kitchen . . . the key word being "reasonably" since soiled dishes were piled in the kitchen sink, wet towels lay on the bathroom floor, and the bed remained unmade with dirty clothes making a trail bespeaking a bone-weary cowboy falling dead on his feet to the mattress at night.

Well, something would have to be done if Charmaine was going to stay there for one day, let alone several weeks. Rusty might be able to live this way, but she couldn't. Besides, Charmaine was a hard worker, trained from an early age to cook and clean and keep busy during the daylight hours when her mother slept. If she hadn't taken care of herself, no one else would have.

First, she gathered up the bed linens and blankets from two bedrooms and all the dirty towels. She took them to the laundry room off the pantry and started her first load of wash. Then she brought in the perishable groceries that Tante Lulu had sent, along with some she had emptied out of her own fridge—milk, orange juice, fresh vegetables, some meats, even some crawfish from a neighbor. Charmaine set the dishes and pots and pans to soaking in scalding hot, sudsy water in the big enamel sink, then left two loaves of frozen bread dough out to rise on the counter in greased loaf pans before preparing a quick crawfish étouffée. She wasn't attempting to please Rusty. It was one of *her* favorites. At least that's what she told herself. She made enough for a half dozen people, in case some of the ranch hands would be eating there, too. Heck, maybe Rusty wouldn't even eat with her. She shrugged. In that case, she would be eating the Cajun dish for days.

By then, the first load of laundry was done. She put that in the dryer and started on a second load. The sweet scent of detergent filled the air, giving her an odd satisfaction. Some folks probably felt like this when they hung their clothes out to dry on the line.

After that she scoured the bathroom sink, toilet, and tub, even the tub surround and floor tiles. The bedrooms got a cursory whisk of a dust cloth on heavy old furniture dark with age. She used a dry mop to remove the curly dirt, or dust balls, under the beds. She would do a more thorough cleaning tomorrow.

Charlie's bedroom door was closed, and she didn't bother to open it. The bedroom Rusty had been using was the one he had used as a boy when visiting his father, as evidenced by a few rodeo posters on the cypress plank walls and Zane Grey novels and a half-deflated football in a bookcase. More recent additions were the myriad animal medicine books, veterinary and ranching magazines, and what appeared to be a large, leather doctor's bag. Besides that, the room contained a single bed against one wall, a large dresser, and a bedside table. She'd been to the ranch a number of times alone, and she had slept in that bed with Rusty on the one occasion when they'd visited his father together. Somehow it hadn't seemed so small then.

Quickly, she pushed those memories aside.

By 6:00 P.M., the kitchen sparkled from her cleaning efforts. The smaller wood table in the kitchen had six chairs; so she'd set place settings for six with the old Fiesta dinnerware and bone-handled cutlery. The wonderful smells of her crawfish casserole and baking bread and a frozen apple pie of Tante Lulu's filled the air.

She was putting the finishing touches on the linoleum floor with an old rag mop when one her favorite songs came on the local Golden Oldies rock station on the radio sitting on the windowsill. While the music blared out, Charmaine danced with her mop. Every time the Beatles sang, "Well, shake it up, baby," Charmaine shimmied around, up and down her mop handle; she wasn't the daughter of a stripper for nothing. Every time the Beatles called out, "Twist and Shout," she did that, too, with her own sexy version of that dance move.

Why she would be in such a good mood, she had no idea. Perhaps a day of hard work with visible effects. Perhaps relief that her money problems were at least in someone else's hands. Perhaps just because it was a good song.

That's when she heard a choking sound behind her and a muttered, "Lord have mercy!"

She came to a screeching halt, midtwist, and turned to see Rusty standing in the archway, staring at her as if she were an alien landed in his kitchen. He wore dusty Wrangler jeans, a black Bite Me Bayou Bait Co. T-shirt, boots, and a cowboy hat. His hands and arms and face were filthy. Days-old whiskers gave him an outlaw look.

Flanking him on either side were a middle-aged black cowboy the size of a tupelo tree, similarly attired and covered with dust, who grinned at Rusty and remarked, "I think I've died and gone to heaven," and on the other side a young man of about fifteen with auburn hair and freckles, also similarly attired and equally dirty, who just grinned.

Aerosmith was singing one of their old songs now,

"Sweet Emotion." Ironic, really, because when she looked at Rusty, despite all their history, she was filled with such sweet emotion she could barely breathe.

Rusty's dark Cajun eyes were welcoming at first, before he scowled, taking in her cleaning efforts with ever-widening lids. Then he sniffed the air, gave her another sweeping head-to-toe scrutiny, and repeated his initial comment, "Lord have mercy!"

Chapter 3

Dirty dancing, for sure . . .

Raoul felt as if he'd been sucker punched to the floor. At the same time, he felt light as a feather, floating up to the sky.

Never in a million years had he expected to walk into the ranch house kitchen and see his ex-wife—no, his wife—in her bare feet, wearing a pair of cutoff jeans that showed off her butt to perfection, and a white, short-sleeved T-shirt with LET ME SHAG YOU emblazoned across the prettiest breasts this side of the Mason-Dixon line. Even worse—or better—Charmaine was pole-dancing . . . with a mop, for chrissake.

And she looked good. Damned good! So good, in fact, that his teeth ached and his knees felt wobbly. Before he did something foolish, like jump her bones, or say, "Welcome home, baby," he snarled, "What the hell are you doing here?"

She blinked at him, then raised her chin. "I'm here to visit. On my lawyer's advice."

Don't you dare blink those puppy-dog eyes at me, Charmaine. I am immune. "Luc told you to come here?"

She nodded. And hitched one hip, leaning against her mop.

I am not ogling her hips. Not, not, not! I am a man with a mission. I am immune. "For how long?" he finally managed to inquire.

"A couple of weeks."

He groaned. He couldn't help himself. *Immunity only lasts so long.*

"Are y'all hungry?" she asked, changing the subject.

"For what?" he blurted out. *Did I really say that?*

"You betcha," Linc and Jimmy—the traitors—said on either side of him.

She means food.

I knew that.

"No," he said, though his stomach was grumbling at the succulent smells that filled the kitchen. *Is that crawfish étouffée I smell? My favorite. What a coincidence! Hah! I better be on guard. Charmaine is pulling out all the stops. For what purpose? Hmmm.*

Charmaine smiled.

He hated it when she smiled. Well, he hated how it made him feel.

She arched an eyebrow at the two men flanking him.

He realized how rude he was being, not introducing them.

"Charmaine, this is Abel Lincoln, better known as Linc." He jerked his head to the black cowboy on his right. Linc had been a fellow inmate of Raoul's who had become a good friend. Raoul was tall at six-foot-three; Linc had a good three inches on him.

"Linc is a musician, Charmaine. You should hear his music sometime," Raoul said.

"Really? I look forward to it."

He told Linc, "Charmaine loves all kind of music . . . as you probably noticed with her mop dancing routine."

Charmaine sliced him with a glower.

Then Raoul motioned with his head to his other side. "And this is Jimmy O'Brien. He's helping out on the ranch till he goes back to school." Jimmy was a fifteen-year-old high school dropout, but he would get his high school diploma, come hell or high water, if Raoul had anything to do with it. Actually, he wasn't so much a drop-out as a kick-out. He wasn't a bad kid, but he'd been hanging with a bad crowd and had been involved in a serious incident of vandalism resulting in thousands of dollars in fines and restitution. His father, a widower at his wit's end, had appealed to his good friend Clarence for help. As a result, Jimmy was working about five hours a day at the ranch to help pay off his fines and completing correspondence courses the rest of the time to keep up to date with his schoolwork. He hoped to return to his father's home in January at the beginning of a new semester, or next summer at the latest.

"Jimmy is our mathematician cowboy," Raoul told Charmaine. "I swear he's a regular Bill Gates when it comes to numbers."

Jimmy appeared about to protest, then shut his mouth with a click.

Raoul looked at Charmaine, sighed, and announced to the two guys, "And this is Charmaine." His heart twisted as he added, "My wife."

"Wife?" Linc exclaimed. "I thought you were divorced."

So did I. "So did I."

"You lucky dog!" Jimmy muttered under his breath, barely loud enough for him to hear.

I don't know about lucky, but I am a dog, for sure, to be looking at her and thinking what I'm thinking.

"Pleased to meet you." Charmaine flashed a big ol' beauty pageant smile at Linc and Jimmy, which wouldn't gain her any crowns but probably their lifelong devotion. Charmaine always did have the smile-thing down pat. In fact, she had a repertoire of smiles for different occasions. Amazing, the things he still remembered about her. Especially the smiles she'd reserved just for him on special occasions.

"My pleasure," Linc said with a courtly bow.

Yep, lifelong devotion.

"Likewise, ma'am," Jimmy said.

Raoul got a perverted satisfaction at Charmaine's face flushing up over being referred to as "ma'am." Raoul was old enough to know that women had a thing about age, and "ma'am" was definitely an age-defining word. For a former beauty queen, he imagined it would be even more offensive.

"Dinner will be ready in about twenty minutes if y'all want to wash up first."

His two Benedict Arnolds nodded eagerly and left for the bunkhouse to wash up. He just scowled. He knew he sounded ungracious, but Charmaine was hauling in his two workers like a couple of bayou catfish. He refused to be her catfish. Not again.

Still, she had gone to some trouble. And he was hungry. "Do you have enough food?" he asked.

"Tante Lulu insisted I load up the car," she answered brightly.

"I wondered about her T-bird out there. Why didn't you drive your own car?"

Pink color bloomed on her cheeks, and he could tell she didn't want to tell him. But she did, finally, with a haughty lift to her chin. "I gave my BMW to Luc to sell.

Hopefully, Bobby Doucet will accept that as part payment on my bill and set up a reasonable plan for repaying the rest. Luc is handling it all."

"A BMW, huh?" He leaned against the archway, crossing his arms over his chest. He was dying for a glass of water, but he didn't want to step on her clean floor with his muddy boots. "You always said that someday you'd own your own house, your own business, and a fancy car. It must've been hard for you to give up the car." He wasn't being sarcastic. They both knew what Charmaine's childhood had been like, and her dreams had been understandable.

"I got all three, Rusty, and giving up the car wasn't all that difficult. I can always buy another."

"Well, I'll go shower," he said, awkward with the silence that enveloped them suddenly.

"Wait a minute." She went out through the pantry, then returned with a pile of folded, sweet-smelling towels.

He narrowed his eyes at her. "You did my laundry?" *Holy shit! She probably did my underwear, too.* "Charmaine . . ." he started to chastise her.

"Oh, don't get in a snit. I did it for me as much as you. Your towels had mold on them, and there were boot prints on your sheets."

"I haven't had much time to—"

She waved a hand dismissively, then shoved the towels into his hands. He spun on his heels, about to go.

Just then Michael Bolton's old ballad "When a Man Loves a Woman" came on the radio. He stopped dead in his tracks, still near the kitchen. It had to be the hokiest chick song ever made, but it was the song he'd always put on the tape deck when he was "in the mood" because he'd known Charmaine loved it, and, frankly, it got her "in the mood." What a stupid thing to recall! She probably didn't even remember. He turned slightly and cast a quick glance her way.

Yep, she remembers.

Charmaine had a fist to her mouth, and tears were welling in her eyes. Hell, he probably had tears in his eyes, too. He exhaled loudly. Less than ten minutes in the same house, and he was ready to take her in his arms.

He set the towels on the dining room table and was about to walk over to her and do just that, muddy boots be damned, but Charmaine put up both hands. "No!" She swiped at one eye, then the other with the back of a hand, smearing her mascara. Only Charmaine would scrub floors in full-battle, armed-to-the-teeth makeup. "I'm all right now. Just a little memory blip."

More like a full power outage for me. "You better go home, Charmaine. Go while the gettin' is good."

She arched her eyebrows at him, back to her haughty ol' self. "Why?"

"Because you are in way more danger here with me, *chère*, than you are from some measly mob."

The way to a man's heart . . .

Charmaine sat at the kitchen table with Rusty, Linc, and Jimmy, all of them sipping at thick Cajun coffee, even Jimmy. She was well satisfied with herself, with good reason.

Every bit of food was gone. Two loaves of the fresh-baked bread. A hot endive salad. A bowl of rice. The whole apple pie. A box of store donuts. And the crawfish

étouffée? Well, suffice it to say, she could have quadru-
pled the recipe, and it still wouldn't have been enough.

There was something about feeding a hungry man that
filled some primordial need in a woman. These men had
been more than hungry. She suspected they'd been living
on whatever they could grab for weeks.

And they all looked so nice. They'd shaved. Well,
Rusty and Linc had. They wore faded but clean clothes.
All their hair was slicked back wetly off their well-
scrubbed faces.

"Can you make meat loaf?" Jimmy asked all of a
sudden.

Everyone turned as one to stare at him.

He ducked his head sheepishly, his face flaming with
embarrassment. "My mother used to make meat loaf and
mashed potatoes and brown gravy. I just thought . . ." He
shrugged.

Charmaine's heart went out to the boy. From what
Rusty had mentioned during dinner and the little he'd disclosed in whispered asides, she'd learned that his mother
had died of cancer a few years back, and Jimmy had
become an increasingly troubled kid. Hanging out with a
wild crowd. Playing hooky from school. Shoplifting.
Running away from home. His father, a feed company
sales rep, was trying to pay off a mountain of medical
bills from his late wife's lengthy illness and probably not
spending enough time with his child, though he was
doing his best.

"I'm sure I could find a recipe for meat loaf on the
Internet." She glanced at Rusty. "You do have an Internet
connection on that computer I saw in your office, don't
you?"

He nodded, equally touched, she could tell, by the

boy's simple request. "It's a dinosaur of a machine, though. Slow as Mississippi mud."

"As long as it works."

"I can help," Jimmy offered.

Everyone looked at him.

"Really. The problem with that machine is they cut some corners so it wouldn't cost so much to build. It's really not a bad machine on the inside. If you put on another half gig of memory, get it a faster hard drive, and put in a sound card and faster video card . . . well, that machine's never going to scream down the walls, but, hey, it wouldn't be half the dog it is."

Three jaws dropped with amazement.

"I knew you were good at math, but I didn't know you could speak another language. Computerese," Rusty remarked.

"Maybe you'd be better off utilizing Jimmy inside instead of working him outside," Charmaine observed to Rusty. Then, changing the subject, she asked Rusty, "Do you have ground beef in the freezer that isn't old enough to walk?"

He grimaced. "I don't know. You'll have to check the freezer package dates."

"You know, I threw away a whole trash bag full of stuff from your fridge. Talk about mold! You could have started a terrarium in there."

"Hey, it's all about priorities. The cattle have to come first if I'm ever going to turn this place around. Man, we must have fifty young bulls strutting their stuff all over the place."

"Fifty bulls are bad?"

Rusty smiled at her.

And her traitorous heart turned over. At just his smile. *Jeesh!*

"Fifty bulls are definitely bad." He smiled some more.

And she developed a sudden fondness for the crinkles that bracketed his eyes and mouth. Really! One smile, and all two thousand of her hormones stood up, and said, "Howdy!"

"And what a bunch of horndogs they are, too. Whooee, those bulls'll screw anything with four legs. I saw one yesterday that tried to mount a wheelbarrow." It was Jimmy giving out that wonderful information.

Linc gave Jimmy a light punch in the arm to shut him up, and the boy blushed even more than he had before. "Sorry, ma'am."

Enough with the ma'am business. I don't need any reminders that the big Three-Oh is coming up. "You can call me Charmaine. And no offense, honey. I know all about horndogs." She gave Rusty, who was grinning to beat the band, a pointed glower.

"Did ya see Rufus today?" Jimmy asked Linc. "I swear that bull has a dick the size of a fireman's flashlight."

Apparently, the boy had a one-track mind . . . and the sense of a flea.

Rusty and Linc put their faces in their hands.

"What? Golly, I did it again, didn't it? I really am sorry ma'am . . . I mean, Charmaine. I know I talk too much. My dad usta say that if tongues were race cars, I'd a won the Nascar. My mom never complained, though. She always said that she liked my babbling."

He stopped suddenly, and silence pervaded the room.

"You should meet my half brother Tee-John," Charmaine said with a laugh. "You would get along so well."

"Why? Does he talk too much, too?"

She ruffled his hair. "Yeah, he talks a lot. He's about the same age as you, and he's always coming out with things that make adults blush."

"Do I make y'all blush?" Jimmy asked with surprise.

"Oh, yeah," Linc said. "Even a black guy like me."

The conversation moved on to ranch stuff then, things like fence posts, tagging, breeding stock, and market prices, none of which Charmaine understood. She just kept the coffee coming.

"We'll send all the bulls and steers to market next week, along with about half the cows," Rusty concluded. "That'll leave us with about three hundred cows. After we buy some new bulls, we should be set to start a new herd."

"I don't 'spect you'll make much on the sales," Linc said. "Never saw a scrawnier bunch of animals, even during a drought one time down in Texas."

"I know," Rusty said grimly.

"Why do you have to sell them if you won't make much profit?" Charmaine wanted to know.

"The bulls have got to go because no one has been tagging and keeping track of the stock for the past couple years. Without the tagging, you might have a bull mounting his sister."

"Or his mother," Jimmy offered.

"So inbreeding is bad in animals, too?" Charmaine asked.

"It can be." Rusty rubbed his chin thoughtfully. "I can't imagine what my father was thinking to let things go so badly. His doctor tells me he wasn't sick."

"What's the cause of death listed on the death certificate? I mean, at the funeral everyone said he had a heart attack. I assumed that was it." Charmaine was as puzzled as Rusty by his father's behavior. Charlie Lanier had loved this ranch and had been proud of carrying on the family tradition. Presumably, five generations of Laniers had held this land, since just after the Civil War.

"Cardiac arrest," Rusty answered.

"Let me guess. His doctor says he had no history of heart disease?" Charmaine remarked.

"Bingo," Rusty said. "But that's a mystery left for later. Right now we have to work on the cattle. Do you want us to help clean up the dishes?"

"Good heavens, no! Go do your cow thing."

They all laughed at her wording.

Linc and Jimmy thanked her once again for the meal and left for the bunkhouse. Rusty stayed behind. Of course he would. This was his home. Where he slept.

Oh, boy!

"Cleaning up keeps me busy. I have too much energy to just sit still. Can I do anything else for you?" Charmaine said nervously.

There was a long pause as Rusty seemed to be considering her offer. Her poorly worded offer.

"Well, we do have a big job tomorrow. Maybe you could help us with that."

"Anything," she said eagerly. "What's the job?"

"Castrating cattle."

"Oh, you!" She threw a wet dish towel at him.

He caught it with one hand and winked at her.

The image of that wink stayed with her long after he was gone.

In the still of the night . . .

Raoul tossed and turned for more than an hour before finally giving up the fight.

Glancing at the lighted dial of his bedside clock, he saw that it was midnight. Only five hours till he had to get up again, but it was useless trying to sleep when all he could think about was Charmaine next door.

He'd heard her shower. And smelled her shampoo even from that distance.

He'd heard her puttering around her bedroom and setting her alarm.

He'd heard her mattress shift when she'd gotten into bed.

He'd heard her flip the pages of a magazine.

He'd heard her flick off her lamp, finally.

And he could swear he heard her breathing now as she slept.

Did she wear a nightgown? Or nothing?

Did she dream about him? Ever?

Was she as hot and bothered by his proximity as he was by hers?

With a whooshy exhale of surrender, he got up and pulled a pair of jeans over his briefs. Barefooted and bare-chested, he padded through the hall down to his father's old office—a small cubicle off the living room. His feet would probably be dirty once he returned to bed, but then again maybe not, depending on whether his very own Cajun cleaning maid had hit this area yet.

The quiet of the house should have been a soothing balm, but he sensed an underlying turbulence. There was trouble brewing. And it wasn't just Charmaine.

He flicked on the desk lamp and booted up the computer. Slipping on a pair of wire-rimmed reading glasses, he began to tackle the receipts and scribbled notes that littered the small room in monumental piles. Each of these he methodically transcribed to the computer in a hunt-and-peck method dating back to the Stone Age of typewriters. The whole job should take him about a year or two at this rate, he figured. By then he expected to be dead of frustration or boredom or out-and-out brain freeze.

He had been working for about a half hour when his head shot up with alertness. He smelled her before he saw her.

Charmaine stood in the open doorway behind him. He spun his swivel chair halfway around to face her.

"Holy cow, Charmaine! Are you crazy? Coming here in the middle of the night, dressed like that?"

"What?" she said, glancing down at the old, oversized LSU T-shirt she wore, and presumably nothing else. The sleeves went halfway down her upper arms, and the hem reached midthigh of her long legs, but she looked sexier than a buck-naked *Playboy* centerfold. "I'm covered. You can't see anything."

I can imagine, and believe you me, I am imagining. "Is that my shirt?" he choked out.

"Yeah. I forgot to pack my nighties."

Nighties? Well, thank God for small favors. "Charmaine, go back to bed. This house is not big enough for the two of us."

She ignored his words and said in a breathy voice, "You're wearing glasses."

Huh? Since when do breathy and glasses go together?

"I wear them for reading and computer work." He took them off.

She moaned softly.

Cocking his head to the side, he asked, "What did I do that made you moan?"

"You took your glasses off."

"Have you been drinking?"

She shook her head. "Is there anything sexier than a man when he takes his glasses off?"

Never rocked my world.

"Especially when he does it kinda slow and looks at a woman when he's doing it, which you did. Sort of implies he's about to get down to serious business."

A torpedo to his groin area exploded with about a million testosterone pellets. *Be still, my heart . . . and other places.*

"Not that I'm interested in that kind of business with you." She flashed him a shy grin.

Charmaine shy? My brain must be fried from all these numbers. She was probably just pulling his chain, but then, you never knew with Charmaine. "You should not be telling me things like that, *chère*. It gives me ideas. And I definitely do not want to be having ideas about you."

"Me neither," she said with a sigh that could have meant just about anything. Her eyes scanned the room then, and she concluded, "What a mess!"

"Yep."

"What are you doing? I could hear your painfully slow tapping all the way to my bedroom."

"Sorry if I woke you. I never did learn to type very fast."

"You didn't wake me."

There was some meaning in those words, as there had been in the sigh, but he wasn't about to investigate. He explained what he'd been doing.

"Hey, I can help you."

I doubt that sincerely, unless you plan on spending a week or so in my bed. No, no, no, I did not think that.

"With your computer," she added. "Not with all that computer geek business Jimmy mentioned, but inputting data is a no-brainer."

Oh. That kind of help.

She pulled over a chair, forcing him to wheel himself a bit to the right, making room for her. Once again, he was assailed by the scent of Charmaine, all flowery and feminine.

"Why would you want to help?" he asked churlishly. It was that or make a grab for her, which he was not going to do. *I hope.*

She gave him a sidelong glance, which pretty much put him in the category of ungrateful cretins, but then she spoiled the guilt trip she laid on him by pointing out, "It's my ranch, too."

With a few quick tap-taps of her fingers, Charmaine familiarized herself with his programs, which really impressed him. "Where'd you learn to do all that?"

She shrugged. "I use different software with my businesses. Before that, I needed to develop computer skills for some of the jobs I took when I dropped out of college."

Concentrating on the screen, she didn't notice the frown that furrowed his brow. Her dropping out of college had been a sore point between them, one of the reasons for their break-up. How could she mention it so casually?

"Stop frowning and hand me some of those papers," she ordered.

Apparently, she was aware, after all.

"It's too late to do much tonight, but give me an idea what you're doing, by going through a couple of papers. I might be able to wade through some of these piles during the day while you're out chasing cows, or whatever it is you do."

He smiled at her assessment of ranch life.

"Don't smile."

"Why not?"

"Because I get butterflies in my tummy when you smile, and then I can't concentrate."

"Oh, Charmaine." *Truth to tell, I get butterflies, too, but they're more like kamikazes, and they're aiming a bit lower in my anatomy.*

"Don't 'Oh, Charmaine' me. Just because you give me butterflies doesn't mean I'm going to do anything about it."

Me, neither. But I'm sure thinkin' about it. "Because you're a born-again virgin?"

"Yeah." She grinned at him before turning her attention back to the screen and tap-tap-tapping some more.

When she yawned widely, he said, "That's it," and reached over to take the mouse out of her hand to log off. In the process, his hand brushed hers. He could swear that just the brush of his palm over the back of her hand threw off erotic sparks.

She turned in her seat to ask, "What are you . . . ?" Her words trailed off as she realized how close his face was to hers.

As if in slow motion, he noticed the two freckles on her nose, which she always hid with makeup, the widening of her whiskey eyes, which were glazing over now with strong emotion, the parting of her lips.

She moaned softly.

That was all the encouragement he needed. Leaning closer still, he pressed his mouth against hers. Not hard. Not gentle. Just a coming-home kind of kiss where body parts once well-attuned acclimated themselves to familiar territory.

She moaned again and opened her mouth more for his exploration.

He moaned, too. Into her welcoming mouth. Releasing the mouse, he used both of his hands to frame her face and kiss her more deeply. So powerful was the draw between them that he felt his eyes burn with unshed tears. This was the way it had always been.

Charmaine ended the kiss, finally, by pressing her hands against his bare chest. His vision blurred, and he was panting like a war-horse.

"That should not have happened," she said.

He nodded.

"It's not why I came here tonight."

He nodded.

"I'm only here for a visit."

He nodded.

"We are *not* going to have sex."

He paused, but then he nodded. *One word from you, though, and I would be on you like a duck on a June bug.*

She stood and pulled down the hem of her T-shirt, which caused her erect nipples to protrude.

Raoul knew something important at that moment. Charmaine wasn't as cool and collected as she pretended.

"Luc is going to file the divorce papers for us." She still fidgeted with the T-shirt.

He nodded. *Why is there a lump in my throat?* "If it's what you want."

"Of course it is," she said, but her kiss-wet lips quivered as she spoke. "It's what you want, isn't it?"

"Oh, yeah." *How the hell do I know?*

Charmaine gave him a long, questioning look, as if waiting for something. Then she left.

He suspected he'd just been given a rare opportunity for a replay in the misbegotten game that was his life. But he had dropped the ball.

Chapter 4

Whoopi-ti-yi-yo, for sure . . .

Trouble hit the next day with a vengeance. Four steer shot between the eyes, and not a clue in sight.

Raoul and Clarence stood next to a widebed, open-sided truck parked in the middle of the field, which had been brought over by the sheriff's office an hour ago. The sheriff would be back soon to ask more questions and take the carcasses in for examination, extraction of the bullets and analysis. A sad waste of time on the part of the sheriff's department. And for Raoul and Clarence when there was so much other work to do. Linc and Jimmy were completing the fence repairs at the opposite end of the ranch, which was where they should be, too.

And all Raoul could think about was Charmaine.

He needed to get laid, badly. It had been two long years since he'd been with a woman. That had to be the reason why his ex-wife—he still couldn't think of Charmaine as his wife—lingered on his mind, like an erotic burr.

And it wasn't just sex. She attracted him in the most idiotic ways. He loved watching her prepare a meal.

He loved the way she listened so intently to Jimmy's rambling nonsense. He loved her love of music—all kinds, not just Cajun. He loved her smiles. Hell, he even loved her frowns. Everything she did, she did with passion.

Something had to give, or he would go bonkers. He shook his head like a wet dog to help him focus.

"Who do ya think done it?" Clarence asked him as they wrapped a rope around one of the steer.

Raoul patted it on the head. Poor animal! *Mon Dieu!* He should be healing animals, not dealing with their deaths. He sighed, then answered. "Got me. But it sure as hell wasn't a teen prank, like cow tipping, as the sheriff implied." Next they used a winch and a forklift attached to a tractor to swing the steer up and onto the truck. Raoul exhaled loudly with disgust. "I suspect it's the same bunch of oil interests that kept pressuring my dad to sell the ranch. Or maybe the people responsible for framing me. Or maybe even the ones who killed my father."

"Or mebbe they're all the same person."

"Could be," Raoul concurred. *What a mess!*

"Hard to believe that oil people would go to these extremes, even killing a fella," Clarence mused.

"Hey, look at that John Grisham book . . . and movie. *Pelican Brief.* They were pretty ruthless in there."

"Guess so." Clarence straightened and arched the kinks out of his back. This was really strenuous work for a man his age, though Raoul would never dare tell him that. One time he had dared, and Clarence told him it was better for a man to wear out than to rust out.

"You really think Charlie mighta been murdered?" Clarence asked.

Raoul shrugged. "I'm still investigating. Hell, we may never know for sure."

"Well, the shootin' of these animals," Clarence said, waving a hand at the dead cattle, "I 'spect it's a warnin' of sorts."

"You're probably right," Raoul said with a shrug.

"On the other hand, mebbe it's those Mafia hit men come to tweak Charmaine." Clarence grinned as he spoke, then spit out a long stream of tobacco juice. Apparently, he didn't consider the loan shark, which Raoul had explained to him, as big a deal as Charmaine did.

Raoul grinned back at him. "You mean, like *The Godfather*, where they put the horse's head in the guy's bed?"

"Yessirree. We better warn Charmaine to be on the lookout fer cow parts." He caught Raoul's frown, then added, "Then again, mebbe not."

"This was a warning for me, not Charmaine," Raoul insisted. Inside, though, adrenaline shot through his system at the mere prospect that Charmaine might be in real danger. He wouldn't admit it to her, but he was glad, in a way, that she'd parked herself at the ranch where he could protect her.

"Yer one lucky fella," Clarence said then.

"Huh?" Raoul couldn't imagine anything about his life the past two years that would fit into the realm of lucky. *Lucky to have been convicted of a felony? Lucky to have spent two friggin' years in the slammer? Lucky to have lost my medical license? Lucky to have lost my father? Lucky to have inherited half of a run-down ranch? Lucky to be climbing the walls with lust?*

"Charmaine," Clarence explained. "Whooee, she is one fine woman, if ya doan mind my sayin' so."

I do mind your saying so. Don't say it. Don't even think it. I'm thinking it enough for both of us. "She's only here for a visit."

"Thass what she tol' me, but iffen yer the man I think ya are, ya kin change her mind."

"Why would I want to do that? No, don't answer that. Charmaine is soon to be my ex-wife. End of story." *And, frankly, I don't know what kind of man I am anymore. Or whether I want to change her mind. Who am I kidding? At the least encouragement, I'd be all over her like dew on Dixie.*

"I could give you pointers," Clarence said. With a little huffing and puffing, they managed to get the second steer up on the truck. Even with the winch and fork, it was hard work lifting these almost two-thousand-pound animals.

"I beg your pardon," Raoul said, once he got his breath back.

"Pointers . . . on how to win Charmaine back." Clarence spit again. "I was quite the ladies' man at one time."

Bet you didn't chew tobacco then.

"Oh, doan give me that look, boy. I still got a little gid-diup in my stirrups. Doan judge me by my age."

"I wasn't judging you by—"

"Oh, yes, you were. But thass no nevermind. The important thing is women go bonkers over cowboys. Always did. You just need to strut yer stuff in yer cowboy gear, and you'll be home free."

"Home free, huh?" *How pathetic can I get? Even an aged Lothario thinks I need help.*

"The most important thing is ya gotta get her back in yer bed. After that, ya gotta make love to her over and over and over till she's walkin' bowlegged. Poke, poke, poke. Thass one thing us cowboys know how to do good. Ride our fillies hard."

Oh, good Lord! He wants me to make Charmaine bow-legged. "Uh, Charmaine might have a thing or two to say about that."

Clarence waggled his shaggy eyebrows at him. "She's a hot tomato, all right. A hottie, as Jimmy would say. Yer dumber'n a cow's patoot iffen ya doan make the effort."

Why don't you say what you really think, old man? "I may be dumb, but you're the one who's dumb if you dare to call Charmaine a hot tomato to her face. I called her a bimbo one time, and she walked out on me." *Now, why did I blab out something like that?*

"Bimbo? Bimbo? Are you nuts, boy? 'Bimbo' is a bad word . . . like . . . like slut. Hot tomato is a compliment."

Unbelievable! Un-be-freakin'-liev-able! I'm standing here, taking advice from a senior citizen cowboy version of Anne Landers. He oughta write a column called "Dear Clarence" or "The Cowboy Confessor." Talk about!

Time to change the subject. "I think you're just wanting me to keep Charmaine around because you like her food."

Charmaine had gotten up even before him this morning and had prepared a huge breakfast of thick Cajun *boudin* sausages, scrambled eggs, toast, her own version of *couche-couche*, which was fried cornmeal mush served with brown sugar, butter, and milk, and lots of thick chicory coffee. Clarence, Linc, and Jimmy were falling in love with his wife just because of her cooking. And the respectful way she treated them. And the fact that she'd offered to do their laundry. And, yes, she was making meat loaf for supper, just because Jimmy had asked.

My life is goin' down the tubes, but we got meat loaf.

How could he ask her to stop doing things that pleased his workers so much? If he wasn't careful, she would be insinuating herself into his life, too, and that would be intolerable.

Wouldn't it?

"There is that, too." Clarence chuckled and spit another stream off to the side. Meanwhile, they heaved the third steer onto the truck by way of the squeaking winch and forklift.

"Huh?" Raoul had been so deep in thought that he'd lost track of his conversation with Clarence.

"You said that mebbe I'm just warming up to Charmaine 'cause I like her food, and I said, 'There is that, too.'" Clarence's cloudy gray eyes twinkled, as if he could read Raoul's mind and knew that it lingered on his wife. And not just her food, either. There was the image of her in his LSU T-shirt. There was the lingering smell of her. There was the kiss.

They swung the last steer onto the truck bed. Both of them whisked their hands together, then removed their heavy work gloves.

"Yer daddy liked Charmaine, too."

Mon Dieu! *He never lets up.* "I guess so," Raoul said. "He gave her half the ranch."

Clarence waved his hand in the air, as if that was of little importance. Well, it was important to Raoul.

"I'm thinkin' he did that fer yer benefit."

Don't ask, Raoul. You are only encouraging him. What did he do, though? He asked, of course. "How so?"

"He prob'ly wanted you two to stay together, and bein' stubborn as you are, the only way he could accomplish that was get you both here on the ranch. Thass why he dint file the divorce papers to begin with."

Hey, I'm no more stubborn than Charmaine. Stubborn is her middle name. Isn't she right this minute cleaning the ranch house when I ordered her not to? Hell, her chin is on autopilot. The least little thing I do and her chin shoots up. "How do you know Charmaine so well, anyhow? We only came to the ranch that one time after we were married."

"Oh, she's been here lots of times. Even after the divorce."

Now, isn't that interesting? I wonder why she was so chummy with dear ol' dad. "Really?"

"Uh-hmm. She was a real basket case after the divorce, of course . . ."

What? Charmaine's the one who left me. I was the basket case, not her. "I think you got the wrong impression."

". . . then over the years she dropped by on occasion, or your dad went to visit her. He was like the father she never had, seeing as how that Valcour LeDeux never wanted much to do with her. His own chile! Can you imagine that?"

Something just didn't fit in this picture, but Raoul had no time to dwell on that. A motor could be heard approaching. Was it the sheriff back so soon? Nope. This vehicle was traveling at breakneck speed. He soon realized it was Charmaine driving his Jeep, like a blue ass fly. He assumed she was driving his vehicle, rather than Tante Lulu's T-bird because it hadn't been totally unloaded yet. In it still were a lifesize plastic St. Jude statue and a hand-carved hope chest. He'd been afraid to ask who they were for.

"Let's move away from here. I don't want Charmaine to see these dead animals," he said.

Clarence nodded, and the two of them stepped forward quickly so that they stood a good twenty feet away from the truck by the time she came to a screeching halt.

"Hey, Clarence. Hey, Rusty."

"Lookin' mighty fine today, little lady," Clarence said, tipping his hat at Charmaine.

The big ol' suck-up! Actually, Charmaine did look good. Since she was driving his Jeep Wrangler with the soft top and open sides, he got a full head-to-toe view of her: her dark hair all big and poufed up like she was about to walk down a runway, her full lips plastered with kiss-me-or-die red lipstick, her breasts pressing out in a baby blue T-shirt that proclaimed HAIR ME OUT, her brighter blue stretch pants that molded her butt and long, long legs, and black sandals that showcased her matching kiss-me-or-die red toenails. Not that he was paying attention to any particular details.

"Well, thank you kindly, Clarence." Charmaine arched a brow at him as if he was remiss in not seconding Clarence's compliment.

"Charmaine, you always look good enough to eat." *Oops! Talk about Freudian slips.* He hadn't meant that the way it sounded. Well, he did think that, but he hadn't intended to say it out loud.

Instead of lashing out at him for his crudity, she laughed. She must have noticed his embarrassment and taken pity on him. Then she surprised the hell out of him by tossing out, "Honey, you look good enough to eat, too. Always."

He tipped the brim of his hat back off his forehead and smiled. "Is that a fact?"

"See," Clarence whispered to him in an aside. "Prime ta be bowlegged. Why dontcha wink at her? Winkin' allus worked fer me."

"Shhh," he said, without bothering to look Clarence's way. *That's all Charmaine needs to hear, and she'll run us both over.*

"Where you off to, missie?" Clarence asked, causing Raoul to break the mesmerizing eye contact between him and Charmaine.

"Yeah, where are you off to?" he inquired, too.

"I need to go into town and buy some supplies."

"Uh, I don't think that's a good idea," he advised.

"Why not?"

"You're trying to hide from the loan shark. Walking into some store, looking the way you do, is like announcing on a loudspeaker, 'I am Charmaine. Here I am. Come get me.'"

Of course, Charmaine homed in on the most irrelevant part of what he'd said. "What's wrong with how I look?"

Oh, sweetheart, how can you even ask? He exhaled loudly. "You look just great. That's the problem."

"Huh?"

"Look, I don't have time for this, but if you insist on going into town, I'll go with you."

"I don't need you to accompany me. I'm a big girl, and . . ."

Just then, her gazed fixed on something behind them. *Uh-oh.*

"Why are those cows sleeping on that truck?" *Uh-oh.*

As one, he and Clarence moved closer together to block her view.

She craned her neck to the left so she could see better. Stubborn wench!

"Are those *dead* cows back there on that truck?" she demanded to know. "Yeech!"

"Dead *steers*," Clarence corrected her. "Shot through the eyes by some slimy varmints."

Sometimes Clarence had a motor on his tongue. *Varoom-varoom!*

Charmaine looked immediately to him. "Rusty . . . ?"

He shrugged.

"Okay, you can come," she said, obviously understanding the potential danger now that she'd seen the dead steers.

"Move over," Raoul ordered.

"Get in the passenger seat," she ordered back.

"Do we have to argue about everything?"

She just arched her eyebrows at him and tapped her long fingernails on the steering wheel.

As Raoul eased himself into the other side of the Jeep, he asked Clarence, "You can take care of the sheriff's questions, right?"

Clarence nodded and called out to him, "Remember my advice. Bowlegged, boy. Bowlegged. Wouldn't hurt to wear yer jeans tighter, either."

Raoul just chuckled at the old guy's perverted humor. Charmaine couldn't possibly understand Clarence's words. Or at least he didn't think she could . . . until she gunned the gas pedal so hard he almost fell out of the Jeep. *Jesus, Mary, and Joseph!* he thought inside in his head, and he was praying, not swearing.

He thought he heard her mutter, "I'll give you bowlegged." And took off like Mario Andretti at the Indy 500.

He just held on tight. What else could he do?

Shopping is the next best thing to sex . . . for a woman . . .

"So, what was that bowlegged business all about?"

Charmaine finally asked that question as she drove down the one-lane road, heading toward the nearest supermarket. She needed to break the silence, which was as thick and tantalizing as the most intimate sexual banter in the confines of the small Jeep.

If that wasn't bad enough, she kept taking her eyes off the road to stare at Rusty, who was a sight to behold in his faded, everyday cowboy work clothes. He had his long legs stretched out as far as they would go, which wasn't far enough in the passenger seat, even pushed all the way back. His left arm rested on the back of the driver's seat, just touching her shoulders with white-hot heat.

"You don't want to know," he said lazily, giving her a lingering sideways glance . . . and a grin. Meanwhile, he twirled a strand of her hair around one finger, over and over, a habit that used to annoy her but now felt kind of nice.

Actually, she *didn't* want to know, but stubborn had always been her middle name. "Yes, I do."

"Clarence was giving me romance advice."

See where stubborn gets you, Ms. Smartie. Next time you'll know to keep your mouth shut. "I beg your pardon," she choked out. "Clarence telling *you* what to do? I don't believe it."

"Believe it." He waggled his eyebrows at her, which prompted her to notice his eyes.

Merciful heavens! What was God thinking to give a man such thick black lashes and such beautiful dark eyes? "Like what?" *Did I really ask him to elaborate? My brain is in hormone overload. I just can't think straight when I'm around him. Never could.*

"Oh, Charmaine. Tsk, tsk, tsk. Watch the road, honey. You almost hit that guardrail." He laughed at the foul word she said, then continued. "If you really must know, Clarence says I should screw your brains out till you walk funny."

"He never did!"

"Yes, he did. Not in those exact words, but the meaning was the same. 'Ride you long and hard till you walk bowlegged.'"

"That was so crude."

"You asked."

They didn't talk much after that till they got to the supermarket, Charmaine having decided to put a zipper on her lips. Besides, she couldn't rid her mind of the image of Rusty riding her hard. They had gone down only two aisles at Albertsons and were in the produce section when Rusty started whining about going home.

"What is it about men and shopping?" Charmaine inquired idly as she examined a bunch of bananas, wondering if she had all the ingredients for Bananas Foster. She had a special recipe from a New Orleans Cajun restaurant. "Women see it for the orgasmic experience it can be, while men regard it as pure torture."

"Hah! The only orgasmic thing I can imagine is you

holding those bananas and me imagining what you could do with them. Holy crap, Charmaine, are you deliberately trying to torment me?"

Surprised, Charmaine looked from Rusty to the bunch of bananas in her hand. When understanding dawned, she flashed him a glower. "Not everything in the world is about sex."

"Maybe not to you," he said and stomped off to the apple section.

She watched him walking, with way too much interest. He wasn't the only one with sex on the mind, truth to tell. His kiss last night had about knocked her for a loop. And staring at his tight butt in those tight jeans right now, well, sex about said it all.

A young college girl noticed, too. The blonde sidled up to Rusty and asked him a question about apples. Apples! Like that was what she was interested in with a drop-dead gorgeous cowboy. And Rusty, the jerk, just tipped his hat back and smiled down at her and answered her questions as if he were suddenly some Johnny Apple-seed or something. Not that Charmaine was jealous or anything. But she was thinking about sashaying over there and walloping blondie over the head with the bunch of bananas she still held in her hands.

"I think the best ones are McIntosh, darlin'," she heard him say.

Darlin'? Oooh, I'd like to wring your neck, you randy, stupid, too-good-looking jerk.

He sauntered back then and dropped a bag of McIntosh apples into their cart. "Shopping's not so bad, after all," he announced.

Forget neck-wringing. Shooting would be better. She

practically growled at him, especially when he winked at her, understanding perfectly that she had not liked what she had just witnessed. "Be careful, stud, or you're gonna land yourself back in jail on statutory rape."

He jerked back as if she'd slapped him. "She's twenty-one. Legal. She told me so. Not that I care. All I did was answer the girl's question."

Uh-huh, and apples and her giving you her age just went hand in hand. "Like you're suddenly the apple expert? And you ask where the sex idea came from? Well, you just said something a few minutes ago about sex being on your mind all the time."

"No, no, no. That's not what I said, sweetheart. At least that's not what I meant. *You* and sex are always on my mind these days."

"Oh," she said, and couldn't help herself from grinning ear to ear. *He still wants me. I mean, I knew he wanted me, but it is so damn good to hear him say the words. How pathetic can I get?* "You are pathetic," she said.

"Yep," he agreed. "And so are you, being jealous of a young twit like that. Talk about! Like I would be interested in her when you're around, waving bananas in my face."

She dropped the bananas into her cart and pushed the cart away. But she was still grinning ear to ear.

Charmaine had the cart half-full and was ready to leave a short time later, but she had lost Rusty back in the paperback book section about ten minutes ago. She finally found him near the front of the store, down on one knee, talking to a German shepherd the size of a pony. Rusty had had a dog just like it when they'd been together, but Eli had been ten years old then, and he'd died about three years ago. At least, that was what Rusty's father had told her. Well, this dog wasn't quite like Rusty's had been since it was a Seeing Eye dog, on a leash held by a middle-aged lady wearing dark glasses and sitting on a bench, talking softly with Rusty.

Charmaine's eyes misted with tears, and her heart clenched with compassion for Rusty. This was how he must look when practicing veterinary medicine. Although he dealt more with large animals, like horses and cows, the principle was the same. He spoke gently, caressed the animal with nonthreatening, expert fingers, examining it for problems, and answered the questions of its mistress. He patted the dog when it allowed him to look inside its mouth, even let the dog give him a sloppy kiss on the mouth.

Rusty stood then. Just before he noticed her, she saw the hopeless stoop of his shoulders and the sadness in his eyes . . . things his pride would never allow him to show under normal circumstances. He desperately missed his work treating sick animals.

When he saw her, he immediately masked over his emotions and asked, "Are we done shopping? I've only had three babes try to pick me up. I'm losing my touch."

"Oh, yeah! Well, I can top that. The butcher asked me if I'd like to see his meat," she said, trying to match his light tone.

He laughed and shook his head at her coarse jest. "And did you check it out?"

"Nah! I told him I've got all the meat I can handle."

"Guar-an-teed!"

Rusty might think he had fooled her, but Charmaine was smarter than the average bimbo. And, despite all her failings, she had a heart of gold, in her own humble opinion. As they made their way to the checkout together, Charmaine made a vow to herself. She was going to help Rusty get his medical license back. He hadn't asked for her assistance, and she hadn't a clue what she could do. But, by God, she was going to do it.

Maybe you should ask me for a little help, a voice in her head said. Charmaine was pretty sure it was St. Jude.

Chapter 5

One ringy-dingy, two ringy-dingy . . .

The phone rang following breakfast the next morning.

Clarence, Linc, and Jimmy had already left for the barn, and Raoul was about to join them.

Since he had already advised Charmaine not to answer the phone, just in case Bobby Doucet got wind of her whereabouts, he went over to the wall phone and picked up the receiver. "Hello."

"Rusty, is that you?"

"Yes."

"Lucien LeDeux here."

"Hey, Luc. Did you want to speak to Charmaine?"

"Yes, but first there are a few things I want to tell you. Is Charmaine nearby?"

"Uh-huh." *What could he possibly want to tell me that he doesn't want Charmaine to overhear?*

She looked at him suspiciously, mouthing, "Luc?"

He ignored her and listened.

"Okay, here's the deal. I sold her car and gave Doucet the twenty thou, and I made him sign a receipt for payment. He was not a happy camper. He wanted all or nothing, with the interest clock ticking away."

"I figured as much." *Lordy, Lordy! Do I really need all this stress in my life?*

"Threatening to go to the police turned him downright mean. I don't think he's Mafia, like Charmaine does, but he's in some kind of lowlife mob that the police would be interested in."

Not The Godfather, *just one of the Houma hood, huh?* "I've never met him before, I don't think."

"You'd remember if you had. He looks like a Cajun Danny DeVito. A short, little bastard, but ornery as a piss ant."

Raoul laughed. "So, what's the bottom line?"

"She has got to stay out of sight for a couple of weeks. Maybe I should find another hideout for her, though. I don't want to get you in trouble. You know, with your parole board."

"Not to worry." *I'm on the side of the good guys here. No harm in that. At least, I think Charmaine is a good guy. Hah! No question about that. Charmaine is very good.*

"I'm going to continue to act as go-between with Doucet, try to set up a reasonable payment plan, but I can't do it if Charmaine comes back to Houma too soon. Do you get my drift?"

"Gotcha." *Charmaine doesn't know how to be invisible in a town like Houma. Hell, she's like a blinkin' neon sign here on a remote ranch.*

"I'm also looking into your felony conviction."

That surprised Raoul. *I swear, Charmaine has the most interfering family in the whole world.* "Who asked you to do that?"

"Charmaine."

That figures. He glared at Charmaine, who was

clearing the table of soiled dishes. She stuck her tongue out at him.

"Well, let me amend that. Charmaine didn't directly ask me to help you. She just mentioned that you'd been framed. I know a good private investigator. Really good. Are you interested?"

"For sure," he said, and jotted down the name and number on a nearby pad. "Though I don't have much cash right now."

"Use my name for a reference. He owes me."

"Thanks for your help."

"One more thing. Charmaine asked me to check out your divorce."

"Oh?" Immediately he felt as if he had a boulder in his stomach.

"You're not."

"I already knew that." The boulder churned, turning him a little queasy.

"Do you want to be?"

Divorced from Charmaine? "Yes. Sure. Hell, I don't know."

"That's the same thing Charmaine said."

Hmmm. Now, that is interesting. He glanced over at Charmaine, who was singing "Laughin' My Way Back to Lafayette" along with Jimmy Newman on the radio and washing dishes in the soapy water of the sink. She kept the beat by rolling her hips from side to side, with an occasional shimmy thrown in. Raoul was pretty sure he was going to have a stroke or something by the time Charmaine left.

If she ever does leave, a voice in his head, or some place, said. He looked toward the front porch, through an open stretch of space between the kitchen, dining room and living room. There he saw a life-sized, plastic statue of St. Jude peering in at him through the window.

He groaned inwardly. *Could it be?*

Nah.

Wanna bet? the voice said.

He groaned aloud then. *I am being attacked from all sides. I do not friggin' stand a chance.*

One ringy-dingy, two ringy-dingy . . .

Rusty was long gone, and Charmaine had just finished her phone call with Luc when the wall phone rang again.

Should she or shouldn't she answer it? Rusty had ordered her not to, but then he was probably being overly cautious. On the other hand, Luc had advised her to be careful, too. Not answering a ringing phone bothered her. Maybe she could just pick it up and wait for the other person to speak first. That wouldn't be so bad, would it? No risk there.

Tentatively, she held the receiver to her ear.

"Hello. Hello. Is someone there? Rusty?"

It was a woman. Charmaine bared her teeth and replied sweetly, "Mr. Lanier is not available right now. Who's calling?"

"Amelie Ancelet. Dr. Amelie Ancelet. Since when does Rusty have a secretary?"

I'll give you secretary, Ms. I-am-a-doctor-bigshot. But then the woman's words sank in. "You're a physician? What's wrong? Is Rusty sick? Oh, my God, was there an accident or something and he's in the emergency room? Did he fall off his horse?"

The woman on the other end laughed. A young laugh. "I'm a veterinarian. A friend of Rusty's."

I'll just bet.

"Who is this, by the way?" the *friend* asked.

Charmaine took great delight in announcing, "Mrs. Lanier."

"Huh?"

"Mrs. Rusty Lanier." *Oooh, boy, I am really pathetic, getting my jollies by proclaiming my wifehood. Not that I'm really a wife, but it does come in handy.*

"Charmaine?"

Red flags went up in Charmaine's head. "You know about me?"

"Of course. Rusty talks about you all the time. His famous ex-wife."

Famous? I can just imagine what he said about me. Well, tit for tat, buddy. I really should not be doing this, but what the hell! "Not so ex, honey."

"I beg your pardon."

You very well should be begging my pardon . . . hitting on a married man. "We're not divorced."

There was a telling silence on the line. *Friends, indeed!*

"Would you tell Rusty that I called? And remind him about the party on Saturday night." Amelie's voice was chilly now.

"Sure thing, Amelie. I'll give my *husband* the message. Bye-bye."

Charmaine shook her head at her own juvenile behavior when she hung up the phone. It was only then that she noticed the St. Jude statue on the front porch where she'd placed it yesterday till she could find a place for it. Good ol' Jude seemed to be watching her through the window. For one brief moment, she thought she heard the statue speak to her.

"Tsk-tsk-tsk," it said.

One ringy-dingy, two ringy-dingy . . .

The next time the phone rang, Charmaine didn't even hesitate to answer it.

"You got flowers on that there ranch?"

"What? Is that you, Tante Lulu?"

"'Course it's me. Who'd ya think it was? Gina Lolla-whatchamahoozit?"

"Where'd you get this number? Luc wouldn't even let me give it to my shop managers."

"I got my ways." She chuckled. "Actually, I'm in Luc's office. Sylvie brought me over. Luc took her down to the file storage room to look fer sumpin. Hah! I know what they's doin' down there. Hanky-panky."

"Auntie, you don't know that."

"Yeah, I do. He was lookin' at her like she was a sweet beignet, and she was looking at him like he was one of them Chippendale fellas and she just happened to have a five-dollar bill in her pocket."

Charmaine couldn't help but laugh. It was true. Married for five years, Luc and Sylvie were still crazy in love with each other. But all that was beside the point. "Why do you want to know about flowers here at the ranch?"

"'Cause I was thinnin' out my flower beds and I got lots of extra plants I could bring fer Rusty's ranch. Irises. Magnolia bushes. Climbing roses. Okra."

How okra fit in with all those flowers, Charmaine

had no idea, and she wasn't about to ask. "I'm not sure about you sending plants to the ranch. Rusty's already upset about all the cleaning I've been doing inside the house."

"Cleanin'? Is the place dirty?" Tante Lulu sounded gleeful at the prospect of a dirty house.

"Filthy. I swear, there are parts of this ranch house that haven't been touched in years. I haven't even started on the living room. Or the third bedroom. Or the pantry."

"Oooh, oooh, oooh. Doan you be doin' any more cleanin' till I get there." Aside from her healing arts, Tante Lulu enjoyed nothing more than a good spring cleaning, and, although it was winter, she would go through the place like a dervish and love every minute of it.

"Tante Lulu, I don't think it's a good idea for you to come here now. You might be followed by Bobby Doucet."

"Hah! I ain't afraid of that dumb dilly. Besides, I got a gun. And I need to get my car back. Oooh, oooh, oooh, I know what. I'll have Remy drive me there in his whirly bird. No one can follow us then." Charmaine's half-brother Remy was a pilot. "Mebbe he'll bring Rachel with him." Rachel was Remy's new wife.

Charmaine groaned. "Tante Lulu, believe me, Rusty is not going to appreciate your coming here. And the helicopter will probably stir up his cattle."

Tante Lulu totally ignored her protests and went on to another subject. "Next week's Thanksgivin'. You got a turkey yet?"

"No, I don't have a turkey, and don't you dare bring a turkey here."

"I wasn't even thinkin' of bringin' a turkey. Betcha I

could talk that Clarence into shootin' me a wild bird, though. Do you have all the fixin's? Nevermind, we kin take care of that later."

"I . . . I . . . I . . ." she sputtered. The idea of a Thanksgiving feast, Tante Lulu style, was more than Charmaine could fathom at the moment.

"The best part is, once Thanksgiving's over, we can start decoratin' fer Christmas. Dontcha jist love this time of year?"

Where in God's name am I going to find Christmas decorations? Charlie Lanier was a nice old man, but Scrooge when it came to sentimental things, like Christmas. There probably isn't a string of lights or a tree ornament on the whole place. Charmaine had to stop this Cajun train, which was Tante Lulu once she got an idea in her head, before it went any farther. "Now, just wait a minute here, Tante Lulu. You can't come here and—"

A dial tone rang in Charmaine's ear. Tante Lulu had hung up on her.

Rusty is going to kill me.

Was that laughing she heard out on the front porch? Had Rusty or one of the guys come back?

Nope, she decided, after going out to check. The only one there was St. Jude.

One ringy-dingy, two ringy-dingy . . .

The phone rang again a short time later, which meant Charmaine had to climb down from the ladder in the middle of the kitchen. She had been cleaning the ceiling fan.

"Hello," she snapped churlishly the instant she picked up the phone.

"Charmaine, what the hell are you doing answering the phone? I specifically ordered you not to answer the phone." It was Rusty.

Like you have the right to order me to do anything. "Then what the hell are you doing calling me?"

"It was a mistake. I meant to call Clarence's cell phone."

Likely story. You missed me, buddy. Admit it. "Where are you anyway?"

"I'm in town. We ran out of fence nails."

"Can you bring home some extra milk?"

After a long pause, he said, "You sound like a wife, Charmaine."

"And that's a bad thing?"

"That is a bad thing."

"Screw the milk then."

"I'll get the damn milk."

She hung up on him.

And she didn't even bother to look toward St. Jude. She knew he would be tsk-ing.

One ringy-dingy, two ringy-dingy . . .

"What now?" she yelled into the phone when it rang several moments later.

"You picked up the phone again," Rusty yelled back.

"What? Now, you're checking up on me?"

"Damn right I am. Do . . . not . . . pick . . . up . . . the . . . freakin' . . . phone. Was that clear enough for you?"

"Sure. Is this clear enough for you? Go . . . to . . . hell!"

She hung up on him again.

Next time the phone rang she didn't pick it up, but not because he'd told her not to. She didn't pick it up because she knew it was him again, trying to get the last word in, and she wanted to annoy him.

There were a half dozen other calls after that, but she turned on the answering machine. People from various oil companies were attempting to contact Rusty. Surprise, surprise.

A cowboy's day is never done . . .

It was seven o'clock before they got back to the ranch house, and the four of them were bone-weary and discouraged with all the work they'd done that day . . . and all the work they'd never gotten to. The Triple L needed more cowboys, at least on a part-time basis, but Raoul just didn't have the cash for that.

"I'll meet you back at the house in a half hour," Raoul told Clarence, Linc, and Jimmy. "After we wash up, we can eat."

"I swear, I'm gonna fall in my bed tonight," Clarence said. "But I caint, not without showerin' first, since Charmaine put clean sheets on my bed. Not that I'm complainin', mind you."

"She dusted and waxed my guitar," Linc added. "No one never dusted and waxed my guitar before."

Apparently, waxing must not be the norm for guitars, Raoul thought, chuckling. But Linc would never dare tell that to Charmaine. Instead, he'd probably hide his instrument.

"I hope Charmaine made somethin' good fer dinner." Jimmy licked his lips in anticipation.

Raoul hated the fact that Charmaine had insinuated herself into all their lives after only three days here. Even he brightened at the prospect of seeing her again, and it wasn't her food that hot-damn lured him.

Linc ruffled Jimmy's dusty hair. "Well, it's not meat loaf leftovers, for sure. You ate all that last night."

Jimmy ducked his head and blushed. Amazing how Jimmy could switch personalities so quickly and so often . . . a regular teenage Dr. Jekyll. Today he'd gone into a cursing rage because he'd been hot and tired and wanted to go for a swim. A swim at this time of the year and in the middle of a job! Talk about! He'd even thrown a few wild punches at Linc when he'd tried to chastise him. And now, he went all red-faced and flustered like any typical kid when teased over a lousy meat loaf. Raoul would like to see Charmaine's reaction if he ever acted out around her. *Whoo-boy!*

As he entered the house, Raoul heard Charmaine bustling around the kitchen. He called out to her, "We're back," but went immediately to the bathroom without waiting for her reply. He did a double take at what he saw. Her stuff was everywhere. Along the lip of the tub were a pink razor, lilac shaving gel, scented liquid soap, something called hydrating lotion and three different shampoos and conditioners. On the small counter next to the sink, he could barely find his electric razor, what with her blow dryer, combs, round brushes of different sizes, a cosmetics bag the size of Vermont, and a bottle of Obsession perfume. He sniffed the latter and realized that it was the same scent she'd worn all those years ago. And, yes, Obsession about said it all, at least on his part.

Looking around the small, suddenly overcrowded bathroom, he realized that Charmaine was taking over his space . . . literally. Putting her mark on every bit of his home. Okay, their home.

Opening the medicine cabinet to get a much-needed aspirin, he got another jolt. A little round plastic case containing a month's supply of birth control pills. Now, why would a born-again virgin need birth control pills? And since she claimed not to have had a date in six months and her new virginity presumably started only a week ago and three weeks worth of pills had already been consumed, a guy could only wonder.

I should not be wondering. I should not care. I need to focus, to prioritize. And Charmaine cannot, will not, be a top priority of mine. No way! He sighed deeply at the jumble Charmaine was making of his life.

After a really long, hot shower, he picked up all his dirty clothes and put them in the hamper. He didn't want Charmaine picking up after him. Next she'd be waxing things he didn't want waxed. Then he wrapped a towel around his middle and walked to his bedroom.

He was tempted to lie down on the bed with its clean quilt and take a nap, but he knew he wouldn't wake till morning. And his stomach was growling with hunger.

Dropping his towel, he went to his underwear drawer and pulled out a pair of briefs. He paused at the scent of flowers that wafted up from the drawer, where she'd neatly arranged all his folded briefs in two long rows. "Jesus!" he murmured under his breath. *Flowers! My underwear smells like flowers*. He soon realized the cause. Charmaine had placed a dryer sheet in the drawer, something she used to do when they were still married. When they were still married and living together as man and wife, he corrected himself.

He noticed something else at the bottom of the drawer. Their framed wedding picture, which he'd placed there a long time ago. He took it out and gazed at it. They'd run away and eloped. No big wedding with long white gown and fancy tuxedo. He'd worn a plain black suit and dark tie. Charmaine had worn a pink frothy dress with long sleeves and a ruffled hem that ended just below her knees. Sheer stockings ended in pink, high-heeled sandals, which she'd worn for him later that night, with nothing else. She'd been nineteen and he'd just turned twenty-one. So young and so damn good looking, both of them. They stared at each other with so much love it made his heart ache.

He exhaled with disgust at his maudlin reverie and placed the photograph back in the drawer, under the briefs. Charmaine had to have seen it when she'd straightened out his drawers. What had she thought?

Enough dwelling on the past! He pulled on his briefs, a pair of clean jeans and T-shirt, ran a brush through his too-long hair, saw that he needed a shave as well as a haircut, but was too tired to do anything about either one. Then he walked to the kitchen in his bare feet.

His eyes about bugged out at the scene before him. Everyone, including Charmaine, sat around the kitchen table which was covered with a tablecloth today. God only knew where Charmaine had found a tablecloth. Two mismatched, lit candles, one blue and one green, sat at either end. A huge tureen filled with what looked and smelled like chicken gumbo held center stage, flanked by about five quarts of dirty rice, corn bread, some kind of lettuce-and-tomato salad, and a pitcher of iced sweet tea. A be-still-my-heart bread pudding cooled on the stove next to a pot of steaming coffee.

The whole scene was something out of The Waltons TV show. *She's killing me here. With kindness, for chrissake. And birth control pills, and lilac shaving gel, and folded underwear, and Obsession perfume.*

"Well, dontcha wanna say sumpin?" Clarence prodded him.

"Uh, everything looks great. Dig in. Don't wait for me."

He glanced over at Charmaine as he spoke and added a silently mouthed "Thank you" just for her. Her response was a little curtsy move with her shoulders.

She sat at one end of the table looking all prettified in full makeup with her hair pulled back off her face with a white ribbon. The white ribbon matched her white shirt, which, for once, had no suggestive logo. It didn't need one. He could see her bra through the thin material. In fact, he could see the lace details on her bra. It was giving him all the suggestive messages he needed and a few he didn't need.

Charmaine was buttering him up for something. He would bet his boots on that. Maybe she just wanted to make up for hanging up on him today . . . twice. Or maybe she planned something else. It was always best to be on guard with Charmaine.

At first, they all ate in silence, satisfying their ravenous hunger and their appreciation for the fine food.

"Jimmy, we gotta have a talk," Linc said. "Today you had a tantrum when we wouldn't let you quit in the middle of a job to go swimmin'. Yesterday, you foul-mouthed that sheriff when he was askin' questions 'bout the dead steers. I admit, the sheriff was rude, but you gotta learn to curb that tongue of yers."

Jimmy glanced toward Charmaine, embarrassed to be reprimanded in front of her. Then he lashed out at Linc. "Yer not my dad. I doan have to do what you say."

Raoul saw the shock on Charmaine's face as she halted halfway between the stove and the table. She was carrying the coffeepot in one hand and the bread pudding in the other.

Before Raoul could speak, Clarence said, "Now, boy, that'll be enough of that kind of talk."

Jimmy started to rise from the table, to flee God-only-knew where.

Putting a hand on Jimmy's shoulder, Raoul forced the boy to sit back down.

"Take yer hands off me, ya scummy ex-con."

Everyone was taken aback by Jimmy's unprovoked anger, especially Charmaine, apparently, because she slammed the coffeepot and dessert dish on the table and stormed around to Jimmy's side. Poking a forefinger in his face, she said, "Listen up, you snot-nosed punk. No one talks to Rusty that way. He's been nothing but kind to you. If you haven't concluded by now that he was framed, then you're not as smart as I thought you were."

Holy shit! Charmaine is coming to my defense like a bleepin' pit bull. Who would have ever imagined? And, dammit, does she think I'm so helpless I can't defend myself against a teenager? He couldn't stop himself from grinning.

Pulling Charmaine away and tucking her behind him, he addressed poor Jimmy, whose eyes were brimming with tears. The kid adored Charmaine and had to be hurt by her attack. He knew from experience that the kid was about to bolt. "Listen, we're not your father, but he gave us the authority. It was either that or send you to juvie hall. Now, you're gonna toe the line, or suffer the consequences. Do you understand?"

Jimmy's lower lip protruded with rebellion, but he nodded.

"First off, you are going to apologize to Linc."

To Jimmy's credit, he appeared shamedfaced. "I'm sorry, Linc. But I ain't no snot-nosed punk." He looked accusingly at Charmaine, who stood to his side now.

"I know that, honey. You were just *behaving* like a snot-nosed punk." Charmaine gave Jimmy a big hug. When she was done, Raoul held out his arms for her to give him a big hug, too, but she walked right past him, sniffing her disdain. Clarence snorted with disgust at his lack of finesse and Linc hid a grin behind his hand.

After that, they dug into Charmaine's dessert and devoured every bit of it. He noticed that Jimmy got an extra large serving.

"Where'd you get the chicken for the gumbo?" he asked Charmaine, just making conversation to take the attention away from Jimmy. "Dare I hope it was one of those mean roosters that've been strutting around out front?"

"Yep. Clarence came up and killed one for me. Even plucked and gutted it. I never would have been able to do it myself." Charmaine patted Clarence's shoulder as she picked up the empty dessert dishes.

The old cowboy beamed under her compliment.

"By the way, your girlfriend called today."

Anyone else would think that Charmaine's remark had

come out of the blue, but not Raoul. He knew damn well she had planned its timing with precision.

"My girlfriend?" Raoul drawled out.

"Musta been Rita," Jimmy said. "The waitress at The Horny Bull."

Charmaine pinched his shoulder. Hard.

Raoul shot Jimmy a dirty look, but Jimmy just batted his eyelashes at him. Retribution came in any form for a fifteen-year-old.

Charmaine narrowed her eyes at him. The expression on her face pretty much put him in the category of . . . well, horny bulls. "No, it wasn't Rita. It was Am-el-ie."

Is Charmaine jealous? Is that possible? Hmmm. "Amelie?" he inquired with a frown, though he knew perfectly well who she referred to.

"Puh-leeze. Don't play dumb with me."

"Oh, you mean Amelie Ancelet."

"*Doctor* Am-el-ie Ancelet. Am-el-ie made sure she pointed out to me that she's a doctor. I'm surprised she didn't spell it for me. You know, we bimbos aren't all that smart."

Raoul laughed. Charmaine really was jealous. Now, wasn't that an interesting turn of events?

Charmaine made a little feral growl in her throat, like a wildcat. "She said to remind you about your date Saturday night."

"What date?"

"Puh-leeze," she said again, and for sure her fangs were about to come out. "The party."

"Oh. That party."

"Yes, the party, you moron."

Clarence, Linc and Jimmy were pivoting their heads back and forth like bobble heads, enjoying the interchange between the two of them. They'd have something to talk about when they went back to the bunkhouse tonight.

Moron, huh? He grinned at the vehemence of the epithet she gave him. Somehow, Charmaine made moron sound sexy. "Her father, Cletus Ancelet, is retiring after forty years as the town veterinarian. Amelie is taking over his practice," he explained. "Anyhow, a big barbecue bash is being held to celebrate Cletus's retirement."

"How nice!"

I shouldn't be teasing Charmaine like this. "Amelie is just a friend."

"Hah! Some men can't see past the smoke some women blow in their faces. Morons! All of them."

"Amelie and I met in medical school. Being from Cajun backgrounds and sharing an interest in animal studies, it was natural that . . . What the hell are you all thinking?"

Clarence, Linc and Jimmy were laughing outright now, with Clarence slapping his knee with glee. He probably figured arguing with Charmaine was two steps away from making her bowlegged.

"And how do you and your cows feel about helicopters?" she asked him way too sweetly, with utter irrelevance.

"Huh?"

"Helicopters? Do your cows mind when helicopters land in their backyard? Do they stop milking or something?"

I sense a little payback coming up. "Hell, yes, they mind. But, Charmaine, there's something you need to know if you're going to hang around this ranch. I don't have a dairy farm. This is a cattle ranch."

She waved a hand airily, as if there were no difference between a milk cow and a beef steer. But then she frowned. "Are you saying I'm a dumb bimbo who can't understand the difference between a cow and a bull?"

"I never used the word 'bimbo.'" *Man, she is obsessed with that one single time I called her a bimbo. Why is it women never forget the things we men say? We forget the things women say right after they leave their mouths.*

"Oooh, boy, you are asking for it. I do not like your attitude."

"Attitude? I don't have an attitude." *You are the one who is reeking with attitude, but I don't think I'll point that out right now.*

"I'm sensing an attitude. And, for your information, buster, I happen to know the difference between a cow and a bull. One has udders and the other has balls. So there!"

Everyone burst out laughing then, except Charmaine, who looked as if she was about to windmill her right arm and sock him a good one.

This was absolutely the most ridiculous conversation, and even though his three workers were enjoying it immensely, he had to put a stop to it. "Um, could we backtrack here? You mentioned a helicopter. Is someone going to land a helicopter on the ranch?"

"Maybe." She averted her eyes guiltily.

"Maybe? Like maybe who? No, don't tell me. Your half brother Remy. He's coming here, right?"

Charmaine nodded with a little gloating smile that turned up her red lips. Jimmy got his revenge by bringing up Rita the hottie waitress. Charmaine got her kicks popping these surprises on him.

I shouldn't ask. I really shouldn't. "Why?"

"He's bringing a visitor."

A door-to-door salesman is a visitor. The Three Wise Men were visitors. We do not get visitors at the ranch. "Would you just spill it, Charmaine? What is all this mystery about? Who's coming?"

"Tante Lulu."

He put his face in his hands and groaned.

"And—"

There was a long, telling silence till he raised his head and asked, "And . . . ?"

"And I think Remy might be bringing his new wife, Rachel, with him. She's a Feng Shui decorator."

"And that is relevant to me how?"

"She'll probably have some ideas for Feng Shui-ing the ranch. She did a great job on my spa in Houma."

Her wacky aunt and a wacky decorator! I think I'll go slit my wrists now. "Aaarrgh! You call your aunt right now and tell her not to come. I don't want a helicopter here. I don't want your interfering aunt here. And I sure-as-hell don't want a Feng Shui nutcase here either."

"Tante Lulu hung up on me, and she hasn't answered her phone since then. Don't worry. They probably won't come till tomorrow or the next day."

Raoul stood and started to stomp off toward the front of the house.

"Rusty? Where you going?"

To the nearest cliff. Where I hope to jump off. "To find that St. Jude statue."

"Why?"

"To pray. If ever there was a hopeless cause, it's me."
And I'm getting hopelesser by the minute.

"Pray for me, too," Charmaine called out, which he thought really odd. "I'm gonna need it."

He wasn't about to ask why. He was no moron.

Chapter 6

It was hot and wet and slippery . . .

Rusty was washing dishes and Charmaine was drying, at his insistence. Who knew dishwashing could be an erotic experience?

Every time Rusty dipped his hands in the sudsy water and ran a soapy sponge over a plate, Charmaine couldn't help but admire his long fingers and the gentle way he handled the slippery plates. She remembered a time when Rusty's fingers had been just as wet and sudsy and gentle, working their magic on her, in a bubble bath back in their tiny apartment. At the sweet memory, her nipples went hard and a soft pulse began between her legs, like a heartbeat.

Sometimes being a twenty-nine-year-old virgin is damned hard. Especially a twenty-nine-year-old virgin with a carnal memory. I better get out my born-again virgin vow and repeat it again . . . and again . . . and again. I will be pure. I will be pure. I will be pure. Charmaine smiled to herself at her impure thoughts.

"Charmaine! What are you dreaming about?" Rusty was staring at her, half-shocked, half-amused. Actually, he was staring at the front of her blouse, where her arousal must have been evident.

"Nothing," she said, averting her face from his too-knowing eyes. *Nothing that I want you to know. You'd pounce on me like a Cajun on a mudbug.* "Tell me more about Jimmy and why he behaved so badly tonight." *Safe subject. Whew!*

"He's a troubled kid. He wouldn't be here otherwise," Rusty said, wiping his hands on a dish towel and leaning back against the sink. "At the least, he's got ADD, an inability to concentrate very well without medication, and at worst, he's emotionally disturbed."

Charmaine nodded. "I understand, somewhat, but that doesn't explain his outburst."

"Frustration, pure and simple. I'm no psychiatrist, but my guess is he has difficulty succeeding in school. Not that he's dumb or anything, far from it. Just that he learns differently, and some schools just aren't equipped to handle special needs kids. Written tests, for example, are a major problem for him. Add to that, his mother dying."

"So you offered to help?"

"Clarence asked for my advice, and we agreed to give it a shot."

"Wasn't that a lot to take on, with all that you have on your plate right now?"

He shrugged. "The boy is the least of my problems. It was worth a shot. If it doesn't work out, he's out of here. His father's responsibility."

"I'm surprised his dad hasn't visited."

"He will, eventually. Probably this weekend. It was agreed, by everyone, that he had to step out of the picture for a while."

"He seemed like such a good kid the first time I met him."

"He is a good kid. Just a little mixed up. Give him a chance."

"Oh, I will. In fact, I have some ideas how I might help him redirect some of his anger."

Rusty turned around and began scrubbing the pots and pans with a steel wool pad. "So, why does a born-again virgin need birth control pills?" he asked all of a sudden.

"I beg your pardon." She glowered at him. "Have you been spying on me?"

"Hard not to notice when your stuff is spread all over the place. I was looking for aspirin."

"Likely story. I take birth control pills just in case."

"Just in case?" He smiled and her heart flipped over. God must have been playing a joke on womankind when He gave Rusty a smile like that. "Just in case what?"

"I get tempted." *And that is the God's honest truth.*

"By me?" He smiled even wider.

The too-perceptive lout! "No. By some drop-dead-gorgeous hunk who drops by one day to deliver fertilizer, or a door-to-door salesman with a pitch to die for, or the butcher at the supermarket whose meat turns out to be extra tempting." *Or a Cajun cowboy with a grin and wink that would melt the most fervent vows.*

"You're afraid of being tempted by me," he insisted.

Bingo! "Am not."

He looked pointedly at her nipples, which were pointing.

Sometimes women are just as bad as men when it comes to body parts giving them away. "Stop that. Stop it right now." She wasn't sure if she was speaking to Rusty or her nipples. Neither of them paid any attention to her orders.

"Stop what?"

Like you don't know! "Smoldering."

His head jerked up with surprise. "Was I smoldering?"

Like the coals in a pig roast pit.

"Clarence says I should smolder more," he said.

Uh, I don't think so.

"I didn't even know I could smolder. Who knew?" He appeared really pleased with himself, that he could smolder.

"Clarence? Don't tell me. He's giving you more romance advice." *I could use a little romance advice. Like, how to withstand a smoldering cowboy.*

"Yep. Bowlegging you and smoldering you. Surefire winners in his seduction book." He waggled his eyebrows at her.

She laughed and shook her head from side to side. "We are a sad pair, us two. The Lady on the Lam and The Smoldering Cowboy."

"Yep," he said again, still idly scrubbing away at the pots and pans and the baking dish.

"Rusty, we have got to clear the air about something."

"Uh-oh."

"You really, really tempt me, but—"

"—but we are not going to make love," he finished for her with an exaggerated sigh.

"Exactly." *Unfortunately.*

"I tempt you?" he asked, homing in on the least relevant thing she'd said. Well, it *was* relevant, but only to the no-sex conclusion.

"Tsk-tsk!" She figured that was answer enough.

"Why? I mean, why the no-sex rule?"

Setting her dish towel down, she gave him her full attention. "I know you think my born-again virgin vow is a hoot, just a lot of nonsense. It is funny, considering my history, I admit that, but it's significant to me."

"Hell, it's significant to me, too." He winked at her.

"Listen, I'm serious here. I'm not good at relationships. Whether they were valid or not, I've been married four times, and all four of them failed for one reason or another. And I've been involved with a few other men, and those didn't last either."

"A few?"

"A few."

"Charmaine, you and I have the hots for each other. We always did, probably always will. Why do you have to analyze things to death? You'll be here a few weeks. What's wrong with enjoying each other while you're here?"

"And then?" Her blood suddenly turned cold.

"We get a divorce." At least he had the grace to blush when he said that.

I feel like crying. I really do. She couldn't get mad at him, though. Other than sex, after ten long years, they had no basis for a marriage. "See, that's where we're different. You want a fling. I want forever."

That got his attention. "From me? You want forever? From me?" His voice was shrill with shock.

You would have thought she'd asked him to cut off his balls and wrap them in a gift box. "No. I mean, not necessarily. Probably not. Aaarrgh! Stop confusing me."

He grinned, as if confusing her were a good thing . . . or as if confusion was her normal state.

"Bottom line. Next man I get involved with, it won't be a fling."

"In other words, back off?"

She nodded. "I know why I don't want to get involved

with you again, Rusty, but what's your problem? You moved beyond bimbos?" *God! How much more pathetic can I get?*

"Charmaine, what is it with you and the bimbo crap? You go for the image, rub it in people's faces, then get offended if they take you for what you are."

Look beyond the facade, Dumbo. Care enough to know me. That's what I want. "I am what I am," she said stubbornly, though that didn't really answer his question.

"Yeah, well, I am what I am, too." Rusty could be stubborn, too. "Truth to tell, honey, there's a lot of my father in me. Once my mother did a job on my father, he shut himself off emotionally. To everyone, including me. He never wanted to risk himself again. He became a bitter shell of a man. I have no desire to get married again. Once burned and all that stuff."

"Your father was as misunderstood as I am."

"I haven't a clue what that means." He shrugged. "So, I'm a bitter young man."

It was a sad picture Rusty painted of himself.

"And that's all you want?"

Rusty stood with his hands in the water for several long moments before he turned to her and suddenly placed his wet hands over her breasts. "Nope, that's not all I want."

Did the man hear one single word I just said? She blinked with shock at the wet hands cupping her breasts.

Before she had a chance to shriek, or bop him on the head with the soup ladle sitting in the draining rack, he moved his hands and fingers over her breasts so that the fabric of her blouse stuck wetly to her. Only then did he step back and look at her.

"Wha . . . why did you do that?"

"Oh, darlin', I've wanted to do that since I stepped into this kitchen tonight and saw you in that see-through shirt. I figured with the no-sex line you just drew in the sand—uh, linoleum—this would be my last chance."

He is incorrigible. "It's not a see-through shirt," she said indignantly, then looked down to see herself clearly outlined as if the white blouse and nude-colored bra were nonexistent. "At least it wasn't see-through before."

"If you're going to slap me, you better do it quick before I kiss you."

Kiss? Oh, no! If he kisses me, I am a goner. "This is a bad idea," she said, even as she allowed him to back her up against the wall.

"It's the best damn bad idea I've had in ages." He nuzzled her neck and nibbled a line from her ear to her chin, then back again. "Uhmmm," he whispered into her ear as he licked and blew and about shattered every resolution she'd ever made not to get involved with him—or any man—again. Four broken marriages and a dozen failed relationships over the past ten years had finally sunk in, or so she'd thought until now.

"Remind me again why you're doing this." She moaned even as she spoke, so intense was the pleasure of his mouth brushing across hers.

"Because you heat my blood and melt my bones. Because you turn me breathless. Because you tempt me."

Sounds good to me. He lifted her by the waist so she stood on tiptoes. Then he used his knees to spread her legs and nest himself against her groin. His erection fit perfectly between her legs. Even with her slacks and his jeans, she felt him. And she wanted him.

He closed his eyes and groaned, a deep, masculine sound, accentuated by the arch of his neck and the press of his belly against her belly. His thick eyelashes lay like jet-black fans on his tanned skin. What an odd thing to notice when her blood felt like molten roux moving through her body!

Opening his eyes slowly, he gazed at her. His dark eyes were hazed with arousal. "Come to bed with me, sweetheart," his voice rasped out, thick and raw.

Does he have to talk? Did he have to ask for my permission? Couldn't he just carry me off like some Cajun caveman, and then later I could say I hadn't actually consented?

"Please."

Oh, God! He had to throw in the please card. She moaned and hesitated just long enough for Rusty to realize that she wasn't falling into his bed. Not that easy.

He stepped back an inch or two and let her lower herself from tiptoes to stand on the floor. Her knees were shaky, but she managed to stand upright.

"I'm sorry, Rusty. It's just that I can't do this again. Not without—"

He put a hand up, halting her words. "I get it, Charmaine. I get it." Turning away from her, he adjusted his pants and walked toward the door that led to the back porch. When he got there, he breathed deeply several times, then said, "You might consider going back with Remy and your aunt when they come here. Luc will find another safe place for you."

Tears were running down her face. Not for herself, but for Rusty. Somehow, she had hurt him, and she didn't know how to fix the pain. With a catch in her voice, she asked, "Why?"

"Because if you stay here, I won't be able to keep my hands off you, born-again cupcake or not."

"Don't threaten me."

"That's not a threat, darlin'. That's a promise." With those ominous words, he moved out into the darkness beyond the porch.

Hot stuff . . . and then some!

It was Saturday night, and Raoul was more than ready to paint the town . . . or a small portion of Lake Charles.

He heard Amelie's horn just as he came out of his bedroom and she pulled into the front yard. He gave only a cursory glance at Charmaine's closed door. Let her sulk. She'd been avoiding him for two days, ever since he'd advised her to leave the ranch when Remy and her aunt arrived, which should be tomorrow. He didn't know if her silence meant she was going to leave or if she was digging in her heels. She'd been warned.

And he didn't want to examine too closely the near panic that overcame him every time he contemplated her actually leaving. He also wasn't examining too closely their explosive almost-sex encounter in the kitchen two nights ago. Whoo-ee! The two of them were like flint on dry tinder. They had to put distance between them, painful as it would be . . . at least, for him.

When he went out on the porch and down to the yard, Amelie waved and got out of her red Volkswagen van with ANCELET VETERINARY CLINIC printed on the side. She gave him a quick kiss on the cheek and hugged him warmly.

"You're lookin' good, buddy. No more prison pallor."

"You're lookin' pretty good yourself, darlin'."

Amelie was a fine-looking woman, short and small-boned, with dark Cajun hair. They'd met in vet school. She'd stuck by him at his trial and the whole time he was in the slammer, with frequent visits. He owed her a lot. But it was true what he'd told Charmaine. Amelie was a good friend. That was all.

Amelie waved at Linc and Clarence, who were sitting on rockers on the front porch, all spiffied up in clean jeans with ironed pleats, thanks to Charmaine, cowboy shirts with snaps instead of buttons, and string ties. He wore jeans, also sporting the freakin' pleats, a light blue T-shirt and a navy blue blazer. That was as dressed up as he got these days.

"What are you guys up to tonight?" he asked, draping an arm over Amelie's shoulder.

It was Linc who answered. "Goin' to The Horny Bull fer a little beer and dinner. Mebbe some dancin', if I can find a gal who's willin'. Jimmy's father picked him up fer an overnight visit, so we're just a couple of wild and crazy guys tonight."

"So what are you two waiting for?"

Linc looked at Clarence. Clarence looked at Linc. Then the two of them looked at him guiltily. "Waitin' fer Charmaine," Clarence finally disclosed.

"What?" Raoul practically yelled. "Charmaine is supposed to stay in hiding, to be inconspicuous. What could she be thinking? The Horny Bull? I . . . don't . . . think . . . so."

"Are you talking about me?" Charmaine asked sweetly, coming out onto the porch. "You must be the *famous* Am-el-ie." She gave a little wave to Amelie. Then her eyes latched on to his arm on Amelie's shoulder, and he could swear she growled. "Good friends, indeed!" she muttered under her breath.

Four jaws had dropped open at the sight that Charmaine presented. She wore skintight, white jeans and red high-heeled cowboy boots, which matched perfectly her red lipstick and red fingernails. From her ears dangled a god-awful bunch of shiny things that looked like fishing lures. Her dark hair was poufed up and out and over her shoulders in a mass of curls designed to look as if she'd just fallen out of bed, but had probably taken an hour to perfect. On top . . . oh, my God . . . on top, she wore a stretchy white, long-sleeved shirt, tucked into her jeans. It was covered with red and gold sequins that would no doubt glow in the dark and sported the logo I AM A TEASER.

In essence, Charmaine represented every man's fantasy of a sex kitten. A wet dream in the flesh.

And Charmaine did it on purpose. She had deliberately made herself into a bimbo. It pretty much said, "In your face, bozo." In the face of everyone, for that matter. Like it or leave it, was the message she proclaimed with this attire, like a blinkin' red light.

"Uh . . . nice outfit," Amelie said, which was laughable coming from her since she wore a very demure jeans skirt down to midcalf and a long-sleeved plaid shirt. Makeup on her was at a minimum. Belatedly noticing the little smirk on her face, Raoul decided that she'd meant her comment to belittle, not compliment. How unlike Amelie!

"Thanks, sweetie," Charmaine replied, in a not-so-sweet voice, giving Amelie a sweeping head-to-toe survey of disdain.

Mon Dieu, next he would be witnessing a catfight.

"You are not going anywhere, dressed like that," he said, dropping his hand from Amelie's shoulder and walking slowly up the wooden steps. He was so angry he could hardly breathe.

To her credit, or to her stupidity, she didn't back up one bit. "I beg your pardon," she said, batting her eyelashes, which were too big to be real. "Who died and named you master? Oops, sorry, have you suddenly decided to become my *forever* husband?"

"Charmaine, stop acting like a child." *But, man oh man, you don't look like a child. Not in those pants you must have painted on. Not in that tease-me shirt that outlines every curve of your breasts. Be still my heart . . . and other body parts.*

She put her hands on her hips. "Get out of my way, cowboy. I'm going dancing."

"You are not."

"Try and stop me."

"Rusty, let her go." Amelie had moved to the bottom of the steps and was tugging on his sleeve. "She's a big girl. You are not responsible for her actions."

"Yeah," Charmaine said. "Let me go, please . . . pretty please."

His eyes bulged and his hands fisted. He probably looked like a lunatic. He didn't care. "Hell, no, I'm not letting her go," he informed Amelie. "For reasons I can't go into, Charmaine's life is in danger. She needs to stay out of sight." He tried to tamp down his temper when he addressed Charmaine. "Now, go back inside and watch TV or something, like a good girl." He immediately recognized his poor choice of words and wished he could take them back.

"Good girl? Are you for real, Lanier?" Charmaine just laughed. "Do they sell oyster shooters at this bar?" she asked Clarence.

"Oh, yeah," Clarence said. He and Linc were enjoying this argument immensely.

"Oh, goody."

I'd like to give you a good dose of "goody," you willful, outrageous bundle of female orneriness. "Listen, Charmaine, if you go to The Horny Bull dressed like that, every cowboy within fifty miles is going on testosterone alert. The cowboy grapevine is going to broadcast your presence. Bobby Doucet is for sure going to hear about your whereabouts."

She totally ignored his warning, but instead homed in on a tiny portion of what he'd said. "That's the second time you've remarked on how I'm dressed. Well, I don't like the way you're dressed either. You look too damn sexy, if you must know. The way your jeans hug your legs and your butt, the way that blue shirt brings out the highlights in your dark eyes, the way your jacket shows off your broad shoulders, the way your belt calls attention to your narrow waist. Yep, every female within fifty miles will go on hormone alert. Men will be fighting with you because their wives or girlfriends have the hots for you. The police will be called. Nothing but trouble. Best you stay home, boy, and twiddle your thumbs."

She was probably being sarcastic, but he couldn't help himself. He grinned. Which caused Amelie to elbow him in the side and Charmaine to gloat and Linc and Clarence to slap their knees with glee. Dumb as a dingo, that's what he was. Naturally, what came out of his mouth was dumb, too: "So, you think I look sexy?"

"As sin," was her blunt reply.

I don't care if she thinks I'm sexy. I don't care if she thinks I'm sexy. I don't care . . . much. He grinned some more.

She just looked sad all of a sudden.

Amelie was right. Charmaine was an adult. If she wanted to get herself killed, it was no skin off his nose. Or it shouldn't be.

"Just be careful," he cautioned Charmaine as he took Amelie's hand and led her to the car.

Charmaine stared at them sadly as they pulled out of the yard. It was an image that stayed with him all night.

Cry me a river . . .

She cried buckets for the first hour after everyone had gone, having decided after all that it might be dangerous to be seen in public.

But Charmaine had never been one to wallow in self-pity for very long. It was, frankly, boring.

So she brushed out her hair and gave herself a hot-oil conditioning treatment.

Then she redid her fingernails and toenails with Peach Passion, no longer being in a Red-Hot Mama mood.

Then she made herself some Bananas Foster . . . and ate three of them, covered with vanilla ice cream and about a pound of whipped cream, all by herself, along with three cups of "burnt roast," the thickest of Cajun coffees.

Then, on a sugar-and-coffee high, she decided to scrub the kitchen floor, pluck her eyebrows, rearrange the pantry, and order some cosmetics off the Internet.

Then, while she was still on the computer, she did about an hour's worth of work, inputting information from the boxes of ranch paperwork that still lined the office in daunting piles.

Then she treated herself to a peach-scented bubble bath while sipping on a glass of beer, which was the only alcoholic beverage she'd been able to find in the house.

Since it was only ten o'clock, and she was still wide-awake, she put on her favorite cow pajamas and fuzzy cow slippers—comfort clothes—and slapped a peach mud facial on her face. Rusty probably wouldn't be back from his date for another couple of hours, she figured, not that she was watching the clock. She expected to be snoring away in bed by then with a beer buzz.

To make sure of that, she went out on the back porch, carrying with her another beer and the portable radio tuned to a local Cajun music station. That was what she needed, a little Acadian *joie de vivre* to lighten her spirits.

"Hi, there, Jude," she said to the plastic statue sitting in the other rocking chair. That was where Rusty had put it, after being tired of it being on the other porch. He claimed it watched him through the front window.

Jude didn't answer her. Surprise, surprise.

"Welcome, folks, to our Cajun country dance party," the announcer on the radio said. "We're gonna have us a little *fais do-do* down on the bayou, guar-an-teed."

Well, I wanted to dance tonight. Guess this is the next best thing. Charmaine loved to dance, and she'd been looking forward to going out tonight. Nothing bad. Just dancing. Her second husband, Justin, had been a really good dancer. His moves had been so smooth, people had stopped to watch. He'd been one good ol' Cajun boy who could charm a woman up one side and down the other till she didn't know her engine from her caboose. Unfortunately, Charmaine had found out that his smooth moves were being spread to engines and cabooses throughout

Louisiana. Justin had been a larcenous rat, as well. When he'd left, he took everything, including the gumbo pot.

Her third husband, Lester, hadn't been a Cajun, but he'd left, too. Thank goodness! He'd been boring as bayou mud.

Her fourth husband, Antoine, had been a Cajun . . . a Cajun nerd. She must have thought she'd be safe with a more serious fellow. Hah! Antoine had some kind of sexual addiction because he'd wanted to make love morning, noon, and night. And he wasn't very good at it, either. Unfortunately, he hadn't been working while he'd been chasing her around the house, except for diddling with his computers, of which he'd had five. When she'd laid down the law, refusing to support him anymore, he'd gone off with some other Sugar Mommy.

And all of them had wanted her to strip for them, like her mother. In fact, Antoine had urged her to strip to support them in a grander lifestyle, as if being a beautician and then shop owner hadn't been enough for him. No wonder she had relationship problems. But that was all in the past. She was smarter now.

She listened appreciatively as various Cajun musicians played old favorites like "Ode to Big Mamou," "Devil's Dream," "Ways of a Cajun," and "Girls Like Cowboys."

She hadn't needed to hear that last song to know just how much girls liked cowboys. She was the worst of the lot. Show her a pair of spurs and a cowboy hat, and she swooned, especially if they were tacked onto a sexy-as-sin cowboy. Like Rusty.

No, no, no, I've had enough of that bum. Giving me orders like I'm one of his cows. As if! Another couple of weeks and I'm out of here. I promised myself some new beginnings, and that's just what's going to happen. A whole clean slate. Minus cowboys. Or minus one cowboy in particular.

Maybe she should become a lesbian. Hmmm. Could a woman *decide* to become a lesbian? She laughed softly as she took another drink from her cold bottle of beer. *Hell, if I can decide to become a born-again virgin, why not a new sexual preference?*

Stop swearing, she thought she heard a voice say. Probably that plaguey St. Jude. She glanced over. He said nothing, just rocked with the breeze, but he talked plenty in her head. *You would not be speaking so lightly of hell if you knew just how bad it is. Whew! Talk about heat. Southern Louisiana in midsummer has nothing on hell. And forget the lesbian nonsense. I have other plans for you.*

Chapter 7

Horny as a bull . . .

"You don't seem to be having a good time."

Raoul was sitting on a picnic bench, leaning his back and elbows on the table with his legs extended and crossed at the ankles. Amelie's comment had jarred him from the reverie that had plagued him all evening.

"I'm having a great time, Amelie. It's just a little disorienting for me. You know, mixing socially with so many people. I'm out of practice." *I didn't get much chance to exchange chitchat in prison. That's for sure. Plus, the people I got to mix with were all men and they weren't your normal barbecue crowd. Murderers, sex offenders, drug dealers.*

"No one made you feel bad, did they?"

Well, there was the time I rejected George the Hammer. And the time my cellmate said I was suffering from delusions about my innocence.

"Here at the party, I mean."

Oh. Here at the party. She looked genuinely offended on his behalf as she sat down and put a hand on his thigh in comfort.

"No, everyone's been really nice." *They whisper behind*

my back, but that's to be expected, I suppose. He glanced once again at Amelie's hand on his thigh. Odd thing about that. From Amelie, it was just a friendly gesture. If Charmaine had done the same thing, he would have taken it as an invitation to sex. Sparks would have been shooting up to his groin by now. His cock would have been singing cock-a-doodle-doos and doing the chicken dance.

"Why are you smiling?"

Uh-oh! "I didn't realize I was."

"Are you thinking about my offer?"

Hardly. Amelie had made him a surprising, generous offer to join her veterinary practice here in Lake Charles, now that her father had retired. He would have to be just an assistant till he got his medical license back, but when he did—and it was heart-lifting to know that Amelie had that kind of confidence in him—he would be a full partner.

"I am, but I've gotta stick with what I said before. I have too much on my plate right now. Getting the ranch back in order. Clearing my name. Investigating my father's death. Straightening out my marriage situation."

Why didn't I just say divorce? Marriage situation? Talk about skirting the issue! He saw a spark of what almost seemed like anger in her eyes at the mention of his "marriage situation," and for the first time wondered if Charmaine hadn't been right in implying that more than friendship existed between him and Amelie . . . or at least on Amelie's part. That suspicion was strengthened when he noticed that her hand still rested on his thigh, up higher.

"Why not just sell the ranch? Cut your losses and be done with it."

He shrugged. "I can't. Not yet. And definitely not to the oil vultures. The Triple L has been in my family for 150 years. I would feel like a traitor selling out."

"Your father never treated you very well. You didn't spend all that much time on the ranch. Does the property hold that much sentimental value for you?"

"Yes," he answered without hesitation.

"I wonder . . . does it have anything to do with Charmaine?"

He frowned. "Hell, no. Her ties are all in Houma and Lafayette, where she owns businesses, and she grew up mostly in Baton Rouge."

"I just thought . . . well, maybe subconsciously you're looking at the ranch as a way of getting back together with her."

Why do women have to analyze everything to death? At first, he was sort of insulted, but he gave her comment consideration anyway. Then said, "No, this isn't about Charmaine. Why would I be looking to hook up with her now when I haven't sought her out in ten years?"

Good question, Lanier. How about it's the first time in ten years she hasn't been married to someone else? How about you've had time the past two years in prison to think about her and what you might have done differently? How about there is still a spark when she enters a room? Spark, hell! More like fireworks. How about I'm as horny as a rutting bull when Charmaine is within a ten-mile radius?

There was a moment of companionable silence as they both watched the other party attendees, about two hundred of Cletus Ancelet's closest friends. A half-consumed side of beef still sizzled on the grate of a stone barbecue pit, where people occasionally came back for another helping. A pigload of side dishes crowded several long tables, along with an assortment of mixed drinks and plenty of beer on ice.

"She certainly is . . . um, interesting."

"Huh? Who?" He scanned the partygoers to see which "she" she referred to.

"Charmaine."

Why is she so fixated on Charmaine?

Probably because I'm so fixated on Charmaine.

"Interesting would be an understatement," he replied.

"I never would have expected you to be with a woman who was such a . . . well, bimbo."

"Amelie! That is a catty remark, especially coming from you." *Be careful, Amelie, I am starting to see a different side of you, and it's not attractive.*

"I'm just being honest, Rusty. My God, did you see that outfit she had on?"

Oh, yeah, I saw it.

"There is no subtlety about her. She's a walking billboard for promiscuity."

Yep, a whole new side. Mean comes immediately to mind. "Hold it now, Amelie. You know better than to judge a book by its cover."

"Are you saying she's not the slut she appears to be?"

That remark went beyond mean into the realm of vicious. Raoul gritted his teeth and counted to ten. "That's exactly what I'm saying." And Raoul surprised himself by how sure he was of that fact. "She likes to be outrageous in her clothing and her actions, but it's all for show."

"Why? That's what I don't understand. Why would anyone deliberately want to look like a floozy?"

I am really uncomfortable talking about Charmaine

with anyone else. Isn't that odd? "I'm no psychologist. I don't have all the answers when it comes to Charmaine." *But maybe—just maybe—if I found out what makes her tick, I might get a clue into a few mysteries. Like why she really left me. Isn't it interesting that I was married to her, crazy in love with her, but didn't really know her?*

"Oh, my goodness. I think I know why she dresses the way she does." Amelie's face lit up as if she'd just discovered gumbo. "Protective coloration," she said gleefully.

"I beg your pardon." *I should cut this conversation short right now.*

"Think about it, Rusty. You and I have both studied animals in college classes. Animals adapt to their surroundings as a defense mechanism, often by changing their color or fur to camouflage them in the wild."

"And you think Charmaine does this to camouflage herself?" *Dumb, dumb, dumb. Keep this conversation going, Dumbo. If Charmaine ever hears about it, she'll cut off my tongue . . . or other body part.*

"More as a defense."

"Hmmm," he remarked noncommittally. But what he thought was, *Oh, yeah. Charmaine, the Cajun Chameleon. She would really appreciate that.* "You might like her if you got to know her."

"I doubt that, Rusty. I can't imagine anything in the world we would have in common."

"I can't say that Charmaine and I are alike in many ways either, but that doesn't mean I don't like some things about her."

"Like what? I mean, really, Rusty, what's to like?"

Raoul didn't understand Amelie's persistence on this subject. It bordered on hostility toward Charmaine, which made no sense unless . . . He looked at her more closely and at the hand that still rested on his thigh. *Holy crap! She's attacking Charmaine because she considers her a threat. Amelie doesn't look at me as a friend, after all. Have I really been that blind all these years?* With a sigh, he said, "Charmaine has a good heart. She is generous to a fault. Although she had a rotten life as a child, moving around so much with her stripper mom and constantly being rebuffed by a dad who wanted nothing to do with her, family is very important to her. She would do anything for Tante Lulu or her half brothers. She even treated my dad as family, and you know how unlikable he was. And kids . . . man, you should see her with Jimmy. She even made him meat loaf, for chrissake. And yesterday she trimmed the kid's hair so he'd look good for his overnight trip. As for the dumb bimbo image, you have got to give her credit for two successful businesses. She's smarter than anyone gives her credit for."

"Well, she can't be that smart if she lost all that money and went to a loan shark."

Raoul was beginning to regret having filled Amelie in on Charmaine's recent history on the ride over here. "Lots of people have lost money in the stock market since the 9/11 terrorist attack. I'd be willing to bet your dad is one of them."

She ducked her head sheepishly, which pretty much confirmed his suspicion.

"Going to a loan shark was dumb, yeah. Her pride probably got in the way. Thought she could borrow some money and pay it back quick without anyone knowing about it. And one more thing about Charmaine, she was Miss Louisiana a few years back. Someone must have thought she had the looks."

Raoul suddenly realized just how much he had been expounding on Charmaine's virtues. In the course of his speech, he had stood and was pacing in front of the picnic table. Amelie was looking at him as if he'd just laid an egg. Which he had.

Mon Dieu! What is wrong with me? "Don't get me wrong, Charmaine has lots of faults, too," he said defensively, but it was too late.

"You're still in love with her," Amelie accused him.

"No! Definitely not! I wouldn't walk into that land mine again. Uh-uh!" His protests sounded hollow, even to his own ears. "Honestly, Amelie, I've been wondering lately if I ever was in love with her. Or her with me. We were really young, and we didn't even know each other that well."

"Okaaay," Amelie said, obviously not convinced.

"I just don't want you to think that any decision I make regarding your generous offer of a partnership has anything at all to do with Charmaine."

She nodded. "And I want you to know that the offer stands, regardless of Charmaine. You're a good vet, Rusty, and I would welcome your help."

He pulled her to her feet and gave her a warm hug. "You are a great friend, Amelie," he murmured against her hair.

He felt her stiffen against him. Finally, she relaxed and said, "I consider you a good friend, too, Rusty."

After that, they decided to cut the evening short. "Do you want me to drop you off at the ranch or at the bar? I suspect you've been worried all night about Charmaine."

Was I that obvious? I guess so. "Drive by the bar and we'll see."

When they got to The Horny Bull an hour later, the lot

was half-full, but Clarence's truck was still there. "You don't have to come in, I'll hitch a ride back with them," he told her. He saw the disappointment on her face, but gave her a quick kiss on the mouth and added, "I'll call you next week and give you an answer, if I can. Thanks for everything, Amelie."

Despite the smoky dimness of the bar, Raoul was able to locate Linc and Clarence right off. They were sitting with two fortysomething cowgirls; at least they were wearing old-time movie version cowgirl outfits. No Charmaine in sight. Not even on the dance floor, where the crowd was doing a lively Cajun two-step to "Diggy Liggy Lo."

Raoul's heart sank. She must have gone off with some guy, was his first thought, but then he chastised himself for the unkindness of that assumption. She was probably in the ladies' room jazzing up her makeup.

"Where's Charmaine?" he barked in a more strident voice than he'd intended when he got to the table.

"Well, hello to you, too," Clarence said.

"Home," Linc said.

"Home?" His heart sank again. "Who took her home? Jesus H. Christ, what is she thinkin', goin' home with some stranger?"

"No one took her home." Clarence glowered at him. "I swear, boy, when did you fall out of the dumb tree?"

"Huh?"

"She stayed home to begin with," Linc explained. "Guess she took yer advice about it bein' too dangerous to come out t'night."

"Poor thing. She really wanted ta go dancin', too," Clarence added. "She was gonna teach me how ta do the shag."

Oh, yeah? If Charmaine's gonna shag anyone, it's gonna be me. Oh, my God! I can't believe I thought that. I do not want Charmaine to shag me. Well, I might want it, but I wouldn't let her do it. I mean, I wouldn't ask her to do it. Aaarrgh!

They both looked at him as if he were some kind of Simon Legree who had wielded a whip over Charmaine. Some image, that!

"I'll go over to the bar and have a beer until you two are ready to go home. I need to hitch a ride with you." He glanced pointedly at each of the women, who had been following the conversation with avid interest.

"Girls, I wantcha ta meet Rusty. Rusty, this here is Wanda," Clarence said, nodding toward a blonde with teased hair and a bimbo cowgirl outfit that would do Charmaine proud. The fringed skirt showed a bit of neon pink thong. She weighed about two hundred pounds.

"And this is Jolene," Linc said, squeezing the shoulder of a mocha-skinned, similarly attired cowgirl with corn-rows in her long black hair and a ring in her one nostril. She was skinny as a fence rail.

Dale Evans must be turning over in her grave.

"Unless you want me to call Charmaine and ask her to come pick me up," he offered as an afterthought. Maybe Clarence and Linc had big plans for these babes. It boggled the mind, but stranger things happened, he supposed.

"Nope, we'll be ready in 'bout fifteen minutes," Clarence said. "Wanda and Jolene was about to leave anyways. They's gotta get up early t'morrow fer the Gumbo Queen contest over in Natchitoches."

As Raoul walked away, he heard the women giggle.

Everything's just peachy, chère . . .

The place reeked of peaches when Raoul got home.

He followed the peach scent, first to the bathroom, then out through the kitchen to the porch, where Charmaine rocked back and forth with big fuzzy cow-clad feet propped on the back porch rail, listening to Fiddlin' Frenchie Bourke belt out "Let's Go to Big Mamou." She wore the most hideous, adorable cow pajamas. The St. Jude statue sat in the other rocker, where he'd put it yesterday. Her date for the night.

"Holy crawfish! The whole house smells like peaches. And out here, too." *Way to go, cowboy! Is that the best greeting you can come up with?*

Charmaine almost tipped over her rocker as she jumped to her feet. "Rusty! What are you doing home so early? Oh, please, don't tell me you brought your date back here for a little cowboy delight."

"No, Amelie dropped me off at The Horny Bull an hour ago. Clarence and Linc brought me home. But really, sugar, *cowboy delight*?" He laughed, then went still. "What happened to your face?"

Charmaine put a hand to her face and shrieked, "You jerk! You cracked it."

"I cracked what?" He quickly glanced about the porch floor to see if he'd stepped on something.

"My peach mud mask. You scared me, and my face moved. It took me a half hour to get it this hard, and now look."

Oh, she means her face. I cracked her face. "I've been hard ever since you got here, and I haven't cracked yet," he murmured.

"What?"

Oops. Didn't mean to say that out loud. "Nothing." He leaned down and sniffed. Yep, her face smelled like peaches. In fact, all of her did. And, man, did he like peaches!

She shoved a half-empty bottle of beer into his hand and stomped past him into the house. Was there anything in the world cuter than cows swinging back and forth on Charmaine's ass?

He followed Charmaine to the bathroom, where she left the door open. Leaning against the jamb, he watched as she looked into the mirror over the sink and began to peel off the mud gunk. Her hair was drawn back off her face with a stretchy headband. Little by little she pulled off all the crap, then rinsed her face over and over with handfuls of cold water.

"The things women do to get beautiful!" he remarked. And wasn't it amazing how he could get turned on by a facial peel? But then he recalled one time observing to Linc in prison that he got turned on by Charmaine's kneecaps, and the back of her neck, and the way she ate crawfish, and . . .

Linc had laughed and said, "In other words, everything about Charmaine turns you on."

She shrugged, still staring at herself in the mirror. "What? The wonderful Am-el-ie has so much natural beauty she doesn't need any help? Pfff!"

I wonder if she's wearing anything under those jammies. "What does that stuff do anyway?"

"Cleanses the skin and tightens pores."

"What's wrong with soap?" *Like I care. What I really want to know is whether every part of Charmaine smells like peaches, and what she would say if I asked to eat her.*

"Too drying."

Not if I . . . oh, she means the soap. Whew! That was a close one. "Yep, that's what I think when I'm in the shower. Will my soap dry out my skin?"

She gave him a dirty look for making fun of her. Imagine the dirty look she'd give him if she knew what he was really thinking. "You *should* be concerned, being out in the sun as much as you are. I could give you a facial, if you're willing."

He scrunched up his nose with distaste.

"It would feel really good."

"I'm sure it would, babe." He actually gave her offer some consideration, that was how pitiful he was. The prospect of Charmaine laying her hands on him held great appeal, but, nah. When—or if—Charmaine ever put her hands on him again, he was holding out for something better than a slathering of mud. "Maybe some other time." Then he said something really stupid as he sniffed the air some more, "I love peaches."

She arched her eyebrows at him and smiled sardonically. "I know."

"Remember the time we drank all those peach margaritas?" *Dumb, dumb, dumb. Have you lost your mind, Lanier, bringing that up?* He gave himself a mental thwap upside the head.

She studied him, as if questioning whether he was serious or not. "How could I forget? It was our honeymoon."

"Our wonderful two-day honeymoon at the Holiday Inn." That was all they'd been able to afford, and all the time they'd been able to take off from school.

He thought she would laugh and make a sarcastic

remark, but instead, she said softly, "It was wonderful to me."

"Me too," he said after a long pause. This was dangerous, dangerous territory. "I'm going out on the porch to finish this beer with Jude."

She nodded.

Whether that meant she would join him once her pores closed up or not, he wasn't sure. If she was smart, she'd skedaddle off to bed. Her bed. If he was smart, he'd skedaddle off to bed, too. Alone.

When was either of us that smart?

Raoul sat on the rocker for quite a while, listening to BeauSoleil sing that classic *"Jolé Blon."* No Charmaine. But that was all right. It was nice to have this quiet time.

He really did love this ranch. Ever since his mother brought him here when he was four, the Triple L had entranced him. A younger Clarence had been around then, and he'd taken him out to the barn to show him some new calves. Actually, he'd probably wanted to protect him from the shouting that was going on in the ranch house. Apparently, his mother had never bothered to inform his father until then that their weekend affair five years earlier had resulted in a son, although she'd made sure Charles Lanier's name was on the birth certificate as father.

The only reason she'd been dropping the Daddy bomb then had been that she needed some place to dump her kid while she went off to Acadia, a French province in Canada, for three months to do research for a masters degree in the history of Cajun culture. She'd needed a babysitter, pure and simple.

His mother had managed to drop him off for three months on that first occasion and periodically for short visits over the years, but only when it had been convenient for her. When his father had tried to gain custody, she'd dug in her heels and stopped the visits altogether for years.

"Why so grim, cowboy?" Charmaine asked, perching herself on the porch rail off to his right. Even with the dim light coming from the kitchen, he could see that her face glowed from her recent ministrations.

Maybe I should let her give me one of those facials, after all. Then again, maybe not.

"Just thinkin' about my dad and my mom."

"Whoo-ee! An explosive combination, those two."

"Yep."

"Do you see your mother very often?"

He shook his head. "Haven't seen her for more than two years."

"Really? I saw her on a local TV station last month. She's making quite a name for herself in academic circles, isn't she?"

He nodded. His mother was the well-known Dr. Josette Pitre. Born and raised on Bayou Teche, she had been and still was a free spirit, a hippie at a time when hippies were already out of style. "She fancies herself the premier expert on Cajun culture, I hear," he said.

"She *has* done a lot to gain respect for Cajuns, not just the language but in art and history and all that stuff."

"Hey, sweetheart, since when did you become a cheerleader for my mother? As I recall, she didn't like you from the get-go and didn't mind telling you so."

Charmaine shrugged with a "who cares" attitude. "Lots of people don't like me."

Like Amelie.

"She couldn't quite get over *her* son marrying a hair

dresser wannabe. Talk about! My only saving grace in her eyes was that I was Cajun. No offense, baby, but your mother is a bitch. That doesn't mean I can't appreciate the good work she's done, though."

There had been a period a few decades back when the public schools of southern Louisiana had tried to wipe out the Cajun dialect and customs from all its native students, considering it inferior to the French language and culture. Eventually, that misguided movement had been reversed, thank God, because of lots of dedicated individuals, including his mother. He'd grown up being fluent in classic French, Cajun French, and good old Southern English under his mother's tutelage. Lot of good that did him when he was sticking his arm up to the elbow in a pregnant cow's ass.

"I suppose you're right, but when I was a kid all I saw was a mother who cared more about research and a career than me, except when she could show me off to her friends by having me recite 'Evangeline' in French." Longfellow had detailed the plight of the Acadians', or Cajuns', historical exile in that well-loved poem. He'd come to hate it.

"Remember when they pulled 'Evangeline' from the English curriculum in high school? Some people need to get a life and leave other people's alone."

He nodded.

"Now I understand. Your mother relishes highbrow stuff. Me, I'm lowbrow, for sure." Charmaine smiled after she spoke. It was obvious she could care less what his mother thought of her. Bless her self-confident soul!

"I kind of like lowbrow," he said. *Way too much!*

"I know," she said, and smiled again.

Does she have any idea how my heart races when she smiles like that?

No, someone replied.

His head jerked to the right. St. Jude just stared straight ahead.

"Back to my mother. You can't be offended by my mother disliking you, *chère*. She's pretty good at spreading her dislikes around."

"Personally, I think she abused you as a child . . . with neglect."

They'd had this conversation before, and he wasn't in the mood for rehashing the old argument. "Some women—rather, some people—sacrifice their personal lives for a greater good." *Son of a bitch! Am I really defending my mother? Wonders never cease.*

"Unlike my mother who sacrificed me for her own good?" Charmaine asked.

"Well, they both did, in the end. But the fact that we were both neglected, in different ways, doesn't constitute child abuse." *I need a psychiatrist.*

"Would you ever do that to your own child?"

"Never."

His mother, now a full professor at Tulane and a well-known feminist, had never married. "Maybe my mother would have acted differently if I'd been a girl." *Yep, a good psychiatrist.*

"Puh-leeze!"

"Really. Sometimes I wonder if my mother likes men at all. Her rage is so bitter about the male species . . . including me." *I had three beers tonight. Could they be causing this running of the tongue?*

"She *was* rather cool to you when we were married,"

Charmaine mused. "I mean, when we were married and living together."

Raoul felt an odd pleasure at Charmaine's remembering that they were still married. "Well, cool turned to ice eventually. She totally cut me off when I was arrested for drug dealing. She never once questioned that I was guilty."

"It's amazing the impact mothers can have on their children," she said, a wistful expression on her face.

"Not just on children. My mother's twisting it to my dad on numerous occasions over the years turned him into a hard, resentful man."

"You never understood your father," she claimed.

He ignored her claim, one she'd made before with no explanations. "I suspect there were a number of affairs but never a marriage for him, either."

Charmaine's eyes suddenly went wide, as if she'd just thought of something. "Rusty! You said you hadn't seen your mother in over two years. Don't tell me. She didn't come to your trial . . . or visit you in jail?"

He shrugged. "I was an embarrassment. She was about to get her professorship, and she couldn't risk the association." *Not that I would have allowed her on my visitor list.*

"Bull crap!"

He smiled at Charmaine's vehemence. "Hey, sweetheart, you didn't come either," he pointed out gently. *Not that I would have allowed you to come to that sordid place, either.*

"That's the second time you've said that to me. I don't recall you asking me to come."

"Would you have come if I'd asked?" *Pointless question.*

"Probably not," she confessed. "I had just gotten married again."

He winced, not wanting to be reminded.

"Oh, don't make that face at me. I imagine you had just as many women in your life these past ten years. You just didn't marry them."

"Were you in love with all of them?" *I do not want to know. Don't tell me. Dumb question. One of many in a long line of dumb questions tonight.*

"No," she said flatly, without hesitation.

Maybe it wasn't such a dumb question. "Any of them?"

This time she did hesitate. "Only one."

Me? Raoul did a mental high five but zipped his lips. Never in a million years would he step into that mortar field.

But Charmaine saved him a response by asking her own loaded question. "Were you in love with any woman during all those years?"

He answered truthfully, "Only one."

A dangerous silence hovered in the air.

Raoul decided it was time to change the subject just as Don Williams on the radio launched into an appropriate "Louisiana Saturday Night." "I meant to compliment you, *chère*."

"For what?" she asked suspiciously.

"Great cows," he said, waggling his eyebrows at her. "Can I hear you moo?"

"You louse!" She reached forward to slap him on the arm, but he grabbed her wrist and pulled her toward him. She landed on his lap. At first, she struggled but, when he assured her, "Relax, nothing's going to happen," she shifted her butt in his lap and laid her head on his shoulder.

And, damn, she felt so good in his arms right then. He closed his eyes and relished the softness of her body and the smell of peaches.

"So, what happened with you and Dr. Am-el-ie tonight?" she asked finally, without raising her head.

"Nothing," he said against her silky hair.

"Nothing?"

"Nothing. I told you, we're just friends."

"Does she know that?"

"She does now."

"Oh."

"She offered me a job as assistant in her clinic till I get my medical license back. Then it would be a full partnership."

"How convenient! And what string would be attached to that generous offer?"

"None whatsoever. I told you, we're friends."

"Uh-huh."

"Are you jealous?"

"Not in the least."

He laughed softly.

"Maybe a little bit, but it passed once you started acting like you were the boss and I was the dumb bimbo, ordering me to stay home."

He considered arguing with her, but decided it was best to pick his battles with Charmaine. Instead, he said, "Thank you."

"For what?"

"Staying home."

"I didn't do it for you. I realized that it was dangerous to go out dancing in a public place."

He did something really stupid then, not that he hadn't said and done plenty of dumb things tonight. A soft ballad started playing on the radio, "Sweet Cajun Love," and he asked, "Would you like to dance now, sugar?"

She pulled back slightly to look at him. After a long moment, she shook her head. "I better take a rain check."

"Why?"

"Because if I dance with you tonight, I'll end up in your bed."

I hope, I hope, I hope. "Not necessarily."

"Liar! I know what a good dancer you are."

He shrugged. "Most Cajun men are."

"Besides, you know what they say about men's opinions of dancing? Just another form of foreplay."

"You've got a point there." He chuckled. "But I'm beginning to wonder . . . would our making love be such a bad thing?"

"Definitely a bad thing. You're forgetting something important here, darlin'."

"And that is?"

"I'm a born-again virgin."

Chapter 8

And then their world turned upside down . . .

Tante Lulu arrived the next day in a whirlwind. Literally.

Remy circled his helicopter over the ranch about noon before landing in an empty field near the ranch house. Empty, that is, after about fifty cows ran like hell for the border.

Charmaine went out to the front yard to meet Tante Lulu, who was dressed today in what she must consider typical ranch attire—blue jeans, a plaid, long-sleeved shirt with snap buttons, boots, complete with spurs, and a cowgirl hat, all purchased in the children's department at Walmart, no doubt.

Charmaine, at five-foot-nine, had to bend over to give the old lady, five-foot-zero on a good day, a warm hug. "Welcome, Auntie," she said. "Oooh, we need to do your hair, honey."

Her black curly hair had about a half inch of white roots showing all around. "Doan I know it! Ain't had my roots done since before yer troubles. Mary Boudreaux asked me at church t'day iffen I was goin' to let my gray hair grow out and start actin' my age. I asked her iffen she was goin' to let those chin whiskers of hers grow down to her saggy boobies."

Charmaine laughed.

Tante Lulu gave her a once-over and asked pointedly, "You still a virgin?"

Charmaine nodded.

"Pfff! That Rusty ain't the man I thought he was then."

"Oh, he's the man you thought, all right. Give me a little credit for being stronger."

"Mebbe he needs some romance advice."

"He's getting all the advice he needs from one senior-citizen love advisor. He sure doesn't need two."

"Who you callin' a senior citizen?" Tante Lulu tapped her chin thoughtfully for a second or two. "You referrin' to that Clarence Guidry? Good, good. That fella knows stuff."

Stuff? I do not want to know what stuff Clarence knows.

"Hey, Charmaine. How's ranch life suitin' ya?" Remy called out.

"Hey, Remy," Charmaine replied, waving to her half brother, who was beginning to remove a bunch of bags and boxes and coolers from the helicopter. *Big* coolers. The coolers must hold perishable food. *Oh, my!*

Remy was a former Air Force pilot who'd been burned badly during Desert Storm. As a result, one side of his face was drop-dead gorgeous; the other side was not. He'd recently married Rachel Fortier, a Feng Shui decorator from Washington, D.C. A yankee, of all things!

"Where's Rachel?" she asked. "I thought she was coming with you."

"No room." Remy rolled his eyes meaningfully toward the overpacked copter. "Rachel and I will be coming back on Thursday, though. For your Thanksgiving feast."

Feast? What feast? "That's nice. A holiday is always more special when there's company." *What feast?*

"Oh, there'll be company, all right. Me, Rachel, Luc, Sylvie, their three kids. Who else, Tante Lulu?" He winked at Charmaine, knowing full well that Tante Lulu had issued all these invitations without consulting her.

Tante Lulu had been standing with her hands on her non-existent hips surveying the ranch. Without turning around, she answered, "Tee-John and mebbe René if he kin get away from his job up North." Any place above Kentucky was considered "up North" to Tante Lulu, a born and bred Southerner. Actually, René was an environmental lobbyist who worked in D.C.

Charmaine began to do a mental calculation in her head. Herself, Rusty, Clarence, Linc, Jimmy, Tante Lulu, Remy, Rachel, Luc, Sylvie, Tee-John, three kids, maybe Jimmy's dad, and maybe René. *Sixteen people. Mon Dieu, it* will *be a feast.*

"What a mess!" Tante Lulu exclaimed with a wide smile on her crinkled face. She was staring at the unpainted clapboard house and the seedy landscaping, surely envisioning all the projects she would be able to take on. The old lady turned to Remy then, who had a huge stack of stuff piled in the middle of the yard and was still unloading, including a St. Jude statue even bigger than the one already here. "When you get done bringin' that stuff in, Remy, how 'bout you shoot me one of them steers. I'm in the mood fer a barbecue t'night. Good thing I brought a batch of my homemade Cajun bastin' sauce." She licked her lips in anticipation. With that, Tante Lulu walked briskly toward the ranch house, already making mental lists, no doubt, of all the things to be done.

Remy looked at Charmaine. "Me? She expects me to shoot a cow? And then skin it and gut it. I . . . don't . . . think . . . so!"

"What's that?" Charmaine asked as he lifted a big chest out of the copter. It was made of wood, highly carved, about the size of a blanket chest. "Oh, my God! It's a hope chest. One of Tante Lulu's famous hope chests." She frowned with confusion.

"It's not for you." Remy grinned.

When understanding dawned, Charmaine grinned, too. "For Rusty?"

"Yep."

"He doesn't stand a chance." *I wonder if that means I don't stand a chance, either.*

"Y'all better stop dawdlin' and hurry on in here," Tante Lulu yelled from the front door. She was already holding a feather duster in one hand and a gumbo pot in the other. An apron was tied around her tiny waist, and a kerchief had replaced the cowgirl hat on her head. "There's a load of work to do here."

Charmaine and Remy exchanged a quick glance. "None of us stand a chance," Charmaine said then.

Invasion of the mind-snatchers . . .

"Are you people crazy?" Raoul bellowed as he ran into the house.

He stopped dead in his tracks when he saw Tante Lulu up on a ladder before the fireplace kissing a deer head. Well, maybe not exactly kissing, but she was face-to-face with the twelve-pointer his father had bagged several decades ago. She seemed to be smelling it or something.

"Yikes!" she yelped. He must have startled her because the old lady jerked, the ladder shook, she grabbed for the antlers, and the ladder clattered to the floor. By the time he got to her she hung from the deer head with her tiny feet dangling about three feet off the floor.

Once he helped her down, with her spurs barely missing his family jewels, the first words out of her mouth were, "You got fleas, boy."

"Huh?"

"And the smell! Pee-you!"

He could feel his face heat with color. "I showered last night, but I've been wrestling steers this morning. Dammit, old lady, it's good, honest sweat."

She shoved him in the chest, which was about how high her head reached on him. "Not you, lunkhead. That deer head has got fleas. And it stinks. Gotta get rid of it."

"That's a family heirloom." *Sort of.*

"Heirloom, schmeirloom!"

He ground his teeth together. "Where's Charmaine?" he inquired, about two decibels above a growl.

"Showing Remy around the barn."

What could Charmaine possibly know about a barn?

"I dint wanna go 'cause it smells like cow poop. Pheeew! How kin you stand it all day long?"

"You get used to it."

"I asked Remy to shoot me a cow, but he wouldn't do it. Can you believe it?"

You're about three days late, old lady. You could have had four dead steers.

"That Remy, he prob'ly shot lots of people when he

was in the Air Force but won't shoot one lousy cow fer his auntie."

He probably shouldn't ask, but he did anyway, "Why did you want Remy to shoot a cow?"

"Fer the bar-be-cue."

"What bar-be-cue? Never mind." *I really don't want or need to know.*

"He wouldn't shoot a chicken either. Talk about!"

Shoot a chicken! I need an aspirin. Bad.

"Soz I tol' him I would do it myself . . . wring the neck of one of those mean ol' roosters I saw out front, pluck the feathers, pull out the guts. Done it plenty a times before, I reckon. Gonna make some Tipsy Chicken fer t'night. Or mebbe I should save that fer t'morrow. Mebbe I should use some of that catfish I brought with me and make up a pot of Catfish Court Bouillion. Whaddaya think?"

I think I've been run over by a cement roller, Cajun style.

"What were you screaming 'bout when you come runnin' in here?"

"That damn helicopter. You can't fly that low over a herd of cattle."

"Uh-oh. Betcha they's gonna stop givin' milk."

He practically crossed his eyes with frustration, though why he would be so surprised at the remark, he didn't know. Charmaine had said pretty much the same thing. "I run beef cattle, not a dairy farm."

She made a moue with her mouth that pretty much said, "Big difference!" Same as Charmaine. They might not be related by blood, but these two were alike in way too many ways. "C'mon, sonny boy, let's have a cup of coffee. I brought you some Peachy Praline Cobbler Cake. I remembered how much you like peaches."

For the first time since he'd heard that whirlybird fly overhead, Raoul smiled. *Oh, yeah, I do like peaches.*

He followed her into the kitchen, her spurs jangling the whole way. She looked like a midget clown he'd seen once at the rodeo. Once there, they were greeted by a blast of "Cajun Madness" on the radio, which Charmaine must have left on. Raoul thought, *For sure!*

"So, how'd you lose your mojo?" she inquired a short time later in that sly manner she had of slipping in a bomb of a question out of nowhere. She'd already plied him with two pieces of cake, to soften him up, no doubt.

He choked on his coffee. "I beg your pardon."

"Mojo. Ain't you ever watched those Austin Powers movies? Tee-John watches 'em on the DeeVeeDeedy all the time."

"I might have seen one or two." They were really popular in prison, where any excuse to laugh was welcome. "But I can't imagine in a million years that you would know what mojo is."

"Mojo is manly magnetism. What draws the wimmen to ya like flies on a honey pot."

He put his elbows on the table and rested his chin on his cupped palms. "I gotta admit, there haven't been many flies on my honey pot lately." *This is the most incredible conversation of my life. Not even the ones I've held with Charmaine—and there have been some doozies—could match this.*

"See. I toldja. Not to worry, boy, I'm here to help. And St. Jude, too."

Well, that sure makes me feel better.

"And lookee over there." She pointed to a big wooden chest sitting in the middle of the dining room. "Thass your hope chest."

I have a headache the size of a bayou barge. If I keep on talking with this dingbat, she's going to make my brain explode. He didn't have the heart to be unkind to her, though, so he tried to talk sensibly to her. "Men don't have hope chests, Tante Lulu."

"The men in my family do. I started you out with a Cajun crazy quilt, some homespun towels, and lotsa doilies."

Yep, that's what I need in my life. Doilies. Then, the first part of what she'd said registered in his increasingly fuzzy head, and Raoul felt oddly touched that Tante Lulu considered him part of her family.

As if reading his mind, she said, "You and Charmaine are still married. I'm thinkin' you should work things out. So, you're family, whether you like it or not."

"I'm not so sure about working things out. Both of us are hesitant." *Resistant would be a far better word.* "Charmaine wants forever, and I . . . well . . ." He shrugged.

"You want a fling?" she guessed.

Tante Lulu always surprised people by being more perceptive than she appeared to be.

"You'll come around," she promised, patting him on the shoulder.

"Uh. One question. How did you know I lost my . . . uh, mojo?"

"Charmaine."

"Charmaine told you I lost my mojo?"

"Nah. Charmaine said she's still a virgin."

"I can tell you, for sure, that Charmaine isn't a virgin."

"A *born-again* virgin," Tante Lulu emphasized. "Anyhows, I'm here now. Me 'n Clarence will help you get your mojo back. Charmaine'll be warmin' yer mattress in no time."

"Tante Lulu! I'm surprised at you."

"Why? You and Charmaine is married. It's not like you'd be involved in any hanky-panky. I mean, yeah, it would be hanky-panky, but it would be legal like."

I do not want my love life directed by this looney bird.

"Do any of those rifles in the gun closet in the living room work?" she asked.

It was always hard to follow a conversation with Tante Lulu because she changed direction so often. "Uh, I think so. Why?"

"Well, if no one else is gonna shoot me an animal, I'm thinkin' I best shoot my own turkey fer the Thanksgiving feast. Mebbe two turkeys, with the mob what'll be here."

Raoul didn't know which question to ask first. "What turkeys?" *There are no turkeys on this ranch, as far as I know.* "What feast?" *This is the first I've heard of a feast.* "What mob?" *Oh, my God! Are there a bunch of people about to invade my home?*

Tante Lulu just smiled. "Not to worry, boy. Your auntie is here now. Everything's gonna be all right."

Raoul was pretty sure everything was not going to be all right. He should tell her to hop back in that copter with Remy and fly away. No busybodies welcome at the Triple L. Instead, he said, "Thank you."

Friends in low—uh, high—places?

Raoul found Charmaine in the barn with Remy.

She was sitting on a bale of hay with a basket of eggs in her lap. Wearing a white blouse pulled off the shoulders and cutoff jeans—cut off way too high, if you asked him, which no one did—she looked like a freakin' Daisy

Mae. And Remy, showing off his good side, from this angle, was leaning against a support beam, listening intently to something Charmaine was saying and smiling down at her. Li'l Abner, for sure. If he didn't know they were half brother and sister, he might have been jealous.

He *was* jealous. Look how relaxed and playful Charmaine was when talking with her brother. She shoved his arm when he said something teasing to her. She giggled at something else he said. On the other hand, whenever Raoul was in Charmaine's presence, she tensed up like a tightened coil. She was wary and distrustful of him, even when he carried on a casual conversation. There was some message in that, he thought. Something to be examined more closely when he had the time.

Remy was the first to notice him. "Hey, Rusty, how's it going?"

He stepped forward, and Charmaine bristled. *What, does she expect me to say or do something to offend her, right off the bat? What the hell is her problem?*

"Gettin' by," he answered. And that was the truth in a nutshell. Not doing great. Not getting buried. Just surviving, day to day.

"Sometimes that's good enough," Remy remarked. And that was the truth, too.

"Well, I think it stinks. Who wants to just get by?" Of course, Charmaine would take the contrary position. He chucked her playfully under the chin, and she bristled some more. For chrissake, she acted like some uptight virgin threatened by anything on two feet with an ounce of testosterone. And he was packing about fifty pounds under his belt. "Oh, don't look at me like that, like I'm some rosy-eyed bimbo who doesn't know sand from granola.

Everyone needs to have a positive attitude. If you don't, it just eats away at you, and you become a bitter old man."

Remy laughed. "I guess she told us."

"Oh, yeah! Looks like I got me a regular Charmaine Vincent Peale here."

She set aside her basket of eggs and poked a forefinger into his chest. "I'm not your anything yet, mister."

Raoul homed in on one word. He was probably grinning like an idiot. *"Yet?"*

"A slip of the tongue," she said as a becoming blush pinkened her cheeks. And her bare neck. And her bare shoulders. And her bare arms. Hell, probably some places he had no business imagining as pink or bare. *Yet.* He wondered idly, or perhaps not so idly, if said skin still smelled like peaches.

"You smell like peaches," Charmaine said, as if reading his mind.

"Tante Lulu plied me with Peachy Praline Cobbler Cake." He waggled his eyebrows at her.

"Well, that's just peachy." She crossed her eyes at him.

Remy looked from him to her, then back again, and let out a hoot of laughter. "Tante Lulu is going to have such a good time with you two." Once he settled down, wiping tears from his eyes, he asked, "Did you contact Frank Zerby, that detective Luc recommended?"

"I did, and he seemed to think he could help me. He offered to take on my case on a contingency basis, letting me pay him off once I'm on my feet again."

"You didn't tell me that you called a detective," Charmaine complained.

"You didn't ask. And besides, it's none of your business. *Yet.*"

She made a tsk-ing sound while he turned to address

Remy again. "Zerby homed in right away on the under-cover detective who claimed to be buying drugs from me. Doug Gaudet."

"I know. Luc contacted Ambrose Mouton, a Houma cop who's a longtime friend of his. Rosie's going to do some investigating of Gaudet behind the scenes. Nothing official."

"I've met Rosie. He's a good man."

"There's something else, Rusty. You may not be aware of this, but I work with the DEA. Mostly big drug busts that require the use of my copter and knowledge of the bayous. Your arrest had nothing to do with the DEA, but maybe I can do some behind-the-scenes investigating of my own. The people involved in drug enforcement have a quiet network of their own. It wouldn't hurt to try, I reckon. What do you think?"

"I appreciate your help, but why would you do that for me? You and Luc . . . all of you?"

"Because you're family, you thickheaded fool," Charmaine answered for her brother. She was shaking her head at him as if he were a . . . thickheaded fool.

"Only till the divorce is final," he pointed out.

Charmaine's face went from pink to bright red. First, she sliced him with a withering glower. Then, she slid off the bale of hay, grabbed her basket of eggs, and proceeded to stomp out of the barn.

As they both watched Charmaine's rear sway from side to side in her short cutoffs—Remy with amazement, Raoul with appreciation—Remy commented to him, "Did anyone ever tell you you're a thickheaded fool?"

"Only St. Jude."

Pushing the limits . . .

Remy left a short time later, wanting to make sure he was home before dark.

Jimmy was a brat at the dinner table that night.

Charmaine couldn't believe that the kid was behaving so badly, especially in front of Tante Lulu, whom he'd just met. He'd apparently been in a snit ever since his father returned him to the ranch that morning. Jimmy had wanted to stay at home and return to his old school and his old friends and probably his old patterns of trouble. When his father had refused, Jimmy had thrown a tantrum, which resulted in Rusty holding him back physically while his father drove off with tears rolling down his agonized face. There had been tears rolling down Charmaine's face, as well.

Now, Jimmy refused to eat Tante Lulu's Catfish Court Bouillion, saying, "I doan like no stinkin' bottom feeders. And I 'specially doan like no catfish stew. Oooh, is that okra floatin' in there? Yuck!"

Charmaine was not fond of okra, either, but it was a staple of Cajun cooking. You could eat around it, without being offensive to the cook.

And talk about offending the cook! Tante Lulu took great pride in her Catfish Court Bouillion. To call it a mere stew had to be an insult to her culinary pride. But, while everyone else at the table—Charmaine, Rusty, Clarence and Linc—rose to their feet, about to chastise the boy on her behalf, her aunt just raised a halting hand in the air. "Everyone, sit down!" Then to Jimmy, she said, "Thass all right, boy. Have a hissy fit, iffen you wants. Ya doan have ta like everythin' in the world. Have a piece of bread and butter."

Jimmy proceeded to spread about a pound of butter on half a loaf of crusty French bread. Then he wolfed it down with crumbs flying everywhere and butter smeared all over his lips and chin. He was pushing the limits of everyone's patience, and he did it deliberately.

Instead of walloping the boy with a wooden spoon, like she would have done to Charmaine or one of her half brothers when they were that age, Tante Lulu just ignored his boorish behavior. But there was an evil glint in her eyes.

Rusty glanced Charmaine's way, and their gazes caught and held. He wore a black T-shirt tonight and old Wranglers. His hair remained too long on his neck, but she wasn't about to suggest that he let her cut it. She didn't dare get that close to him. Not when the expression in his beautiful eyes was so hungry. Not when she was feeling so hungry herself. And the appetite she referred to had nothing to do with food.

She'd changed from shorts to jeans before dinner because of the nightime chill, which had hit of a sudden, but she still wore the white blouse with the elastic neckline, which she had noticed Rusty noticing earlier. The capped sleeves weren't pulled down off her shoulders anymore, but her neck and arms were exposed, and Rusty's gaze kept drifting to those areas. If she were being honest with herself, she would have to admit that she'd worn it deliberately, without a sweater, which was really more appropriate for the weather. But she'd wanted to tease him. Why, she couldn't really say.

It was an impossible situation. Like Thomas Wolfe

said long ago, "You can't go home again." That was for
sure. *Not that Rusty is home to me.*

Not exactly.

Not hardly.

Well, maybe a teeny tiny bit.

Aaarrgh!

A voice in her head said, *Ditto on the aaarrgh.* Probably that pesky St. Jude again. They now had his statues
on the front and back porches thanks to Tante Lulu's
latest addition. He was getting to be a real pain.

"You two gonna stare at each other googly-eyed forever?" Jimmy asked impudently, jarring them from their
erotic eye play.

Tante Lulu chuckled. Linc and Clarence just grinned.

"Rusty, you want seconds, yes?" Tante Lulu inquired
then.

Rusty nodded and she ladled more into his soup plate,
then handed him a slice of bread, which he buttered
sparingly.

"Clarence, how's yer rheumatiz?" Tante Lulu asked as
she sat down for the first time to take a few bites herself.

"Not so bad," Clarence answered. "That liniment you
mixed up fer me las' year fixed it up real good. Does it
really have alligator piss in it?"

Tante Lulu grinned impishly. "I was jist joshin' you."

"Guess ya got me that time," he said, chortling with
glee as he slapped a knee.

Hmmm. Charmaine hadn't even realized that Tante
Lulu knew Clarence. After all, the Triple L was quite a
distance from Bayou Black. But then, Tante Lulu's *traiteur* skills had been sought far and wide, especially when
she was younger.

Tante Lulu jumped up and proceeded to give Linc and

Clarence seconds, without their even asking. But then, they weren't protesting. She ignored the sulking Jimmy as if he weren't even there.

"Linc, will you come back this evenin' after chores and play us some of yer music?" Tante Lulu requested.

Linc sat up straighter. "How'd you know 'bout my music, Miz Rivard?"

"Why, Charmaine was tellin' me whilst we were preparin' dinner that you play the guitar and write yer own music, jist like one of yer famous ancestors. I'd be pleased to hear you."

"Well, ma'am, I'd be pleased to play fer ya." Linc's shoulders went back with pride, making Charmaine a little ashamed that she hadn't asked him to play herself during the past few days. "I'm a bit rusty, though. Don't be expectin' much."

"All he plays is that blues stuff," Jimmy complained.

"What you want him to play, you? That knocker garbage?" If there had been a wooden spoon within reach, she probably would have whacked him this time.

"Huh?" everyone at the table said.

"What knocker?" Jimmy asked. "You mean boob? I never heard of boob music."

"No, I don't mean boob," Tante Lulu said, giving Jimmy a dirty look. "And watch yer mouth, boy. They's ladies present."

Charmaine had been interpreting for Tante Lulu since she was a kid. "I think she means rapper music, not knocker music."

"Rap, knock . . . whass the difference?" the old lady asked.

Jimmy opened his mouth, about to say something, but Linc squeezed his arm in warning.

"Eat up, honey," Tante Lulu said to Rusty, patting him on the shoulder as she passed by on her way to the counter. "I got more of that Peachy Praline Cobbler Cake fer dessert. Only good boys what eats their dinner gets to have a sweet afterward."

Ah! So that is her game plan with Jimmy. A little sweet revenge, Tante Lulu style.

"More peaches. Yippee. And, man, I have been a very good boy," Rusty said to Tante Lulu, but he was looking at Charmaine while he spoke. "Haven't I, Charmaine?" Then he winked.

Gawd, I hate it when he winks. Well, not exactly hate. I actually like it too much, and that's why I hate it. I am not making sense. But then nothing I do makes sense when Rusty is around.

In the end, the lure of Tante Lulu's dessert proved too much for Jimmy. "Mebbe I'll have a little taste of that catfish crap . . . uh, stew," he offered.

Tante Lulu poured a huge ladleful into his bowl, including a piece of okra floating on top, and watched as he ate every bite. "Thass a good boy," she said finally, giving him a little hug from behind. "Now, you wantin' some dessert or not?"

"Yes, ma'am."

"You can call me Tante Lulu like everyone else, or Auntie."

The boy beamed at her with adoration, especially after she gave him a generous slice of cake topped with vanilla ice cream.

"Hey, you didn't offer me ice cream," Rusty complained.

"Mebbe you weren't *that* good of a boy." Tante Lulu glanced pointedly from Charmaine to Rusty. "While I'm here, I might as well put together some of my herbal remedies," she said in one of her usual swift changes in conversation. "I'm thinking of brewing up some cow-pen tea and some pizzle grease."

"Don't ask," Charmaine muttered under her breath.

But of course no one listened.

"What's cow-pen tea?" Clarence asked.

"And pizzle grease?" Jimmy wanted to know.

Tante Lulu beamed at their interest in her *traiteur* abilities. "Cow-pen tea is a medicinal tea thass been around fer more than a hundred years. Made from brewing up cow poop, it is. And pizzle grease is the bestest ointment, made of the fat culled from boilin' up hog pizzles. 'Course cow pizzles would prob'ly work just as good."

Four male jaws dropped open.

"Is she serious?" Rusty whispered to Charmaine.

She nodded.

But Tante Lulu heard his remark and said, "Tsk-tsk! Ya shouldn't be puttin' down the old remedies. Sometimes they work best."

They might work best, but Charmaine was pretty sure that no one sitting at the table would be willing to try them anytime soon.

After Rusty, Clarence, and Linc took Jimmy out to the barn to feed the horses and do a last-minute check on the herd, she and Tante Lulu did the dishes and cleaned up the kitchen, chatting the whole while. Then they took cups of coffee out to the back porch to catch up on the news.

"Seen any of the Dixie mob around here?" Tante Lulu asked.

"Nope. Knock on wood."

"No sense doing that superstitious stuff. St. Jude is the

answer. Always." She glanced over to the statue, which had been moved to the corner of the porch. "What say we build us a grotto to St. Jude tomorrow, right there in middle of the yard? I brought some bedding plants, and we can transplant a few bushes. Good idea, huh?"

Not a good idea. Rusty will have a fit. "Uh, sure, great idea."

"Luc said ta tell ya he would discuss yer situation in detail when he comes on Thursday. I think he has a plan fer repaying the whale."

"The shark," she corrected. "A loan *shark.*"

"Why are people always correctin' me? I knew it was a shark. Geesh!"

"That's good news anyway. That Luc has a plan." *Wish I had a plan. For my money woes. For my career. For my life.*

"You sure yer shops are okay without you?"

Charmaine nodded. "For a short while, they will be. And my two managers can contact me through Luc if there's a problem."

"Mebbe Luc's plan is to pay off sharkie from the shop profits."

"I wish! No, Bobby Doucet made it clear that he wasn't going to accept any long-term payment plan. And neither was I if that thousand dollar a day interest was piling on." Between the two shops, she usually pulled in fifty thousand in net profits per year, even after her own generous salary, but that wasn't enough.

"You gonna invite yer mother here fer Thanksgiving dinner?"

Charmaine laughed. "No, I am not. She wouldn't want to come. I'm not even sure if she's still in Baton Rouge. Last I heard, she and her boyfriend du jour were talking about opening a male strip club." That was a year ago, and their meeting had ended in an argument when she'd declined to invest in any more of her mother's born-to-fail, usually seedy ventures.

"Really? A *male* strip club?" Tante Lulu asked with way too much interest.

"Uh-huh. Chippendudes, or some such thing. Actually, there were supposed to be Chippendolls, too." *Gawd!* Charmaine shivered at the mental picture. She'd seen the inside of way too many strip joints over the years. She'd seen the inside of way too many male and female G-strings, too.

"You should invite her," Tante Lulu insisted.

Do you never give up, old lady? "You've already invited too many people. There wouldn't be room for more."

"They's always room for more, honey. And you should call Fleur. She's still yer mama, no matter what."

"Some women give birth, but they don't have the mother gene. She never wanted a child. She never wanted me. I was a doll for her to dress up as a clone of herself . . . a ten-year-old painted doll in hooker clothes. She thought it was a hoot. The kids at school thought . . ." Charmaine let her words trail off. *What is wrong with me? I never talk about that. Old history. Why dredge it up now?*

Tante Lulu reached over and squeezed her hand. "Now, now, sweetie. She caint hurt you anymore."

Charmaine swiped at her eyes. Amazing, that her mother still had the ability to hurt her, even when she didn't even try.

"Call her, baby. You'll feel better if you do."

Charmaine didn't see how that was possible. Still, she said, "I'll think about it."

"So, do you still love the cowboy?"

Oh, boy! Another subject change. And a doozie this time. "Which cowboy?"

"For shame, girl! They's only one cowboy you'd be interested in. The one with the mojo."

"I thought you told him that he lost his mojo. At least that's what he told me when he came in for dinner." She smiled as she remembered the chagrin on Rusty's face that anyone would think he'd lost his masculine appeal.

"Hah! That boy's got mojo coming out his pores. I jist said that to shake him up a bit. You better lasso him in afore some cowgirl comes along, sees him for the prime animal he is, and ropes him first."

Oh, yeah! That's me. Dale-damn-Evans without her horse . . . or lasso, for that matter.

"You dint answer my question."

I know I didn't answer your question, you busybody you. I was hoping you'd forget. Other old folks get memory loss; you get sharper with age. "I'm not sure I ever loved him. I was only nineteen when we were married. What did I know about anything?"

Tante Lulu shrugged. "I doan know 'bout that. You two seemed crazy in love to me."

"Maybe it was just lust." *Or maybe not.*

"Lust is good, too. Take a word of advice from a meddling old coot. Love is rare in this world today. If there's even the tiniest chance that there's a spark of love left 'tween you two, you're a fool not to jump on it."

Charmaine nodded, not about to argue with that sentiment. The question was: *Do I still love him?*

Chapter 9

When curiosity bites you in the butt . . .

Raoul was approaching the back porch from the side of the house when Tante Lulu asked Charmaine if she still loved him.

He should have made his presence known. What did it matter if Charmaine did or did not love him? She'd already told him point-blank that she wanted more from a relationship than he could offer. And, hell, he'd be begging for heartache if he got involved with her again. Still, curiosity got the better of him, and he stopped in his tracks, listening.

When Charmaine said, "I'm not sure I ever loved him," it felt as if a knife twisted in his heart. *Not true, Not true*, he protested, but then he reminded himself that he'd said almost the same thing to Amelie when she'd asked if he still loved Charmaine. *Did I really love her then? Did she love me? And what about now? Is there still some love left? Do I want there to be?*

He wished he hadn't stopped to listen. He wished he hadn't heard the question. And he for sure wished he hadn't heard Charmaine's answer.

Truth was, sometimes curiosity came back to bite a nosy guy in the butt.

What is wrong with me? On the one hand, I want her so bad I'm a walking hard-on. On the other hand, I wish she'd leave and find some other schmuck. One side of my brain says, "Go for it, bucko. Take whatever you can get." The other side says, "Slow down, cowboy. Sometimes riding the bull isn't worth the pain." What is wrong with me?

I know, I know, said the voice in his head, or rather St. Jude standing over there in all his plastic glory, staring ahead like a . . . statue.

"Well, keep it to yourself. I don't want to know," he muttered.

"Who ya talkin' to, buddy?" Linc asked. He'd just come up beside him, carrying his guitar in one hand and a battered old trumpet case in the other. Following close behind were Clarence, with a plug in his mouth, and Jimmy, with a frown on his mouth.

"Just myself," he answered.

"Women'll do that to a fellow," Linc opined.

Raoul jerked his head toward Linc with surprise. "Who said a woman was involved?"

"Don't have to. Anytime a guy starts talkin' to himself, a woman must be involved."

"That's 'cause Rusty hasn't been takin' my advice," Clarence said, apparently overhearing enough to get the gist of the conversation. "Bowlegged, boy. Bowlegged."

Raoul rolled his eyes at Linc, who just grinned at him.

"Whattya mean? Bowlegged?" Jimmy wanted to know.

The three adult males smiled but remained silent. But Mr. Plastic said in his head, *I know, I know.*

In his own head, Raoul sent this silent message. *Why don't you go find someone else to plague? Some hopeless cause somewhere else, like Iraq.*

You're as hopeless as they come, St. Jude informed him drolly.

I'm losin' my frickin' mind.

A mind is a beautiful thing, but it ain't everything, boy.

A short time later, they settled on the back porch, and Raoul tried his best not to look at Charmaine, who batted her black eyelashes at him with the innocence of a born-to-tempt siren. While his mind was engaged thus in testosterone overload, Tante Lulu sucker punched him with the question: "How's about we invite yer mother fer the Thanksgiving feast?"

Raoul didn't know what aspect of that seemingly casual suggestion scared him most. The prospect of being in the same room with his nonmaternal mother. The prospect of his mother coming back to the ranch she hated after all these years. Or the prospect of a "feast" of any kind being held here. He opted for the safest answer, "Uh, I don't think she'd be interested. She's a vegan."

"Thass okay, boy. Some of my best friends are Lutheran."

Raoul's jaw dropped open. The other three males on the porch snorted with mirth. And Charmaine, ever kind to her adopted aunt, explained, "A vegan is a vegetarian."

"Why dintcha say so, you lunkhead?" Tante Lulu said to him. "Bless her heart, Josette allus was like buckshot in a huntin' rifle. Scattered, yer mother was. Goin' off on one cause or 'nother, without direction."

Leaving me behind.

"I reckon some wimmen jist doan have the mommy

gene. Remember the time when you wuz 'bout seven she forgot you at a rest stop when she went on one of her research trips?"

He nodded. *Oh, yeah, I remember. Seven years old and left behind. Talk about!*

"So, you gonna invite her?"

"No."

"Mebbe I'll give her a call."

"No."

"What do vegans eat anyhows?" she asked Charmaine, totally ignoring his protests.

"Bark and seeds and grass, I think," Charmaine answered, giving him a saucy wink.

"Let's get one thing straight," Raoul said, in as firm a voice as he could manage, "I do not want or need a Thanksgiving feast here. I have nothing to be thankful for this year."

"Me neither," Charmaine piped in.

Tante Lulu gasped with shock. "Can you believe these two?" She glanced over at St. Jude, as if seeking his opinion. Jude still stared straight ahead. "Bless their hearts, dumb as dirt, both of 'em."

Yep, you-know-who concurred.

Singin' the blues . . .

Linc surprised them all.

Oh, Rusty and Clarence and Jimmy had probably heard him sing and play the occasional melody before, but not like this. Tonight he was not Linc the Black Cowboy. He was Linc the quintessential artist, a musical performer, in his real element.

He carried with him an ancient-looking case, presumably holding a trumpet, the instrument that had been the specialty of one of his Civil War era ancestors, but his instrument of choice was the guitar. He adjusted the strap of a vintage Gibson acoustic and tested the strings. With head tilted to hear the tiniest nuances of sound, he became a different person. As if he were in his own world, he smiled softly, a musician focused on his craft.

Charmaine sat on a glider with Tante Lulu, a wool throw draped over both their shoulders against the chill. Jimmy sat in one rocker and Clarence in the other. Rusty half sat on the porch rail.

"My great grandfather many times removed was Abel 'A. B.' Lincoln, a New Orleans musician," Linc related as he began to strum on the guitar. "I was named after him."

"How many years ago was that?" Jimmy asked.

"Many, many," Linc answered with a chuckle. "About the time of the Civil War and twenty years after. He died in 1885 when he was about my age."

"I think I've heard of him," Charmaine said.

"Maybe you're mixing him up with one of yer ex-husbands," Tante Lulu quipped.

Charmaine elbowed her for teasing.

"I have a few old journals of his," Linc went on. "Plus, I've checked out some historical society books on early blues musicians." He began to sing, faintly at first.

> *"If you were a bayou, my friend,*
> *And I were a fish, my friend,*
> *I would swim you, my friend,*
> *Because I love you so . . ."*

"If you were mud, my friend,
And I were a pig, my friend,
I would wallow in you, my friend,
Because I love you so . . ."

"If you were the sky, my friend,
And I were the wind, my friend,
I would billow for you, my friend,
Because I love you so . . ."

"What kind of songs are those?" Jimmy complained. "Pigs, and mud and stuff!"

"Like rap music that praises big butts and gangs is any better?" Linc laughed. "Actually, these were lyrics that slaves in the cotton and sugar fields used to chant. It's hard to tell which were passed on by oral tradition and which were original to A. B. In truth, I suspect that everyone added a new lyric as they went along, including A. B. It's just that he was the one to write them down."

He sang several other songs then, including some by Billy Bolton who was considered the father of the blues back in the nineteenth century. Then he played a poignantly melodic song, about peaches, of all things, which caused Charmaine and Rusty to look at each other and smile.

"You're playin' in my orchard,
Now don't you see.
If you don't like my peaches,
Stop shakin' my tree."

"And that goes for you, too, *chère*," Rusty told her with a wicked wink. "You better stop shakin' my . . . tree." He stared pointedly at her blouse as he spoke.

She tilted her head saucily, and asked, "Or?"

"Or else," was all Rusty would say. But that was enough. She felt the promise of *else* in every erotic spot on her body, of which there were about a thousand.

"Have any of you ever heard the song 'My Simone?'" Linc asked.

She, Rusty, and Clarence all said, "Yes." Tante Lulu asked, "Didn't Louis Armstrong sing that song?"

Linc nodded. "Bessie Smith's version was probably the most famous. And lots of other artists did it, too." Linc sang the beautiful song then with all the emotion his husky voice could drum up and all the pain of his genetic memory of A. B.'s love for a woman he could never truly have.

"Did your ancestor write that song?" Rusty asked in the heavy silence that followed the song.

"He did." Linc raised his chin with pride, before adding, "Simone ran a sporting house in Nawleans after the Civil War. They loved each other but could never marry because she was white and he was black. He wrote this song about Simone . . . just before they both committed suicide."

"Tsk-tsk-tsk!" Tante Lulu said at the sadness of such an act.

"Oh, Linc!" Charmaine got up and went over to lean down and give him a hug. When she straightened, she told him, "You should be writing all this down. Put it in a book. Or make a record."

"That's just what I was doing before I was . . . incarcerated," Linc answered while he started to take off his guitar strap.

Charmaine was confused. Rusty had already told her that Linc had been convicted of embezzlement . . .

money he'd stolen to support a cocaine habit. He'd been clean for five years now, but before hitting bottom he'd lost his job, his wife, and his home. Something was out of kilter in this picture, though. She just couldn't reconcile a talented musician and author with a ranch hand.

"What did you do for a living before you went to prison, Linc?" Tante Lulu was obviously as confused as she was. It was none of their business, of course, but both of them stared at him expectantly, waiting for his answer.

"College professor," he answered bluntly. "Music history at Tulane."

Charmaine gasped with surprise.

Tante Lulu nodded as if she'd suspected as much.

Clarence and Rusty appeared already to be aware of his background.

Jimmy would have been more impressed if he'd said rock musician. In fact, Jimmy's attention centered more on Charmaine now as he inquired, "Is it true you was once Miss Loo-zee-anna?"

"Yep."

"Holy smoke!"

She chuckled at his raised eyebrows.

Rusty just smiled, knowing she would be irritated under other circumstances by Jimmy's golly-gee reaction to her as a beauty queen. But he was just a kid.

"Jeesh! You wore a bathing suit and a gown and all that stuff? Like a movie star or sumpin'?"

"For sure, I did."

"Wow!" He was gaping at her as if she were some dumpy old broad who'd never be able to squeeze her bod into a revealing outfit fit for a beauty pageant. Well, she couldn't get too offended. To him, a girl of twenty would seem old.

"What did you do fer talent?" Clarence asked.

She brightened. "I sang."

"You did?" Linc was looking at her with interest. "What did you sing?"

"That old Billie Holiday number 'The Man I Love.'"

"You sang the blues?" Linc's jaw dropped with shock, that the two of them would have so much in common.

"Yep. I wanted to do a Cajun song, but this is Loo-zee-anna, after all. There were plenty of Cajun and Creole songs, even one girl playing the accordion and another with a *frottoir* for accompaniment. A *frottoir* is an over-the-shoulder washboard." The latter explanation she added for Jimmy's benefit because he was frowning with confusion.

"But the blues?" Linc was shaking his head with disbelief. "I just didn't expect the blues from you."

"Why? Because I'm always so happy?" *Just call me Loo-zee-anna Pollyanna.*

"Probably because he expected you to do something more outrageous," Rusty offered. "Like Madonna in a cone cup thingee."

"*Mais oui.* Me and Madonna. Like a virgin." She stuck her tongue out at him, which caused him to grin. Not the reaction she'd been hoping for. "Actually, I thought about doing 'Twist and Shout'. You know, the one with 'Shake it up, baby!' That would have given me an opportunity to dance and strut my stuff." She flashed Rusty a dirty look before he could add another rude comment—about all the stuff she had to strut, no doubt. Or about her dancing with a mop. "But my coach advised me to go for a less flamboyant persona."

"I doubt those prissy ass judges, bless their hearts, could have taken yer shakin' it up, honey," Tante Lulu said. If it had been Rusty offering that opinion, she might have hit him. Since it was Tante Lulu, she just smiled. Which just encouraged the old broad. "I 'member the time you and me entered that belly dance contest in Lafayette. Lordy, Lordy, that one geezer on the judging panel about swallowed his false teeth when he saw yer belly button ring."

Everyone chuckled, except Rusty, who asked, "You have a belly button ring? Can I see?"

"Yes, I have one. No, you can't see it, Mr. Lech." *But maybe someday. If you're lucky. If I'm lucky. Oh, boy, I am losing this battle to be pure.*

"I'm thinkin' 'bout gettin' one myself," Tante Lulu said. "Did it hurt?"

"Why would anybody deliberately poke a needle in their skin? And, hell's bells, Louise," Clarence told Tante Lulu, "I could give ya a piercing and save ya a trip to town. We staple ID rings onto the steers' ears every day. Can't be any different than a human skin piercing."

"Uh, I'll think about it," Tante Lulu said with a slight shiver. "Besides, it's hard ta find my belly button these days fer all the wrinkles in my tummy."

Not a picture any of them wanted in their heads!

"You never got pierced when you were with me," Rusty pointed out in a little boy whiny voice.

Geesh! The things he fixates over!

"Did you?"

As if he wouldn't have known! The man knew every inch of her body back then. Every freakin' inch. "I got my navel pierced because I was depressed over my second divorce. Justin was the most charming of all my husbands. My oh my, that man could talk a woman into anything. And he was a great dancer. Unfortunately, he was doing the mattress bop with everything that wore a dress." Charmaine could see that Rusty was annoyed by her bringing up one of her ex-husbands, which pleased her in an immature way. But when had maturity been her strongest point? So, she barreled ahead. "I got the tattoo after I kicked out my third ex-husband, Lester."

"A tattoo?" Rusty mouthed silently at her. Then, out loud, "Where?"

I thought you'd never ask. She glanced down near the crotch of her jeans, then back up. Holding his gaze, she smiled.

He gulped several times and looked as if he'd swallowed his tongue.

Everyone was chuckling at the interplay between the two of them, though Rusty, sitting directly across from her, had been the only one to see the direction of her gaze.

"Then, after Antoine, my fourth husband, I . . . oh, never mind. I shouldn't discuss that in mixed company."

Rusty didn't say anything. She suspected his tongue was still stuck to the roof of his mouth.

"Atta girl," Tante Lulu encouraged her, sensing that she was on a tear, deliberately teasing Rusty so.

"Don't stop now, darlin'," Rusty groused, once he'd dislodged his tongue. "Tell us what you got after your last divorce. I can see you're just dyin' to blab it to one and all."

Gleefully, she informed him, "I bought myself a toy."

"A toy?" he practically choked out, suspecting a trap she had set for him. Smart guy!

"A boy toy?" Tante Lulu whooped. "I'd like to get me one of those."

"No, I didn't get myself a boy toy." She tried to appear offended but ended up laughing. "A mechanical toy, so to speak."

Jimmy continued to frown as he tried to follow their conversation. "Like a Game Boy?"

"You could say that," she answered with her tongue firmly planted in her cheek.

"Sometimes, *chère*, you are not happy till you go too far." Rusty's shaking head and chastising words were belied by the wicked grin that lifted the edges of his lips. "Dare I ask what you got after your first divorce?"

"The biggest heartache of my life," she blurted out before she had a chance to bite her tongue. *Could a woman die of overcrying? I almost did.*

For some reason, Rusty looked surprised.

"Will you sing your pageant song for us?" Linc asked then. "I don't recall the music precisely for 'The Man I Love,' but I could provide some background chords."

"Me too," Clarence said, pulling out his harmonica.

"Oh, I don't know if . . ." She hesitated. It had been a long time since she'd sung before an audience, and never professionally. But this was just friends and family. And she'd sung this particular song for Rusty before . . . in private. She hadn't met him yet when she'd entered the pageant or reigned as Miss Louisiana. "Sure. Why not?"

She thought she heard Rusty moan under his breath. She wasn't sure if he moaned over the possibility of her making a fool of herself or over the possibility that she would shake him up even more than she already had. She decided to assume the latter.

Going to the doorway where she would be backlit by

the lamp hanging over the kitchen table, she posed herself against one side and pulled the elastic neckline of her blouse down over her shoulders. Good move, that, she concluded when Rusty moaned again. "Picture me in a long slinky, flame red dress. Off the shoulders like this blouse, but form-fitting from the bodice to the toes of my red-sequined stiletto heels. The whole point was to look like an old-time torch singer."

"We get the picture," Jimmy said enthusiastically, though he'd probably totally missed the image she was going for. Rusty didn't, though, as was evidenced by the arousal that glazed his dark eyes, causing them to go half-shuttered as he studied her. She noticed that his hands were folded over his lap. Clenched.

Linc was already playing soft chords on his guitar as an introduction, but then he seemed to change his mind. Setting his guitar aside, he leaned over and took out the trumpet. Lipping the mouthpiece, he tested it several times, then let loose with a long wail of pain in the vein of the oldest blues known in the South. New Orleans at its best. Clarence, not to be outdone, blended in with a trill on his harmonica in perfect counterpoint to Linc's rhythm.

It was showtime!

And then she blew them all away . . .

Raoul was still in love with Charmaine.

He knew that the instant she began to sing, poignantly and from the heart, of the man she loved. Someday that man would come along, and when he smiled at her, she would know. They would both know. He'd take her hand,

and no words would be necessary. When that man came, she would do her best to make him stay.

Tears burned in Raoul's eyes as he wondered why she hadn't stayed. Why hadn't he made her stay?

Charmaine wasn't a great singer, but she was good. Her normal voice had a melodic range, but when she sang, it went all husky and smoky as a Bourbon Street nightclub. A torch singer's vocal cords, for sure.

The last time Charmaine had performed this song for him she'd been standing in their Baton Rouge bedroom, wearing a sheer, floor-length black negligee with tiny, tiny straps. He'd been lying on the bed, wearing nothing. There'd been no doubt then that "The Man I Love" had been him. She'd enjoyed re-enacting all her pageant roles for him, including that showstopper of a song. In retrospect, he probably hadn't been appreciative enough. He'd always remember her that night, though. Always.

Now, Charmaine was approaching the last line of the last stanza, arms extended outward. She crooned in a soul-reaching wail, "I'm waiting for the man I love."

Mon Dieu, how I love her! he thought. *And how I wish I were that man she is waiting for.*

She did a cute little bow to each of them when she finished.

A stunned silence followed.

Jimmy was the first to speak. "Cooool! You're as good as J.Lo." They all smiled at what had to be a high compliment from the boy.

Linc put down his trumpet and went over to take both of Charmaine's hands in his. "That was wonderful."

"Really?"

"Really. I'm surprised that you never pursued a music career."

Charmaine's gaze connected immediately with Raoul's. Was she expecting him to disagree? "Yeah, you were great, darlin'. *As always.*"

She beamed then, as if his words really mattered, as if he complimented her so rarely that she was surprised now. His heart wrenched at that possibility.

There was a rustling then as people started to rise and gather up their stuff. When Linc bent to put his trumpet back in the case, an old sepia-toned photograph fluttered out. Raoul picked it up and glanced quickly at it before handing it back to Linc. It was two black men flanking a white one, probably a Creole, all of them in 1800s style clothing. "Who are they?" Raoul asked.

"That one there is the ancestor I told ya'll about. Abel Lincoln," Linc said, pointing to one of the black men, who bore a slight resemblance to him. "And that's A. B.'s twin brother Cain." He also resembled Linc, of course. "In the middle is Etienne Baptiste, a friend."

"Let me see," Charmaine said. At one glance, she exclaimed, "I've seen this picture before."

"I doubt that," Linc responded. "As far as I know, this is the only photo of A. B. Lincoln, except for a hazy one of him and Simone that hangs in the Louisiana State Museum as part of an exhibit on Storyville brothels."

"No, really, Linc. My sister-in-law Sylvie has a copy of this photograph framed in her family room. That guy, Etienne, is one of her ancestors. His family used to own a sugar plantation on Bayou Black."

Linc still looked skeptical.

So, Charmaine told him, "I'm going to have Sylvie bring the picture when she comes on Thursday. Maybe I'm wrong. But I don't think so."

Everyone went off then, saying their good nights, even

Tante Lulu, who went inside to take a bubble bath, or so she said. Raoul wasn't sure why he hung around. He had nothing to say to Charmaine that he hadn't said before. His realization that he still loved her didn't alter the fact that theirs was a doomed relationship. Too many obstacles. Too many unresolved problems. When Luc arrived on Thursday, he would probably be carrying divorce papers for them to sign.

He felt as if there were a vise around his heart. He could barely breathe.

"What's the matter?" she asked, stepping closer.

He moved to the side and put out a hand to halt her progress. If she got close to him now, he was pretty sure he would grab hold of her and never let go. Panicked, he said the first thing that came to his mind, "I won't be home for dinner tomorrow."

She tilted her head to the side.

"We're taking the cattle to market tomorrow . . . about three hundred head. A half dozen hired hands will be here at dawn with horses and trucks to help round them up and load them for transport."

"And that will take all day . . . and evening?"

"Well, Clarence and Linc and Jimmy might be back by dinnertime, but I have some appointments afterward."

"What kind of appointments?"

How like Charmaine, he thought with an inner smile. She just barreled ahead, never questioning whether it was any of her business or not.

"First, I have to meet with my parole officer."

"Why? Is something wrong?"

"Just a regular meeting. Then I have an appointment with that detective that Luc recommended."

"Let me come, too."

"No," he said flatly. "This is about the investigation into my alleged crime. It has nothing to do with you. Luc is working on your problem."

"Maybe I could help . . . with the parole officer, too. Really. I could say lots of nice things about you."

"Believe me, Charmaine, you do not want to meet my parole officer. Deke Devereaux is not fond of me, and I guarantee he would treat you with the same disrespect he gives me. He is a little runt of a bully who enjoys the power his job gives him."

Her face grew stormy. "I'm a big girl. I can handle myself. Maybe I'm just the person to put him in his place."

That's all I need. A pit bull female coming to my defense. He decided to home in on something else. "What nice things would you say about me?"

"Lemme see. You're nice-looking, in a rugged sort of way."

"That would impress the hell out of Devereaux."

"You work hard."

"He doesn't give a rat's ass about hard work. He would think that's a minimum requirement for an ex-con . . . which is how he refers to me every other word."

"You look like hell on wheels in tight, faded jeans."

He grinned. "Oh, baby! You should not tell me things like that."

Charmaine moved one step closer.

This time he didn't move. He could smell the floral scent of her shampoo. He could feel her body heat.

Dangerous, dangerous, dangerous.

"Sometimes I wonder . . ."

"What?" she asked, looking at him like a cold drink on a hot Loo-zee-anna day. It wasn't hot tonight, but it felt steamy as all get out.

". . . why we ever broke up."

"Oh, Rusty, we were always breaking up. The least little thing caused us to argue. I'd run off to one of my girlfriends' for a day or two. Or you'd go to a frat house, or sleep on the couch."

"Yeah, but the makeup sex was mind-blowing."

She smiled sadly. "It was that."

"I guess I never really understood how that last argument snowballed into your leaving for good. And don't quote me that bullshit about my calling you a bimbo. That was anger speaking, and you know it."

"You were upset about my quitting college and going to work."

"A real ogre I was, wanting my wife to get a college degree."

"College was always more important to you than it was to me." She put up a hand to stop him from arguing with her. "Really, you had a dream to become a veterinarian, but there was no clear career goal for me then. I was taking a bunch of liberal arts courses with no goal in sight. Pointless."

"And what was the point in your taking a job at a strip club instead?"

She gasped. "The Blue Pelican was not a strip club, and I would not have been a stripper. I would have been a waitress earning good tips."

"You might as well have been a stripper as wear one of the outfits the girls wore there. Jesus, Charmaine, why do you think half the college boys hung out at the Pelican? Because of their greasy burgers?"

"I . . . would . . . have . . . been . . . a . . . waitress," she said through gritted teeth.

"Why?" It's not as if he hadn't asked that question a hundred times before.

"Because I needed the money," she practically shouted.

He could tell that she immediately regretted her outburst. But, Holy Moses, this was something new. "Your father was paying your college expenses. Why did you need the money?"

"Forget it," she said and started to go into the house.

He grabbed her arm. "Truth, Charmaine. I deserve the damn truth."

"My father cut me off, you big baboon. Now, let me go."

"Why did your father cut you off?"

"Does my father ever need a reason for the things he does?"

"Well, no," he started to say, but then he noticed the way Charmaine's eyes shifted nervously. She was hiding something. Something important. "Spill it. *Por l'amour le Dieu*, spill it."

Tears welled in her eyes and seeped out. "I can't."

"Yes, you can, baby," he said, taking her by the forearms and forcing her to meet his scrutiny. "Tell me."

Just then, Tante Lulu stepped through the doorway, reeking of peach bubble bath, and asked, "So where am I gonna sleep t'night?" She was wearing pink foam rollers in her hair and pink Barbie pajamas and some kind of white goop on her face.

Charmaine stepped away from him quickly, and said, "I'll fix a bed for you on the living room sofa for tonight. Tomorrow, we'll clean out Charlie's bedroom for you to use."

The two of them scurried off then.

Charmaine probably thought she'd had a narrow escape.

It was just a temporary reprieve. For ten long years, Raoul had wondered if there might have been some hidden reason why Charmaine had left him. Maybe now he would get the answer.

'*Bout time*, the bane of his life expounded.

Chapter 10

Mr. Clean had nothing on them . . .

The next day, just past dawn, they treated the much-expanded Triple L crew to a breakfast Tante Lulu style: fried tasso, a highly seasoned Cajun ham, red-eye gravy, biscuits as light as a bayou cloud, grits, fluffy scrambled eggs, and gallons of coffee. Then Charmaine followed in the wake of the old lady on the mother of all cleaning sprees.

Before the men had left for the day, Charmaine had asked them to take the hand-woven Cajun carpets out of the living room to the side yard, where they now hung over the clotheslines for scrubbing. They were old and worn, but still fine, probably made by Rusty's grandmother on the loom she'd seen stored in the loft of the barn.

Before they got started, though, Tante Lulu asked her to tackle her roots. Tante Lulu, known for her outrageous appearance, had decided to be a redhead in line with her kick-ass cowgirl persona of the moment. While Charmaine worked on her at the kitchen table—work that was so familiar to Charmaine she could do it with her eyes closed—they chatted amiably.

"I think you and Rusty should have a big wedding this time."

Charmaine almost dropped the small bowl of dye she held in one hand. Then she chuckled. Leave it to Tante Lulu to surprise her like that. "There is no 'this time,' Auntie."

"Hah! I seen the way that boy looks at you, like a hobo on a hot dog. And yer no better. Lordy, Lordy, if he was a sweet praline, you'd be lickin' him up one side and down the other."

"Tante Lulu! I'm shocked at you."

"Doan be takin' that attitude with me, girlie. Yer more shockin' than I ever was. I'm learnin' new antics from you, day by day. If it hadn't been so long since I had a man in my bed, I'd even try that born-again virgin thingee of yers. As it is, my thingee is prob'ly dried up 'bout now, like a raisin."

Charmaine couldn't help but laugh.

"I allus felt bad that I wasn't there to help you with yer weddin' to Rusty, but I gots plenty of time now. How 'bout Christmas? Wouldn't that be a great time to have a weddin'?"

Charmaine groaned with dismay. Putting a hand on Tante Lulu's shoulder, she squeezed gently. "Thank you for caring so much. But Rusty and I have too many obstacles between us. Besides we're still married, so another wedding would be redundant, don't you think? Ha, ha, ha."

"Renew yer vows then. Iffen anyone needs a new beginning, it's you. You caint fool me, girl. I doan care if you got obstacles up the kazoo. Iffen you two still love each other, and I 'spect you do, there could be a mountain sitting on yer toenails, and it wouldn't matter. Speakin' of nails, I need to do mine to match my hair. You got any of that Chili Pepper Red? Thass my favorite."

Tante Lulu had a way of rambling from one subject to another to distract a person, but Charmaine was not about to be distracted. "Listen, I don't know how to make this more clear. Luc will be bringing the divorce papers with him on Thursday. We will probably sign them."

"Probably? *Probably* never made the gumbo boil." She cackled at her own joke.

Charmaine closed her eyes briefly with frustration, then tried a different tack. "Wishing something were so, doesn't make it happen."

"Hah! Doan I know it, sweetie. Wimmen gots to make their own destiny. The question is: Are you woman enough?"

"I don't have a bleepin' clue," she said.

Well, here's a clue, that wretched voice in her head said. *God gave you a second chance. You gonna flub it again?*

Now, that was food for thought . . . that her divorce to Rusty never having been finalized was actually a celestial intervention.

Finally! Someone's listening to me.

"Mebbe you ought to ask St. Jude for help," Tante Lulu suggested.

Righto!

Was her aunt reading her mind now? Scary prospect, that!

Once Charmaine was done dyeing and styling her aunt's hair, they cleaned the living room, starting from the raftered ceiling and working downward. It really was a charming room, much in the style of that old *Bonanza* TV series. Lots of wood and exposed beams and

Western-style furniture. The only modern feature in the big room was a large-screen TV, which was at least ten years old.

After lunch, while her aunt was taking a nap, Charmaine went to work in Rusty's office again. She was making progress and uncovering some interesting information. For years, as much as a decade ago, oil companies had been contacting Charlie Lanier, trying to obtain the oil rights under the Triple L, if not the land itself. A familiar saying in these parts, and in Texas as well, was that the successful rancher had a wife who worked in town or at least one oil derrick on his property for the steer to scratch their butts on. The point was that a little bit of oil drilling didn't hurt. In fact, it allowed the rancher to stay afloat financially while cattle prices fluctuated.

Unfortunately, or fortunately, Charlie hadn't shared that opinion. He'd refused, adamantly, to sell or lease his land to the oil interests. Some of the letters from the oil companies, including her father's own Cypress Oil, were testy the past year, borderline threatening.

Could an oil company have been responsible for Charlie's untimely death?

Sounded logical. But they had to know that Rusty would be the heir. And he would follow through on his father's wishes.

Oh, my God! Not if Rusty was in jail. Not if he was on nonspeaking terms with his father. Not if they didn't know the terms of his will, splitting everything between her and Rusty.

Good heavens! Could those same oil interests be responsible for putting Rusty in jail, wanting him out of the way?

She would have to show these papers to Rusty tonight. No, tomorrow. He had said he'd be back late tonight. Charmaine was uneasy about the worried look she'd seen on his face that morning when he'd left the house. Yes, this news could wait till the morning.

After Tante Lulu's nap, they began to tackle Charlie's former bedroom, which obviously hadn't been touched in ages. While Charmaine took the curtains and the bedding, including a beautiful old patchwork quilt, to the laundry room, Tante Lulu began to put Charlie's clothing and boots and hats into a large cardboard box. They would offer them first to Clarence and Linc, and the rest would go to Our Lady of the Bayou's annual rummage sale, if Rusty approved, of course. It was only when they flipped the mattress, preparatory to vacuuming out the box springs, that they got their first shocks of the day.

Sitting on top of the box springs was a yellow manila envelope containing fifty thousand dollars in savings bonds.

Their second shock came when they pulled a shallow wooden box out from under the bed and discovered dozens of letters, at least fifty, which had been sent to Raoul Lanier and marked MAIL REFUSED, some of them more than twenty-five years old.

"Mon Dieu!" Charmaine exclaimed. "And all these years Rusty thought his father made no contact with him."

"This calls for a cup of burnt roast," Tante Lulu declared and walked off toward the kitchen to brew the strong Cajun coffee. Charmaine followed after her, stunned.

Soon they were seated at the kitchen table, sipping at hot coffee and munching on last night's leftover *Les*

Oreilles de Cochans, or pigs' ears cakes. Charmaine's tongue practically curled around the rich Cajun delicacy—deep fried twists of dough coated with cane syrup and nuts.

What to do with everything they'd just discovered?

"Well!" Tante Lulu said, as if that said it all.

"Rusty will be so pleased," Charmaine said. "I think."

"Well, why wouldn't he be? Fifty thousand buckaroos is a lot of cash to put this ranch back on its feet."

"Twenty-five thousand, not fifty," Charmaine corrected her.

"Oh. Thass right. Charlie's will left everything half and half. Does that mean you'll be hightailin' it back to Houma, now that you can pay back the fish?"

For some reason, that prospect did not delight Charmaine, as it should have. "I don't know."

Tante Lulu grinned, as if *she* knew. "Ain't you afeared of having yer kneecaps broken or the Mafia puttin' a horse's head in yer bed, or sumpin'?"

"Yeeeees," she said uncertainly. "But I've always believed in putting money to work for me. Maybe there is a better use for my half."

"Better than having kneecaps?"

Charmaine licked the syrup off her fingers one at a time. "I've been thinking . . . it's only an idea at this point . . ."

"Uh-oh! The last time you had an idea for making lots of moola, you lost yer shirt."

"This is different."

"It allus is. So, tell me. What's yer idea?"

"What would you think about turning the Triple L into a dude ranch? You know, hunky cowboys teaching rich city ladies how to ride horses. Stuff like that. I think it would be a way to make the ranch profitable again. And maybe we could even have a beauty spa here, too. Really, it's a good idea. It would bring in a lot more steady income than stinkin' cows."

Tante Lulu looked at her as if she lost one of her last screws and said, "Ooooh, boy!"

St. Jude probably rolled his eyes, too, and said, *Ooooh, boy!*

In the still of the night . . .

Raoul was mentally and physically beat by the time he arrived home at midnight.

All the lights were off, except for a lamp in the living room. Even before he glanced around, he detected lemon wax in the air and knew that his very own Molly Maids must have attacked the room. It looked great, better even than it had when he'd been a boy and his Dad employed Clarence's late wife as a housekeeper. He'd told Charmaine that she didn't have to do all this housework, but did she listen to him? Hah! Not about this or anything else. Add Tante Lulu to her team, and he might as well wave a white flag.

As he stood under the steaming shower, he cataloged the events of the day. The cattle had brought in a depressingly low price, only thirty thousand dollars in profit for three hundred animals. How was he ever going to build up a new herd on that? Or buy feed? Or pay Clarence and Linc their back wages? Or get the much-needed new carburetor for his Jeep. Or pay the past due electric bill. Forget about the taxes. And there was always the possibility that Charmaine would demand her half.

After he'd sent everyone home about 6:00 P.M., he'd gone to see his parole officer. Not an experience he'd ever want to repeat, though he would have to, monthly, for the next year. He'd developed a sudden talent for grinding teeth. Devereaux had been especially obnoxious, deliberately trying to prod a reaction from him that could result in a red mark in his file. In particular, Devereaux had delighted in his crude observations over his still being married to Charmaine, a former Miss Louisiana. Apparently, there was something crudely funny about beauty queens and ex-cons.

The only highlight of the day had been his dinner meeting with Frank Zerby, the detective Luc had recommended. Zerby had impressed him with his professionalism and the work he'd done thus far, investigating the police officer who'd been a prime witness in his conviction, as well as the oil interests who'd been harassing his father for a long time. There was no doubt in Zerby's mind, and in Raoul's now that they'd talked, that he would get his conviction reversed eventually. Zerby would also help him uncover details about his father's death but warned him that he might have to request an autopsy.

But first, he had to turn this ranch around. And decide what to do with an ex-wife who was not an ex-wife. And plan a future that right now looked like a freakin' dead end. And face a houseful of people in three days and pretend to be thankful. How had his life gotten so hopeless? He was thirty-one years old, but he felt about ninety.

After the shower, he made his way back to his bedroom in the dark, where he just about knocked himself out when he tripped over some large object. Hopping about on one foot and swearing under his breath at the pain in his bruised shin, he flicked on the light and saw that someone had placed Tante Lulu's hope chest at the foot of his bed. "Sonofabitch!" he said aloud now, an all encompassing exclamation of disgust over the day's events, the already swelling bump on his leg, and the ridiculous piece of furniture. Once he'd satisfied himself that he wouldn't die from his injury, he went over and lifted the lid. Inside were layer upon layer of embroidered bed linens, towels, hand-woven Cajun blankets, a quilt, and doilies. And from all of them wafted up to him the scent of roses. A quick examination showed there were dryer sheets mixed among the fabrics. He realized then, with hysterical irrelevance, he supposed, that Charmaine must have learned this trick from Tante Lulu.

After that, he lay in bed for more than an hour, exhausted but unable to sleep. Finally, he pulled on a pair of boxer shorts and padded off to—*where else?*—Charmaine's room. Not the wisest decision in the world, but being wise was beyond his grasp tonight with all the grief that weighed him down.

A full moon allowed him to see somewhat. Charmaine lay on one side with her hands folded together prayerlike under one cheek. A slight breeze drifted through the two open windows, but it was warm and muggy tonight. As a result, she was uncovered, wearing only a red nightshirt, which had ridden up her thighs to expose the edge of her white panties. No, on closer examination, it wasn't a nightshirt. It was another old LSU T-shirt of his. Why that should be an adrenaline kick in his groin was beyond him. All he knew was that he got immense pleasure from her wearing an item of his clothing. Way pathetic in the *Playboy* book of cool, he would imagine. Not that he had been cool for a long time, if ever.

He smiled and eased himself carefully onto the double bed behind Charmaine. When he was up against her spoon fashion, he laid one arm over the pillow on which her head rested and the other arm over her hip, with his hand spread over her cloth-covered belly. Only then did he sigh softly. It was like coming home . . . just what he needed tonight.

Luckily, Charmaine didn't wake up and belt him one. He would just rest here for a moment. Just one blissful second . . . or two . . .

He awakened God only knew how much later with a jolt. He was lying flat on his back. Charmaine was plastered all over him like honey on a hot rock, and he meant that in the best possible way. Her face was nestled in his chest hairs. One leg had wedged itself between his thighs with her knee resting up against his . . . well, what a more poetic person might have called his Longfellow.

The steady breath of her deep sleep against his heart brought tears to his eyes. For a long time, he'd needed to hold her like this, more than he'd realized. He gently kissed the top of her hair and ran a hand over her back from shoulder to waist and up again.

"Ummmm," she moaned appreciatively.

He stilled his hand, not wanting to awaken her. She'd bop him from here to Opelousa if she discovered him in her bed.

"You smell like Irish Spring," she murmured sleepily against his chest.

Uh-oh! I've been caught. "Irish? Darlin', there isn't a drop of Irish blood in this old body. I'm pure Cajun."

"Irish Spring, silly. Soap."

"Oh, you mean that green bar in the shower." *Great! We're going to discuss soap. What next? Deodorants?*

"What are you doing in my bed?"

Oh, shit! Here comes the bop. "I got home late and was checking on you and . . . hell, it was just too damn tempting to resist."

"I was tempting?"

"As sin." *Now there's a good sign. She cares whether I consider her tempting. Or maybe she's just asking so she can give me an extra bop.*

"How did it go today?" She was still lying across his body with her head on his chest.

So, no bop. At least not right away. "Don't ask."

"Did you sell the cattle?"

"We sold them."

"For how much?"

"Not enough. Not even close."

"Oh, Rusty. What are we going to do?"

I like the sound of that "we" in there. I shouldn't, but I do. "Just keep plugging away."

"Well, guess what, baby? I've got something to make you happy."

There's only one thing that would make me happy right now. Is that what she's offering? On the other hand, this is the kind of land mine women plant in the path of men all the time. Say the wrong thing and you are dead meat. He chuckled at his own warped speculations.

She slapped his shoulder. "Not *that,* silly."

Oh, yeah. Silly me for thinking that getting laid would cheer me up. "I never thought you were offering yourself up as a Happy Meal," he lied.

"When—or if—I ever decide to offer myself up, there will be nothing subtle about it, big boy. You will know."

He laughed. That was the best thing about Charmaine—her unsubtlety.

"The truth is, Tante Lulu and I found some . . . uh, stuff today that might help your whole dismal situation."

Is that what I am? Dismal? Geeshum-golly! Horny as hell, and dismal to boot. "Listen, Charmaine, I don't want to talk about the *whole dismal situation* tonight. I want to forget. Just for tonight."

He could feel her body go still. Then she did the oddest thing . . . well, odd, considering their conversation, their past history, her new virginity, the whole schlemiel: She used one forefinger to circle his nipple. Slowly. Circle after circle. Soft as a butterfly's wing. Then she leaned over, wet the same nipple with her tongue, blew him dry, and began to suckle him. Yep, nothing subtle about Charmaine.

"Jesus, Mary, and Joseph!" He about shot up off the bed. Stars appeared before his open eyes. And his Longfellow became an even longer fellow.

"Are you forgetting yet?" she whispered huskily as she looked up at him with seeming innocence.

Even as he choked out, "Forgetting what?" Charmaine swung her leg up over his hip and sat on his belly. If that wasn't enough to blow his torpedo, she began to pull her T-shirt—*his* T-shirt—up over her head. She probably did it quickly but it sure felt like slow motion from his perspective, which was clouded by about a thousand volts of testosterone. "Are you trying to kill me, *chère*?"

"With kindness," she answered.

This is kindness. I wonder what happens when she gets generous?

She was naked now, except for a pair of plain white, low-riding underpants and a teeny-tiny, blinkin' gold hoop in her belly button. She raised her hands to fluff out her hair, which caused her pretty breasts to jut out even more. She probably did it deliberately, if that little Madonna smile on her lips was any indication.

Who the freakin' hell cares! He reached up to touch her breasts.

She slapped his hands away. "No way, cowboy. This is my rodeo."

Okaaaay. "Aren't you a mite worried about losing your . . . um, virginity? Riding the bull is hard on the . . . doohickey." *Good thing I remembered Tante Lulu's word for it. One slip of a crude word here and I would have been out of the rodeo. No doohickey for me.*

"Not to worry. We're just going to fool around. Correction. *I* am going to fool around. You're just going to lie there nice and still and do a little forgetting. Are you all right with that?"

Women just don't get it. Men, dolts that we are, will take whatever we're offered in the way of sexual favors. We're very easy to please in that regard. Very. And telling a guy you want to do him is definitely not a turnoff in any male dictionary I've ever read. Knowing all that, though, he said, "Well, I don't know." *Men, bless our doltish hearts, don't want to appear easy, either.*

"I don't know" was apparently a green light to Charmaine because she placed her hands on either side of his head and half lay on him, with her nipples nestled in his chest hairs. She even brushed herself from side to side to give him the full effect. "Do you like that?" she asked in a sultry, hot silk voice.

"Are my eyeballs rolling around in my head like a pinball machine?"

She laughed. Then, just before she placed her lips over his, she murmured, "I love your mouth."

"I love that you love my mouth," he murmured back.

"I just want to kiss you."

He couldn't have spoken then if he'd wanted to. And he didn't—want to, that is. He was too busy holding on to the bedsheets.

Charmaine licked his lips. Not little catlike laps either. With wide swathes of her tongue, she wet him down. Then she bit him for smiling. Then she glided her mouth over his till they fit together perfectly. Then she inserted her tongue in his mouth, deeply. When he tried to reciprocate, she pulled back, but he was so far gone by then, it didn't matter much.

"My show," she insisted, lacing her fingers with his and placing his hands above his head.

"Whatever you say." *I'm no dummy.*

"Are your ears still so sensitive?"

Oh, boy! "Nope. Not anymore." He got rock hard just thinking about how sensitive his ears were and all the ways Charmaine knew to heighten that sensitivity.

She did every one of them now, one by one, as if she were following the Cosmo Step-by-Step Guide to Driving Your Man up the Wall. She blew into his ear. She nipped his lobe, then sucked on it. She inserted the tip of her sweet tongue inside. Ear sex, to be sure.

He bucked his hips up off the mattress, hoping Charmaine would take the hint and let him take over.

"Uh-uh-uh!" She unlaced her fingers from his but ordered him, "Leave your hands above your head." She scooted herself farther down his body so that she sat on his thighs now; along the way her behind brushed over his erection causing him to groan aloud.

She just smiled, like the born seductress she was.

And, *Dieu,* she was so beautiful, with her wild black hair and dancing eyes. Her breasts were full . . . so full they overflowed his palms . . . at least, they used to. They were high, considering their size, and tipped with large pink nipples, which were erect now . . . hopefully because she was as aroused as he was. *No, no one can be that aroused,* he decided. Charmaine prided herself on a small waist, much like Southern belles of old, but her hips flared out nicely. She was slim but curvy, no anorexic model type. Pure woman.

"Honey, let me . . ." he said in a husky voice he barely recognized. "I need to touch you."

She shook her head. "Not yet. I need to touch you first."

But she wasn't doing any touching. She was just staring at him, all over. "You are so beautiful," she said, mirroring the same sentiment he'd just thought about her.

"Men are not beautiful."

"You are. I remember the first time I ever saw you. You were walking ahead of me across campus. You wore a white T-shirt and tight jeans. I took one look at you, and I told my roommate, 'That guy has a butt to die for.'"

"You did not!"

"Yes, I did. That's the one thing about you that all the women comment on. Even today. Your rock solid tushie."

I have something else that's rock solid. Wanna see? "My ass? My ass is my best asset?" *Women! Go figure!*

"Yep. Then when you stopped that first day and turned around to talk to someone, my heart about stopped. You were so freakin' handsome I about wet my pants."

"You sweet talker you!" He was laughing on the outside, but inside his male ego grew about a mile. "Why didn't you come up to me that day?"

"Are you kidding? You were a big man on campus, and I was a lowly freshman."

I don't know how big I was then, but I sure as hell am big now. Big as in hard. As in hard-on. "Charmaine, you were never a lowly anything a day in your life. You ooze self-confidence."

"On the outside."

"You were already a former Miss Louisiana by then. Don't pretend that you were unsure of yourself."

She shrugged. "Around you, I was."

He let that interesting admission go for the moment. "I remember the first time I noticed you. It was spring of my junior year, and you were working on some kind of charity car wash. About half the guys from the football team had their cars lined up because of you. When I got there, I couldn't believe my eyes. You were wearing denim cutoffs—Daisy Maes, I think they were called—and a red tube top. Half your body was covered with soap suds, and you were laughing. I probably fell in love with you on the spot."

"Hah!" she said, but he could tell she was pleased. "And when did you fall out of love?"

He didn't answer. He couldn't. What he did say was, "Touch me."

"Where?"

"Oh, baby. Everywhere."

And she did. God bless her, she did. He spread his thighs, and she knelt between them. When she leaned forward, her breasts swayed. He'd forgotten how much he loved to see her breasts sway.

His hands were still raised above his head, but his fists were clenched. She used her fingertips and her hands to caress his shoulders, and upper arms, and paps, even his underarms. All the time she made little appreciative sounds.

She licked his nipples, and he dug his short fingernails into his palms. "Please . . . don't . . . stop."

With a saucy chuckle, she tugged at his nipples with her teeth, which caused his fingernails to dig deeper. Then she used the tip of her tongue to make a trail from the middle of his chest down to his navel. "You should get pierced."

"Where?" *If she even hints that I should get a ring in my cock, I am out of here.*

"Here," she said and stabbed his navel with her tongue.

Hot damn! Who knew I had an erotic zone there. Hell, it feels like I have ten thousand carnal hairs in there, and she's got every one of them on red alert.

She was on all fours over his body with her mouth just above his belly. Glancing up at his face, she asked, "Did you like that?"

Ha, ha, ha, ha, ha! "It was okay."

"Well, then, maybe you would like this better," she said. Sitting back on her haunches, she tugged quickly on the waistband of his shorts and drew them down to his thighs, then all the way off, all this before he could say, "Hells bells and hallelujah!"

He jackknifed to a sitting position. "Enough! I want to participate in this game."

She shoved him back down. "No. My game. My rules. Relax."

It was hard for him to put two syllables together with his cock standing up like a tupelo tree and every nerve ending in his body standing to attention, but he did. "Relax? Are you freakin' serious?"

"Don't question a gift horse, sweet cakes."

"This is some kind of rodeo where the cowboy is

gifted with a horse," he teased, folding his arms behind his head.

"And that's not even the main attraction."

"And that would be?"

She smiled mischievously at him. Then she raised her arms over her head in a long, posed stretch, after which she flexed her fingers in front of him in an exaggerated fashion, like a pianist about to give a magical, musical performance. Then and only then did she take his most prized body part in hand and for damn sure performed her own brand of magic. She stroked him, she churned him, she licked him up one side and down the other. When she finally took him in her mouth, he died a little bit and went to heaven.

Just before he came about an hour later—give or take about fifty minutes on the man-exaggeration-scale—she shimmied up his body and kissed him deeply.

He exploded his insides onto her stomach. Sheer unadulterated ecstasy.

He could hear his heavy breathing in the silence that followed. And he could swear he heard some heavy breathing from Charmaine, too.

"*Merci, chère,*" he said, kissing the top of her head.

"Ummmm," she answered sleepily. She was splayed over him with her legs bracketing his thighs.

"I made a mess on you. How 'bout we take a shower together, then it's your turn."

"Sounds tempting, but not tonight."

"Huh?" *Now this is a surprise. Since when does a woman do me, then hightail it out of Dodge without a little satisfaction of her own?* He shouldn't be upset, but he was. "Did I just get a pity fuck?"

She stiffened and raised her head to look at him. "As I

recall, there was no fucking going on. As I recall, I'm still a born-again virgin."

"Dammit, Charmaine," he said, "is that what this was all about? Have a little action without crossing the friggin' line you've drawn in the sand."

She sat up and rolled off him, grabbing for his T-shirt, which she held against her stomach. By the slump of her shoulders, he could tell he'd hurt her feelings.

I screwed up again. Damn, damn, damn! Why can't I just shut up? "I'm sorry. But one-way sex has never been my thing. I wanted you . . . still want you . . . more than I wanted to be done."

"It was a gift, Rusty. Can't you just accept that?"

Well, I sure made things better by talking some more. Why not just keep it up? Alienate her totally. So, he did. "Hell, no! I'm not a kid to be handed a lollipop and patted on the head . . . or my cock, in this case."

She gasped at his crudity. "Why? Most men would."

Because I probably still love you, that's why. "I'm not most men. You couldn't have wanted me very much if you could just stop there." He knew that wasn't true. He might have been in a testosterone haze, but he hadn't been so far gone that her arousal hadn't been evident to him. Angry, he jumped off the bed, about to stomp off to the bathroom when he stopped and pointed a finger at her. "Stay here. Don't you dare move."

She raised her chin and glared at him, but she said nothing. *Dieu,* if she only knew how she looked, sitting there all defiant and half-naked.

After he pissed and washed his hands and cock, he wet a clean washcloth and prepared to go back to Charmaine's bedroom. When he opened the bathroom door, he almost ran over Tante Lulu who stood there about chest high to him, wearing the same pink tube thingees in her red hair. *Red hair? Lordy, Lordy!*

"Tsk-tsk! You almost gave me a heart attack, boy."

"What are you doing up this time of night?"

"Hah! When you get to be my age, you have to pee every other hour. What you doin' with that washcloth?" she asked, a sly cast to her eyes.

"Uh, I spilled something," he said, and, boy, was that the understatement of the year.

"I'm sure you did." She cackled with glee.

Raoul belatedly remembered that he was naked and he draped the washcloth over his lower half, but not before the old lady commented with a lascivious glance downward, "Great wee-wee!" just before she sashayed past him into the bathroom, slamming the door behind her.

Raoul's jaw dropped. *Wee-wee?*

But then that infernal voice in his head remarked, *Not so great, actually. I've seen better.*

Go away!

You should have seen the wee-wee on Adam. God was being generous in those days. And Goliath! Saints preserve us! Oops. I forgot. I am a saint.

Raoul shook his head slowly from side to side and wondered when his life had taken a detour to Bedlam.

Chapter 11

Still in the still of the night . . .

The door opened without so much as a knock just as Charmaine had made her way to the dresser in the dark. It was Rusty, of course.

"Are you back to hurl more insults at me?"

"No."

"What are you doing here . . . again? I thought you went to sleep."

"Yeah, right. That's what I'm in the mood for. Sleep. What are you doing up?"

"Looking for a nightie to put on."

"Why would you be putting a nightie on?"

"To sleep."

"Yeah, right," he said again.

He reached down and swiped a wet cloth against her stomach. She flinched at the cold and with shock at his action. Then, before she could say, "Buzz off, bozo!" he put his hands on her waist, lifted her high off the floor, turned, and tossed her onto the bed. He followed immediately after, covering her with his naked body, then immediately adjusted himself, side to side and up and down so that his chest hairs abraded her nipples and his erection rested between her legs.

"Tante Lulu saw me naked," he told her out of the blue.

"Just now?"

"Uh-huh."

"Uh-oh!"

"She said I have a great wee-wee."

"How great was it at the time?"

"Not so great. In fact, it was more of a limp dick."

"Poor dickie!"

"He's not so poor now," he said, bucking himself against her a few times for emphasis.

"Rusty, why are you doing this?"

"What kind of wuss do you think I am? Where, in what far reaches of that scattered brain of yours, could you imagine that I would let you do me, then shove me out the door?"

"It wasn't like that."

"I don't give a flying fig how it was. All I know is the game is only half-over. Are you ready for the second half?"

"I'm still a born-again virgin. That matters to me."

"Okay. Agreed. I think this born-again virgin stuff is a load of crap, but I promise you'll be 'intact' when you get up tomorrow morning. In fact, you can keep your panties on. We're going to make love, though. That's a promise, too."

"I like being in bed with you," she said by way of concession. And that was the truth. She'd loved waking up earlier and finding him in her bed, sleeping. She loved the smell of his skin. She loved the weight of him now, pressing her to the bed. Charmaine liked men, in general, but this was different. This was Raoul . . . rather, Rusty.

"I feel like I've been wanting you forever." He nuzzled her neck as he spoke.

She tingled all over, whether from his sweet words or his nuzzling, she couldn't say. Probably both.

"Did you dunk yourself in peach water again?" He was sniffing her neck and her shoulders and hair.

"Peach bubble bath."

"I love peaches." He licked her neck to show just how much.

"I know." And she felt his lick all the way to her toes.

Arching himself up on braced arms so that he could look at her directly, he said, "Honey, I want to make this last so long and go so slow that you will be begging me to take you."

"But you won't."

"I won't."

"Go to it then, cowboy."

He smiled down at her then—such a relaxed, take-no-prisoners smile that she couldn't help but think that this was the Rusty she had known before—not the frowning, always disapproving Rusty of the past week.

He shimmied himself a bit down her body so that his face was directly over her breasts. "Do you have any idea how much I wanted to touch these before? What torture it was not to?"

No words were necessary from her because he had already cupped her breasts from underneath, raising them higher so that the nipples just peeked over the top—nipples he proceeded to strum with his thumbs.

"Aaaahhhh!" she squealed and reflexively arched herself upward, as if trying to avoid the delicious contact. "Torture goes both ways," she gasped out.

"Is that torture?" he asked as he continued to play with her.

"Sweet torture," she admitted.

He smiled with pure male satisfaction. He kneaded her breasts with his whole hands. He rubbed the nipples with his closed fingers. He pulled and tugged and finallyfinallyfinally he put his mouth to one of them, sucking rhythmically.

Charmaine, to her mortification, began to come in a matching rhythm of erotic waves, starting in her womb and rippling outward. Some men bemoaned their hairtrigger ejaculations. Charmaine bemoaned her hairtrigger orgasms . . . at least where Rusty was concerned.

Rusty must have sensed what was happening with her because even as he began to give equal suckling attention to the other breast, he lowered his arms and spread her thighs wider, tugging her knees up and her heels back to meet her buttocks. All of her female parts were exposed then, albeit under cover of her panties, as she undulated wildly against his belly. Her climax came quick and ended quickly, but it satisfied her deeply, turning every bone and sinew in her body to mush. Her eyes fluttered shut, seeking sleep.

"That was Number One, babe. Are you ready for Number Two?" Rusty's voice was thick and raw as he asked his question.

Her eyes shot open.

He knelt between her legs now. Her feet were on the mattress, her knees still spread wide. He used a forefinger to flutter the little ring in her belly button, but that was not where he was looking. Nope, it was her panties that held his attention, or one particular, very wet portion of her panties.

Holding her eyes, he ran the back of his fingertips from her navel to her belly, over her crotch, all the way down.

She whimpered.

He licked his lips.

"Where's your tattoo, Charmaine?"

"Huh?" The line he'd just drawn on her lower half was sizzling and yearning for a repeat, and he got a sudden interest in tattoos. "Oh, that tattoo. You can't see it."

"Why? Where is it?"

She used a forefinger to tap a spot at the very lowest part of her belly, about an inch away from the crease with her thigh.

His eyes went wide.

"But you can't see it now, even if I took off my panties."

"Why?"

"I would need to have a Brazilian bikini wax for you to see it."

"What the hell's a Brazil wax?"

She used a forefinger again to draw him a picture . . . on her underpants.

His eyes went even wider.

"Let's go do it."

"Do what?"

"Give you a Brazil wax."

She laughed. "Get a life, buddy. I wouldn't let you near me *there* with hot wax . . . or a razor. Not with those shaky hands."

He glanced quickly to his hands, which weren't shaky at all. But they probably would be if she were dumb enough to give in. Which she wasn't.

"Maybe another time," he said way too easily. "I'm really hungry now."

Disappointment riddled through her, which was silly. He'd just given her a great orgasm. Since when did she get so greedy? "I think there's leftover beans and rice in the fridge."

"Not for food, silly." He tapped her playfully a little north and left of her tattoo, which caused her to about have another orgasm.

"These aren't edible underpants," she cautioned in an embarrassing squeak.

"We'll see about that." If she wasn't turned on enough by that remark, he added another equally titillating one, "I think my tongue has a hard-on."

And Charmaine, not to be outdone in the outrageous department, said, "I think I know the very thing to do with a tongue hard-on."

A short time later, Rusty was chirping, "Number Two!" and Charmaine was gasping for breath. "Very good, Rusty! But, now, I think I've had enough for one night."

He winked down at her. "Oh, *chère,* I've only just begun.

And Charmaine, after hearing Rusty announce gleefully two hours later, "Number Four!", was beginning to think that the Cajuns took that old phrase of theirs way too literally, *"Laissez les bons temps rouler."* She had had the good times literally rolled out of her. Cajun style, guar-an-teed!

But she was still a born-again virgin. Talk about!

I've got good news and I've got bad news . . .

Raoul was the first one to arrive at the breakfast table the next morning. Life had dealt him some bad breaks yesterday, but the night had ended well. Correction. The night had ended with a blast, and he was feeling goooood.

He smelled the coffee before he entered the kitchen and saw a midget with red corkscrews all over its head stirring a pot on the stove. On her body the midget-aka-Tante Lulu was wearing a black cat suit. And what a sight that was with her nonexistent butt and boobs!

"'Morning," he said cheerily as he poured himself a cup of thick black coffee.

"Good mornin', sunshine," she replied, turning toward him. She wore red lipstick today, which, backdropped by her white skin, resembled blood. So, of course, smart fellow that he was, he said, "You lookin' mighty fine today, Miz Rivard."

"Hush yo' mouth, boy." She preened with pleasure at his compliment. "You wants some *couche-couche* for a start, yes?"

He nodded and she ladled out some of the fried cornmeal topped with a dollop of butter and sweet cane syrup. He took it to the table, wondering, *Why does she go in for these outlandish outfits?* But he immediately chastised himself. *What do I care? She's a nice old lady who's being nice to me, and her adopted niece was especially nice to me last night, and . . .*

"Glad to see yer smilin' today, sonny boy," Tante Lulu said, sitting down at the table next to him with her own cup of *cafe au lait*. "Me, I was wonderin' . . . what's yer opinion 'bout a Xmas weddin'?"

"For who?"

"You."

He choked on his coffee as it went down the wrong pipe. "I'm already married."

She waved a hand airily as if that didn't matter a bit. "Thass what Charmaine said."

"You talked about this with Charmaine?"

"I sure-God did. I tol' her and I'm tellin' you . . . you gots to renew yer vows if this marriage gots a chance."

"Where did this idea come from? Is it because I was with Charmaine last night?"

Her entire face lit up with pleasure, which was a sight to see with the red curls bobbing, her white vampirelike skin, and the crimson lips. "You was with Charmaine las' night? Glory be! I'm gonna light a candle next time I go to church to thank St. Jude."

"I wasn't with her like that." *Not exactly.*

"Does she still have her doo-hickey?" She narrowed her eyes at him suspiciously.

How do I answer that question? No, she doesn't have her original doo-hickey. Yes, she has her born-again doo-hickey.

"It doan make no nevermind. The point is, iffen you love her, you will want to do this."

What about her loving me? Don't you think that would be a major consideration?

"Besides, I ain't never had a Christmas weddin' in our fam'ly, and I already gots ideas fer decoratin' yer living room fer the reception. Unless you wants to do it all at Our Lady of the Bayou Church, but thass a ways from here."

"Hold your horses, lady. There is not going to be a wedding that I know of, and certainly not one so soon as Christmas, and I really don't want you planning anything on your own, and—"

As if he hadn't said a word, she continued, "Father Girard, the new priest at Our Lady of the Bayou, is an old boyfriend of Charmaine's. Betcha he'd love to be the minister."

Isn't everyone an old boyfriend of Charmaine's? And I just bet he'd love to minister to her. And who the hell cares? I am not going to let anyone rain on my parade today.

Which Charmaine, of course, proceeded to do by strolling into the kitchen wearing white athletic shoes, latex running pants that showed every inch of her body from waist to ankles, including the goose bumps on her ass, and a long-sleeved, white, form-hugging shirt proclaiming DON'T TANGLE WITH ME. Her hair was big and wild. Her face was fully made-up, complete with red lipstick, just like Tante Lulu, except totally different.

She looks wonderful. Good enough to eat. Oops, I already did that. All this he thought with a smile on his face. At first.

It wasn't her appearance that rained on his parade. Hey, if he had his way, he'd like nothing better than to jog on back to her bedroom with her and show her just what kind of exercise he could give those running pants. No, it was what she eventually said that caused a dark cloud to come over him.

"Hey, Rusty," she drawled out, slow and sexy, looking back at him over her shoulder as she poured herself a cup of coffee. As only a born-to-tease seductress could do, Charmaine let him fill his eyes with her backside, which filled the stretch pants so nicely. In fact, she dropped a spoon—deliberately, he was sure—and took a nice long time bending over to pick it up.

Tante Lulu giggled, watching the direction of his stare. *Great! Caught in mid-ogle.*

"Are you finished with breakfast?" Charmaine asked once she was standing again.

Huh? Hell, no! I barely started. But he nodded. *Maybe she's looking for some exercise, too.*

"Can you bring your coffee into the office? I have some important things I need to discuss with you. *Very* important. I have good news and I have bad news." She looked so serious that he felt his stomach drop. His parade suddenly slowed down. Could he take any more bad news on top of yesterday's events?

They both walked into the small office, which was surprisingly tidy. Charmaine must have done a lot of work here the past two days. Closing the door behind him, he set his coffee cup on the desk, sat down in the swivel chair, then pulled Charmaine onto his lap. "If I kiss you, will I have red lipstick all over me?"

She looped her arms around his neck and smiled saucily. "Would it make any difference?"

"Hell, no!" he said even as he was lowering his head.

"It's kiss-proof," she said against his mouth.

"Wanna bet?" he countered, already nibbling at the edges of her bottom lip. "You taste so freakin' good."

"It's just coffee," she murmured.

"Uh-uh! It's you."

Charmaine was the one to break the kiss first. She pulled away—and hot damn, she was right; her lips were still hot-as-sin red—and told him, "There really is some serious business I need to discuss with you."

"More serious than sex in a swivel chair."

"I already told you I can't have sex with you."

The born-again virgin crap again! "It depends on your definition of sex." *If oral sex isn't real sex in Clintonese, then swivel sex sure isn't real sex in my language.*

Get real, the voice in his head said.

"Tsk-tsk-tsk!" Shoving away, Charmaine stood about two feet away from him.

"Okay, I'll behave. What's the all-important business we have to discuss."

"First, look at this file."

Briefly skimming through the contents of a bulging manila folder, he saw numerous letters and jotted Post-it notes regarding phone calls from various Louisiana oil companies, including Valcour LeDeux's own Cypress Oil. They dated back at least ten years but were heaviest the last year of his father's life. All of them indicated a desire to purchase mineral rights or outright land from Charles Lanier.

"This is nothing new, Charmaine. I've been aware of their interest for a long time. *Dieu*, just since you've been here, there's been phone calls and letters, directed at me this time. Apparently, they aren't aware yet that you own half the ranch since the probate papers haven't been filed."

"Yes, but don't you see? There's a pattern here. Increasing pressure on your father to sell. Getting you out of the way. Your father conveniently dying. It's worth investigating, don't you think?"

"I suppose so. Actually, I've discussed this to some extent with Zerby . . . my suspicions about the oil pressures. But you're right, sweetheart, he needs to see the file, as well." He smiled at her. "Now, can we have sex?"

"No, that was the least of the business I have to discuss

with you." She handed him a boot box, her eyes misting with tears, which caused him to go on immediate alert. "Maybe now you'll be a little less hard on your dad for all his years of neglect."

Hesitantly, he took off the lid. Inside were dozens of letters. Maybe even a hundred of them. All still sealed. All with a return address for Charles Lanier, Triple L Ranch. All addressed to him. All of them stamped MAIL REFUSED, except for the most recent ones sent to the state pen, which were marked UNDELIVERABLE, whatever that meant. Some of the letters were more than twenty-five years old and some as recent as a year ago, according to the post office marks.

His heart suddenly started racing, and, yeah, his eyes were burning with unshed tears, too. It took all his self-control to get his emotions banked. Later, he would read the letters, every single one of them, and perhaps finally get some clue to his dad's behavior.

But there were other things to consider regarding these undelivered letters. "That sorry bitch!" he said, referring to his mother, and "Those bastards!" referring to whatever miscreant at the prison had been paid off by the oil scumbags to deny him mail.

"There's more, baby," she said. "I've given you the bad news. Well, good and bad. Now, here's the really good news." She laid a yellow manila envelope in his lap.

He arched his eyebrows at her in question.

"Go on. You'll be happy."

He doubted that. Still, he opened the envelope and out spilled a pigload of savings bonds.

"There's fifty thousand dollars there." Charmaine was practically jumping up and down with glee.

Hell, he felt like jumping up and down with glee. "What does it mean?"

"It means yesterday wasn't such a bad day after all."

He looked at her and said huskily, "I already knew that last night."

"Oh, you!" she said, blushing prettily.

Charmaine blushing? Man, I'd like to see that more often.

She plopped herself back on his lap, and he swiveled them around a few times.

"This is just the jump start I need to get this ranch back on its feet," he said.

"Uh, hold the train, cowboy," Charmaine said, putting a foot down to the floor to stop the swiveling. "Half of that bounty is mine. So I have a say in how it would be used."

He had to admit it, he'd forgotten. But that didn't matter. "It's to your advantage, too, to have the ranch prosper. Oh, I see. You want your half to get the Mafia off your back."

"Not necessarily." She drew each of the words out slowly, while she batted her eyelashes at him.

Raoul knew from past experience to be wary when Charmaine batted her eyelashes.

She jumped off his lap, pulled over a straight-backed, wooden chair, and sat down facing him, knee to knee. "I have some ideas about how we can turn the ranch around."

Whoa! There are a whole lot of red flags in that one little sentence. Like "ideas", like "we" and like "turn the ranch around." But he wasn't all that concerned. This was Charmaine. She knew zippo about running a ranch. Hell, she barely knew a cow from a bull.

"Okay, I'm all ears, darlin'," he said.

"You know that the price of cattle is volatile. There are very few ranchers anymore who make a profit from beef alone. So, I was thinking . . ." She paused in a ta-da fashion. "How about ostriches?"

"Huh?" He sat up straighter. She couldn't possibly be suggesting . . . "What about ostriches?"

"Let's buy a bunch and raise them here. Oh, don't look at me like that, Rusty. I did some research yesterday on the Internet, and the city restaurants are buying up specialty meats like that for huge prices . . . maybe ten times the price per pound of beef."

"Have you lost your friggin' mind?" he practically shouted. "This is a cattle ranch. You don't run cattle and ostriches together."

"We could run a fence across the middle of your . . . uh, spread . . . is that what you call it?"

"A fence across the middle of my *spread*? I repeat, have you lost your friggin' mind?"

"You won't even think about it?"

He could see the hurt on her face, but dammit, why was she interfering in his business? Oh, he knew she owned half, but she should let him run the place. "No, I won't even think about it."

"Not even if it could save the ranch?"

"Charmaine," he said with as much patience as he could garner, "if I were going to sell out what this ranch has always represented, I could just give it lock, stock, and barrel to the oil companies. Let them rip it all up, and I could retire in style. Is that what you want me to do?"

She lifted her chin haughtily, and, for sure, she was offended now. "You know how I feel about my father and what he did to the bayou by drilling on our lands. All my life I've fought the stigma of what he did. My brothers feel the same way. How could you even suggest that I would want such a thing?"

"I'm sorry. I knew that. You just surprised me with that ostrich nonsense."

She nodded her acceptance of his apology, though he could tell she didn't like the "nonsense" reference.

"Actually, I was pretty sure you would say no to the ostriches, and it was my second-best idea, anyway. My first idea is really good. Wanna hear?"

What could he say? "Sure."

"A dude ranch," she said bluntly.

He closed his eyes and counted to ten.

"To be more specific, a beauty spa dude ranch."

He decided to count to twenty.

"Oh, Rusty, have an open mind about this. We could hire some real hunky cowboys . . . you know, cover model types, but they would have to be ranch hands, too. Well, they would have to at least be able to ride a horse."

"*Hunky* cowboys?" he sputtered.

"Women would flock here in droves."

"Yep, I really want a flock of females running amongst the cattle. They'd spook 'em for sure."

"They could ride horses. Once they've taken riding lessons, of course."

"*Who* would be giving riding lessons?"

"And we could turn that big shed into a spa, complete with whirlpools and saunas and massage tables. Not to mention hairstyling stations."

"And where would we be parking the tractors and hay wagons, once you take over the shed?"

She waved a hand dismissively as if that were a minor point. "Rachel could come up and design the whole thing, Feng Shui style. Wouldn't that be great?"

She wants to Feng Shui a shed. Have I died and gone to Bayou Bedlam? What he said was, "Just great!"

Charmaine missed the sarcasm, though, because she barreled ahead, "I researched dude ranches on the Internet, too. Guess what some of these places charge per person for one week? Five thousand dollars. And I figure we could handle a dozen guests at one time, especially if we put an addition on the bunkhouse."

Five thousand dollars! That got his attention. "You've got to be kidding."

"Really. And this fifty thousand dollars could be the seed money we need for starting such a project." She pointed to the pile of bonds on the desk.

"Charmaine," he started to say, prepared to let her down easy.

"Don't decide now. Think about it."

He took a deep breath and exhaled loudly. He couldn't let her get her hopes up. "It's not going to happen, Charmaine."

"It's a good idea," she argued.

"It's a dumb idea."

Her nostrils flared and she practically breathed fire. "Dumb? Why? Because it came from me?"

"Yeah. Maybe. You don't know anything about running a ranch, whether it's cattle or sheep or freakin' dude cowgirls." He tried to calm himself down, to refrain from saying the things he would have said to a man standing before him.

"Oh, yeah! Well, I know a hell of a lot more than you do about running a business. And don't you dare bring up the loan shark. That was a blip on my success radar. I have built and expanded two businesses from scratch. And they're successful, you thickheaded idiot."

"They're beauty parlors, Charmaine. There's a big difference between teasing hair and castrating a cow."

He stood.

She stood, too.

Nose to nose now, she seethed at him. "They are both businesses. And if there's one thing I know in this world, it's how to run a business."

He pulled at his own hair and yelled, "They're not the same!"

"You know what? You don't respect my talents at all, do you? You think a woman like me couldn't have a bleepin' intelligent idea in her empty head if she tried. You think I was a bimbo, am a bimbo, and will always be a bimbo."

"I never said that."

"You didn't have to," she said on a sob. Then, pivoting on her heels, she stormed out of the office. They probably heard the door slam all the way to Lafayette.

Raoul sank down to the chair with a long sigh. *I came in here thinking I might get lucky and nab a little swivel chair sex. What just happened?*

You-know-who had the answer, of course. *You ever seen that movie* Dumb and Dumber? *Yoo-hoo, Academy Awards! I have a nomination for Dumbest.*

Chapter 12

And that's no bull . . .

Midmorning, they delivered the seven prime bulls he'd bought on credit yesterday. The only difference was that yesterday he hadn't been sure how he would pay for the necessary additions to his herd; today he knew he had a little leeway in his financial morass.

Jimmy was off working on his correspondence school exams. It took every bit of strength and a lot of cursing for him, Clarence, Linc, the delivery driver, and his helper to get the bulls out of the truck and into the pens set aside for them. Bulls were a stubborn breed, by nature. The only thing more stubborn in his opinion was Charmaine in a snit, which she was now as she strolled by on the way to the henhouse with Tante Lulu, both of them carrying egg baskets.

"Hubba hubba!" the driver said.

"Sonofagun!" the other guy said.

He wasn't sure if they were exclaiming over Tante Lulu in her cat suit with her bright red curls, or Charmaine still wearing her so-tight-I-can't-breathe stretch pants and the DON'T TANGLE WITH ME shirt. They were both equally outrageous and loving every bit of it. There was a time when Raoul would have been outraged over some guy drooling over Charmaine. Not anymore. He supposed he had mellowed over the years.

Or maybe I just don't care.

Nah! I care.

He assumed he wasn't getting a repeat of last night's action anytime soon, though.

Well, so be it. If it took a dude ranch to get back in Charmaine's good graces, he was S.O.L.

They finally got the seven bulls settled in their new surrounding, separated from the females of the species for now. No sense starting a stampede on the first day. Especially that one bull. With the size of his . . . uh, wee-wee, girl cows were going to take one gander, yell, "How's it hanging, big boy?" and hot foot it off to Texas.

He was leaning against the fence rail smiling at his own joke when Charmaine and Tante Lulu passed by on their return trip, both baskets half-full of eggs. He decided to be a nice guy and ignore Charmaine's snotty attitude. "Hey, Charmaine. Wanna name one of the bulls for me?"

She gave him a haughty once over without stopping and said, "Up yours."

He laughed. "Uh, I don't think that's a good bull's name."

"Bullshit!"

"Lots better."

Linc and Clarence whooped it up with laughter on either side of him. Tante Lulu chirped in with, "Definitely lost his mojo! Name my bull! Is that the best you can do? Talk about!"

Once Charmaine and Tante Lulu were back in the house, he turned to Clarence and said, "She wants to turn the Triple L into a dude ranch."

Clarence's jaw dropped open, and he almost lost the wad in his cheek.

"She wants me to hire hunky cowboys to take the female guests out riding and roping cattle and stuff."

"I'm kind of hunky," Linc said. The amazing thing was, he wasn't even smiling as he said it. When Raoul and Clarence just gawked at him, Linc added defensively, "Some women have called me a hunk."

"How long ago was that?" Raoul asked with a laugh.

"Not that long ago," Linc proclaimed.

"Well, I doan think I've ever been hunky," Clarence said dolefully. "Doan get me wrong. I got plenty of action in the bedsheets in my day, unlike some folks I know." He looked pointedly at Raoul. "But I doan recall any wimmen callin' me a hunk. Does that mean I'm gonna get fired?"

"No one's getting fired. I just thought you'd like to know why Charmaine's having a hissy fit. We better get back to work now."

As they walked away, Linc asked Clarence, "How does my butt look from back there? I did lots of squats when I was in prison. That helps a lot."

"I doan give a squat how many squats you did," Clarence said. "You are not a hunk."

"I don't know about that," Linc persisted. "Having a good butt is the first requirement for a hunk. I think."

"Hah! If thass the case, I might as well give up now. I lost my butt about 1982. Jist started saggin' one day, and before I knew it, kaplooey! It was gone."

"You can buy underwear with padding in the ass area," Linc told Clarence.

"Really?" Unbelievably, Clarence appeared interested. *Maybe men are really as dumb as women claim we are.* "I only said that Charmaine suggested a dude ranch," Raoul tried to explain, "not that it would ever happen."

But nobody listened to him. Clarence and Linc had moved on to discussing the pros and cons of putting a sock in the crotch of their jockey shorts. A bulge was apparently a definite hunk requirement.

Aaarrgh! He and St. Jude both thought that at the same time. Scary, huh?

And then the big boys arrived . . .

Charmaine was still bristling over Rusty's cavalier disregard of her dude ranch proposal by early that afternoon.

She and Tante Lulu were making a grocery list for the Thanksgiving feast to be held two days hence. Truth to tell, Charmaine wasn't feeling very thankful. She still owed a ton of money to the loan shark. Her relationship with Rusty was hanging in limbo, or worse. Tante Lulu was making her nervous about all the food she was planning to cook, and she wouldn't shut up about a Christmas wedding.

"I still think we should shoot one of them cows and dig a pit in the backyard down by the bayou. If Rusty won' do it, I will." Tante Lulu just never gave up. She'd been harping on the beef barbecue idea since yesterday. "Let that big ol' side of beef cook over the hot coals fer two days. Lot less trouble than stuffing a couple of turkeys. Although we could do the birds Cajun style. Inject 'em with marinade and deep fry 'em in hot oil. Yum! Whaddya think, sweetie?"

I think I'm getting the mother of all headaches . . . or the mother of all P.M.S. . . . or both. "Whatever you decide is okay with me . . . except for shooting a cow. I won't have any part of that."

"Didja hear that?" Tante Lulu asked. "Sounds like a car out front."

Since Rusty and the guys had ridden horses out to the north pasture to introduce the seven new bulls to the herd, it couldn't be them. She and Tante Lulu made their way through the living room to the front porch.

"Son of a bitch!" the old lady swore, which was really out of character for her, except when you considered who she was calling a son of a bitch.

Therefore, Charmaine concurred, "Son of a bitch!"

It was her father, Valcour LeDeux, getting out of a black limo, along with three other men, all of them dressed in tailored suits that combined probably could have paid off her loan shark.

"What are you doing here?" Charmaine demanded of her father.

"What are *you* doing here?" her father demanded back.

"You're not welcome here. Go the hell away." She sniffed the air dramatically. "Have you been drinking? At 11 A.M.?"

He was still a good-looking man, despite his years, but his cheeks and nose were indeed flushed. Perhaps that was a permanent state for His Alcoholic Highness.

"We're here to see Lanier about some ranch business," he said.

"Is that a fact? Well, Daddy Dearest, Rusty's not here; so you can discuss your ranch business with me," Charmaine said.

"Funny bizness is what it is if it comes from you, Valcour, you slimy toad, you." Tante Lulu stepped up to stand beside Charmaine, regarding Valcour like one of the cow pies that littered the Triple L Ranch pastures.

"You!" Valcour spit out, regarding Tante Lulu with equal venom.

"Any business you have to discuss with Rusty can be said to me," Charmaine said. "He won't be back till late this afternoon, and you will for damn sure be gone by then."

"Val, let me handle this," said one impeccably groomed gentleman as he stepped to the forefront. He had thick white hair styled, no doubt, by one of the New Orleans celebrity hairdressers at five hundred dollars a pop. "I assume this lovely lady is your daughter and the other lovely lady is Miz Rivard of Bayou Black. I've heard so much about both of you." Charmaine recognized the jerk from newspaper photos as one of the top execs at Cypress Oil.

Tante Lulu snorted her disgust and stomped back into the house, leaving Charmaine alone on the porch. That was okay. Charmaine was a big girl. Her father couldn't hurt her anymore.

"Ladies, let me introduce myself. I'm Winston Oliver, CEO of Cypress Oil, and these are my associates Pierre Pitot and Max Elliott from our Dallas office."

Big whoop! "I don't care who you are. You are not welcome here."

"Charmaine, behave yourself, and go call Lanier," Valcour said. "He's been ignorin' our letters and phone calls. It's time for a one-on-one with that ex-con ex-husband of yours."

"Daddy, *you* behave yourself. Rusty is a better man than you on his worst day. And, no, I'm not going to call him back to the house. Anything you have to say about the ranch can be said to me."

"And why is that, girlie? You spreadin' yer legs fer convicts now, too? Ha, ha, ha." He looked to his cronies who had the grace to appear embarrassed by a man speaking thus to his daughter. Little did they know!

"If I was sharing a bed with Rusty, and I'm not saying we are, it might be because we're still married. Surprise, surprise! Furthermore, I own half the ranch." That was way more information than she should have revealed, but her father had always had a talent for pushing her buttons.

"What?" her father practically squealed. The three other men appeared stunned, then pleased by the news. They probably figured that family ties would work to their advantage.

"If you own half of this ranch, then you damn well better sell us the mineral rights," her father concluded, dumb ass that he was.

"And why would that be?"

"Because you owe me, dammit. So stop jerkin' us around." He turned to one of the gentlemen who stood in the background, which might very well be a bodyguard and not an executive, and told him, "Get the papers out of the limo so my daughter can sign them."

"You are unbelievable. A real piece of work." She waved to the man who had just emerged from the limo with a folder in hand. "Hey, you. You just hand those little ol' papers to my father so he can shove them where the sun don't shine."

"You allus did have a gutter mouth," her father remarked with disgust. Amazing how a low-life like him could be disgusted by anything.

"Can we come inside and discuss this?" Mr. Oliver inquired in a patently sly manner.

"No, you cannot come inside. My aunt and I are busy. We were just about to go off to shoot a steer for Thanksgiving dinner." She spun on her heels, about to walk back into the house, pleased with her outrageous pronouncement.

Well, not so outrageous when she saw Tante Lulu standing in the open doorway with a rifle aimed at the group in the front yard. The rifle was almost as big as she was.

"Does she know how to use that thing?" Valcour asked Charmaine.

Tante Lulu probably couldn't hit a bull in the ass with a bass fiddle. "A crack shot," Charmaine said.

All four men turned green.

Especially when Tante Lulu let loose with one shot, which put out the headlight on the limo.

"Jesus H. Christ, are you nuts, Louise?" Valcour exclaimed.

"Let's get out of here," Mr. Oliver said.

All four of them scurried back into the limo and raised dust as their squealing tires backed up, then flew down the road. Her father leaned out of the window at the last minute and yelled, "This isn't over yet, you bitch."

"Which one of us was he calling a bitch?" Charmaine asked.

Tante Lulu shrugged, a huge grin on her face.

"Were you aiming for the headlight?"

"Naw. I was aimin' for Valcour's too-too."

At first, Charmaine's jaw just dropped, but then she grinned, too. She and Charmaine gave each other high fives, followed by little Snoopy dances of victory. After that, buoyed by their brave actions, they went back into the house to finish their grocery lists.

All in a day's work.

More almost-sex . . .

"You did what?" Raoul raged at the two dingbats when he got back to the house by midafternoon.

"I took a shot at Valcour's too-too and hit his head-light, instead," Tante Lulu said, not one bit repentant. She was sitting at the kitchen table making a grocery list that looked about two feet long.

"You hit his *what*? Headlight? What body part in your convoluted language is a headlight? Did you hit his belly button or one of his nipples? *Dieu*, Valcour would like nothing better than to sue the skivvies off you, old lady."

"Who you callin' an ol' lady?" the old lady inquired.

"You are such a dolt." Charmaine laughed at him while making that pronouncement. She was polishing some silverware for the upcoming friggin' feast. He didn't even know silverware that needed polishing existed at the ranch. "Tante Lulu knocked out one of the headlights on the Cypress Oil limo."

Oh. "How was I supposed to know that?" he stormed, his face heating up with embarrassment. "The two of you are proud of your actions. Like a Cajun version of Lucy and Ethel, you are. Did it ever occur to you that an ex-con can't afford to have the police called to his home? Did you think about what effect a weapon on my property might have on my parole?" He glared first at Charmaine, then at Tante Lulu, the prime perp in this case.

Charmaine at least had the grace to appear surprised, then guilty about not having considered the consequences to him.

Unlike the redheaded Cajun Rambo midget who glared right back at him. "Doan you be lookin' at me like you jist ate a green persimmon," Tante Lulu chastised him. "Those men were actin' threatenin'-like, and I know better than most that Valcour doan hesitate to raise his hand to his daughter . . . or his fist. Wouldja have felt better iffen you came back to see Charmaine's blood on the porch?"

Fists? Blood? Raoul's eyes shot to Charmaine, whose chin was raised haughtily, daring him to say anything more. *Oh, Charmaine.*

"Don't you dare be pitying me," she snapped.

"Why? You might end up with a little pity action, if you know what I mean." If he didn't tease, he might just cry . . . on her behalf. *Fists? Her father had used his fists on her?*

"I know what you mean, and forget about it. Us no-brain bimbos, who wouldn't know a spreadsheet from a bed sheet, aren't into *that*."

Back to the dude ranch business again. As if! But, man, she's like a puppy tugging on a guy's pant leg. Tug, tug, tug.

"Charmaine and me gots to go shopping tomorrow fer the Thanksgivin' feast," Tante Lulu said. "You gonna be our bodyguard, or do we gots to ask Clarence?"

"Give your list to Clarence. He and Jimmy can go for you in the morning after their chores."

She looked as if she might protest, but then she shrugged and said, "Mebbe thass best. We have lots of things to do here today, me and Charmaine." She paused dramatically and added, "Like shoot and dress a steer. And dig a barbecue pit."

"There will be no shooting of animals on this ranch,"

he said as firmly as he could, then turned and made his way toward his bedroom. He planned to spend the next two hours there delving into his past, a task he did not relish. The reading of his father's letters.

He read only the first few from twenty-five years ago before stopping to stare off into space. They were so poignant with a father's obvious love for a son he'd only discovered he'd had and the agony of separation. That was when something disturbing happened.

A gunshot. And it came from behind the house.

His first thought was, *If they shot a steer, I'm going to shoot them.*

His second thought was, *Oh, no! Maybe Valcour and his cronies came back. Or the Dixie Mafia discovered Charmaine's whereabouts and they shot out her kneecaps . . . or worse.*

Like lightning he rushed through the house and out the back door, grabbing a rifle along the way. He hit the back porch running, then skidded to a stop. His heart was racing so fast he thought he might have a heart attack.

Tante Lulu was standing in the backyard near the bottom of the steps, flanking one of two improvised tables—discarded wood doors over sawhorses. She and Charmaine must have dragged them from the barn to use for the big hoopla feast, which was apparently going to be outdoors. Tante Lulu just grinned at him. "Ain't Charmaine sumpin'?"

"Oh, yeah, she's something," he said grimly as he walked over to Wild Bill Charmaine. She was holding a smoking pistol in one hand as she regarded the humongous snake at her feet—a water moccasin of about six feet, not counting its head, which Charmaine had blown off. The reptile must have come up out of the bayou, though it was the first poisonous snake he'd seen this close to the house.

I can't believe this. I'm seeing it, but I still don't believe it. "Have you lost your freakin' mind, Charmaine? Why didn't you call me when you saw the snake?"

"Why?" She blinked at him with genuine puzzlement. "Do you think I need a big ol' man to take care of little ol' me? Do you think I can't handle the job myself?" She looked pointedly at her weapon and the dead snake.

I feel like taking her by the neck and shaking some sense into her. Or taking her by the neck and kissing her to make sure she's still alive. But first, I've got to get my heart rate down below supersonic. "Where'd you get the gun?"

"I always carry a pistol in my purse."

Just great! "Why? So, you can shoot one of the Sopranos when they show up?"

"Hell, no. Although it's a thought. Oh, stop glowering at me. I'm a single female living alone on a remote bayou. My half brothers taught me how to protect myself when I was a teenager."

But not from a father's fists. "Well, you almost gave me a heart attack," he grumbled.

"Didja think we shot a cow?" Tante Lulu cackled, having come up beside him.

Well, come to mention it . . . "No, I didn't think you shot a cow," he lied.

"Whooee, thass a big one." Tante Lulu stared with gruesome fascination at the snake, which was still twitching in its headless death throes. She had a broom in one hand and a plastic trash bag in the other. Within minutes, the snake was off to the trash barrel, and he and Charmaine were left alone.

"You scared me, sweetheart. That's why I yelled at you. I thought you might have been hurt," he said softly, stepping toward her.

"Was that an apology?" She put a hand on one hitched hip. "Well, no need to worry about me. Us brain-dead bimbos get along just fine." She unhitched her hip and took a step backward when she belatedly noticed his advance.

Not afraid of a venomous reptile, but she's afraid of me.

He took two steps forward then, staring at her lips, which were red and parted.

She backed up three steps and hit the trunk of an ancient live oak tree dripping Spanish moss.

"Be more careful in the future, honey. No more shooting. I wouldn't want anything to happen to you." He leaned down slightly and closed his eyes briefly as he inhaled the floral scent of her hair.

"Why? Don't act as if you care. Do you care?" She sounded breathy and excited.

Please, God, let her be excited.

Uh, I don't think that's the kind of thing you should ask God for, St. Jude said.

"Do I care? *Mais oui, chère.*" He burrowed his fingers in her hair to hold her face in place, then rubbed his lips back and forth across hers. He moaned his appreciation of the sheer, exquisite pleasure. Then, oh God above, then he kissed her with all the yearning that seemed to overflow in him all the time. And, oh God above, she kissed him back with equal yearning. When he drew back, he gasped out, "Why is it . . . why is it that every time I kiss you, it feels like coming home?"

"Don't try to sweet-talk me," she said and grabbed his

head, pulling him back for another kiss . . . a kiss that about sucked all the oxygen out of his lungs and every blood vessel in his overheated body.

"Nobody in the world kisses like you, darlin'. Nobody. Let's go to my bedroom. Let's forget the whole friggin' born-again crap. Let's make love till the cows come home, and the chickens and the hogs and the goats and the birds. Let's forget the past and make some new memories. I . . . need . . . you . . . so . . . much." With each choked-out word, Raoul showered her face and neck with kisses. His hands roamed over her body wildly.

When she whimpered and arched her neck for more kisses, he put his hands on her butt and lifted her so that her legs wrapped around his hips and her cleft rode his erection.

"I am so tempted, but I think—"

"Don't think."

"But—"

"No buts."

"Forever . . . I want forever this time."

"I swear to God, Charmaine, this feels like forever."

She laughed in a suffocated manner. "You just want to get laid."

"Yeah. Forever."

She laughed again. "You don't take me seriously. You think I'm just a brainless bimbo."

Hell and damnation! She is going to talk this thing to death. Only she could talk down a hard-on. "I've developed a fondness for bimbos. And I don't know how much more serious I can get at the moment." He ground his hips against her in emphasis.

"Yeah, but will you respect me in the morning . . . as a business partner?" Charmaine wiggled her hips slightly to keep herself from slipping. That slight abrasion of her latex crotch against his denim one felt like an electric shock of the best possible kind. It would take no effort on his part at all to eat the spandex out of the joining of her thighs if it would mean that he could plunge himself into her hot sheath.

But no, sanity was returning. Dammit! He pulled back slightly and rested his forehead against hers, panting for breath. When he was able to speak, he said, "So you want forever *and* a dude ranch. A little greedy, don't you think?"

She put a hand to his cheek gently. "I'm worth it, Rusty."

"I know that way too well." Even so, he released his hands from her butt and let her slide to the ground with a painfully pleasurable drive-by over his erection. Setting her at arms length away from him, he added, "But I don't much relish trading sex for favors."

"Don't insult me by implying that I would prostitute myself that way. Bimbo or not, if I made love with you, it would be because I wanted to. Period."

"Enough with the bimbo rant! I used that word to you once ten years ago. Are you going to punish me for that for the rest of my life?"

She ignored his words and continued her explanation. "Try to understand this, Rusty, because it's important. You may call it born-again crap, but what it means to me is that next time I get involved with a man it's going to be more than a roll in the hay, married or not. And that man has got to value me for being more than a good lay. I am smart, and I am sexy. Both of those attributes are equal."

"Did I just get a lecture here?" he asked, smiling.

"Uh-huh. Is it sinking in yet?"

"It's starting to. But you know, honey, that respect thing goes both ways. I'm a trained veterinarian, and I know a hell of a lot more about ranching than you do. It's about time you started giving me credit, too. And, furthermore, you walked out on me ten years ago. You were the one who threw in the towel. Talk about unresolved issues!"

She appeared about to argue, then changed her mind. Instead, she nodded.

He reached out a hand and ran the pad of his thumb over her kiss-swollen lips.

She sighed.

"What if I said that I think . . . that I think . . ."

"Spit it out, cowboy." She gazed at him with such soulful intensity that his heart about flipped over.

". . . that I think I might still love you. Would that melt any ice?" He'd thought this when they'd engaged in almost-sex the night before, but he hadn't planned to say it out loud. It just slipped out.

"Oh, baby." She was the one who ran the pad of her thumb over his kiss-swollen lips then. And he was the one to sigh. "It would melt a mountain of ice, a continent. But love is not enough. Teenagers think it's the end-all and be-all. I certainly did when I married you in a heated hurry. There has got to be more this time."

It's all I've got to offer, though. And still it's not enough. He stepped back from her and put his hands in the air in a surrender gesture. "So be it. But I'm warning you, babe. No more twitching your tail in my face."

"I do not twitch."

"You twitch all right. Bottom line: You don't want to have sex? Fine." *Well, not so fine, but you don't have to know that.* "Just don't keep passing the platter if you don't want me to eat."

Nice analogy, boy. Real nice! the burr in his brain said.

"Are you saying I'm a tease?" She bristled like a cat in a roomful of rocking chairs.

"Don't put words in my mouth. Just know this." He pointed a forefinger at her for emphasis. "I'm not a college kid anymore that you can twist around your little finger. The next time I put my mouth on yours . . . if you don't bite off my tongue . . . I'm probably going for the real deal. And I don't mean dry humping against a tree trunk."

"Is that a threat?"

Oh, yeah. "Take it any way you want, sweetheart." He pivoted on his bootheels and stomped away, pride intact. Or, with as much pride as a guy could have with a half-blown erection still sticking out of his jeans like the prow of a ship.

Windows to the past . . .

Raoul spent the rest of the afternoon locked in his bedroom reading old mail. It was an enlightening experience.

There were letters and birthday cards and Christmas greetings. Even the gifts his father had sent over the years had been returned and stored in the attic, according to what he read. Teddy bears. A child's cowboy outfit. Drums. A BB gun. Some Western comic books. An Atari game system. Why his father had never given them to him on his rare visits he had no idea. Probably pride. Or misplaced revenge against his mother. Maybe just embarrassment.

His father had not been a gushy man, in person or in his letters. Some would have even described him as cold, especially in later years when bitterness clouded his thinking, but Raoul was beginning to get a better picture. A young man of eighteen having to take over a ranch when his parents were suddenly killed in an auto accident, the constant struggle to keep the ranch afloat, no social life to speak of, a one-night stand with a young woman that resulted in a baby he never knew . . . till its fourth birthday, years of a tug-of-war just to visit with his child. His father had been hurt so many times that he fought in the only way he knew how. If he didn't show his emotions, he'd figured he couldn't be hurt.

His father never used the word "love" in his letters, but Raoul no longer doubted that he had loved him. It was there between the lines. And in his actions.

When he finished the letters, he swiped at his eyes, threw the box on the bed, then opened the door and hollered at the top of his lungs, *"Charmaine!"*

Within seconds, she came running toward him from the kitchen, her hands all floury. "What? What's wrong?" She looked his face over with concern, probably noticing the aftereffects of his tears.

"Did you know that my father paid for my college scholarship? The one I was offered after I lost my football scholarship for dropping out of school when you dumped me?" He took a deep breath following his long-winded question.

Her face flushed with guilt. "He asked me not to tell you."

Secrets! More secrets! "Why?"

"Oh, don't ask me that now." She groaned.

"Why?"

"Because then I'd have to tell you why *I* had to drop out of school."

That was not the answer he'd expected. His eyes went wide with shock. "What did *your* dropping out of school have to do with *my* dropping out of school and my father secretly funding my education, which, by the way, the ranch could not afford."

"Oh, if you must know, my father—snake that he was and is—pulled the financial rug out from under me. He wanted me to use my influence with you and your father to sell him the ranch, which I wouldn't do."

Son of a bitch! Longtime puzzle pieces began to fall into place. "And that's why you were getting a job in a strip joint?"

"It was not a strip joint, I tell you. But, yes, that's why I needed to work." She blushed and lifted her chin so high it was a wonder she didn't get a nosebleed.

Control your temper, Raoul cautioned himself. *Don't scream or punch the walls or drive off in a rage. Just calm the hell down.* He inhaled and exhaled several times. "And you didn't tell me all this at the time . . . because?"

"Because you would have felt responsible for me, and you would have dropped out of school."

I feel like hurling the contents of my stomach. "Which is precisely what I ended up doing."

She threw her hands in the air with disgust, causing flour to flutter all over the place. "How was I supposed to know that?"

How about because I told you I loved you every pathetic chance I got? "Let me get this straight. My father knew that Valcour was pressuring you to get to him, and he did nothing to stop it?"

"He didn't know then. He found out later. That's why he always liked me, I think. He was a self-sacrificing

kind of guy, and he probably saw some of that in me."
She shrugged. "It's probably why he lied about the
divorce papers being filed. His small way of making up
for problems he felt that he had caused, no matter how
indirectly."

"I just don't understand why I was kept out of the
loop. Why didn't he trust me enough to tell me? Why
didn't you?"

"It seemed best at the time."

*Best for who? Not me. Your leaving me was definitely
not the best thing for me.* "So, the financial hole this
ranch is in started when my father came to my assistance?
So, the oil vultures have been after my father all this
time? So, you and my father were in cahoots, never
deigning to let poor ol' Raoul know what was going on?
So, everything I ever thought about my dad and you was
a sham?"

"Let me explain—"

"No, let me explain. You stood outside just two hours
ago preaching to me about respect and trust and how you
couldn't enter a relationship without those two essential
ingredients. Well, screw you, Charmaine. You *and* your
hypocrisy."

She gasped.

But he didn't care. He was on a roll. "What kind of
respect and trust did you show me? You didn't think I
could handle the truth back then when we were kids. You
didn't think I could handle the truth these past ten years.
And you sure as shootin' didn't think I could handle the
truth this past week while you've been living under the
same roof with me."

"Are you two havin' a lovers' spat?" Tante Lulu asked
during the short spurt of silence between his outbursts.

They both turned to look at the old lady standing in the dining room doorway, staring at them with concern.

"*No!*" he and Charmaine shouted at the same time.

Raoul turned his attention back to Charmaine. Wagging a finger in her face, he warned, "Stay away from me, Charmaine."

With those words, he stomped out of the house and to the barn, where he saddled a horse and rode off at a fast gallop, needing to let off steam.

It must have been the wind that caused his eyes to tear up.

Chapter 13

And then she got mad . . .

Charmaine bawled her eyes out for a long time . . . about five minutes.

Hurt and disappointment riddled her body and mind to the point where she shook and actually felt sick to her stomach. *He said he loved me . . . well, he said that he thought he might still love me. Same thing. But that didn't sound like love spewing from his lips. More like hate. Just like a man! First hint of trouble and he's out of there.*

Then anger took over. *How dare he call me out for doing the noble thing? Who the hell does he think he is? St. Rusty?*

Then determination kicked in. *He's gonna be sorry. Yes, he is. Stay away from him? Hah! He's not gonna know what hit him. Thinks he can tell me what to do. Hah! Just watch me.*

"Tante Lulu," Charmaine said, coming into the kitchen where the old lady was still writing out a grocery list. "Did you by any chance bring that belly dance outfit with you?"

Tante Lulu just grinned. "Thass my girl!"

And then he got mad . . .

Raoul rode his horse hard, till he and Dark Star were both saturated with sweat. Only then, out of concern for the animal, did he head back to the barn.

A series of emotions roiled through him as he walked the horse dry in the main aisle of the barn, then proceeded to brush him down. A quick survey of the barn showed that the three horses used by Clarence, Linc, and Jimmy were still gone. Thank God for small favors.

He took extra special care in grooming the horse. It was as close as he got to ministering to animals these days. God, how he missed being a vet! And now this mess with Charmaine!

He wasn't a guy who liked to analyze his feelings. Most men didn't. They put it up there with other unfavorite things like shopping and plucking their eyebrows. But he was analyzing now, and he was not a happy camper.

First, he was hurt. Profoundly hurt. By both his father and Charmaine. His father had taken so many actions over the years, manipulated him in a sense, without his knowledge. Why had he felt the need to protect him so? Had he considered him a weakling who couldn't handle the stress? At the very least, why had he never told him that he cared?

But his father wasn't around to answer his questions or be punished for his omissions or his orneriness. Charmaine was.

Mon Dieu, she complained all the time about his considering her a brainless bimbo. Well, tit for tat was apparently her modus operandi because he sure felt like a male bimbo . . . a bimbob, or himbo, or whatever the hell they called it. Too dumb to live and handle the problems life dealt him. Talk about!

The second emotion to sucker punch Raoul was anger. Blood boiling, punch-the-walls, I-could-scream-with-rage anger. How dare she make decisions on his behalf? How dare she omit telling him life-altering news? She was not his mother or his guardian. She'd been his wife, and he'd trusted her. No more!

Determination became his primary focus now. If he'd been wavering over a renewed relationship with Charmaine, that foolhardy notion fizzled out like foam on day-old beer. The sooner they got divorced and she moved out of his life, the better.

In the meantime, he was going to make her so sorry, and she better not come waving that sweet ass in his face, either. Or her tempting breasts. Or her kiss-some lips. Nope, he was immune.

An odd thing happened then. He could swear he heard the horse laugh at him. But maybe it was St. Jude.

It wasn't me. Although I do think you're a horse's ass. Aaarrgh!

Misery loves company . . . depending on the company . . .

Rusty was behaving like a real horse's ass.

And Charmaine was so miserable she could cry . . . or die.

He didn't show up for supper last night or for breakfast this morning. How was she supposed to torment him with her new push-up bra that promised a "voluptuous cleavage" if he never got to see it? How was she supposed to flaunt herself in front of him, making him sorry he would never have her? How was she supposed to ignore him if he wasn't there to ignore?

Clarence and Linc had arrived for both meals with their hair slicked back off their faces, reeking of Old Spice and wearing jeans so tight they could barely sit at the table. Jimmy couldn't stop himself from snickering.

"You look mighty fine again today," Tante Lulu told Clarence and Linc.

"You look like dorks," Jimmy disagreed.

Tante Lulu swatted him with a dish towel and cautioned, "Hush!"

"Thank you kindly, ma'am," Linc said.

"Any chance we look a little bit hunky?" Clarence asked with a flushed face. Charmaine noticed that he didn't have a plug in his cheek today. That was one thing to be thankful for.

"You mean like a Polish fellow?" Tante Lulu frowned with confusion.

"No, not like a Polish fellow," Clarence snapped. Then he softened in tone and explained, "Like that Diet Pepsi guy on the television . . . or those cover models on romance novels. Oh, not young like them, but . . . you know . . . virile."

"Clarence, if you were any more virile, we'd have to lock you up," Tante Lulu said.

Understanding dawned slowly for Charmaine, who realized that this was all about the dude ranch and hunk cowboy proposal she'd made to Rusty. He must have told them about it. These two nitwits must be trying to turn themselves into hunks to hold on to their jobs. Geesh!

Later that morning, Charmaine and Tante Lulu stood on the front porch, waiting for Clarence to come back and take Tante Lulu to the grocery store. She had a daunting list in hand, which would require his pickup truck to haul it back, her T-bird being too small to contain it all.

Charmaine was going to stay behind with her own list of duties, which the old lady had prepared for her:

1) Iron four tablecloths.
2) Make up with Rusty.
3) Take pies out of oven when timer goes off. Put in new pies.
4) Make up with Rusty.
5) Cut up dry bread for stuffing.
6) Make up with Rusty.
7) Bring three jars of canned peaches up from cellar.
8) Make up with Rusty.
9) Check for snakes.
10) Make up with Rusty.
11) Scrub out kettles for deep-frying turkeys.
12) Make up with Rusty.
13) Take peach bubble bath, paint finger- and toenails peach color, and wear an I-can-make-yer-eyes-bug-out outfit.

Charmaine had to laugh inside. *I wonder if Auntie wants me to make up with Rusty.*

Even then, Tante Lulu had some last-minute instructions, "Doan fergit to take some beefsteaks out of the freezer to thaw. Iffen we caint cook up a side of beef to go with the turkeys, we kin at least bar-b-cue some steaks. And mushrooms . . . I gotta remember to buy fresh mushrooms. Caint have steak without mushrooms."

"Everything's going to work out, Auntie. Stop worrying." She squeezed the old lady's shoulder.

"Well, of course, it'll all work out. Things allus does. And that goes fer you, too, girlie. God has a plan fer you, and fer a certainty Rusty plays a part. I guar-an-tee. Jist doan fret so."

"In other words, let things happen?"

"Heck, no! God helps those what helps themselves. Dint I lay out that belly dance outfit fer you?"

Speaking of outfits, Tante Lulu was wearing her "Goin' Shoppin'" outfit today. She still had the same red curls, which was unusual; Tante Lulu usually liked to change styles or colors every day, but she'd been extra busy this morning. As for clothing, she wore a senior-citizen adaptation of cargo pants and a fishing shirt, the common denominator being lots of pockets and loops for holding things, like a slim tablet with her lists, a pen, calculator, packet of tissues, reading glasses, sunglasses, recipes. In addition, she carried a purse the size of a bayou barge. On her feet were comfortable running shoes. Tante Lulu took her shopping seriously.

Charmaine's heart expanded with love, just looking at the kooky old bird. She adored her, idiosyncracies and all.

Just then, they heard a motor approaching. But it wasn't Clarence. A large, old-fashioned Winnebago being pulled by an ancient Chevy Impala with more rust spots than paint sputtered down the road.

Charmaine was the first one to recognize the latest arrival. Her eyes darted accusingly to Tante Lulu.

"Now, doan get riled up. I jist happened to give her a call yesterday and . . ." Tante Lulu, the traitor, shrugged.

It was her mother, Fleur Robicheaux, better known on

the stripper circuit by the single name "Fleur." And she wasn't alone. She'd brought with her a man, presumably her latest companion. Her mother *always* had to have a man in her life.

As the two of them opened the creaking doors of the vehicle and climbed out, Charmaine and Tante Lulu both groaned.

Her mother was wearing a one-piece, leopard print leotard. It was sleeveless and low cut and covered only by a wide cinch belt. Matching leopard print hoop earrings the size of mason jar rings hung from her ears. She wore high-heeled leopard print sandals. Her bleached blond hair was piled atop her head and held together with a leopard print scrunchie. Her makeup was a work of art, if one admired plasterwork.

To give her credit, her mother had a great body for a woman of forty-six. And her skin had not a wrinkle to show for her years, thanks to meticulous creaming and possibly some plastic surgery.

The companion, on the other hand, couldn't be more than thirty. He wasn't very tall, and he had the body of an overmuscled weight lifter. In fact, his biceps were about the size of Charmaine's thighs. His hair was bleached blond and long, down to his shoulders. He wore leather pants and a white T-shirt sporting the logo MOTHER TRUCKER. A toothpick dangled from his loose Elvis-like lips in a manner he probably considered sexy.

Barbie and Ken, they are not. Lordy, Lordy.

"Charmaine!" her mother shrieked and ran toward her in a hobbled, short-stepped manner thanks to the stilettos, arms spread wide.

With a sigh, Charmaine went down the steps and into her mother's hug. "Fleur," she said—her mother insisted that she not be called Mother—"what are you doing here?"

"Tsk-tsk? Doan you be rude, sugah. Why am I here? To see my baby girl of course." Her mother kissed her on each side of her face, the kind of kisses that didn't involve skin touching.

Noticing Tante Lulu still standing on the porch, mouth agape, which was the usual reaction her mother garnered, her mother said, "Miz Rivard, how you doin'?" She blew air kisses her way.

"Jist dandy." Tante Lulu threw air kisses back. Her mother failed to catch the sarcasm of the gesture.

"And I want y'all to meet my new friend. This here is Dirk Denney. Ain't he a sweetie?"

He's a sweetie all right. Oh, God. With a name like Dirk, he wouldn't be a porno star, would he? I wouldn't put it past her.

Dirk stepped forward. Well, actually, he swaggered forward. "Well, hello there, pretty ladies," he said to Charmaine and Tante Lulu both. He spoke in a low—yep, Elvis—drawl.

Forget the porno business. Maybe he's an Elvis impersonator.

"This here is Louise Rivard. Everyone calls her Tante Lulu. And this here gorgeous girl is my daughter Charmaine. You'd never know she's only twenty, would you?"

All right, Mom's been telling people she's only thirty-six again. Hard to explain away an almost-thirty daughter when you're thirty-six.

"Oh, yeah! She's very well preserved," Dirk remarked, giving her a way-too-personal head-to-toe survey. The push-up bra wasn't wasted on him. That was for sure.

Tante Lulu snorted her opinion of the whole business. Then staring at Dirk's T-shirt, she asked, "You a trucker?"

He glanced down at the logo and laughed. "Nope. I'm a personal trainer. Fleur hired me to get her in shape."

Uh-oh! Charmaine and Tante Lulu both exclaimed at the same time, "For what?"

"My nude layout in *STUD* magazine." She made the announcement in a ta-da fashion, fully expecting them to gush with enthusiasm. When they just gasped, she went on, "It's gonna be a special issue called 'Ageless Beauty.' Women from various professions who have managed to maintain their sexy bodies. They're gonna have Gina Romano, that sexy Hollywood actress from the eighties who was famous for those nude scenes; Brassy Bush, that double-jointed porno star; Mona Lewsky, that woman who had an affair with a senator; and there's even gonna be a former Olympic gold medalist in gymnastics, but I forget her name. And me, I'll represent the stripper profession." She beamed at all of them.

After a prolonged silence, Tante Lulu said, "Thass jist peachy."

Charmaine was horrified. She was almost thirty, no matter what her mother proclaimed, not a little girl of ten, but the woman still managed to find a way to humiliate her. Would it never end? Charmaine could just imagine the snickers she would hear behind her back. The licentious looks from men who would uncover her with their eyes wondering if she was the same as her mother. The tasteless jokes. "When's this photo shoot going to take place?"

"Two weeks, but there's a problem."

"Cellulite," Dirk pronounced gravely, as if he'd just

announced that Fleur had cancer. "Her butt and thighs are riddled with it. Looks like friggin' cottage cheese."

"And you came here . . . why?" Charmaine asked, uncaring how rude she sounded.

"To jog. And ride horses. And stuff. I need a private place to work out." Her mother had never worked out a day in her life. In fact, the most physical exercise her mother had ever engaged in involved bumps and grinds . . . or pounding a mattress under some man's body.

"You came to the Triple L Ranch to get rid of your cottage cheese . . . uh, cellulite? In two weeks?"

Her mother nodded enthusiastically.

"I do a great massage for pounding out those ripples," Dirk boasted.

"And I bought about two hundred dollars worth of cellulite removal cream," her mother added.

"Mebbe I'll work out with you," Tante Lulu mused, a forefinger pressed thoughtfully to her lips. "I've been noticin' a little cellulite on my hiney of late. Truth to tell, my buns looks like they have about a thousand dimples. Like golf balls."

That is not a picture I need in my mind. And I've got news for you, Auntie. You lost your hiney about twenty years ago. Charmaine began to laugh hysterically. Turns out the Triple L was being turned into a spa of sorts, no matter what Rusty wanted. She couldn't wait to tell him.

Misery, Part II . . .

Charmaine tracked Rusty down that afternoon, despite his best efforts to avoid her. It wasn't that she wanted to have anything to do with the stubborn mule, but she had some things to tell him that couldn't wait.

She was still wearing her push-up bra, but that was just because she'd forgotten to take it off. At least consciously. She'd already dropped her plan to torture him with her sexual appeal. He probably wouldn't notice her sexual appeal, anyhow, in the haze of anger he'd chosen to cloak himself in.

She walked to the back of the barn, where Clarence had told her she would find him. He had a horse's hoof resting against his thigh and was scraping some yucky stuff out with a metal tool . . . probably poop or dried mud. Yeech!

The second he raised his head and watched her approach, she realized her mistake. He for damn sure did notice her sexual appeal, as evidenced by his gaze instantly riveted on her chest. She smiled inwardly with pathetic satisfaction and said, "I need to talk to you, Rusty."

"Go away," he said. "I warned you before. Stay . . . away . . . from . . . me."

Charmaine gave Rusty a closer study then. He looked awful. His eyes were bloodshot. There were dark circles under his eyes. Day-old whiskers darkened his cheeks and chin.

"You look awful," she blurted out.

"Thanks. You, on the other hand, look sensational. What's with the push-up action?"

For sure, I got his attention. "Were you out on a bender last night?"

"Nope. Should have been, though, 'cause I couldn't sleep a wink."

Oh, Rusty. Why was it that a guy could be the biggest

creep in the world, but tell a gal that she caused him to lose sleep, and her heart melted with sympathy? Well, she couldn't let him distract her from her mission. "I need to tell you a few things."

He turned his back on her and continued to work on the horse's hoof.

"My mother has come for a visit. I just thought you should know."

"Who else would travel in an aluminum foil box on wheels, except your ditzy mother?"

Okay, so he already knows Fleur is here. Is that any reason to be such a jerk? Yeah, I consider my mother a ditz, too, but it sounds different when he says it. Probably he puts me in the same class.

"She brought her boyfriend with her. Dirk Denney."

That got his attention. He straightened, then turned slowly to look at her, carefully keeping his eye contact above her neck. "Dirk? Please don't tell me—"

"No, he's not an X-rated actor. He's a personal trainer."

"And you're telling me all this . . . why?"

"Because I don't want you to think it's part of my plan."

He put his tool down on a bench, then washed his hands in a bucket of water, drying them on his pant legs. Leaning against a support beam, he asked real soft, "What plan would that be?"

He was stubborn as a cross-eyed mule. He looked hung-over from lack of sleep. He wore nothing spectacular . . . just a plain black T-shirt, faded jeans and scuffed boots. But, mercy, he was absolutely gorgeous. A devastatingly fine specimen of manhood. Temptation pure and simple.

It took her several seconds to recall his question. "No plan. I mean, you might think I have a plan, but I don't. I just made a business proposal to you, but it wasn't a plan." Even to Charmaine, that sounded weird.

"Aaaah, so we're back to the dude ranch nonsense."

"It is not nonsense." Charmaine inhaled and exhaled several times to dampen her temper. She hadn't come here to argue with the lout.

She noticed that Rusty, despite his best intentions, was watching intently as she inhaled and exhaled.

Good!

But there was a look of disgust on his face.

Not good!

Was he disgusted with her or with himself?

Whatever.

"Look, let me tell you all of it. Then I'll be out of your way. My mother is doing a nude pictorial for some magazine about overaged sex goddesses. Problem is, she has cellulite, and her boyfriend is going to help her get rid of it. In two weeks. Here at the ranch, or till I kick her out . . . or you kick her out. Plus, Tante Lulu thinks she has cellulite, too."

His jaw dropped with shock.

"I was as shocked as you are."

"That Tante Lulu has cellulite?"

"Of course not. I'm talking about Fleur. Believe me, I didn't invite her. Tante Lulu did. For Thanksgiving. But you can't really blame her. She didn't know what my mother was up to. The minute my mother told me all this, I knew . . . I just knew . . . you would think it was part of some plan of mine to turn this into a dude ranch/health spa/exercise club."

At the end of her rambling explanation, Rusty's jaw still hung open with shock.

"Don't worry, though. I won't let her stay two weeks."

"I hope the hell not," he said, finally snapping out of his trance.

"You don't have to yell." *Although I would yell in your circumstance.*

"*Mon Dieu*, Charmaine, how many people has the old lady invited here?"

"I have no idea," Charmaine murmured. *A lot.*

"What?" he barked.

"I don't know for sure. The only other additions to what you already know are Jimmy's dad, but I doubt he can come since Jimmy told me he's in Brazil right now on his job, and maybe your mother."

"WHAT?"

I thought I'd be able to slip that last one in. Guess not. "Settle down. I don't think she actually called her. She knows how upset you are over the letter business and stuff."

"Settle down? Upset?" he sputtered. "You and Tante Lulu have got to stop interfering in my life. I mean it. Just know that, if my mother shows up here, I will be leaving. Because if I stay, in the mood I'm in, I may very well kill her. Did I make myself clear?"

As a Bayou Black sky on a cloudless day. "Anyhow, I just thought you ought to know about my mother."

Tears welled in her eyes, and she feared they would overflow. She couldn't give him the satisfaction of seeing that. One more humiliation in a week of humiliations! It had taken her almost ten years to build up a good business reputation and down the tubes it went with one bad turn to a loan shark. *Humiliating.* She'd tried four times to hold a marriage together and failed. *Humiliating.* Her mother was a stripper and apparently would continue to strip, one way or another, till she dropped dead. *Humiliating.* Rusty had shown with words and actions that he didn't want her anywhere near him. *Humiliating.* Turning quickly, she started to walk away, while her dignity was still intact.

He grabbed her upper arm, pulling her to a halt. "You're crying," he accused her. "And you hardly ever cry."

"I am not crying," she said, even as a big fat tear slid down her face.

He used the thumb of his other hand to wipe it away, still holding on to her arm to prevent her escape. "Don't think you can sway me with tears."

Hmmm. I didn't think of that. "Who's trying, you big baboon?"

"Why are you crying?" the big baboon asked.

"Not over you, that's for sure."

"It never occurred to me that you would cry over me."

"And why is that?" she asked contrarily. *Clueless . . . the man is clueless. I cried a river over you, baby.* "Do you think you're the only one who was hurt over our breakup? Do you think you can holler at me, and my feelings won't get hurt? Do you think I don't feel bad that you feel bad? Do you ever even goddam think?"

"Huh?" He stared at her as if she'd lost her mind. It felt as if she had. "The breakup was ten years ago. And you left me."

I am so sick of that same old song. "Let me go, Rusty. I'm thinking about driving back to Houma tonight. I'm tired of this whole stinkin' mess."

"What stinkin' mess?" When she flashed him an "Are

you for real?" glower, he elaborated, "Are you talking
about the loan shark mess . . . the no-divorce mess . . .
the I-lied-to-my-husband-but-so-what mess . . . the
Thanksgiving feast mess . . . or your mother mess?"

What a mess! "All of the above. And add to it the four
failed marriages mess, the price of cattle mess, the my-
husband-hates-me mess."

He cocked his head to the side. "You said you weren't
crying over me. At least one or two of those messes
involves me. And no way are you skedaddling off to
Houma, babe. Me, I am not facing all these nutcake relatives of yours alone."

Okay, you have a point there. "I'll stay till after
Thanksgiving then."

"And the loan shark?"

Don't remind me. "I don't freakin' care. Frankly, I'd
rather face the Mafia thugs than . . ." She let her words
trail off.

"Than what? Me?"

That's the sixty-four thousand dollar question. "Just
forget about it."

"I don't hate you."

It was her turn to say, "Huh?"

"When you were listing all your woes, one of them
you named was my-husband-hates-me. Well, I don't."

The floodgate let loose then. Tears streamed out of her
eyes without control.

"*Now* what did I do to turn on your faucets?" he asked
on a groan, pulling her into his embrace. "You're crying
because I don't hate you? Talk about! I can't win for
losing, babe."

"You're driving me crazy," she wailed, and wrapped
her arms around his waist, pressing her face against the

curve of his neck. He smelled of horse and sweat and man. Eau de Raoul. They ought to bottle him.

"No, no, no. *You* are driving *me* crazy." This was the point where he should be shoving her away. This was the point where they should both come to their senses. This was the point they kept coming back to, over and over and over . . . then stopping.

But neither of them wanted to break the embrace. And that was all it was. A man comforting a woman in distress. With soft kisses on her hair. Soft murmurs of "Shhh. Don't cry, you." Soft strokes of hard hands running from her shoulders to her waist, over and over. They meant nothing.

She sighed. "Why does everything have to be so difficult for us?"

"Got me, babe. Know this: I would crawl over broken glass for you, if needed, but I won't—I *can't*—exist in the chaos that surrounds you."

"I can't help the people and things around me. It's who I am."

"I know that." He kissed her hair again, a little harder for emphasis. "And I'm not saying it's a bad thing *for you*. It is a bad thing *for me* . . . at least at this point in my life. I have enough turmoil to handle. My father died while I was in prison, and I'm just now starting to grieve over him, especially after reading those letters. I suspect they'll have to exhume my father's body for an autopsy. Not a pleasant prospect, that. Getting my conviction reversed is going to be messy, to say the least. *Dieu* only knows how long it will take to get my vet license back and the ranch back into shape. Stress City, that's me right now."

"And I just add to the stress by suggesting you turn the place into a dude ranch?"

"You got it."

"And you won't even consider that my proposal has merit?"

"Charmaine . . ." he cautioned. "Living with you is like living on a roller coaster."

"Hey, there are a lot of ups and downs with you, too. One minute you're breathing-smoke mad at me, and the next you're looking at me like a little boy with his nose pressed to the window of the candy store."

"Mais oui!" he said and she heard the smile in his voice. "But then your candy, she is mighty sweet."

She pushed away from his embrace but held on to his hands. They were arms length away from each other now. "Okay, I'll back off then. What do you want me to do?"

"What I want and what I consider best are two different things." His dark Cajun eyes were hot and needy as he spoke. She knew what he wanted without the words being spoken. "Take your half of the bond money and go home. Pay off the loan shark. Be happy."

There were so many mistaken notions in his words that Charmaine didn't know where to begin. When did home start to feel like the ranch instead of her cottage on Bayou Black? When did not paying off the loan shark lickety-split stop scaring the daylights out of her? When would she ever be happy again if he wasn't around? Foolish as it might be, she was about to tell him just that, but someone entered the barn behind her.

"Yoohoo," the feminine voice yelled. "Charmaine? You in there?"

It was Tante Lulu.

She let loose of Rusty's hands.

He gave them an extra squeeze before he let go.

Standing next to him, they waited for the old lady to approach.

She'd changed from her shopping outfit to house slippers and a loose, flowered housedress—sort of a muumuu-type garment. Her red curls were confined under a scarf. This attire could represent either a frenzy of cleaning or a frenzy of cooking. Probably the latter.

Huffing for breath after her trek from the house, Tante Lulu said, "Charmaine, you gots to get yer be-hind back to the house. Yer mother wants you to blow-dry her. She and her boyfriend jist used up all the hot water takin' a shower . . . *together*, I think. Turns out Dirk the Jerk won't be eatin' our turkey and other vittles tomorrow. He doan eat nothin' but organic crap. 'Scuse my language, Rusty, but sometimes a lady's jist got to use dirty words to express herself. Anyways, Dirk brought his blender into the kitchen and he's whippin' up carrots and celery fer his own dinner. Talk about! And Fleur wants ta know if I can make her up a special diet version of the leftover jambalaya we're havin' tonight. I tol' her, 'Yeah, right. When old strippers shimmy through the pearly gates, thass when I'm gonna make diet jambalaya.' Then she said a dirty word to me. Suck is a dirty word, ain't it?"

After that lengthy tirade, Charmaine looked at Rusty, and he looked at her. Even though they were both accustomed to Tante Lulu's outrageous personality, she'd turned them speechless this time.

Finally, Rusty whispered in her ear, "See what I mean? Chaos."

That was so unfair. Blaming her because her mother stirred up trouble wherever she went, or that Tante Lulu wouldn't stand still for any of it. "What do you expect me to do?" she asked Tante Lulu.

"Go back ta the house and give Fleur what-for." She sank down onto a low bench and crooked her finger toward Rusty. "Besides, I gots to have a talk with yer husband."

Uh-oh, she thought.

"Uh-oh," he said, and sat down next to the old lady, who had a determined gleam in her eyes.

Charmaine left the two of them alone, but she decided to skirt around the back porch on her return to the house. It was time to visit the patron saint of hopeless causes, *M'sieur* Jude.

Chapter 14

I'm trapped, and I can't get away.

How could a six-foot-three, 210-pound guy who'd been in prison for chrissake be trapped by a senior citizen half his size wearing a flour sack? But Raoul was, and he didn't know how to escape without offending the basically kindhearted old lady.

Sitting on the bench next to her, feeling a bit like Mutt and Jeff with their contrasting heights, he braced himself stoically for whatever she had to tell him. It wasn't going to be good, he could tell.

"You havin' trouble gettin' it up, boy?"

At first, his eyes went wide with shock. Then he closed them and counted to ten. This was worse—*way worse*— than he'd expected. "No, Tante Lulu, *it* is doin' just fine."

"Then why aren't ya shakin' the bedsheets with Charmaine?"

Shakin' the bedsheets? Well, at least she didn't use a vulgar word for it, or refer to my cock as a wee-wee again. "Don't you think that question is a little personal?"

"Personal, schmersonal! Charmaine is miserable. Yer miserable. Why aintcha doin' somethin' 'bout it, you?"

"And you think shakin' the bedsheets is the answer?"
God, if only life were that simple!

"It's a start. Listen, boy-o, I'm an old lady. I know better'n most that life's too short to dawdle, and you been doin' way too much dawdlin'."

"Me? Charmaine was busy getting married three different times while I was off . . . dawdling?"

She turned and wagged a finger in his face. "Listen up, and listen up good. Do you know the one thing all of Charmaine's husbands had in common?"

Holy hell! What a question! I do not need to know all the finer points of Charmaine's men.

"They all looked jist like you."

Once again, Raoul was stunned speechless. And the old lady was standing up, about to leave him hanging in the wind. "Whoa! What does that mean?"

"It means that Charmaine never got over you. It means that she's been lookin' fer you in every man she meets. It means ya better get off yer duff before she finds another look-alike and this one turns out better than a stubborn ol' ex-con cowboy. Think about how yer gonna feel if that happens . . . again."

With that parting shot, she was off.

But she'd given Raoul food for thought.

And then the REAL chaos began . . .

The guests began to arrive at 9 A.M.

Even before Charmaine went out on the front porch, the squealing laughter and rapid-fire chatter of three little girls told her it was Luc and Sylvie and their brood. She watched as they emerged noisily from their minivan.

Who would have ever thought that the "bad boy of the bayou" would one day drive such a conservative Soccer Mom vehicle?

The men had left hours ago, after a cold breakfast, to work in the west pasture, where the new bulls were going to be given a second stab, so to speak, at some lucky females. Rusty had waggled his eyebrows as he invited Charmaine to come watch, but she'd politely declined. And wasn't it strange how Rusty had been regarding her so quizzically since yesterday when he and Tante Lulu had shared a mysterious tete-a-tete?

In any case, Charmaine and Tante Lulu were alone in the ranch house, there being no respite for ranch work even on Thanksgiving. But the men had promised to return early, hopefully by late morning. Jimmy was especially excited because Tee-John would be coming; finally, someone close to his own age.

Her mother and Dirk probably wouldn't get up till noon, considering how everyone in the house had been subjected to the tinny sounds of the Winnebago bouncing on its ancient springs all night long from their enthusiastic lovemaking, highlighted by many feminine refrains of "Oooh, oooh, oooh!" and masculine yells of "Yes, yes, yes!" At one point, Tante Lulu had stuck her head out the window and hollered, "Go to sleep, you! Much more, and *I'll* be having an orgy-asm."

Now, Luc carried one-year-old Jeanette in his arms, though she squirmed to be let down and join her sisters, Blanche Marie and Camille, three and two, respectively. All of them wanted to go over to the corral to see the horsies.

"Kin we ride horses today, Aunt Char? Kin we? Kin we?" Blanche begged.

"Sure thing, sweetie pie," Charmaine answered, scooching down and giving the little girl a hug. "Rusty and his cowboys went out early to get their chores done, but they'll be back soon. I'm sure they'd love to give you a ride." *I hope. On the other hand, if Rusty's concerned about chaos, what could be more chaotic than teaching little girls to ride a horse? I wonder if there are any ponies here. I wonder if it makes any difference.*

"Me too," Camille said.

"Of course, Cammie," Charmaine agreed. *Hey, the more the merrier, or more chaotic.*

"Me, me," Jeanette chimed in, not understanding what she was asking for but wanting to be included.

"Hey, girl!" Luc greeted her. "You are lookin' *good.*"

"Thank you very much," she said with a little curtsy, then gave her half brother a quick kiss on the cheek. She wore a corset-type blouse over a gauzy, midcalf gypsy skirt. Luc was looking mighty fine, too, in khakis and a golf shirt.

"Welcome, Sylvie," she said then to Luc's wife, who was fighting to hold the two little girls in tow. The prospect of real horses was apparently overpowering. Despite their mother's admonitions, they kept tugging on her hands to be let loose.

"Hi, Charmaine. Happy Thanksgiving," Sylvie said with a laugh and a shrug. Sylvie looked good, too, in brown linen slacks and a beige silk blouse. Her hair was swept up off her face in a girlish fashion. Very attractive! But then, Sylvie always did look good, especially together with Luc. The Creole/Cajun combination was something else!

Just then, Blanche spotted Charmaine's outfit. She

stopped dead in her struggles, gave the skirt a critical eye, then asked, "Does your skirt twirl?"

"Gee, I don't know," Charmaine said.

"Mine does," Blanche informed her, breaking away from her mother's restraint and spinning around several times to show how her miniature cowgirl outfit with its flared skirt did indeed twirl.

"Mine, too." Camille did several twirls, as well, in her matching costume. They had certainly come prepared for a day at the ranch, even Jeanette. Who knew there was a place that sold these things in such small sizes!

"Twirling is a requisite for dress purchases these days," Sylvie told her. "Not just Dale Evans attire."

"But of course," Charmaine agreed, and spun along with the little girls. Turns out her skirt did indeed twirl.

They were all giggling when Tante Lulu came out on the porch. "Happy Thanksgiving, everyone." Today Tante Lulu had opted for a dark blond wig in a short wedge style, which was actually very tasteful. On her feet were white support shoes because of the excessive time she expected to be on her feet. Black polyester slacks and a black-and-white polka-dot shirt were topped by a red apron that read CAJUN COOKING . . . YUM! She turned to Sylvie and asked, "Darlin', did ya bring yer special pecan pie?"

"Two of them," Sylvie answered. "Plus, a sweet potato pie."

"One pecan pie is for me," Luc said, coming up behind his wife and giving her a swift kiss on the back of her neck.

"Oh, you!" Sylvie said. The love between these two, though married for four years now, was palpable in the air, and a joy to witness.

Will I ever have that kind of love?

Yep, the voice in her head replied.

Promise?

It's not polite to ask a saint for guarantees.

"Good, good," Tante Lulu said, regarding the pies, though she'd already prepared a ton of desserts herself. Then she gave Luc, Sylvie, and the three little ones gushy kisses before turning on Luc. "I wants you to do me a favor."

"Uh-oh," he said.

"I wants you to go shoot me a steer fer the bar-be-cue."

"Whaaaaat?" Luc squealed.

"Jist kidding. Caint anyone take a joke anymore? Me, I wants you to bring two kettles from the barn out to the backyard. Start the fires so we can deep-fry the turkeys. I already injected them with the Cajun spices, and they's all ready to go. Start the fire on the grill, too. Fer the steaks."

"What are we feeding here? An army?"

"Yep, a family army."

"What can I do?" Sylvie asked.

"How do ya feel 'bout peelin' taters?"

"Just great," Sylvie said with a laugh.

"By the by," Tante Lulu addressed Sylvie, "you brought any of that love potion stuff of yers here? Charmaine, bless her heart, she needs it bigtime."

Sylvie was a chemist for a pharmaceutical company. She'd become famous a few years back for an alleged love potion she'd developed. Nothing had ever come of it so far except a lot of publicity.

"Oh! I do not," Charmaine said. "Need a love potion,

that is." But they were all laughing by then, including Charmaine, who actually thought, *Hmmm!*

Remy and Rachel arrived next on his Harley. Every time she saw her half brother, Charmaine always marveled how godly handsome he was, but from only one side of his scarred face. Rachel, his new wife, had recently done a masterful job decorating one of Charmaine's shops. The two of them had recently returned from their honeymoon and couldn't keep their hands off each other, even as they got off Remy's motorcycle.

That's all I need. More lovey-dovey couples to make me feel bad.

"Hey, Charmaine," Remy said. Then he swung her around in a big hug with her feet off the ground.

"Hi, Charmaine," Rachel said, smiling at her husband's antics. Rachel took two bottles of wine out of the leather side bags and offered them to her as their contribution to the feast.

"Go on to the backyard. Tante Lulu is enjoying her day as commander-in-chief," she told them.

Remy and Rachel laughed with understanding. Everyone knew that Tante Lulu loved being in charge of a family event.

Just before they left, Rachel remarked to Charmaine, "I heard that Tante Lulu brought Rusty a hope chest."

"Yep," she answered.

"Dead as a bayou catfish, that's what Rusty is." Remy laughed. "Once auntie delivers the hope chest, it's a done deal."

I only wish! Charmaine thought after they left, then immediately corrected herself. *No, I don't wish.* After a pause, she added, *Do I?*

René and Tee-John were the last to arrive. Tante Lulu was going to be so surprised to see René, the middle brother. He was a Washington, D.C., environmental lobbyist for Louisiana fishermen. He rarely got home these days.

Tee-John, at fourteen, was looking just as good as all his brothers. While Luc, René, and Remy all shared the same mother, and of course the same father, Valcour LeDeux, Tee-John was the product of Valcour and his longtime common-law wife, Jolie, whom he'd married only four years ago. They, and Charmaine, weren't the only products of Valcour's virile seed, which he'd spread indiscriminately over the years. No one knew for sure exactly how many children he had.

"Did you bring your accordion?" she asked René after all the greetings were over. "We're hoping for a little family entertainment tonight. You probably aren't aware, but Rusty has some accomplished musicians here on the ranch. Linc is a wonderful classical guitarist, and Clarence plays a mean harmonica."

"For sure. I never travel without my trusty accordion," René replied. He used to play in a low-down Cajun band called The Swamp Rats, and could always be called on for some musical fun.

"Yuck! Accordions and harmonicas! You people ever heard of MTV? Get with the times," Tee-John said and ducked as René leaned over to swat him upside the head.

René looked at Charmaine and winked. "Can you imagine the torture of riding in a closed vehicle with this character for more than an hour? Me, I mus' be a saint." In an overloud whispered aside, he informed her, "His latest question was what I thought about piercing a penis with an industrial-sized bolt. Talk about!"

"Well, geeshamighty, how's a guy to know these things?" Tee-John whined with a devilish gleam in his dark Cajun eyes.

"A bolt in your too-too? The things men'll do!" Charmaine pretended to shiver.

"Not this man," René said, crossing his legs with exaggerated pain.

"Where did you hear about such a thing?" she asked Tee-John.

"Bourbon Street. There was this piercing shop, and the guy there even showed us his bolts. Awesome!"

"Tee-John, you have got to stay away from Bourbon Street. That is not real life there." René was laughing as he spoke.

"Yeah, well, this guy says it feels great . . . all that extra weight there all the time. Plus, he said the women love it. Double the pleasure and all that good stuff. What do you think, Charmaine? You ever done it with a guy with a bolt?"

René was bent over at the waist, slapping his thighs with glee, now that Charmaine was the target of Tee-John's curiosity.

And everyone thinks I'm a scandal for having my navel pierced. "No, Tee-John, I can't say that I have. And take my advice. No . . . bolts."

Tee-John grinned then. It was always hard to tell whether his incessant, outrageous questions were serious, or teasing.

"What's with the tin box on wheels?" René asked then.

Charmaine rolled her eyes. "My mother and Dirk," she told him, then quickly added, "Don't ask."

As she walked around to the backyard with the two of them, arms looped over each other's shoulders, Tee-John commented, "Dirk, huh? Betcha he knows about penile bolts."

They all groaned, including—*she could swear*—the St. Jude statue, which had been moved to the side yard.

Charmaine spent a short time with Luc getting updated on her loan shark situation. Bobby the Prick had accepted, reluctantly, the twenty thousand from the sale of her BMW, but he hadn't yet accepted Luc's contention that the clock had stopped ticking on the remaining thirty thousand she owed. In fact, since the loan originally had been twenty thousand, he was trying to negotiate down the balance, which might just happen with Luc's good friend police detective Rosie Mouton putting on his own brand of pressure.

"So what do I do in the meantime? Can I go home?"

Luc shrugged, then scrutinized her carefully. "Do you want to go home?"

I do and I don't. How's that for clear as Mississippi mud? "I have to go back at some point soon, if for no other reason than to check up on my businesses."

Luc handed her a folder and said, "These are reports from the spa in Houma and the shop in Lafayette. Except for routine problems, which are described in here, they seem to be doing all right without you . . . in the short term."

"Yeah, but I need to prepare quarterly tax reports, end-of-the-year P&L's, a bunch of stuff."

"Wait a little longer if you can," he advised.

If I can. "And if I can't?"

"Maybe Rusty could go back with you."

She snorted her opinion.

"No smooth sailing with you two yet?"

Are you kidding? "More like ship wrecked and drowning quick."

"Maybe you need to kiss the St. Jude statue a few times." He pointed to the second statue, which was tending one of the grills.

"You've been hanging around Tante Lulu too long." She leaned over and gave Luc a quick kiss on the cheek. "Thanks for all your help, brother dear."

"No prob, sis. There is one other thing, though." He handed her a second folder. The pensive look on his face boded ill for her mood, which wasn't all that great to begin with.

Opening it slowly, she saw that it was the divorce application.

"Don't get excited," he cautioned. "I'm not asking you to sign it right now. In fact, I don't want you to sign it now. Think it over carefully. Then we'll talk some more."

She agreed with a silent nod of her head. After that, they got caught up on old news. His recent vasectomy. Remy and Rachel's plans to adopt a child, or children. Her father's visit to the ranch. The dead steer.

Seated at another table outside were Sylvie and Linc. Linc and Clarence were gussied up today according to their vision of hunk cowboys. Pristinely brushed cowboy hats, shirts with two pockets and snap buttons, string ties, neatly pressed Wranglers, slicked-back hair. *Lordy, Lordy!* But how adorable that they cared enough to make the effort!

Too bad Rusty doesn't give my ideas as much credibility.

Sylvie brought with her some old scrapbooks belonging to the Baptiste family. Turns out Charmaine had been right about having previously seen the picture of his ancestors Cain and Abel Lincoln. The black twins, a physician and a musician, had been best friends with the sugar planter Etienne Baptiste. Charmaine heard Sylvie graciously offer to lend Linc some ancient journals belonging to her family in which his ancestors were mentioned. Linc said he might just resume work on his book about early-Louisiana black musicians with all the new material he'd been given.

In the midst of all these revelations, they all got another shocker . . . well, Linc got the biggest shocker of them all. A late-model Mercedes sedan pulled up out front. They could see it from the backyard since it was forced to park off to the side.

Tante Lulu came up behind Linc and put a hand on his shoulder. "Linc, bless yer heart, you got a surprise comin'."

"Huh?" He was already bedazzled by all the wonderful information Sylvie had been giving him. But then, as if in slow motion, his head turned to look where the rest of them were now staring.

A well-dressed black man emerged from the vehicle and started to walk toward them. It could have been Linc, except for the khakis with their razor pleats, the designer loafers and the golf shirt sporting the crest of an exclusive Beverly Hills country club.

"It's Linc's twin brother," Tante Lulu announced. "Dr. Cain Lincoln. He's a bone doctor out in Los Angel-less."

The two brothers approached each other slowly, tears welling in both their eyes.

"You stubborn jackasss," Cain choked out, pulling Linc into a tight hug. "Why didn't you tell me where you've been? I could have helped."

"I dug the hole I was in. I needed to climb out myself,"

Linc answered. "But, man, it's good to see you again. How are Phyllis and the kids?"

"Phyllis is still practicing pediatrics, and the girls are at UCLA. Sonia told me about the divorce, and about your being in prison." Sonia was Linc's ex-wife. "Dammit, Linc, I would have gotten you a good lawyer. I would have visited you in prison. I'm your brother. We stick together."

"I needed to do it alone." Linc looped his arm around his brother's shoulder, though, and hugged him warmly. Then he looked over at Tante Lulu, the interfering old biddy. "I don't know how you managed to learn I even had a brother, let alone locate him, but thank you."

"Humpfh!" Tante Lulu said, clearly pleased by his words. "Thanksgivin' is a time fer family."

Sylvie came over then, while the two brothers got caught up on the happenings of the past few years. She saw Linc showing his brother some of the journals and albums Sylvie had brought with her. "Isn't it amazing how history comes full circle?" Sylvie mused. "Linc's ancestors who we were just talking about were twins, too. One was a physician and one was a musician, just like Cain and Linc."

After that, Luc went inside with the other men. Charmaine, Tante Lulu, Sylvie, and Rachel worked on setting the numerous tables and preparing the food. It was going to be a spectacular feast, in the Cajun tradition of there being no such thing as too much food.

Turkeys oozing Cajun spices were about to be deep-fried. Beef steaks were marinating and ready to be placed on the barbecue. In the warming oven in the kitchen, or waiting to be reheated in the microwave were four kinds of dressing: corn bread, rice, oyster, and boudin sausage.

For a starch, there was about a barrel of mashed potatoes and an equal amount of dirty rice. The vegetables included bacon and collard greens, black-eyed peas, smothered okra, candied yams, string bean casserole, and cranberry sauce. Most amazing to Charmaine were the twelve different desserts: pecan (two), peach, sweet potato and pumpkin pies (three), praline cheesecake, rum-soaked bread pudding, a red velvet layer cake, fresh fruit salad, and rice pudding à la Falernum.

A lot of this work had been done by Tante Lulu, but Charmaine had helped till late last night, too. Plus, Sylvie had made some of the pies, and Rachel had prepared a lot of the items, too, sending them in René's vehicle since she'd come on the Harley with Remy.

Charmaine would have liked to think they would be eating leftovers for a week, but these were Cajuns, and they enjoyed good food. Much of it would go today.

When it appeared that everything was prepared that could be for now, and there was a time for a short respite, Sylvie and Rachel cornered Charmaine. Sylvie carried a pitcher of watermelon margaritas, and Rachel carried the frosted, salted glasses. Tante Lulu had gone inside to join the young ones in a brief nap before meal time.

"It's time for us to have a little girl-to-girl, girl," Sylvie said, pouring a drink for Charmaine and handing it to her. They all sat down on folding lawn chairs.

"Oh?" Charmaine said.

"I have got to tell you, I used to think that Luc was the best thing since sliced bread, and he is, of course, but, ooh la la, that Rusty is drop-dead, fan-me-with-a-feather, hot-damn gorgeous," Sylvie pronounced, pretending to fan her flaming face.

That was a lot coming from a woman who used to be

clinically shy. In fact, she'd been treated for chronic shyness by some psychologist at one point. Shyness therapy, of all things.

"Really, Charmaine, when he walks into a room, every feminine heart flutters . . . even the married ones," Rachel added, "but don't tell Remy I said that." She fanned her face, too.

"We heard about your born-again virginity, and we want the scoop. *All* the delicious details," Sylvie demanded. "How's it going?"

"Let's just say that when you're almost thirty virginity isn't all it's cracked up to be."

"Oooh, I don't know about that. Anticipation and all that good stuff," Rachel remarked.

"*Mais oui*, there is much to be said for anticipation." Charmaine had only taken two sips from her drink, and Sylvie was lifting the pitcher to pour her more. What did these ladies think she had to reveal? "However, I'm discovering that I'm the horny one in this picture. And horny isn't much fun unless there's an end in sight, if you know what I mean."

"That's all? That's all you're going to tell us? I'm disappointed," Rachel said. "I expected to get some graphic details here."

"Well, there is one thing to be said for born-again virginity," Charmaine began hesitantly. She took an extra long time to lick the salt off her lips. Sylvie and Rachel leaned forward with interest. "Sex without consummation."

"Huh?" Sylvie and Rachel both said.

"You would be amazed at the number of *inventive* ways there are to have sex—and we're talking mind-blowing, orgasmic, I-need-a-cigarette sex—without losing one's virginity."

Sylvie and Rachel's mouths both dropped open.

"Holy catfish!" Sylvie finally said.

"Do tell," Rachel said.

There was a whole pitcher of margaritas imbibed by the three of them by the time Charmaine finished, amidst much giggling, outright laughing, and a few sighs.

In the end, Charmaine said, "So, what do you think?"

"I think there are going to be two Cajun rogues attacked by their wives tonight," Sylvie said.

"And she doesn't mean Rusty," Rachel added.

On the other hand, Charmaine thought.

Chapter 15

*We are fam-i-ly . . . and fam-i-ly . . . and
fam-i-ly . . .*

By early afternoon, Raoul was sitting in the great room of
the ranch house, sharing long necks with Luc, René and
Remy, the drone of football play-by-play in the background. Every man's vision of a great Thanksgiving.

Linc, Cain, and Clarence were at the other end of the
room, legs propped up on hassocks, watching the NFL
game on TV, also sipping at cold long necks. They were
all being denied lunch to build up big appetites for the
main meal, except for Cajun hot nuts and some chips and
dip.

Linc and Clarence looked like old fools—*if you ask
me . . . which nobody did*—in touristy type cowboy shirts
and hair combed back with so much hair goop they would
probably melt in a good sunlight. But it was kind of
touching that they were trying to please Charmaine by fit-
ting in with her dude ranch idea. Hell, they were probably
trying to impress him, too, thinking he would fall right in
with Charmaine's cockamamie ideas. *Yeah, right!*

The women were out in the backyard preparing for the

late-afternoon feast. They'd shooed all the guys away, probably so they could rake their men over the coals. Raoul wondered idly if Charmaine considered him her man. Okay, not so idly.

Jimmy and Tee-John were horseback riding. The three little girls were taking a nap on Charmaine's bed following an hour of hard horseback riding on the slowest nag on the ranch, which had mostly involved Raoul leading the horse around a small circle in the paddock and the girls squealing with delight. Actually, they got as much pleasure from chasing chickens and going out to look at some cows.

Too bad big girls aren't as easy to please as little ones. Not that I have any particular big girl in mind.

God does not like fibbers, you-know-who said in his head.

Fleur and Dirk had not yet emerged from their sardine can of love. So much for her hard exercise regimen! Well, actually, maybe she had been getting a hard exercise regimen, though Raoul had never heard of sex curing cellulite. Could be a new invention.

"What are you smilin' about, Lanier?" Remy asked. "Charmaine must be treatin' you better these days?"

"Hardly." *I may as well be a born-again virgin, too, for all the action I'm getting. Not that action with Charmaine would be a good idea. Well, it would be a good bad idea, if that makes any sense, which it doesn't.*

"Not to worry. Tante Lulu brought him a hope chest," Remy told his brothers with a decided twinkle in his eyes.

All three men grinned at him.

"What? What's so funny?"

"You are such dead meat, you," Luc said. "Speaking from experience."

"I am not afraid of that old lady," he boasted.

"Dead meat," Luc repeated.

"Seriously, Rusty, you best throw in the towel now," René advised. "When Tante Lulu pulls out the hope chest, the writing is on the wall."

"But wait, you haven't heard the best part," Luc contributed, looking at each of his brothers. "Sylvie told me that Charmaine is a born-again virgin."

"No way!" René said.

"Exactly what is a born-again virgin?" Remy wanted to know.

"She might even have her doo-hickey sewed back up," Luc contributed.

Everyone turned to Raoul with eyebrows arched in question.

"She has good reasons for doing this," he said and couldn't believe he was actually defending such as asinine decision.

Their eyebrows remained arched, now with disbelief.

"Charmaine has been shakin' her bootie like a wild thang since she was fourteen, no offense intended, Rusty. Suddenly, she's turned into Miss Pureheart?" It was René voicing this skepticism.

Raoul took a long swig of beer, then replied, "Charmaine is a drama queen. I suspect she's always been all vine and no taters."

"What the hell does that mean?" Luc asked.

"She's had a reputation for being a bad girl since she was a kid, mainly 'cause of her stripper mama. Charmaine decided early on that she might as well play the game if she already had the name. Except, for the most part, she just pretended to play . . . if you get my drift."

The odd thing was that they all nodded as if that made

perfect sense. *I'm in real trouble if I'm starting to make sense.*

"Actually, a friend of mine described her behavior perfectly. It's called protective coloration. That's a technical term for animal behavior." Raoul was on a roll now. "You see, animals adapt to their surroundings as a defense mechanism, often by changing their color to camouflage them in the wild. A sort of defense mechanism. That's what Charmaine does with all her outrageous clothing and behavior. It's just a defense."

Now all three men stared at him as if he'd lost his mind. Maybe his roll was actually a dip.

"What a load of bullshit!" René concluded.

"Who was this friend who described Charmaine like that? Betcha it was a woman." Luc stared at him, then hooted with laughter when Raoul's face heated up. "It was. Oh, *Dieu*, this is priceless."

"Take my advice," Remy said gently, even as his lips twitched with laughter. "Don't expound that bit of wisdom to Charmaine. If you did, I would have to nominate you for the Dumb Man of the Year award."

Luc pulled his briefcase closer to him on the floor and pulled out a file. "Changing the subject . . ."

Thank you, God!

"I've got some news," he said.

"Good news?"

Luc shrugged. "Could be." He handed the file to him, most of which had been prepared by the P.I., Zerby, and waited for him to read it over.

"This guy is good," Raoul said finally. "So, he thinks the cop Gaudet is working with Blue Heron Oil. And he believes Blue Heron Oil might have been responsible for my dad's death, even if only indirectly."

"Yep," Luc replied.

"At least it's not Cypress Oil. As much as Charmaine dislikes her father, she would be devastated if he was involved in this dirty mess."

"The goddam oil companies! They think they're God," René practically snarled. "Every friggin' one of 'em comes in, rapes the environment, then skips off, leaving the bayou to die off. I am so sick of it all."

Everyone sympathized with René and his fervor regarding the rapid decline of the southern Louisiana ecosystem, whether the culprits were oil companies, other industries, sport fishermen, or developers. The problem was, greed and profit always won out in any battle with the so-called tree huggers.

People like René did make a difference, though. Slow progress but progress nonetheless. Raoul admired the guy for his ideals and for his willingness to fight for those ideals.

"My DEA contacts weren't of much help," Remy said, "except that one of their snitches is supposed to meet with me this week. He might be able to help, especially if he can establish a connection between Gaudet and the oil crooks."

"I really appreciate everything you've all done for me. I mean, I'm overwhelmed."

"Hey, you're family," René proclaimed, and the others nodded.

Not really, Raoul thought, but it sure felt good. He turned back to Luc and tapped the folder in his hand. "So, what do we do with all this? Is it enough to reverse my conviction? Can we go to the D.A. now?"

"Just a little bit longer. I have a friend at one of the banks where Gaudet has a checking account. If we can get a paper trail on excessive deposits, that would clinch the case. There is one thing, though, Rusty."

"Yeah?"

Luc pulled out another folder and handed him a paper and pen. "You need to request an autopsy on your father's body."

"Oh, man!"

"I know how you feel, but we don't want any loose threads here. When we present the D.A. with our evidence, we've got to have covered all loose ends."

He nodded and signed the paper quickly. Just then, he looked up and noticed Charmaine standing in the archway of the living room. There was a stricken expression on her face just before she spun on her heels and bolted back toward the kitchen area.

He frowned, but then he decided she must be upset over the prospect of exhuming his father's body. Hell, it was distasteful to him, too.

"One more thing," Luc said and handed him yet another folder.

Lawyers and their folders!

This time Raoul got a bit of a jolt. Inside were the new divorce papers for him and Charmaine to sign.

"You want to sign this now?" Luc inquired, a mocking tone in his voice.

Raoul let out a loud exhale. "Give me the papers to look over. I'll send them back to you."

"Yeah, right," Luc said, clearly unconvinced.

René and Remy were smiling, as if they didn't believe he would sign them either.

It would be the best thing he could do for Charmaine, to sign the papers and let her start over. But not yet. Oddly, he liked being her husband, even if in name only.

For a little bit longer, anyhow. In the meantime, he excused himself. There was one thing he could do for her now.

He went to his office, where he placed twenty-five thousand dollars in bonds in an envelope he marked, "For Charmaine." Then he headed toward her bedroom, where he planned to leave the "surprise" on her bed.

But he was the one who was surprised.

Charmaine was there, and she looked like sweet temptation with a frilly skirt and a corset top that sucked in her abdomen and waist and pushed her breasts up and out. He didn't know if she was supposed to be a gypsy or a peasant girl or a happy hooker, and he didn't care. She'd obviously been crying.

"Honey, what's wrong?" He grabbed a couple of tissues from the box on the dresser and reached out for her.

She took the tissues but swatted his hands away.

Dabbing at the wetness and smeared mascara under her eyes, she told him, "It's just smoke burning my eyes. Someone needs to go out there and slow Tante Lulu down. She's practically got a bonfire going on the barbecue grill."

He narrowed his eyes suspiciously but accepted her story. "Here," he said, handing her the envelope. "This should make you feel better."

She peeked inside and tossed the envelope behind her on the bed. "What's that supposed to be? A divorce settlement?"

"Huh?"

"Did Luc give you the divorce papers?"

"Yeah, but—"

She waved a hand dismissively.

Oh, no! He must have given the papers to her, too. Did

she sign them? Without even talking it over with me? Dammit! "We need to talk, Charmaine."

"No, what we do not need to do anymore is talk. Everybody talks to me. Everybody tells me what I should do. Well, I'm sick up to here of talking." She sliced a hand dramatically across her neck.

"I haven't a clue what's going on here."

"You gave me the money. It's a done deal."

"What's a done deal? I've been worried about you. It's not safe for you back in Houma, or anywhere away from this ranch. Hell, not even on this ranch. Those Dixie Mafia thugs could show up at any time. This money will buy your safety."

Tears were welling in her eyes again and there sure as hell wasn't any smoke in this room . . . except for that steaming out of her nostrils. "Screw the money. Screw the Mafia. And screw you."

"Is that an invitation?" he tried to joke.

"I swear, you could be a prime exhibit in the Clueless Hall of Fame." *That's just what Luc said . . . except he mentioned the Dumb Man of the Year award. Same thing.* With that, she opened the door and stomped out, leaving him standing there, stunned and . . . well, clueless.

Luc just happened to walk by then, on the way to the bathroom. Spying him standing there in the open doorway like a dummy, he backtracked a couple of steps. "Was that my sister I just saw flying out of here breathing fire, or was it Gypsy Rose Charmaine?"

"I haven't a clue." And that was the truth.

"You didn't tell her that she's like a lizard camou-flaging herself, did you?"

"No! But I feel as if I was just hit by a two-by-four,

and I have no idea why. Guess I just don't understand women."

"Join the club," Luc said.

The pilgrims had nothing on the Cajuns . . .

Tante Lulu's Thanksgiving feast was a resounding success, to no one's surprise, least of all Charmaine, and they hadn't even started.

By four o'clock, everyone was scurrying about with platters or seated on chairs and improvised benches around the backyard—all seventeen of them—waiting for the food to be served.

"Now, wait a minute, everyone. First, we gots to say thanks," Tante Lulu announced after ringing a dinner bell to quiet everyone down. "Me, I'll go first. Thank you God fer this fine food and fer our family and friends joined here today. This year I'm 'specially thankful fer Rusty to be here with us, out of the slammer, and that Charmaine's got both her kneecaps. Yer next, Luc."

"Why do I always have to go first?" Sylvie pinched him, and he said, "Ouch!" Then, "I'm thankful this year that I have three healthy little girls and that I got snipped so now Sylvie and I can make lo . . . ouch!" Sylvie pinched him again, and he sat down, smiling innocently at her.

"I'm thankful this year that Luc has retained his sense of humor," Sylvie said, "despite his having been snipped." It was Luc's turn to pinch Sylvie, who sat down with a soft yelp.

"We better eat pretty soon, or the food will get cold," René griped. To which, Tante Lulu just frowned. And he contributed, "I'm thankful to be back in the bayou I love."

"Thass nice," Tante Lulu said, patting him on the back.

"I'm thankful to have gained a wife this year," Remy said, leaning down to buss Rachel on the lips.

"Hey, you stole what I was going to say," Rachel complained. "Oh, well, I'm thankful, too, for having found Remy this year."

"Found? Found? What? Like I was lying around like a log just waitin' to be tripped over?"

Rachel kissed him to shut him up, which everyone thought was a good idea.

Tee-John stood to speak, and Tante Lulu yelped, "Whass that you have on? And you, too, Jimmy O'Brien? Fer shame!"

"Oops!" Tee-John said, looking guiltily over to Jimmy, who sat next to him. Tee-John wore a T-shirt with the crawfish logo SHUCK ME, SUCK ME, EAT ME RAW! and Jimmy wore one, probably a gift from Tee-John from one of his Bourbon Street excursions, that read, PINCH ME, PEEL ME, EAT ME! Charmaine wasn't sure who was being the bad influence on whom in this picture.

"Tee-John," Tante Lulu cautioned.

He stood up again and blurted out, "I'm thankful it's Thanksgiving and Tante Lulu won't whomp me." He grinned mischievously at her.

Jimmy stood and said, "Me too."

After that, it was Fleur's turn. She and Dirk had finally emerged from their tin cave about an hour ago, beaming in the afterglow of their seemingly nonstop lovemaking. Fleur was dressed to the gills today in her version of a cowgirl outfit. It involved lots of fringe around a décolletage that defied gravity and tight, tight jeans. Charmaine had no idea how her mother was going to fit any food inside her body without all the seams giving way.

A little bit ago, Dirk had apparently tried to start Fleur on a jogging regimen, but she soon discovered that jogging caused perspiration, or glowing. Southern girls did not sweat, they glowed. That was apparently unacceptable to Fleur, who'd declared that Dirk must find her a cellulite-removing exercise that didn't cause glowing. *Geesh!*

Dirk made Charmaine a bit uncomfortable. When he wasn't holed up with her mother, he watched her intently all the time. And he hung around like a shadow at every opportunity. It wasn't as if he was interested in her, sexually. But he was interested, for some reason.

Now, Fleur stood before the assembled family and said, "I'm thankful to be with my little girl today." She looked over at Charmaine and smiled in the most needy way.

"I think I'm going to puke," Charmaine said under her breath.

"Don't be so hard on your mother," Rusty advised. He'd insisted on sitting next to her on the bench, way too close, and kept harping on wanting to talk to her.

Hah! "Don't preach to me, buster, not when you have so many unresolved issues with your own mother." *Besides, I'd rather not talk to you at all, you . . . you jerk! Don't come sniffing around me, you hound dog, not after you signed those divorce papers.*

"I don't have any unresolved—"

"Shut up!" *Before I cry.*

"Don't you think you're being a little unfair to me?"

Unfair? she shrieked silently. *Unfair is God putting temptation in my lap, then telling me not to touch because it is all over.* That was what she thought. What she said was, "Shut up before I hit you."

The fool grinned as if she'd said she would kiss him. *I didn't, did I?* Really, Charmaine couldn't wait till this whole feast was over so she could crawl into bed and cover her head with the sheets. She did not want to think about what she'd seen earlier. Rusty had been signing some papers when she'd walked into the living room. Divorce papers, she was sure. Especially when he'd capped it off by giving her all that money.

Rusty elbowed her. "You're daydreamin', darlin'."

She was going to say something vulgar to him, but stopped herself when she figured he would probably take it as a compliment and continue with that silly grinning.

Dirk the Jerk, dressed to the nines—*not!*—in a white wife beater T-shirt and black jogging shorts, had the nerve to say, "I'm thankful for all the women in the world with cellulite so that my business is booming this year."

His words were met with communal boos and hisses from all the ladies and laughter from the men.

Clarence was thankful for his home at the Triple L and the good honest work provided there.

Linc glanced over at his brother, then at Tante Lulu. In a choked voice, he said, "I am thankful this year to have been given back a piece of my past."

Charmaine stood, without prompting, knowing she couldn't escape. "I'm thankful, too, that I still have my kneecaps. And I'm thankful to have such a warm, though often irritating, family. That's all." She plopped down with a huge sigh.

Rusty stood and cleared his throat. She knew how hard this kind of thing was for him, but, really, he was the host of this shindig, even if Tante Lulu had engineered it all.

"I'm thankful that you are all here today, sharing our food and goodwill. And this year I'm especially thankful for . . ." He paused, looked down at her as if unsure whether he should say what he was about to say, then shrugged his shoulders in a "What the hell!" manner and concluded, ". . . Charmaine."

Thunderous applause greeted his statement as everyone hooted and cheered and food started to circulate around the tables.

Charmaine stared at him, and said, "Fool!"

He waggled his eyebrows at her.

And, God help her, her crazy heart did flip-flops.

Okay, that's it. That's my cue. No more Mr. Nice Guy . . . rather, no more Ms. Nice Girl. Time for the old Charmaine to take control.

"Why are you looking at me like that?" the Jerk-of-the-Month asked. Mr. I-can-divorce-you-twice without even blinking.

"Like what?" she inquired, giving him her ultra-innocent, eyelash-batting look, the one that had won her Miss Personality in the beauty pageant.

"Like your brain is churning with plans."

She smiled then. "Oh, yeah, baby, I've got plans."

He laughed. "Should I be scared?"

"Guar-an-teed!"

A man's gotta do what man's gotta do . . .

Raoul had plans. Big plans.

Sometime between his confrontation with a tearful Charmaine in her bedroom and the plethora of thanks by practically everyone in the universe at the feast, he had decided to take back control of his life. His wife had been holding the reins thus far with her "I am a born-again virgin" crap. Enough! He was the man. He was driving this wagon from now on. And no artificial hymen was going to barricade the road.

Unfortunately, her family wasn't cooperating.

By six o'clock, the Thanksgiving party was still going strong, and people were talking about the musical entertainment about to begin. *Holy stinkin' cow patties! A regular Roman orgy of a food feast they'd just had! Talk till their tongues got tired! Now music! What next? The chicken dance? The Hokey Pokey? The River Dancers flown in to raise some dust? Why not truck in some Angola prisoners for an impromptu rodeo?*

He looked around the backyard of his beloved ranch and relished the sweetness of having a home . . . no, this particular home. The ranch house might be in disrepair, but the setting was spectacular, in his opinion. There was the prairie, which was characteristic of this region of Louisiana, but there was a slow-meandering bayou, as well, with all its myriad birds and wildlife, even the occasional gator. It was not a lush, tropical paradise dotted with swamps, like Bayou Black, where most of the LeDeuxs lived, but it was marshy in spots, which didn't seem to bother the steers.

And look there at that small raft of water hyacinths floating by. As beautiful as the lavender flowers were, they were the bane of all bayous in Louisiana. It had all started in the most innocent way at the 1884 International Cotton Exposition of New Orleans. Japanese exhibitors handed out samples of a flowering aquatic plant native to Latin America. Unfortunately one single plant could producing sixty-five thousand plants in a single season and thus had posed a problem for Louisiana ever since by clogging waterways and cutting off sunlight necessary to aquatic life. They were almost impossible to control.

He had to laugh when he saw René, ever the environmentalist, walk over with a rake and use the handle to lift the pesty plant mass out of the water. With a scowl of distaste, he carried it over to a nearby burn barrel.

As Raoul continued to scan his homestead, he began to wonder, belatedly, about all the electric Christmas lights that had been strung in the trees. Could it be possible . . . oh, *Mon Dieu* . . . they were going to be hanging around till it was dark! At this rate, the gang would be here not just when the cows came home, but when the cows went out again at dawn.

Raoul was, frankly, all partied out. It was past time for him to act a man and stop letting Charmaine run this show that had become their private life. Days ago, he'd made a silent decision about his relationship with Charmaine, without even realizing it. The capper had been Tante Lulu's revelation about Charmaine's other husbands, and then his shock and dismay when Luc had handed him the divorce papers, papers he knew he would not sign. Not unless Charmaine insisted he do so.

So, now he had plans—big plans—for another kind of party. A private one. And he wished everyone would just go home.

He yawned loudly.

He shuffled his feet.

He kept looking at his watch.

Did anyone take a hint?

Nope. Not one single person was budging. Not one single person said, "Well, I guess we better get going." Not one single person said, "I didn't realize how late it was. Gotta hit the road." In fact, Tante Lulu came up and said, "Bide yer time, boy. There's plenty of time fer hanky-panky."

Oh, shit! Was I that obvious? "Was I that obvious?"

"Nah! I jist have a sense fer these things. And stop worryin' so. Worryin' never made the gumbo boil, and it ain't gonna make the day go faster. Now prayin', thass another matter entirely. Doan never hurt to pray."

"Have you been reading my mind?"

She jiggled her eyebrows at him, then turned more serious. "Me, I have one regret today. That I dint get yer mother here."

His brain practically exploded at that suggestion. He counted to three to prevent himself from yelling at the meddling broad. "You didn't call my mother . . . please tell me that you didn't call my mother." What would be worse to Raoul than his mother showing up in his present mood would be his mother not showing up after having been invited.

"I dint, but I shoulda. Oh, doan get yer feathers all ruffled. I knows how angry you are right now, but she's still yer mama, and you should make it up."

"If and when I *make it up* with my mother, it should be my decision," he asserted.

But the old bat was already floating off to interfere in someone else's business. Raoul decided to "float off," too. He had much to do before his personal party, like end-of-the-day ranch work, and he wasn't sticking around for all the niceties of excusing himself.

Before he left, though, Tee-John and Jimmy came up beside him. They caught him in the act of getting one last ogle in at Charmaine in her sexy gypsy outfit. He was speculating idly what she wore under that take-no-prisoners corset blouse. Probably nothing. And how about below?

"We have some advice for you," Jimmy said.

Uh-oh! "What kind of advice?"

"Chick advice," Tee-John said.

Double that uh-oh. "Can I assume that you mean male-female-type advice? If so, forget about it. If I didn't listen to old codger advice from Clarence, I'm not about to listen to two wet-behind-the-ears, snot-nosed kids whose only knowledge of women comes from *Playboy* and clueless movies."

"I'm not snot-nosed," Jimmy said.

"You'd be surprised what I know," Tee-John said. "Anyhow, this is what Jimmy and I wanted to tell you to do . . . if you want to win Charmaine back."

"Who says I want to win Charmaine back?" *Do cows crap? Do bulls fornicate?*

"Are you kiddin'? Ever heard of 'hot tongueing?' You look at Charmaine like she's an ice-cream cone and—"

"I get the picture," he interrupted. *Man, I am one pathetic SOB, if teenagers can tell what I'm thinking.*

"You gotta treat Charmaine like a crawfish," Jimmy hinted, winking at him in the most ridiculous fashion.

"Yeah, a crawfish," Tee-John added, with a wide, mischievous grin.

"And that's your great advice? Crawfish? I have important business to take care of, and . . ." He let his words trail off as he noticed the two of them standing with hands on hips, chests thrust out, and smirks on their faces. They looked down at the vulgar sayings on their shirts, then at Charmaine, then at him, and smirked some more.

Good thing the two of them darted away then,

laughing their fool heads off. If he'd been able to reach them, he would have thrown the dirty-minded duo in the horse trough.

Raoul left then, discreetly, telling Clarence and Linc that he didn't need their help. When he returned two hours later, he discovered, to his horror, that the band was revving up for its third musical set . . . if you could call René on the accordion, Linc on the guitar, and Clarence on the harmonica a band. Charmaine had apparently been chiming in occasionally as the singer with a sexy-as-sin voice that could melt the brass off a doorknob, or turn some knobby body parts to brass.

I wonder how many of those watermelon margaritas she's downed.

I wonder if I should chug down one or two . . . or ten myself.

Nope, I need a clear head for my big plan . . . big being the operative word.

No one had even noticed his absence. That wasn't quite true. Charmaine had her head tilted to the side in question, but maybe it was just the effect of the margaritas. She was on the dance floor—the open area of the backyard where the tables had been pushed back—and she was dancing alone. Well, not quite alone. Luc and Sylvie's three little girls were dancing around her, all of them moving to the music in a way that caused their skirts to twirl about. Each time Charmaine twirled, a little more of her bare calves were exposed.

Man oh man, I really like to run my hands over those calves. The skin is so soft. Charmaine has really nice calves, trim and muscle toned. Her ankles aren't too shabby either, and her thighs, and . . .

The girls looked up at her adoringly as she taught them

some silly dance steps that involved shifting from foot to foot and moving their hands and shoulders in a swaying motion.

It was seductive as hell coming from Charmaine, and he didn't need much seducing at this point.

Luc and Sylvie, Remy and Rachel, Dirk and Fleur, Tee-John and Tante Lulu were out there dancing, too, to "Cochan du Lait." A semifast Cajun two-step that involved some fancy footwork and swinging of the women under the men's arms. They were all smiling at each other and laughing and having a grand ol' time. *Family*, he realized in that instant. This was how real families behaved when they were together. An experience he'd never known he'd missed . . . till that very moment.

He tried to remember any Thanksgiving celebration in his past. There had been some, but nothing like this. Plain turkey dinners with his dad and Clarence and Clarence's late wife were the closest he could recall, but they had been preceded and followed by ranch work. No daylong hoopla. No family joy.

Next the "band" began to play that raucous "Knock, Knock, Knock," which had an even more upbeat tempo. The kids didn't understand the lyrics about a Cajun fellow in the doghouse with his wife again, but they loved the bouncing about and yelling out the refrain "Knock, Knock, Knock" at René's urging to the group.

Tante Lulu, bless her heart, was having the most fun of all. She kept one hand on her blond wig as she whirled about and another hand on the waistband of her black slacks, which kept slipping down over her nonexistent butt as she shimmied and danced.

After that, the "band" segued into "Louisiana, the Key to My Soul," a much slower ballad, which Raoul took as his cue, especially when René looked his way and nodded. With a deep inhale for courage, Raoul walked up to Charmaine, held out his arms, and said, *"Chère?"*

She hesitated, that odd hurt look back in her eyes. It was the same stricken expression he'd seen earlier in her bedroom when she'd tossed his money aside. He didn't yet understand what that had all meant.

Raoul's heart stood still at her hesitation, but then she stepped into his arms, and he let loose the breath he'd been holding. She looped her arms around his shoulders and rested her face in the crook of his neck. He twined his hands together behind her waist and tugged her closer. Her hair was a cloud of black silk teasing his senses. He fancied that her filmy dress twined itself about his jeans and that she pressed herself even closer to him, breast to chest, belly to belly, groin to groin. Probably wishful thinking, but what the hell! He also felt enveloped by her perfume, Obsession, which she must have sprayed on her hair and neck.

Dancing with Charmaine was a trip to the past. A form of foreplay. An exercise in wonderful torture. Raoul was confident in his dancing abilities. He was no expert, but he was Cajun, and Cajun men were born with a rhythm gene that the rest of the male population hadn't discovered yet. And they didn't mind admitting that they loved to dance.

They said nothing to each other, but their bodies spoke volumes. As he swayed and dipped her luscious body, he told her how much he had missed her. As she followed his lead, adding some moves of her own, Charmaine told him that she'd missed him, too. Lots.

By the time the song ended, Raoul realized that his hands had moved of their own volition and were caressing her back and shoulders and waist and hips. And Charmaine wasn't a sweet innocent in this dance-lovemaking. Subtly she rubbed her breasts against his denim shirt and undulated her hips against his burgeoning erection. He doubted she even realized what she was doing. She was as lost as he was·in this prelude to love-making.

René and his happy musicmakers moved without pause from one slow ballad to another, in this case "Jolé Blon." Halfway through the song, Raoul drew his head back so he could look down at Charmaine. Her closed eyes drifted open as she gazed up at him in question.

He kissed her then, in front of everyone. He couldn't help himself. It was a deep kiss but gentle, nothing that would embarrass him or Charmaine in front of all her relatives. She tasted of watermelon and lipstick and Charmaine. A potent combination. They continued to sway from side to side in a pretense of dancing as they kissed, and, yes, Charmaine was kissing him back. *Thank you, God!*

This time, it was Charmaine who pulled back. "Rusty?" she questioned. "What is this about? From one minute to the next, you keep changing your tune. You want me here, you want me gone. You say you care about me, then you treat my opinions like bimbo drivel. You act as if you want to make love with me, but you keep pushing me away. Then you top it all off by saying that you are thankful for me. *Me!*"

"Let's get one thing straight. There has never been a time when I haven't wanted to make love with you."

"Sex," she said sadly, though not really in a condemning way.

"More than that, honey. Way more than that."

"How about the papers you . . ." She stopped herself.

"What papers?"

"Never mind," she said, shaking her head vehemently. "That is one subject I do not want to discuss tonight." She inhaled and exhaled several times as if to gather courage. "Time to put up or shut up, cowboy."

"Huh?"

"Let's go," she said, stopping in the midst of their dancing. People continued to dip and sway around them.

"Huh?" he said again. This was a shocker. "Let's go" was supposed to be his line. He was the one who had planned to seduce Charmaine tonight, to abduct her if necessary. "Go where? Oh, you can't think I'm going into the house and make love with you . . . with all these people out here? That would be worse than your mother and Dirk in the wicked Winnebago."

She shook her head. "No. Someplace else."

He was about to question her more, but stopped himself. "We need to talk about this." This put a whole new twist on his big plan. Should he insist on going through with his original plan, or fall in with hers? Assuming she had a plan and wasn't just pulling his chain.

"We definitely do not need to talk anymore. Talk is what gets us in trouble . . . me, anyway." She took his hand and tugged.

He, dumb slob that he was, dug in his heels.

The expression on her face wavered between "I want him bad" to "This is a bad idea" to "Make up your mind, big boy."

His hesitation caused her to call him a foul name that surprised him, even coming from Charmaine. But then, she did the most surprising thing of all.

She pulled out her small pistol from a pocket in her skirt and aimed it straight at his wildly beating heart.

"You're coming with me," she informed him. "No more games. No more hesitating."

"But—"

"No buts either."

He hadn't been about to argue with her. He'd been going to tell her that force was not necessary with him . . . that he was more than willing. "Put the gun down, baby. Is it loaded?" At the narrowing of her eyes, he suspected that it was. *Damn, she is acting crazier than usual.* "Put the pistol down. I'll come with you."

"I'm not taking any chances. Turn around and start walking toward your Jeep out front."

"Everybody is looking at us," he said in a suffocated whisper.

"So what?" She pressed the weapon into his back, prodding him forward.

No one rushed forward to help him . . . not that he really needed help, but Charmaine might slip and his butt would be history. Behind him, the whole LeDeux clan and their guests hooted and laughed their encouragement at his "kidnapping" by his wife.

"Way to go, Charmaine!" Luc yelled. "Ouch! Why'd you jab me with your elbow, Sylvie?"

"Make him beg, Charmaine," Rachel offered. "Ouch! Why'd you jab me with your elbow, Remy?"

"Doan you mess this one up, Rusty," Tante Lulu advised.

"Crawfish! Think crawfish!" Tee-John and Jimmy shouted at the same time.

René had the "band" start playing another song while

he belted out, "Love is better . . . the second time around . . ."

"Bowlegged, boy! Bowlegged," Clarence called out.

Raoul knew they were all laughing at them, in the kindest way, but it was humiliating. He should have been the one in charge. As usual, Charmaine had surprised them all.

On second thought, I don't freakin' care. Charmaine is going to be in my arms tonight, come hell or high water or pistols. The night is young. And I am so hot and bothered I can't see straight.

The first day of the rest of their lives was about to begin, albeit in a most bizarre fashion.

He hoped.

And bizarre could be good.

He hoped.

Chapter 16

The bed does WHAT?

Charmaine, still barefooted, forced Rusty to drive them down the road a bit to the nearest motel, a place called The Lucky Duck.

The motel looked reasonably clean to her, from the outside, which was all that mattered for what she had in mind. But she should have been alerted by the neon sign out front in the form of Daisy Duck in a thong bikini with blinking breasts and by the desk clerk who asked if she wanted the hourly or nightly rate, neither of which were cheap. Of course, Rusty's barely suppressed laughter should have been a clue, too.

"Holy shit!" he said as he entered the room first with her pressing a pistol in his back. It was only when he stepped aside that she got her first view of the "Duck Pen," as their room was called. Other rooms were called "Quack, Quack," "Feather That," "Waddle Room," "I Like Mud," and "Beak Me."

Her response was, "Holy catfish!"

She took one look at the circular platform bed with the mirror on the ceiling, the picture on the wall of a naked couple cavorting on a swing, and the locked glass case sporting what had to be X-rated toys, then bolted for the still-open door. Rusty jumped in front of her and slammed the door shut, barring her escape.

"Let me go," she said, tears of frustration welling in her eyes. Why did things always seem to go wrong for her? Even when she tried to be high-class—*though kidnapping a man didn't qualify*—she ended up in low class situations. As far as dumb went, this ranked right up there with loan sharks. No wonder people called her a dumb bimbo. "Let me go," she repeated.

"Not a chance," he said. The grin on his face merited at least a punch in the stomach.

He didn't even flinch.

"You knew what this place was, didn't you?"

"I suspected." He still grinned.

The louse! "And you didn't tell me?"

"Why would I do that?" *Grin, grin, grin!*

"You've been here before?" she accused him.

"Never, but Clarence told me about it. He got Daffy's Den one time."

Charmaine did not want to think of Clarence in a porno motel. Or who the ducklet was that he'd brought here. On the other hand, he might have been with his wife, she supposed.

Rusty took the pistol out of her hand and laid it gently on a nearby dresser. "Dare I hope that thing is unloaded?"

"Of course it's unloaded. I'm not that much of an idiot." She narrowed her eyes at him then. "You knew it was unloaded . . . and came anyway?"

"I'm no fool." He wasn't grinning anymore. He was dead serious.

Can anyone be more embarrassed than me? I've been roped, tied, and hornswoggled, without even knowing it.

"I guess I'm the fool then. You were just playing a game with me."

"The only game I have in mind hasn't begun to play out, darlin'." He put a hand to the front of her blouse and tugged on the laces. The bow came undone. "I've wanted to do that all day," he murmured.

She tilted her head in question.

"Hey, if you hadn't acted so quickly, you would have found out that *I* had a plan to kidnap you tonight. Take you to an old lineman's shed and . . ." He let his words trail off with a sheepish shrug.

Don't tell me. I made a fool of myself for nothing. "And?"

"Seduce you into agreeing to having sex with me."

"That was your plan?" *Sounds like a plan to me.*

"Well, toss a few candles and wine in, and that's about it."

She flashed him a look of disgust. But what she really thought was, *How sweet!*

"Give me a break, honey. I didn't have much time. It was a spur-of-the-moment idea. Not making love with you—that wasn't spur of the moment. I've been thinking about that for a long time. How about you? You put a lot more planning into this?" he asked, indicating the Austin Powers type bachelor pad with a wave of his hand.

Oh, yeah! Downtown Charmaine chose even lower-down digs for her seduction. Not! "No, I didn't do much planning. Obviously. My only goal was to get away from the ranch and all those people and . . ." Like Rusty, she let her words trail off.

"And?" he inquired huskily. While she'd been watching his face, he'd been busy. Somehow the laces had come undone from her blouse, which was gaping apart now, half exposing her breasts. Her only saving grace was the hungry look on his face as he stared at her *there*. But then he raised his head and asked her again, "And?"

With a loud exhale of surrender, she admitted, ". . . and seduce you into having sex with me."

He thought a moment, then beamed at her.

"It's not funny."

"Who's laughing? I'm just happy."

"Well, I'm not happy. What a place to have reunion sex!"

"Reunion sex? We're going to have reunion sex? Holy freakin' hell!" He was smiling softly at her and beginning to ease her blouse down to her waist. The smile left his face as he stared, avidly, at her bare upper half. "You are so beautiful."

Rusty had always liked her breasts. They were among her best assets, she had to admit. But he was too far ahead of her in this love play. "Tsk-tsk-tsk!" she said. "Really, Rusty, what a place to lose my second virginity! We should go to that lineman's shed."

"Uh-uh! I've got you half-naked, which is more than I've accomplished in ten years, except for that night of almost-sex, which hardly counts. I am not leaving this room till you're bowlegged . . . till we're both bow-legged. No way am I risking your changing your mind." He reached out for her, but she ducked under his arms.

"I need to think," she said, backing up a step.

"Don't you dare start thinking." He followed after her. "You and I need to stop thinking and stop talking and start acting with—"

"Our body parts?" She wasn't really mad at him for thinking that. After all, this was to be their last hurrah.

He'd already signed the divorce papers. She'd decided that if they were going to be separated for good this time, she deserved one last fling with him. Forget forever. She was going to make this the best one-night fling in history.

"With our hearts, baby. With our hearts."

Oh, my God! I can't believe he said that. He is good!
"Good answer! Real smooth."

"I've been practicing smooth." His words were teasing, but the expression on his face was serious.

Really good! She let him take her in his arms. She even let him push her down onto the bed and fall on top of her.

The earth moved for both of them then.

Or was it the vibrating bed?

Shagadelic, for sure!

Raoul was lying flat out on the bed with Charmaine beside him. They were both staring up into the ceiling mirror, vibrating their asses off. They were laughing their asses off, as well.

Does she have any idea how tempting she looks? Barefooted and bare-breasted, she wore only the gauzy, flowered skirt. Her breasts were magnificent, large and firm. Like inverted champagne glasses, they were, with their puffy areolas. Her feet were pretty, too, long and narrow, with painted red toenails. Her dark hair lay in curly disarray on the pillow. Her eyes were misty with tears of mirth. Her red lips parted, displaying even, white teeth as she laughed.

He, on the other hand, was fully clothed, including his

boots. But he wasn't taking a chance of leaving the bed, in case Charmaine decided he was a dumb dolt after all, that any juice he had wasn't worth the squeeze.

I want her so bad, but I have got to tread carefully here. No mistakes. The least little wrong move, and she will bolt like a wild horse. He rolled over on his side and looked down at her. Charmaine stared up at him, wide-eyed. Her lips were still parted, but in a different way now. In anticipation. *I hope.* "I'm scared," he told her.

That surprised her, he could tell. "Why?"

"I'm afraid I'll say the wrong thing. Or do something to make you run." *It's a curse all men have. Dumb man tongue.*

"Bolt? Like I did before? No, I'm not going anywhere this time. Unless you say the B-word."

"Bimbo" is hereafter wiped from my dictionary. He laughed. "I won't. You can be sure of that."

She reached up and began to tug his T-shirt out of his jeans. He helped and tossed it back over his shoulder. He had no idea where it landed and didn't care. Charmaine was looking at him as if she liked what she saw and for the first time in a long time he was glad of the hard work at the ranch, and on the prison farm, which had honed his body down to almost zero fat and one hundred percent muscle.

Never shy, inside or outside of bed, she put her hands up to his neck and pulled him down. Then she rubbed her breasts back and forth across his chest hairs, the whole time making little kittenish mewls of pleasure.

He could feel the points abrading his skin and saw stars for a moment behind his closed lids. "Jesus, Mary, and Joseph!" he exclaimed. "You take my breath away, babe."

She smiled that secretive Madonna smile of hers. "That's my goal, baby."

He settled his lips on hers and inhaled deeply, relishing the scent of her. Obsession perfume and Charmaine skin. She moved her mouth beneath his and darted out her tongue to lick his lips.

His cock about jumped out from behind the zipper of his Wranglers. He was pretty sure it was singing, "Hallelujah!"

"Mmmmmmm," she said.

"Mmmmmmm," he said back.

He was going to have to slow down somehow. But he couldn't stop the runaway train that was his libido. Not now. Not ever, where Charmaine was concerned.

"Kiss me some more," she urged.

Like I need any urging! "My pleasure," he murmured and rubbed his lips across hers till he got the perfect fit. He opened her wider and plunged his tongue inside. *Sweet. So . . . very . . . sweet!* He withdrew, then plunged again. This time, she sucked on him, locking him in place.

He heard a low humming sound of pleasure in her throat. *Or is it my throat? Or is it this frickin' vibrating bed?*

Meanwhile, her hands were busy, caressing his shoulders, sweeping over his back, cupping his buttocks. Somehow, he had come to be resting between her spread thighs, and the best part of him was planted against the best part of her. Well, not necessarily the best part of him, but the part that was growing to monumental proportions and throbbing to beat the band. He hoped she was throbbing, too. He suspected she was by the way her lower body kept jerking against him.

He drew back, despite her hands, which urged him back. Her lips were already kiss-swollen and her eyes glazed over with passion. He probably looked the same.

Moving lower to territory he loved, he gazed at her breasts for a moment, then examined the familiar terrain with his fingertips. Shaping her. Tracing her. Flicking her. Even pinching her. All accented by her moans of encouragement. Finally, he put his mouth to one pink nipple and took her, areola and all, sucking deeply. He felt the tip against the roof of his mouth. He wished he could swallow all of her.

She bucked against him and murmured, "Too much, too much. Wait. Stop. Oh, no, don't stop. Oh. Oh."

Then he suckled her other breast.

By then, she was flailing futilely from side to side, trying to escape his ministrations, but digging her fingernails into his shoulders at the same time.

Faster than a Cajun could peel a crawfish, he removed her skirt and panties. Then he rolled off her and directed in a voice he barely recognized for its huskiness, "Look in the mirror, sweetheart, and see what I see."

Her arms rested loosely above her head on the pillow. Her full lips moved and made small panting noises. Her nipples and breasts were engorged from his ministrations. Her legs were spread slightly in invitation. Her belly button ring gleamed in the soft light.

"Oh, my," she said.

That about said it all.

"Don't move," he ordered and stood, quickly toeing off his boots, then shucking his jeans and briefs. He stood before her for a moment, wanting her to see just how much he desired her. His cock was rock hard and bigger than it had ever been, blue veins standing out in urgency. A blue steeler, for sure.

"Oh, my," she said again and smiled.

He smiled, too, and moved on top of her. Putting his hands under her butt cheeks, he raised her slightly and used his knees to spread her thighs. Taking his cock in hand, he placed himself at her entrance, then looked up at her. "I love you, Charmaine."

"Ooooh, don't say that."

Damn, damn, damn. I picked the wrong time to spill my guts.

"You'll spoil it," she groaned.

He groaned, too. And his cock would have groaned, too, if it could. *Dumb man tongue, for sure.*

"I know you signed the papers today. I know it will be over after today. Don't pretend."

Huh? "What papers?" he asked, recalling she'd mentioned papers before. *I can't believe we are having a conversation when my brain and other body parts are about to explode.*

"The divorce papers."

"Huh?" he said aloud this time, and frowned. "I never signed any divorce papers. Those were autopsy permission forms."

It took only a second for his words to sink in. "Really?"

"Really. You thought I signed divorce papers?"

She nodded, tears in her eyes.

He said the only thing he could think of at the moment. "I love you, Charmaine." *I hope my timing is better this time.*

And she smiled.

Unable to wait any longer, he thrust into her hot, spasming sheath, which was surprisingly tight for a born-again virgin. When she said, "Oh, Raaa-oooul," he knew by the use of his given name that the timing had been just right. After that, he wanted to tell her how good she was, how great it felt with her vaginal muscles clasping and unclasping him in welcome, but he couldn't speak above a whimper.

Charmaine did her orgasms the way she did everything in life. With gusto. She arched her hips off the bed, moving his much larger body with her, propelled by the strength of a massive adrenaline rush. She dug her nails into his butt till she drew blood. And she screamed out, "Raaa—oooul!"

Ya gotta love a girl who could stun a guy mid-come, Raoul concluded. Ya gotta love a girl who could make a man believe in multiple orgasms . . . *for men*! You gotta love a girl who isn't afraid to be insatiable.

Ya gotta love Charmaine.

And that was the last thought Raoul had before a mind-blowing explosion that seemed to impress the hell out of Charmaine. It sure impressed him.

Easy Rider . . .

Charmaine was flat on her back on the circular bed, which was still vibrating. She stared up at herself in the ceiling mirror and had to admit, *I look hot!*

Really, she was the *Penthouse* version of "Woman Satisfied." Every man's fantasy. Heck, it was every woman's fantasy, too, to be wiped out this way by man.

Raoul slept beside her, wiped out as well. She gave herself a mental slap on the back for achieving that feat.

And, yes, she was thinking of him as Raoul, not Rusty, again.

He said he loved me. Forever? Or is this just a fling? Will he listen to my ideas for the ranch now? Or go on as usual? Stop it, Charmaine. You've been given a gift. Stop asking for more. Take it one day at a time.

When she glanced up at the mirror again, she did a double take because Raoul was staring upward, too. And it wasn't just his eyes that were upward.

She smiled at the mirror.

He smiled, too.

"I'd like to have a picture of us like this."

"Me too. Actually, someone's probably taking our picture from a peephole somewhere."

She shrieked and tried to duck under the sheet at the bottom of the bed, but he laughed and pulled her back. "I was just kidding."

He settled her so that she lay half-on, half-off his body. Leaning down, he pressed a quick kiss on her lips. "Thank you, *chère*."

"For what?"

"For the most spectacular sex of my life. For giving me your virginity . . . again."

She slapped him playfully on the chest for his teasing. "It *was* spectacular, wasn't it?"

"*Mais oui*, sugar."

"Say it again."

He knew without asking. "I love you."

Tears filled her eyes and she told him, "You know, you could get almost anything from me with those three words."

"Something to keep in mind." His eyes twinkled mischievously.

She slapped him playfully again.

"You say it," he demanded then.

She knew it wasn't those three little words he was looking for, at least at this moment. She twirled his chest hairs with a forefinger, then gave him what he wanted in a sex-laden croon: "Raaa-oooul."

He smiled, and his already half-erect penis stood up, ready to boogie.

"Like that, do you?"

"Are you speaking to me? Or Longfellow?"

"Both." She laughed. "You still use that ridiculous name for *it*?"

"*It* likes that name."

"So, cowboy . . . ?" she drawled out.

His eyes went wide with suspicion at her tone.

"Remember when I suggested a dude ranch to you and you told me I know diddly-squat about a ranch?" She swung her leg over his hips and straddled him.

She could tell that his attention was divided between her question and her position atop his family jewels. "Oh, no! You're not going to pick a fight with me *now*, are you?"

"Nope. I just wanted you to know that this cowgirl knows more about ranching than you think I do."

"Oh?" He was clearly interested now, his eyes going from her breasts to the part of her body pressing him down.

"For example, I know how to ride," she boasted, lifting herself up, then onto him.

His eyes appeared as if they were rolling back in his head for a second, which she took as a good sign. In truth, the way Raoul filled her, stretching her inner folds . . .

well, the whites of her eyes might very well be showing, too.

He put his hands on her waist and adjusted her better, then said, "Prove it."

"Them's fightin' words for a Cajun gal."

"Prove it."

And she did. *Giddiup. And then some.*

Feathering her nest . . .

Who knew there were that many ways of making love? Well, he'd known but never experienced the whole she-bang all in one night.

It all started when he was awakened from a sound sleep. Okay, he had been knocked unconscious by two drain-your-brain-of-blood orgasms, thanks to Charmaine, bless her heart. He'd been dead to the world, probably snoring, when he'd sensed his dick getting wet . . . and hot. He recalled seeing an episode of ER one time where some cuckoo bird had decided to dip his wick in hot oil to see how it felt. Ouch! But this was different. Not blistering hot. More like warm . . . blistering only in the sexual sense.

He opened his eyes slowly to the most amazing sight. Charmaine drizzling oil from a small bottle, which she'd obviously purchased from the X-rated toy case, onto his Longfellow. Then blowing on it.

He raised himself on his elbows and asked in a choked voice, "What *are* you doing?"

"It's hot oil. Well, it's not hot oil when you put it on, but it gets hot when you blow on it. Are you hot yet?"

He smiled. "Oh, yeah." *Talk about a blow job!*

After that, he used the remainder of the oil to heat her up. She especially liked it when he spread her wide and dripped the oil onto that little bud between her legs, which was getting bigger. Especially when he gave her a little tongue action to accompany the blowing.

Of course, they had to wash off all the oil in the super-size shower stall in the bathroom. He showed Charmaine how to have sex standing up with her arms braced on the tiles above her head and him coming in from behind. Both of their knees collapsed on them, and they landed on the floor, laughing. He figured, *While we're down here, what the hell!* So, they ended up having doggie sex on the floor of the stall with water pelting them all around. Charmaine didn't seem to mind. *What a gal!*

They both slept for a while then. But he awakened about two hours later, surprised to see by the bedside clock that it was only 2:00 A.M. What's a guy to do at 2:00 A.M. in a porno motel when his woman is fast asleep? Check out the toys, of course.

Raoul couldn't decide between the vibrating lips, the velvet handcuffs, or the condoms with little prickles all over them. He settled on the shrink-wrapped gift box of feathers. The directions said: "Use your imagination."

Okaaay!

Imagine that! . . .

Charmaine was awakened by the sound of chuckling. Male chuckling.

Lying on her back, flat as fritter, she cracked open one eyelid to see Raoul kneeling on the bed beside her examining a plastic case. And chuckling.

"What's up, cowboy?" she inquired.

He glanced down at his penis and said, "Nothing. Yet."

"Uh-oh!"

"Is that uh-oh good, or uh-oh I've had enough of this cowboy?"

"Never enough."

He smiled. And what a smile. It was one of those crinkle-the-eyes, dimple-the-edge-of-lips smiles. One of his specialties, though he probably didn't know that.

"What's that?" she asked, looking pointedly at the plastic case he was now opening.

"Feathers," he said. "The only directions say, 'Be creative.' What do you think?"

"I think you should be creative." She half sat up in bed with her head propped on two pillows. And waited.

First, he took out a hard-bristled feather, like that of a chicken or duck. Brushing it lightly around her lips, he raised his eyebrows in question.

"Nice," she said. Most people didn't realize how sensitive lips were to mere touch. Charmaine knew because every time she outlined her lips with her trusty lip brush she got a little mini-thrill. *Hey, when you're a born-again virgin, you get your thrills any way you can.* "Let me," she said, then used the same brush to outline his lips.

"Very nice," he agreed. His penis liked it, too, although she hadn't ventured anywhere near its territory.

Next he took out a feather with long hairs, like a hundred silky threads. He brushed her body from shoulders to toes, over and over again, giving special attention to her breasts and groin.

She reciprocated, but since he was still kneeling, went only from shoulders to knees, over and over, with special floaty strokes over his Longfellow, which was becoming quite a long fellow *again*.

Raoul was breathing heavily in the quiet room when he took out a small three-pronged feather thingee, which was apparently battery-operated. When he vibrated it across one nipple, then the other, she about shot up off the bed. "Holy moley," best summed it up for her.

When she used the same thingee on the tip of his erection, he stuttered out, "Holy . . . holy . . ." grabbed the apparatus, and tossed it over his shoulder. The case with the remaining feathers fell to the floor, obviously destined for another day, as Raoul fell on her, spread her thighs and entered her in one fell swoop.

Once she finished one bout of spasming, he settled himself deep inside her and said, "I love you, *chère*."

"I love you, too," she said, caressing his face gently. Then, she added with what she hoped was a chuckle, "Prove it."

He proceeded to with slow, excruciatingly pleasurable strokes. Filling her. Then almost pulling out totally. Filling her. Then almost pulling out totally. Repeatedly. Forever.

Charmaine once had a client, a sex therapist, who claimed that in the average sexual encounter the man thrusts 125 times. She'd believed then that the woman had been pulling her leg.

Now, she believed she'd been telling the truth.

In the end, she screamed and raised her hips high, forcing him to go faster. "Harder," she demanded.

"Like that?"

"Faster . . . dammit . . . faster!"

He laughed, a raw masculine sound of satisfaction. "Like that?"

She couldn't speak, so intense was the grasping and ungrasping of her inner folds around him.

He couldn't speak then, either.

Except in the end when they both gasped out, "I . . . love . . . you!"

Chapter 17

Then the cow you-know-what hit the fan.

"I didn't know the sun rose this early," Charmaine said with a wide yawn.

Raoul was driving them back to the ranch, relishing the feel of her fingers laced with his . . . an oddly innocent and yet appropriate end to their wild night. He hadn't wanted to leave their love nest, corny as it had been. It was only four-thirty, but he needed to be back at the ranch when work started for the day. There was too much for Clarence and Linc to handle on their own, even with Jimmy's help, after yesterday's holiday.

But what was that about sunrise? He looked over to the horizon where Charmaine pointed. Then did a double take.

"That's not the sun. It's a fire. And it appears to be at the Triple L," he said, trying unsuccessfully to control the panic in his voice. He pressed the accelerator to the floor.

Charmaine held tightly to the roll bar as they sped down the single lane road. "Oh, my God! A fire? And Tante Lulu is there all alone . . . assuming everyone else has gone home. And my mother and Dirk, of course. Oh, my God!"

When they screeched into the front yard, Clarence, Linc, Jimmy, and, yes, Tante Lulu, were watching the barn being consumed with flames. On the porch stood Fleur and Dirk, their Winnebago having been moved to the back yard. One fire truck was already there wielding its water hoses in hopes of confining the blaze, the barn itself being an obvious loss. Other fire trucks with squealing sirens could be heard approaching from neighboring towns.

"Anyone hurt?" Raoul yelled out to Clarence before he even turned off the ignition.

Clarence shook his head. "Everyone's safe."

"The Thanksgiving guests left soon after nightfall," Linc elaborated. "The old lady's the one who first discovered the fire . . . 'bout 2:00 A.M. Said she got up to go to the bathroom and looked out the window. No one knew where you were, so we couldn't call you. Anyways, we got all the stock out. Except for singed hides on some of the horses, they all made it out in time."

Raoul released the breath he hadn't realized he'd been holding. The veterinarian in him would have been especially horrified at all those animals suffering so.

"Arson, I assume?" Raoul was addressing Clarence once again.

Clarence shrugged. "Too soon to tell, but that would be my guess." Clarence had seen a lot in his time, but his hands shook now.

The whole time they talked, Jimmy stared fixedly at the fire. He was probably scared to death. Someone would have to take him aside and talk down his fears, as soon as things calmed down.

Charmaine was hugging Tante Lulu and crying. Tante Lulu chattered away excitedly, explaining what had happened and when. While she certainly wouldn't wish a fire on him, the old lady must certainly be revved up by all the commotion in their lives, compared to her normally mundane life. At least, there had been commotion ever since Charmaine had arrived. And, actually, chaos seemed to follow Tante Lulu, too, from what he'd heard.

The other fire trucks arrived and began immediately to set to work. One of the men asked Raoul where there was a water source so they could connect their hoses, and he showed them both the well and the bayou stream.

On the way back, he noticed something odd. Dirk had pulled Charmaine aside and was yelling at her, nose to nose. "Where the hell did you go?" Fleur was over talking to one of the firemen, who appeared impressed with her questions . . . or perhaps it was her attire. A red negligee through which her black bra and thong panties were visible.

"What business is it of yours where I go, you overblown pipsqueak?" Charmaine yelled back at Dirk.

"I thought you were just playing a prank on that husband of yours. With a pistol, for chrissake! I had no idea you two were leaving the ranch. I never would have let you go, otherwise. What a pair of dimwits!"

"I beg your pardon!" Charmaine said, frowning with confusion.

Had the body builder been ingesting too many steroids or something? Because he sure was acting strange. How dare he take that tone with his wife. *How dare he?* "No, *I* beg your pardon," Raoul said, shoving Charmaine to the side and belting the pipsqueak in the face, knocking him to the ground.

Immediately the jerk's nose started to bleed. Pulling a

handkerchief out of his pocket, he pressed it to his nose and stared up at him, shaking his head. "You are going to regret that in a minute, buddy."

"I don't think so. No one talks to my wife like that."

"Do you really think this is the time for fighting?" Charmaine asked. "And by the way, Raoul, I can fight my own battles."

He and Dirk both ignored her.

Dirk got to his feet, warily keeping his distance from him. "Come over to the side of the house with me. I have something to show you."

"What? Is this some kind of bodybuilder trick?"

But Dirk the Jerk had already walked away from him and stood waiting over by St. Jude. They were about the same size. He dabbed at his still bleeding nose, then tugged a wallet out of the back pocket of his running shorts—that's all he wore, presumably having been called from bed in the middle of the night.

He shoved the open wallet in Raoul's face before he had a chance to sock him again.

"FBI?" Raoul exclaimed with shock. "You're with the FBI?"

"Shhh. I'm working undercover. We've about nailed a certain sector of the Dixie Mafia, and Charmaine's case might just be the nail in the coffin, so to speak."

"Whose coffin?" he wanted to know, beginning to suspect that Charmaine was in as much risk of physical danger as she'd originally thought. And the FBI was using her.

"I was sent here to watch over your wife till things come together."

"Does her mother know about this?"

"Yep. Fleur's been really cooperative. She's concerned

about her daughter's safety. Wanted to do whatever she could to help."

"Cooperative, huh? Isn't it a little bit unethical for an FBI agent to get involved sexually while on a case?"

"Huh?"

"Fleur. Remember her. Your girlfriend. Oh, don't deny it. You two make so much noise shaking that tin bus that the cows are getting horny."

"Get real! Fleur is old enough to be my mother. We were doing calisthenics."

Raoul's jaw dropped open with surprise. "So, she really isn't doing a nude pictorial?"

"Oh, she's doing it, all right. And she really is worried about cellulite."

Despite the grimness of the situation surrounding them, they smiled at each other.

"Hey, sorry for punching you," Raoul said, extending a hand for a shake.

"No problem. I would have done the same for my wife," Dirk said, "except that she holds a black belt in karate, is a captain in the Army, and could defend herself."

So could Charmaine, and she doesn't know karate from Tae-bo. "I assume you don't want anyone to know your real identity," Raoul said as they walked back toward Charmaine, who was talking to Jimmy, a reassuring hand on his shoulder. He saw Tante Lulu and Fleur heading into the house. He would bet his boots that a barrel of coffee, turkey sandwiches, and leftover pie would soon be made available to the firemen.

Jimmy had just walked away and they were almost back to Charmaine when Raoul heard an odd noise.

"Duck!" Dirk screamed.

Raoul made a flying leap for Charmaine, thus taking the bullet in his left shoulder. For several moments, he just lay there, crushing her to the ground, while shouts and running feet surrounded them as others rushed to find out who had fired the shot. Tears filled his eyes, not because of the pain, but because he could have lost Charmaine in that moment of carelessness.

There was no doubt in his mind that the bullet had been intended for Charmaine, possibly because the FBI had gotten involved, though she didn't even have a clue about that. The barn had been a warning to him, but the bullet had been more than a warning for Charmaine. Someone had tried to kill her.

It wouldn't happen again.

"Get off me. I can't breathe," she said, shoving at his chest. "Has everyone lost their minds?" When she saw the blood seeping through his shirt—the bullet must have come clean through his shoulder, back to front—she changed her tune. "You've been shot," she wailed. "I've got to hurry and call an ambulance."

He had to grab her with the hand on his good side. "I don't need an ambulance, but we need to get you inside, away from the sniper." With that, they both ran for the house.

The Triple L was no longer a safe haven for Charmaine, Raoul soon realized. He would have to get her out of there immediately.

But how did anyone get Charmaine to do something, unless she wanted to? Now that they'd rediscovered their love for each other, he knew without a doubt that his wife would dig in her heels if she thought he was in the least danger.

Even as they hugged once they entered the living

room, to reassure themselves of each other's safety . . . even as Tante Lulu morphed into healer mode and bandaged his bullet wound, with the help of some folk antibiotic, which he prayed God wasn't made with cow shit . . . even as Charmaine fussed over him like a mother hen, Raoul was making plans.

Charmaine would be leaving the Triple L within the hour, and possibly leaving his life forever. It was the only way.

Heartaches by the dozen . . .

"I won't go," Charmaine said forcefully. She couldn't believe that Raoul actually thought she would, after their night of lovemaking . . . just because there was trouble at the Triple L.

"Yes, you will," Raoul said, just as forcefully. "Dirk and Fleur have already loaded up the bus. Tante Lulu is packing for herself *and* you since you won't help her. The fire chief and the sheriff are outside waiting to talk with me. It's eight o'clock, way past time I got out to pasture and helped Clarence and Linc with the cattle. Thank the stars that Jimmy's uncle came to take him away from this mess for the time being. Now, do as you're told . . . just this once."

"Why should I?"

"Because I asked?"

"Not good enough. Come on, Raoul, I'm made of tough stuff."

His face went steely and unbending. His hair was tousled. Soot marked parts of his face and arms and most of his clothing. He looked like he'd been through the wringer, which he pretty much had been. No way would she abandon him now.

"Charmaine, I have enough on my plate now without worrying about you. I want you to leave."

"I can help."

Off to the side, she saw Tante Lulu come out of one of the bedrooms, lugging a big suitcase. Her worried eyes connected with Raoul's, and they nodded at each other in the oddest way. As she passed by them on the way out, the old lady patted Raoul on the shoulder and murmured something that sounded like, "Do what ya has to, boy."

"Charmaine, honey, I don't want to hurt you."

That got her attention, his words and the doleful expression on his face. She sensed what was coming. *Don't say it, Raoul. Just don't.*

"It's over." He reached out for her, but she slapped his arms away. He didn't try again.

How many times do I have to get burned before I finally avoid the fire? When will I ever learn? "How can it be over? It just began . . . last night." She hated the fact that her voice cracked on those last words.

"It was a fling. You knew that—"

It wasn't a fling. It wasn't. "No. No, I didn't know that."

"Please don't make this hard."

"What? I should make it easy for you to be a bastard?"

He winced, but it didn't alter his next words. "If we hadn't had the fire and the shooting here last night, you and I probably would have had a good ol' time for several more days . . . or weeks. But all this crap changes everything."

"How does it change everything?" *My God! Have I no pride at all?*

"I don't have time for a fling right now. So it's over. Forgive me, babe, but it's over, and I want you to leave."

"You said you loved me."

He said nothing. *Nothing!*

"I don't understand."

"I don't want you, Charmaine. Go away. Can I be any clearer than that?"

She felt as if a vise were clamped around her heart. Tightening, tightening, tightening. She stared at him with disbelief. "Don't do this, Raoul. Because if you do, I will never forgive you. Some words can never be taken back. Never."

He inhaled and exhaled, visibly shaken. But then, he said, "So be it."

Charmaine turned away from him and walked stiffly toward the waiting motor home, tears streaming down her face. She'd always thought that a broken heart was an expression, not a real physical malady. She knew different now.

If only she had turned around, she would have seen that she wasn't the only one with tears . . . or a broken heart.

But she didn't turn around.

Tears on his pillow . . .

For two weeks, Raoul operated like a zombie.

Christmas would be here soon, and he couldn't have been more crotchety than Scrooge himself. He really was turning into his father, bless his bitter soul.

He met with fire inspectors, police, his increasingly sadistic parole officer, the FBI and Jimmy's dad. If all went as planned that week, he would soon have his conviction reversed, much to Devereaux's chagrin, he was sure. Gaudet was going to face his own prison time for giving false testimony in his drug trial and accepting bribes; there was no longer any doubt about that. And Blue Heron Oil had their high-priced lawyers scurrying like rats to cover their tails. The oil company hadn't murdered his father, though they probably had contributed to the stress leading to his heart attack, autopsy results showed. The oil company must be responsible, however, for the dead steers and the barn fire and a whole slew of other crimes. Jail time and fines out the kazoo were on someone's horizon.

Much of the progress made in his case had been due to Charmaine's family—Luc and Remy, with their police and P.I. contacts, even Tante Lulu, who kept him up-to-date on everything, except Charmaine. His wife was a taboo subject suddenly for the old lady.

Jimmy's dad had elected to let his son return to the ranch this week and stay till January, now that he knew the whole story. It appeared as if the danger was about over.

Raoul had followed up on a bit of advice Charmaine had given him one time regarding Jimmy. Instead of having the boy spend his half days engaged in physical labor on the ranch, he had put him to work at the computer, logging in the cattle data. The kid was amazing. A real genius with numbers.

Right now, the gang was coming in for supper.

As all four of them sat down at the kitchen table, Jimmy moaned. "SpaghettiOs and hot dogs? Again!"

"Just eat it," Raoul said.

"Ya caint have meat loaf and mashed potatoes and

gravy every day," Clarence said with seeming innocence. The old faker! He knew full well that there had been no home-cooked meals at the ranch since Charmaine had left.

I guess I'm not the only one missing Charmaine.

They all dug in to the not-so-gourmet meal. Hungry men would eat just about anything. If Jimmy weren't here, they'd probably be having it with beer.

"I saw you got a letter today from that publisher," Raoul said to Linc. "Good news?"

"Pretty good," Linc answered. "They want to see a full proposal. That means an outline and a couple chapters. But they are definitely interested."

"Way to go!" Clarence said, clapping Linc on the shoulder.

"Does that mean you'll be leaving the ranch?" Jimmy asked Linc, obviously concerned about losing a pal . . . although he himself would be going back home next month, with the promise that he could return next summer.

"Naw, you can't get rid of me that easy," Linc said, ruffling the boy's hair, which was overlong now that Charmaine wasn't there to trim it. *Why does everything keep coming back to Charmaine?* "I can write in the evenings. I've never been much for TV anyhow."

After dinner, Raoul asked Jimmy to come into the office with him. He sat down before the computer, which was already booted up, and motioned for Jimmy to sit beside him.

Jimmy stared at him quizzically. They'd already completed the ranch business on the computer this morning.

"I want you to help me with something on the

Internet," he announced. "How do I do a search on a particular subject?"

"Go to Google or Yahoo." He leaned in front of him and typed in a web address. When they were there—wherever that was—Jimmy asked, "What subject do you want to research?"

Raoul sighed loudly, then said, "Dude ranches."

Hideout Hell . . .

"I am so angry I could wring your neck," Charmaine said, fisting her hands tightly to her sides.

"Well, at least you're not crying. Geesh, I never saw anyone cry as much as you." This not-so-wise pronouncement came from Dirk the Jerk who was lazing about in a hammock at the RV park where they'd been hiding out for more than two weeks. And talk about annoying! The pest stuck to her like a shadow everywhere she went, which was never far. And her mother was just as bad. Fluttering around her like a mama bird with sudden maternal instincts. "Betcha your tear ducts have finally dried up from overuse. Betcha you could bottle those tears and sell 'em to some fancy cosmetics company. Betcha you could get a job on one of the soaps where turning on the tears at will is considered a great talent."

Betcha you have a death wish. She made a low, growling sound in her throat.

Which must have alerted the dumb dude that he was in potential trouble. He wiped the smirk from his unshaven face. He'd stopped shaving a week ago, probably to fit in with the other lowlifes at this lowlife RV camp who sat around all day in folding lawn chairs, drinking beer and belching. It was a perfect hiding spot. The only danger to Charmaine here was flying beer caps. "Okay, what's the gripe this time?"

"Where's the car?"

"What car?"

She made the low, growling sound again. "That rusted-out rattletrap that is usually attached to the rusted-out Winnebago."

He smiled at her description, which was not a good thing to do, considering her mood.

"Your mother drove it to Houston."

Is that why she asked me to do her hair and makeup? "Why?"

"For the photo shoot."

Yep! "And Tante Lulu?" Charmaine suddenly realized that the old lady was missing, too.

"Fleur is dropping her off along the way. Your aunt has some patient with cataracts that needs her help."

Wait a minute. I know I just woke up, but my brain isn't so fuzzy that I don't realize something strange is going on here. "I thought it was too dangerous for us to leave this godforsaken place."

"It was."

"*Was?* Your neck is looking more and more tempting."

"Luc phoned this morning to say that we can get out of hiding after the court papers are filed today."

"Phone? What phone? I didn't know we had a phone."

"Remy is on his way to pick you up"—he glanced down at his wrist watch—"in about a half hour."

"And y'all just let me sleep through these events in that steambath on wheels? And my mother and Tante Lulu left without telling me all this?"

He shrugged. "Your aunt said you needed to rest . . . after all that crying."

Like my aunt is the expert on what is good for me! "And whose idea was it to leave you behind with me?"

"Mine." He beamed at her. As if she ever in a million years would relish his company! "And, by the way, you might want to be nicer to me . . . once you find out who I *really* am."

Like I care! She narrowed her eyes at the obnoxious oaf.

He continued to lie, all relaxed and gloating, on the hammock, while he pulled a wallet out of the back pocket of his jeans. Flipping it open, he handed it to her.

She couldn't believe what she read. "FBI? You?"

He pretended offense by clapping a hand over his wounded heart. "Why is that so surprising?"

"Because you are so annoying."

"What? FBI agents can't be annoying?"

I am not in the mood for jokes. "You are sleeping with a woman old enough to be your mother."

"I am not sleeping with your mother. She's my cover."

Cover? Cover? "Well, cover that," she said, flipping over the edge of the hammock, thus tumbling him to the ground. He just laughed as he got to his feet and recovered his wallet.

"God, my wife would love you."

"You've got a wife, and you're boinking my mother? Forget about annoying. You're despicable." *Men! God must have created them to torture women.*

"I told you, your mother and I are not involved . . . that way."

"So, let me get this straight. You and my mother are in cahoots . . . for what reason?"

"To protect you till the FBI arrests some major players in the Dixie Mafia."

"Would that include Bobby Doucet?"

"It would. He was taken into custody this morning. Charged with loan sharking, attempted murder, and a half dozen other crimes."

Nice for someone to include me in the loop. "Does that mean I won't have to pay him any more money?"

"Sounds that way."

She had to smile at that. "You're still an annoying pip-squeak."

"I love it when you sweet-talk me."

"What is your wife . . . a masochist?"

He grinned. "Sometimes."

She thought of something else. "How many people know you're with the FBI?"

"Only a few."

Don't ask, Charmaine. You don't really want to know. "Would one of them be Raoul?"

His face flushed, but he didn't answer.

"Tante Lulu? Luc? Remy?"

His face turned redder, but still no answer.

She shook her head sadly at the circumstance she found herself in. Everyone she knew and loved had kept her out of the loop. Why? Could it be because they considered her too dumb to handle the situation? Too untrustworthy? Too insignificant? "I still want to wring your neck, but you'll have to stand in line. A few other people are going to come first."

The implications of what Dirk had just told her spun in Charmaine's head. She could barely comprehend it all. So many questions remained unanswered.

Most important, why had Raoul sent her away? Had

there been another reason? Had she been tricked by him, just as she had by everyone else around her?

Being blue on Bayou Black . . .

Finally, finally, finally. Charmaine had her life back.

She was again ensconced in her home on Bayou Black.

But it didn't feel like home anymore.

She was free to go into her shops and resume work.

But she couldn't drag herself out of bed.

She was blessedly alone for the first time in a month.

And the quiet was driving her bonkers.

It had been two days since Remy picked her up in his helicopter and brought her back here. The first thing she'd done was disconnect her phone and unplug the answering machine. She'd ordered Remy to relay a message to all her meddling relatives: "Leave Charmaine alone."

Which they had done.

Darn it!

Charmaine had thought she needed time to sort out all the confusing questions in her mind. But all she had thought about was Raoul, which made her more confused than ever.

So now she did the one thing she never thought she would. She reconnected her phone and called Tante Lulu.

The phone picked up on the first ring. "Hallo!"

"Tante Lulu, it's Charmaine."

"It's 'bout time you called, girlie. I bin worried 'bout you, but Remy made me swear an oath not to bother you till you wuz ready. I 'bout peed my pants waitin'."

Charmaine took a deep breath, then asked, "What's new?"

Tante Lulu chuckled with glee. "I'll be right over. I got gumbo and Lost Bread right out of the oven. And a new St. Jude statue fer you . . . a teeny tiny one that can fit in yer purse."

In some cultures, chicken soup was the solution to all problems. In Tante Lulu's world, it was gumbo. And St. Jude.

Within an hour, Tante Lulu arrived. She must have been gardening when Charmaine had called because she was wearing bib overalls and rubber shoes. On her head was a big straw hat over black-as-coal hair. *Lordy, Lordy! I wonder who dyed her hair. The shoe repair guy? It looks like bootblack.*

The first thing Charmaine did was sit down on the front steps with the old lady and cry her heart out. Again!

"Now, now, everythin's gonna be all right." She patted Charmaine's back like she was a little girl. How many times had Charmaine done this over the years? Tante Lulu was more like a mother to her than her own mother, though Charmaine had been taken aback by the news that her mother had come to the ranch with the FBI guy to protect her. "Have a good cry, then pull yerself t'gether. Yer a strong woman. Time ya picked yerself up and stopped wallowin'."

Well, no pity from that quarter. And, really, Charmaine did not want pity.

"Ya go take yerself a nice, hot bubble bath while I fix us up some lunch. Take a glass of wine in with ya. I brought some of my dandelion wine from last year's batch."

A short time later, a much-refreshed Charmaine sat down at the kitchen table with Tante Lulu. Crawfish gumbo steamed in the bowl in front of her with a hunk of fresh bread to one side and another glass of dandelion wine to the other. To her surprise, Charmaine found that her appetite had returned, and she consumed everything that had been placed before her.

"Did ya see this?" her aunt asked, shoving yesterday's edition of the Houma newspaper in front of her. The headline read, "Local Mafia Thugs Nabbed," while the photo showed Bobby Doucet and some of his cronies being led off to jail in handcuffs. FBI agent Dirkson Denney was quoted profusely in the article and attributed with a prime role in bringing the bad guys to justice. Charmaine's name was not mentioned, but Remy had told her that she might be asked to testify when it came to trial. She'd told him she would do so gladly.

"How'd you get your car back?" Charmaine had noticed Tante Lulu driving up in the infamous T-bird.

"Clarence drove it to my house last week and left it there while we was in hiding. That was great fun, wasn't it? All of us crammed in that Whinny-bago?"

Oh, yeah. Great fun!

Silence hung in the air between them then as Charmaine pondered whether to ask the next question or not. She had to, of course. "How is he?"

"Who?"

"Pfff! You know who."

Tante Lulu patted her hand. "He's fine."

"And that's all you're going to say?"

"The lawyers from Blue Heron Oil are scurryin' aroun' like rats, tryin' to avoid jail time and big fines, but they pretty much admitted intimidating Charlie Lanier before his death, killin' those steers, and settin' the fire."

"What a bunch of scuzzbags!"

"Speaking of scuzzbags, yer father, ever the one fer good timing, went out to the ranch last week and tried again ta get Rusty ta sell. Dint even bat an eyelash at the burned-down barn."

"And?"

"And Rusty tol' him to go ta hell."

Charmaine smiled. Even when she swore, Tante Lulu was adorable.

"That cop that got Rusty busted fer sellin' drugs has been busted himself now. When the dust settles down, I 'spect there'll be other cops what was on the take from Blue Heron. But the most important thing is Rusty got his conviction reversed. Went to court and everythin' yesterday to get it all settled."

And he didn't feel the need to tell me.

But my phone was off the hook.

That wouldn't have stopped me.

"So now he can be a veterinarian again, I suppose." Charmaine imagined that would make him happiest of all. Finally, he would get to do the work he loved most. Maybe he would even leave the ranch to Clarence's management while he went off to Lake Charles to set up a practice with the good Dr. Amelie.

"I doan know 'bout that. He's bin callin' Luc all the time, askin' 'bout you. Then he started callin' me yesterday after I got back. He's worried 'bout you, honey."

"Who?"

"Rusty, thass who!"

"Puh-leeze! He's just feeling guilty over the way he

treated me." *He screwed me in bed, then he screwed me again by kicking me out of his life.*

"Prob'ly. He asked me to ask you to call him . . . when yer ready."

"Is he nuts? What would ever make him think that I would contact him? Bad enough that I begged him not to send me away! Now he expects me to crawl on my knees and swallow my pride again? No way!"

"I doan think he meant it that way."

"I think he meant it exactly that way. He probably wants me to give him back that envelope you packed for me with twenty five thousand dollars in bonds. Now that he's had a chance to think about it, he probably thinks he deserves all of it. The louse!"

"Where you goin'?"

Charmaine had hopped up from the table and probably had a maniacal gleam in her eyes. "You were right. I've been wallowing too long. Time for me to get on with my life. I'm going to my shops to check up on things. Then I'm going shopping."

"Oh, thass a good idea. Shoppin' always gets me out of the blue slumps. Buy yerself a pair of shoes. That'll make ya feel good. Red ones. With high heels."

"I forgot. I sold my car. Can I drop you off and borrow your car till tomorrow? I need to buy myself a new car."

As they walked out the door a short time later, Tante Lulu asked her, "What kind of car you gonna get? Another BMW?"

"Nope. A Corvette."

Tante Lulu smiled and gave her a high five. "Red, I hope. Ta match yer new shoes."

"For sure. This is a new beginning for me."

"Uh-oh, the last time you had a new beginning, you

became a born-again virgin. And look how that turned out."

"This is a different kind of new beginning. I'm gonna get me a Corvette, then I'm gonna find me a new man."

Charmaine wasn't sure if it was Tante Lulu or the statue in her purse that groaned then.

Chapter 18

Everybody is an Ann Landers . . .

"If you want to know what I think, Rusty—" Clarence started to say.

"I don't. Just sit down and eat your supper." *I am sick, sick, sick of everyone telling me what to do to get Charmaine back. If she wanted me, she'd fight to get me back. If she loved me, like she said, she'd forgive me. Shouldn't she figure out by now why I behaved like a horse's ass? If I am as hopeless as everyone says I am, St. Jude would be here with a herd of saints fighting on my behalf.*

Even to himself, that line of thinking sounded lame.

And a disgusted St. Jude said in his head, *I'm here, I'm here already.*

"Grilled cheese and tomato soup!" Jimmy grimaced with distaste.

"Shut your mouth, boy," Linc told him. "At least it's not SpaghettiOs again."

"I wish we had a Domino's nearby," Clarence said wistfully.

"Well, we don't. So there." Raoul sat down and ate with as much enthusiasm as he could garner for such fare.

They had all been spoiled in one week by both Charmaine and Tante Lulu's cooking.

"Anyhow, we gotta find a way to get Charmaine back," Clarence continued.

"*We* don't gotta do anything," Raoul grumbled.

"Well, if you're sittin' here waitin' fer stuff to happen, maybe *we* should take over," Clarence said huffily. "Mebbe I should pay her a visit in that beauty spa of hers."

"Don't you dare."

"Hey, I can be subtle when I wants to be. I'll jist make an appointment fer a massage."

"That's subtle, all right."

"They give massages there?" Linc asked with great interest.

"I could offer to help her with her business computers. She tol' me one time that she had a problem with Excel." That was Jimmy's solution to Raoul's lovelorn dilemma.

"None of you are going to visit Charmaine on my behalf."

"Nothin' dumber than a man who won't accept a helping hand," Clarence pronounced, eating up his grilled cheese and setting aside the soup, which Raoul had scorched . . . slightly.

"If y'all must know, I tried to call Charmaine yesterday, and she hung up on me," he admitted.

"Well, I would have hung up on you, too." Linc gave him a look that pretty much put him in the category of dimwitted losers. "What's it been? Two weeks, and this is the first you've called?"

"It's been two weeks and four days. Not that I'm keeping count. And I did call two days before that, but she wasn't in. I left a message on her answering machine asking her to call me back. Which she didn't."

"Surprise, surprise," Linc muttered.

"Bowlegged, boy. I keep tellin' ya, thass the trick," Clarence said.

"How the hell am I going to do that when she won't let me near her with a ten-foot pole?"

"You got a ten-foot pole?" Linc asked.

"Very funny!"

"I don't get it," Jimmy chimed in.

"Good!" they all said.

Just then, the phone rang. *Maybe it's Charmaine. Please, God.* When Raoul picked it up, he discovered it was Luc. *Thanks a lot, God.*

You're welcome.

"Huh?"

"Are you talkin' to us or the guy on the phone?" Clarence wanted to know.

"Just God."

"I think he's goin' off the deep end," Linc remarked to Clarence.

For sure.

"Hey, buddy, how's it going?" Luc asked on the phone.

"Just super."

"That bad, huh?" Luc was laughing. "I got the information you wanted on filing a civil suit against the police department and Blue Heron Oil. I'll be ready to file by Monday."

"Okay." He hesitated, then asked, "How is she?"

"Bleepin' effervescent on the outside, and miserable inside."

Raoul had no idea what an effervescent outside would be like on Charmaine, but he was kind of glad she was sharing his misery inside. *Pitiful, pitiful, pitiful.*

"She bought herself a red Corvette, red high heels and a mini-dress that will make your tongue hang out," Luc told him, way too gleefully.

"Is that supposed to make me feel good?"

"No, that's just leading up to the bad news."

I don't know if I can take any more bad news. Oh, please, God, don't let her have gotten married again.

Oh, ye of little faith, God or St. Jude or his plain ol' conscience said in his head.

"Spill it," he said finally to Luc, even as he braced himself for the worst.

And it was.

"Charmaine signed the divorce papers today." There was a long silence before Luc added, "You better get your butt in town."

"Why?" *If she signed the papers, her mind is made up. Too late! Too friggin' late!*

"Tante Lulu has called a family meeting. Tomorrow evening. Seven o'clock. Her house."

"Why?" *I sound like a toddler with that incessant "why" question, or a dumb dolt.*

"To help you get Charmaine back."

"I keep telling everyone I don't need any help—"

But Luc had already hung up on him. Was it a family trait?

Charmaine is going to divorce me.

What am I going to do?

A voice in his head suggested, *Try prayer.*

There's no place like home, except . . .

Charmaine sat on the front porch of her cottage on Bayou Black, waiting for her date to arrive. Jake Theriot, a long-time friend since high school, who also happened to be her stockbroker.

She loved this bayou setting. In fact, it was what had sold her on the house when she'd bought it three years ago.

The cottage itself was nothing special . . . a one-story home in the old Cajun style. The split plank, horizontally arranged logs with their white chinking were quaint, especially with the red shingled hip roof, matching red shutters, and the long *loggia* or porch that ran across the back, facing the water.

But it was the setting that had made her sigh the first time she saw the place. A short stretch of lawn, which required constant cutting in this humid climate, led down to a narrow bayou stream. Every species of wildlife seemed to inhabit her small piece of paradise, including the occasional alligator, which ambled up to the house for some shade. Right now a blue heron couple, male and female, were building a nest in a dead oak tree half-submerged in the water slightly downstream. As they worked diligently, supposedly for an upcoming increase in their family, the birds twined their necks around each other. A heron version of foreplay, she supposed. Or maybe just love, she liked to think.

The bayou was such a microcosm of life itself. Never ending. Except for the house and manicured landscape, this was the way it must have looked a thousand years ago. It would be here in pretty much the same condition a thousand years into the future. Life went on.

And that was precisely what Charmaine had decided about her own life. She had to stop thinking about Raoul and what might have been. Christmas was ten days away, a season she usually loved, but she had barely been able to put up the decorations in her shops, which was a business necessity. She hadn't had the energy to buy a tree for her own home, whereas she usually had one up a month before the holidays. She and Tante Lulu were alike in that regard. So, Remy and Rachel had brought one over yesterday and set it up in the living room for her. Maybe tomorrow she would decorate it.

No, enough wallowing! Enough postponing! She would go inside now and begin trimming the tree till her date arrived. Yesterday she had signed the divorce papers. Today she was going out to dinner with a good friend, who might become more than that.

She'd gotten the miniature lights on the tree and had just opened a box of old ornaments when she heard a car pull up. "Come on in, Jake," she yelled out. "I need some help getting this star on top." The tree was seven feet tall, a short-needled blue spruce, which would touch the ceiling once the star was on. Much too big for this small room, but just right in her opinion.

"Jake who?" she heard behind her.

Charmaine jumped with surprise. It wasn't Jake, of course. It was Raoul.

"What are you doing here?" she snapped. *Nice welcome. Well, he doesn't deserve a welcome . . . nice or otherwise.*

He looked awful. Dark circles under his eyes. A one- or two-day-old beard on his face. His T-shirt and Wranglers were wrinkled, as if he'd taken them out of a clothes basket. He carried a dusty cowboy hat in his hands. His boots were scuffed, as if he'd just come from work on the ranch. And he'd lost weight.

Despite all that, he was bone-melting handsome . . . to her, anyway.

"What are you doing here?" she repeated.

He looked pointedly at her in her new red dress and high heels, at the Christmas tree, then back to her. "Come to help you decorate your tree?"

She could swear she heard the St. Jude statue in the corner say, *Is that the best you can do?*

Dog days of winter . . .

"Here. Let me put that up for you," Raoul said, setting his hat down and taking the star out of Charmaine's hand.

She stood there, hands on hips of a skintight red dress that reached mid-thigh, showcasing mile-long, silk-clad legs and red high heels that gave a guy ideas. Her black hair was piled atop her head in a sort of bun with little curls springing around her face. Her mouth, which was scowling at him right now, was painted a sinful crimson. "I asked you a question, Raoul. What are you doing here?"

He was done putting up the star, which he recalled buying for her their first, and only, Christmas together. It had been a cheesy Wal-Mart purchase—cheap tin covered with glitter—but it still looked good.

He turned to her and said, "Why did you sign the divorce papers?" He could tell his abrupt question surprised her.

"Why wouldn't I?"

"Maybe because you still love me." *I hope.*

"Is that what you think?"

"It's what I know." *I hope.*

"You sent me away. You said you didn't want me."

"I lied."

She shook her head firmly, causing the curls to bounce. "That's bull. I told you then, Rusty, that I would never be able to forgive you if you sent me away then."

"You're back to calling me Rusty again."

"Like that's important now!"

"It's extremely important. Let's pretend the last three weeks haven't happened . . . except for our night at The Lucky Duck, of course. I wouldn't ever want to forget that." He smiled in hopes of softening that scowl on her face.

It didn't work.

"Don't even go there," she said through gritted teeth. "It's over, cowboy. Go home. Let's get on with our lives. I have a date arriving any minute now."

"A date?" he practically bellowed. "You're a married woman, and you're dating? I'm sorry, but dating is not allowed. No way!"

"You went on a date with Amelie."

"That was not a date. That was just friendship."

She inhaled and exhaled several times as if exasperated with him. "We are not really married and haven't been for ten years."

"Oh, yes, we are." He raised his left hand for her to see the gold band on his fourth finger.

"Where did you get that?" At least he'd surprised her again.

"I've always had it." It was one of the matching bands they'd bought in a pawnshop before their wedding. "Bet you still have yours, too."

The blush on her cheeks told him he'd struck home with that lucky guess.

"I'm not signing the divorce papers," he told her.

"Doesn't matter. The divorce will go through without your consent."

Boy, is she stubborn! "But it will take a helluva lot longer."

"And what would that accomplish?"

"Time. Time for me to park my butt on your doorstep and explain why I did what I did. Time to beg for forgiveness. Time to seduce you all over again. Time to build you a dude ranch."

Her head shot up at that last time bomb. "That is a low blow."

"No, it's not. Jimmy and I have been doing research—"

"Jimmy and you?" she interrupted.

"Yeah. What a kid! We've been doing all kinds of research on dude ranches. Jimmy does all the ranch paperwork now, on the computer. You were right about utilizing his talents better."

"You are a piece of work, Lanier. Do you really believe that the key to my heart is a dude ranch?"

How would I know? If I had all the answers, I wouldn't be here, practically on my knees. Give me a clue, baby. What is it you really want? "Everyone misses you at the ranch. Clarence is driving me nuts with all his advice on how to get you back. Says I handled things all wrong with you, which I did. Linc has a publisher interested in his book and wishes he could discuss it with you. Jimmy yearns for your meat loaf and says he's sick of my cooking. Everyone misses you."

"Everyone?" Her arched eyebrows gave him a clue that he'd made an important omission.

"Especially me. I miss you most of all."

"For my cooking?"

He grinned. Maybe he was making some headway. "And those frickin' dryer sheets that smell up my underwear. And all your cosmetic junk that clutters the bathroom. And the way you look in my T-shirt. And your mop dancing. Especially your mop dancing. Will you do that on our wedding night . . . our wedding renewal night . . . except naked . . . and wearing those red high heels? And I miss your snake shooting. And—"

She was back to frowning again. No headway after all. *Note to Raoul: No sense of humor today in Charmaine.*

"I want you to leave," she said, steely-voiced.

"I want to kiss you." Sometimes a guy just needed to get directly to the point.

"Don't you dare." She started backing up.

He followed after her. "I gotta dare. What flavor is that lipstick anyway?"

"Blood . . . because that's what you're going to taste if you put those wicked lips of yours anywhere near mine." Her back hit the wall right next to the tree.

She thinks my lips are wicked. That's a good sign, isn't it? He shrugged and pressed his advantage by putting his hands on either side of her head, thus trapping her. "Sometimes a little blood is worth the battle."

He bent his knees slightly so he was level with her, then pressed his mouth gently against hers.

She moaned. *No question there. That is definitely a good sign.*

He moaned, too . . . because he thought it might be a good thing to do and because, truth to tell, he couldn't help himself.

The scent of the Christmas tree, the scent of her perfume, the sound of the bayou stream outside, the chirping of birds—all these assailed his senses. But mostly, he just lost himself in the feel of her parted lips under his. It might sound hokey, but he felt like swooning at the sheer pleasure of being with Charmaine again. "I love you, *chère*," he murmured against her open mouth.

Instead of being pleased at his words, she jolted upright and shoved him in the chest, hard.

"What?"

"Don't say *that*."

"Why?"

"Because love is forever, and you don't know how to love beyond the moment. Because I don't want to be hurt by you again. Because—"

"Hey, Charmaine," a voice called out from the other side of the screen door.

It must be Charmaine's date. *What bloody great timing!*

Charmaine slipped under his arms and headed for the door. He pressed his forehead against the wall and groaned. When he turned, he saw a dude in khaki pants, loafers without socks and a designer T-shirt. He had a receding hairline, which gave Raoul immature satisfaction, but he supposed the guy would be considered handsome by some women.

What bothered him most of all was that Charmaine was going out with him in that dress. *She should dress like that only for me.*

He pressed his hands into fists and willed himself not to use them on the guy, who was an innocent party in the picture.

"Rusty, I'd like you to meet Jake Theriot."

The dude nodded at him, a questioning tilt to his head.

"And this is Rusty Lanier."

"That's *Raoul* Lanier," he corrected. "Charmaine's husband."

Theriot's chin dropped downward, and Charmaine's chin went up sky-high with indignation.

He picked up his hat and was halfway out the door when he turned. "A bit of advice, Theriot. You can take my wife to dinner or a movie, but if you lay a hand on her I'm gonna have to hurt you."

"I don't believe it," Charmaine called after him. "You are such a dog in the manger."

"Believe it, babe," he called back without turning around. Jamming his hat on his head, he added, "And if I'm a dog, keep in mind one thing. I'm *your* dog."

The man needs a plan . . .

Raoul went to Tante Lulu's house for the family meeting, against his better judgment. But, hell, his judgment hadn't counted for squat lately anyhow.

And, yes, the entire family was there. Tante Lulu, Luc, Sylvie, Remy, Rachel, René, even Tee-John. Of course, like all Cajun events, food played a big part. As they sat around her kitchen table, the old lady served them pork grillades over cheese grits with sides of collard greens, black-eyed peas, and buttered yams. For dessert she made Peach Crisp topped with vanilla ice cream especially for him because of his love of peaches. He suspected she was buttering him up for something. In any case, he planned to take the leftovers home to Clarence and the gang.

"Okay, what's yer plan?" Tante Lulu asked him once the table was cleared.

"Huh? What plan?"

"You don't have a plan?" Luc said.

"How are you going to get Charmaine back if you don't have a plan?" Sylvie asked, ever the methodical scientist.

"He must have some ideas." Rachel turned to him, then shook her head at what must have been a blank look on his face.

"Tsk-tsk!" René contributed.

"Maybe you shoulda taken my crawfish advice," Tee-John said. At Raoul's frown, he said, "Then again, maybe not."

"Not to worry. Luc and Remy were in the same predicament at one point, and we helped 'em out." Tante Lulu beamed at all of them. "With a little help from St. Jude, of course."

Of course.

"Yeah, but we had to do our Cajun version of the Village People for both of them, and I think that shtick is getting old. We need a new routine." It was René who was speaking and tapping his chin pensively.

"Are you sure you've tried everything already to win Charmaine back?" Sylvie wanted to know.

"I'm really out of ideas," he confessed. "I even told Charmaine that I would consider her dude ranch/health spa idea, and she wasn't swayed a bit. I would have even gone for the hunk cowboys. Talk about!"

"Dude ranch?" Luc asked incredulously. "At the Triple L?"

"A health spa?" Sylvie asked with equal incredulity. "At the Triple L?"

"Hunk cowboys?" Rachel giggled, even when Remy nudged her in the ribs. "At the Triple L?"

"I could be a hunk cowboy," Tee-John boasted.

Then all of them looked at each other and smiled. Except Raoul, who hadn't a clue why they were all smiling at him.

"Hunk cowboys riding horses," Tante Lulu announced with glee.

"Riding down the main street of Houma," added Sylvie.

"Luc and Remy could carry a banner that says, 'Triple L Dude Ranch and Health Spa'," added Rachel.

"Maybe René's old band, The Swamp Rats, could be playing their instruments," added Tee-John.

"While we're on horseback?" René's eyebrows were raised in disbelief, but he clearly loved the idea.

"Clarence and Linc and Jimmy will want to be hunk cowboys, too," Tante Lulu pointed out.

"Maybe we could hire a couple of college students, as well," Sylvie said. "And don't forget to include me and Rachel and Tante Lulu."

"For sure," Tante Lulu agreed. "We can be hottie cowgirls."

"I think this is the dumbest idea I've ever heard of," Raoul said. "Absolutely not! Never! No way!"

"Oooh, I have a good idea." Rachel was jumping up and down in her seat. "Rusty could come riding his horse at the end, right into Charmaine's shop. He could scoop her right up into his arms and carry her off!"

"Into the sunset?" Sylvie sighed.

"To have his way with her." Tante Lulu sighed, too.

"Are you people for real?" Raoul said, but not one of them listened to him.

"So when should we do it? How 'bout this Saturday? It'll be the week before Christmas, lots of people out shoppin', but what the hey!"

"No!" Raoul yelled because no one was listening to him.

"You got a better idea? You unwillin' to try everything possible to get Charmaine back? You gonna let yer pride get in the way?" Tante Lulu scrutinized him closely. When he sat silent, she said, "We'll do it then!"

Raoul put his face in his hands, unable to comprehend the amazing spectacle these looney birds were planning, with him as the centerpiece.

A dozen St. Jude statues positioned around Tante Lulu's house started laughing, or at least it seemed so to him. But maybe he was just having a mental breakdown.

When cowboys come to town . . .

Charmaine was in her Houma shop when the hoopla outside first began.

It was the Saturday before Christmas, one of the busiest of the year for her spa and all the businesses in the downtown area. So at first the sound of music didn't draw her attention away from the French twist she was putting in Mrs. Sonnier's hair.

After a few moments, though, the fact began to creep into her subconscious that this was rowdy Cajun music, not the usual Christmas fare. And there were a few Rebel yells tossed in, along with the occasional "Yee-haw!" Not to mention the little boy standing near the front desk with his mother, chattering excitedly, "Horses, Mommy. Lotsa horses, Mommy."

Now, the Rebel yell was not uncommon in the South, nor was the jubilant "Yee-haw!" But horses in downtown Houma? At Christmas time?

The fine hairs stood out on the back of Charmaine's neck in warning.

They wouldn't. Would they?

He wouldn't. Would he?

"Holy catfish! You gotta come see this, Charmaine." It was her receptionist, Alice Mae, motioning her excitedly to the front of the spa.

"What is it?" she asked. *I don't really want to know.*

"Some kind of parade or rodeo or somethin'. But, Lordy, Lordy, I ain't never seen so many good-lookin' cowboys in all my days, and I'm a regular at the Angola prison rodeo."

"This is the craziest Santa Claus parade I've ever seen," Mrs. Sonnier said, coming up beside her.

"Caint be the Santa Claus parade. They held that two weeks ago. Remember. George Thibodeaux was Saint Nick and he was drunk and puked on one of the elves," one of her hairstylists, Edie Beatty, informed them.

"I know what it is. It's them crazy LeDeuxs up to their usual antics." Mrs. Sonnier glanced sheepishly at Charmaine and added, "No offense intended, dearie."

"What usual antics?" Alice Mae wanted to know.

"Haven't you ever seen them do the Cajun Men? They dance and sing and strip. Whoo-ee!" Edie said.

That was when Charmaine started to weep. She sensed what was about to happen, but she was frozen in place.

It had been difficult for her these past weeks: being kicked out by Raoul, his calling her before hanging up— a necessary but hard, hard thing for her to do—his leaving a message on her answering machine, which she hadn't returned but had wanted to, very badly; his actu- ally coming to her house and looking like sin in a pair of cowboy boots. Now this. How much more could one girl handle?

There were dozens of really good looking cowboys riding horses down the middle of the street. They were dressed to the nines in cowboy widow-bait clothes: snap button shirts, string ties, cowboy hats, tight, tight jeans, boots and jangling spurs. They tipped their hats at the men, threw tiny candy canes to the children, blew kisses to the ladies, all accompanied by grins and winks.

And there were a few cowgirls, as well—in particular Tante Lulu, Sylvie and Rachel in rodeo outfits with lots of fringe and tooled-leather boots. Charmaine hadn't even known that they knew how to ride.

Following the ladies, carrying a huge banner between them, were Tee-John and Jimmy. The banner read "The Triple L Dude Ranch and Health Spa."

René and his old band members from The Swamp Rats were playing rowdy Cajun music and singing, even as they rode their horses. Mixed in with the Cajun music was the old country and western hit "Mothers Don't Let Your Babies Grow Up to Love Cowboys." Certainly appropriate.

Other hunk cowboys—and, yes, that was what they were—included Luc, Remy, Clarence and Linc. Unbelievable!

But then Charmaine saw the last cowboy riding up.

It was Raoul, and he'd never looked more devastatingly handsome in his life. Grim-faced and serious, unlike the other participants in this parade, Raoul clearly would rather be anywhere else than there, making a spectacle of himself . . . and her.

That was when Charmaine began to weep profusely.

He rode his horse right up in front of her, with all the

other parade participants crowding the street behind him. Extending a hand to her, he asked, "Are you coming with me willingly, *chère*, or do I have to kidnap you?"

"You're making a fool of yourself."

"I know."

"And you don't mind?"

"No, I just love people pointing at me and giggling. I mind. But I'd do anything for you. Even make a horse's ass of myself."

"Well, I refuse to be an active participant in this . . . this spectacle."

Meanwhile, The Swamp Rats had swung into the hokiest version of "The Cajun Cowboy," a play on that old Glen Campbell hit "Rhinestone Cowboy." Tante Lulu, Sylvie and Rachel had gotten down off their horses and were doing this she-bob kind of dance move to the beat of the music, like idiot back-up Motown singers.

Disgusted, Charmaine spun on her heels and started back into the shop.

To her surprise, Raoul was following after her. *On his horse!*

"If you bring that horse in here, I swear I will shoot you *and* the horse." The horse looked as surprised as Raoul did. On those words, she stomped to the back of the spa, planning to hide herself in a closet or something till everyone left. *Once again, I will be the talk of the town.*

Raoul followed closely on Charmaine's heels. No way was he going to let her get away without hearing him out, not after he'd let that crazy family of hers talk him into their scheme. They would all probably be arrested soon. At the very least, he'd seen the local news media out there with flashing cameras.

He caught up with Charmaine at the back of the shop. He grabbed her by the forearm and saw tears running down her face. *Great! I go to all this trouble . . . to make her cry.*

She squirmed, trying to get away from him.

He demanded, "Stand still. I have a few things to say to you. Then you can go home and bawl your eyes out." *Maybe I'll go home and bawl, too.*

Just then, he noticed a lot of customers and employees in the shop, gawking at them. And Tante Lulu, the old busybody, the instigator of this whole mess, was there, too.

He opened a door, figuring it was a storeroom or something, and proceeded to pull Charmaine in with him for a little private talk. When the heat hit him, he realized it was a sauna. *Oh, well!* He slammed the door after them, then heard a key turn in the lock.

Tante Lulu called out, "I'll be back in an hour, Rusty. Do yer thing."

What "thing"? I don't have a "thing."

Charmaine stared at him as if he'd gone mad, which he had. She tried the door, found it locked from the outside, said a bad word, then glared at him, as if he'd been the one to lock them in. He might have if he'd thought of it first. At least she wasn't crying any more.

"Man, it's hot in here," he said, fanning his face with his hat. He sat down on one of the benches built into the back wall. "When does it cool down?"

She sat at the other end of the bench from him. "It doesn't."

Uh-oh! "Why do people come in here?"

"To cleanse their pores."

"By sweating like pigs? You're kidding."

"And to relax the muscles after a workout."

"I can think of other ways to relax my muscles . . . and yours."

He saw a small smile twitching the edges of her mouth, which he hoped was an indication of her softening toward him. Either that or she was laughing at him.

Charmaine wore a white T-shirt with the logo "Shear Pleasure" tucked into a short, stretchy black skirt that came barely to her knees. Sheer stockings covered her long legs, which ended in the same pair of red high heels she'd had on the other night. *Why would a sane person wear high heels to work?* Red lipstick and nail polish matched her shoes, and her hair was big and curly in her usual bed-mussed style.

She looked hot, hot, hot, and he didn't mean that temperature-wise. But she was staring at him, arms folded over her pretty ol' breasts, like he was a piece of cold meat.

Where to start? "Charmaine, I'm sorry. I didn't mean what I said."

"Which time would that be? Ten years ago when you called me a bimbo? Or three weeks ago when you told me I meant no more to you than a good lay . . . though you, of course, called it a short-term fling. Same thing."

If ever I need help, St. Jude, it's now. Help me choose the right words.

You're on your own, buddy.

He inhaled and exhaled, then began. "First of all, I've taken back that bimbo statement every way I can. I'm not going to apologize for it anymore. And, frankly, I kind of like the bimbo attitude you flaunt at everyone." He put up a halting hand. "Don't get all riled up. Let me finish.

'Bimbo' is just a word. I accept that some people consider it an insult, but dammit, you don't. Admit it. You make it your own word and toss it back in the face of anyone who dares to disagree. So, while I promise never to use the word in anger to you again, you've got to agree not to keep rubbing it in with me."

She must have been impressed with his spiel because she nodded after a while. "You been practicing this speech, cowboy?"

Only night and day. "No. It just spewed out of my mouth."

"You done good."

So far, so good. "It is hot in here," he said then, tossing his hat to the floor and pulling his black T-shirt over his head.

"What are you doing?" she asked, panic in her voice.

Why panic? He glanced over and saw that she was staring at his bare upper body. With interest. And it had thrown her off guard. He grinned inwardly with satisfaction and willed himself not to gloat. He toed off his boots and tossed his socks aside. "I didn't know that toes sweated. Man oh man, it's hot in here." He gave her what he hoped was an innocent look and suggested, "Why don't you take off some of your clothes? You're sweating, too."

"Women don't sweat. We glow."

Sweat, glow . . . take off the damn clothes, sweetheart. But what he said was, "You must know why I told you to leave the ranch."

"I know why you think you did it. To protect me. But I'm not buying it . . . and if you dare to pull that zipper on your fly down any farther, I'm not talking to you anymore. It will be a quiet hour in here."

Like I would stop now! Like I am on a roll. Or a roller coaster. Big difference! "Why aren't you buying it?" Meanwhile, he continued to undo his jeans and shimmy them off, kicking them aside. He still wore his briefs, which were sopping wet in the heat . . . and, he hoped, kinda transparent. He saw her look *there* once, quickly, then turn away with a flushed face. Charmaine had always liked his body. He hoped she still did.

"Because there are a hundred other ways you could have gotten me off the ranch. You could have tied me up and tossed me in the Winnebago. You could have told me that you needed me to take Tante Lulu to safety. You could have told me the truth."

I could toss you over my lap right now and have wild sex with you. "I didn't think of those things. I was in a panic, babe. Someone had just shot at you. I realized that in that instant of my carelessness, you could have been dead. I should have been protecting you, and I failed. And that shook me up." His voice cracked with emotion at the end.

Her face softened somewhat, then hardened up again. "You might very well think that was your motive, but I believe that in a panic situation like that, true feelings come out. I don't doubt that you care about me, in your own way, and that you were worried about me, but bottom line, you did not want forever. You wanted a fling. Don't interrupt me," she said when he was about to disagree with just about everything she said. "I don't blame you for the fling thing. I'd already decided to have a fling myself when I pulled that pistol on you. In the end, though, I realized that I deserve better than that."

"Yes, you do, Charmaine, and that's what I'm offering you."

He could tell that she didn't want to ask, but she did. "What do you mean?"

"I love you. I want to be with you. Forever."

She said nothing, just stared at him.

He'd stated his case. There was nothing more to be said. He wasn't going to beg . . . well, he would beg if he thought it would work, but he was pretty sure Charmaine wouldn't like begging.

Her silence spoke volumes. She wasn't going to forgive him. She didn't love him anymore. Hell, maybe she never had.

It was going to be the longest hour in history if he had to sit here in the quiet after spilling his guts and baring his soul. If women only knew how much control they had in man-woman relationships!

God, it's hot in here. He reached for his T-shirt to dry his hair and face, then rubbed it down his arms and over his chest. Mid-rub, he looked up to see Charmaine staring avidly at his actions. Then she licked her lips.

Okaaaay. She likes to watch me . . . touch myself? He wondered if he could pull off his next move, then shrugged. *What do I have to lose?*

Standing up, he shimmied out of his briefs, not surprised to see that he was already half-erect. He noticed something important then: Charmaine wasn't squealing over his nudity. That had to be a good sign. She might not love him anymore, but she liked some things about him. It was a start.

"Do you know what's a favorite male sexual fantasy?"

That got her attention. "I don't want to know."

She wants to know, all right. "They like to watch—"

"Like that's something new!"

"—their women touch themselves."

She pretended to examine her fingernails with disinterest in what he was saying.

"I was wondering if women like to watch their men? Touch themselves?" *Did I really say that? Where do I come up with this stuff?*

She didn't respond to his question but she'd stopped checking out her fingernails.

He filled a ladle with water from the bucket on the floor, water that was presumably used to toss onto the hot coals and cause steam. Then he leaned back against the blistering hot wood of the sauna, buck naked, with sweat running off his skin in rivulets and dumped the water over his head, to cool himself off, which it did not do. Then he began to touch himself.

I hope I'm not making a fool of myself. Hell, I've already made a fool of myself. How much worse can I look?

He traced his lips with a forefinger and said, "When I touch my mouth, I imagine that you're kissing me. Those soft kisses you give at first, when you're exploring just how far you can push me."

She watched him and licked her own lips.

"I love you, Charmaine." He stretched his arms overhead, then ran his palms over his arms, from wrist to shoulder, from armpit to inner wrist, as if he were washing himself.

Her nipples bloomed under the tight T-shirt.

He touched his own nipples, and, holy hell, it felt good. Real good. "Imagine I'm doing this to you, honey," he said softly. "And imagine how much I love you."

She was imagining. He could tell by her parted lips and the way she arched her back slightly.

He swept his palms over his upper abdomen and his

belly, his hips and buttocks, always getting close to, but not touching his cock, which liked what he was doing. A lot.

She liked it, too. A lot.

Standing, she leaned back against the opposite wall and whimpered, "Why are you torturing me?"

I'm torturing her? Whoo-ee, I'm better than I thought. "Because I want to make love to you, but since you won't let me touch you, it's the next best thing. Take off your clothes, baby, please."

"No," she said, at the same time lifting her T-shirt over her head and shoving her stretchy skirt to the floor, then kicking it aside. She wore only a white lace bra and bikini panties under panty hose, along with the red high heels.

His Longfellow showed his appreciation by growing another inch . . . or five.

"I love you," he said, and began his whole touching routine all over again, starting with his lips. There was no way he could touch his penis at this point without ending the game too soon.

But the game took on a new twist as Charmaine mirrored his actions. Touching her lips. Her arms. Her breasts. Her flat belly.

"Take it all off," he gasped out.

And she did, God bless her.

"Put the shoes back on," he urged.

And God bless her again, she did as he'd asked. She was curved in all the right places, her breasts a visual delight, the dark curls at her groin an almost painful temptation.

"You look like one of those Vargas pictures in *Playboy* magazine," he told her in a testosterone-husky voice. "The perfect pinup."

"Is that a compliment?" she asked shyly.

"For sure." Then, "What do you want me to do now?"

"Touch yourself."

I thought you'd never ask. He did as she'd instructed, watching her the whole time. He would probably embarrass himself any second now, but he didn't care. He was going to do everything she wanted. He was determined not to make any mistakes this time.

"I love you," he said again as sweat rolled off him in waves and he felt as if his eyeballs were going to roll back in his head.

Sweat rolled off her, too. Rather, she glowed to beat the band.

"I know," she whispered.

"What?" he asked, not sure he'd heard right.

"I love you, too. I'll probably regret this five minutes from now, but . . ." She opened her arms to him.

He was across the small space separating them before she could blink. In an even shorter time frame he had her braced against the wall, her legs wrapped around his waist, and himself embedded deep inside her.

He could have wept for the sheer ecstasy of being inside Charmaine. He could not speak, but he did moan a long, "Aaaaaaaah!" As he pounded into her—she would probably have splinters in her backside, but he couldn't slow down for the life of him—he kept repeating, "I love you."

And she kept murmuring, "Shhhh."

Outside the sauna door, the band was playing yet another rendition of "The Cajun Cowboy." They must have moved the frickin' parade inside the beauty spa. Did they bring the horses in, too? He couldn't think about that now.

Wet, slapping sounds resounded in the room from their slick skins meeting and from the moist sounds of their ardent lovemaking. Sweet, sweet raw sex!

As she entered her second orgasm, milking him with mind-blowing ecstasy, he choked out, "Forever. I promise."

"Shhhh," she whispered again. "I love you, too. We'll work it out."

His strokes became shorter and harder.

"Come home with me," he yelled out then as he came into her with hot spurts.

And she did, in fact, come home with him . . . in more ways than one.

Epilogue

The Cajun Cowboy takes a bride . . . again . . .

Raoul and Charmaine Lanier renewed their wedding vows on Christmas Eve at the Triple L Ranch, just as Tante Lulu had planned all along.

The inside and outside of the ranch house were decorated to the gills with more lights than Bourbon Street during Mardi Gras. In fact, a fuse had blown three times so far, throwing them into total darkness. The Christmas tree beside which they'd spoken their vows with the blessing of Father Girard, who'd come up from Our Lady of the Bayou Church, was so big it had taken three men to get it inside. There was enough food cooking back in the kitchen to feed three armies, including meat loaf and a peach wedding cake, of all things.

But Raoul could not care. Charmaine was back in his arms again, and he was never going to let her go.

Clarence acted as Raoul's best man, and he looked so spiffy in his tuxedo with a string tie that a few old ladies in the audience were heard to comment, "What a hunk!" Luc, Remy, Tee-John, and Jimmy were groomsmen or ushers—equally hunkish, in everyone's opinion. Linc sang the lyrics to a song he'd written just for them, "Love

Renewed," accompanied by soulful accordion music provided by René.

Later they played the peach orchard song, which Linc's ancestor, A.B. Lincoln, had sung at another wedding more than 150 years ago. Raoul was heard to say, "I can't wait till you shake my tree, Charmaine." And Charmaine responded, "Wait till you see the peaches I have for you, baby."

They planned to spend their honeymoon at The Lucky Duck motel in the special "Webbing Suite."

Charmaine's maid-of-honor was Tante Lulu, who beamed through the entire event, as if she'd arranged it all. Which she had, of course, with the help of St. Jude, who stood next to the priest, beaming, as well. Her bridesmaids were Sylvie, Rachel and two of the hairdressers from her salon. Luc and Sylvie's three little ones were flower girls, twirling their long dresses through the whole ceremony.

The bride wore red. Yes, red. A thigh-high sheath dress, which hugged her body, with a square neckline and cap sleeves. Demure, by Charmaine's standards. On her feet were Raoul's favorite red high heels.

Before the ceremony, she confided to Raoul, "I'm not wearing anything underneath." To which he was said to smile and reply, "Me neither."

The bride was given away by her mother Fleur who planned to open a stripper school in New Orleans, thanks to the expected publicity from her soon-to-be published nude photo shoot. Charmaine was heard to comment, "Whatever!"

The groom's mother did not attend owing to previous commitments, but she did send her good wishes. Raoul was heard to comment, "Whatever!"

For a combination Christmas/wedding present, Charmaine gave Raoul a German shepherd puppy to replace the one he'd had years ago. Raoul gave her the architectural drawings for the dude ranch/health spa that would open here at the Triple L next fall. They would operate it together, with him running a veterinary clinic on the side. There would be more than enough money for all this with the civil suit settlement they expected to receive from the police department and Blue Heron Oil.

Everyone was at peace and happy at this special time of the year and at this most special event.

Except Tante Lulu.

She nabbed René as he was about to raise a toast to the newlyweds. "Have I given you a hope chest yet, boy?"

Everyone who overheard exclaimed, as one, "Uh-oh!"

Note to the Reader

Dear Reader:

I hope you liked Charmaine's story in *The Cajun Cowboy.* I grew to love her outrageousness in the other books of this LeDeux family series, but I never intended to write a separate novel for her. A heroine with four husbands? Not very sympathetic, I thought . . . originally. But as the books, and her character, developed, I knew she deserved her own story. It was such fun telling this tale of a good-hearted "bimbo" and a sexy-as-sin cowboy. And what's not to like about Raoul Lanier?

As always, I consider the Cajun culture and the southern Louisiana landscape almost like characters themselves. I love the fact that Louisiana is such a diverse state, most noted for its picturesque bayous, but just as beautiful are its prairies. Many people are not even aware that cattle ranches exist in Louisiana, and yet some say it was the birthplace of the Old West.

I try to get things right, but many of you told me that a true Southerner would know that you don't peel okra. Ooops! My apologies. Can you tell I've never eaten okra?

Please check out my Web site for Cajun links to wonderful music, recipes, cowboy clubs, charities, gift shops, and humor. And another contest.

Next up is René's story, which is called *The Red-Hot Cajun.* All I can say is it's an especially hot summer in Terrebonne Parish, Tante Lulu has developed a sudden crush on exercise guru Richard Simmons, René is burned-out from his lobbyist work and hiding out in the bayous where he is building his own log home, and a bunch of wacky environmentalist friends kidnap a celebrity TV reporter and dump her in René's lap. Literally. I promise you this: The LeDeux family is back, and René is the hottest of the bunch.

After that, who knows? Do you think Tee-John will have grown up by then? I already have some ideas about the rogue he will become. How about you?

I enjoy hearing from readers and wish you much good reading in your future, hopefully with a bit of humor tossed in.

Sandra Hill
PO Box 604
State College, PA 16804
Web site: www.sandrahill.net
email: shill733@aol.com

About the Author

Sandra Hill lives in the middle of chaos, surrounded by a husband, four sons, a live-in girlfriend, two grandchildren, a male German Shepherd the size of a horse, and five cats. Each of them is more outrageous than the other. Sometimes three other dogs come to visit. No wonder she has developed a zany sense of humor. And the clutter is never-ending: golf clubs, skis, wrestling gear, baseball bats and gloves, tennis rackets, mountain-climbing ropes, fishing rods, bikes, exercise equipment. . . .

Sandra and her stockbroker husband, Robert, own two cottages on a world-renowned fishing stream (which are supposed to be refuges), two condos in Myrtle Beach (which are too far away to be used), and seven Domino's Pizza stores (don't ask!). One son and his significant other had Sandra's first grandchild at home with an Amish midwife. Another son says he won't marry his longtime girlfriend unless they can have a Star Wars wedding. Another son at twenty-three fashions himself the Donald Trump of central Pennsylvania. A fourth son . . . well, you get the picture.

Robert and Sandra love their sons dearly, but Robert says they are boomerangs: They keep coming back. Sandra says it must be a sign of what good parents they are, that the boys want to be with them.

No wonder Sandra likes to escape to the library in her home, which is luckily soundproof, where she can dwell in the more sane, laugh-out-loud world of her Cajuns. When asked by others where Sandra got her marvelous sense of humor, her husband and sons just gape. They don't think she's funny at all.

Sandra is a *USA Today, New York Times* extended and Waldenbooks best-selling author of seventeen novels and four novellas. All of her books are heavy on humor and sizzle.

Little do Sandra's husband and sons know what she's doing in that library. <grin>

More
Sandra Hill!

❧

Please turn this page

for a preview of

THE RED-HOT CAJUN

available soon

from Warner Books.

Chapter 1

The long hot summer just got hotter . . .

"That Richard Simmons sure is a hottie."

Whaaat? René LeDeux put down the caulking gun he'd been using to chink the logs of his home-in-progress, and stared in astonishment at his great aunt Louise Rivard, who had made that astounding revelation. Tante Lulu, as she was known, lounged in a hammock in the front yard, cool as a Cajun cucumber.

René wore no shirt, only cargo shorts, a tool belt, and work boots, in deference to the scorching heat—the hottest summer in Louisiana history. He swiped the back of an arm across his forehead, as much to gather patience as sweat, before speaking. "Tante Lulu! Richard Simmons is not a hottie. Not by any stretch of anyone's imagination."

"He is in mine. Whoo-ee! When he wears those short-shorts, I just melt."

Now, that was an image he did not need—his seventy-nine-year-old great aunt in hormone overload. Talk about! But it did explain her attire: a pink headband encircling tight white curls, a red tank top with the logo EXERCISE THAT!, purple nylon running shorts, and white athletic shoes with short anklets sporting pink pom-poms on the back. She was a five-foot-zero package of wrinkled skinniness, the last person in the world in need of a workout. That she was a noted *traiteur,* or folk healer, while at the same time a bit batty, was a fact he and his brothers had accepted all their lives.

He adored the old lady. They all did.

He started to walk toward her and cracked his shin against the big wooden box in the middle of the porch. "Ow, ow, ow!" he squealed aloud—screaming much fouler words in his head—and hopped about on one foot.

"I tol' you ya shoulda put yer hope chest inside," Tante Lulu said as she raised her head slightly to see what all his ruckus was about. "Doan want to get rain or bird poop on it or nuthin'."

Actually, inside wasn't much better than outside when it came to René's raised log house. He had the roof and frame up, but no windows. It was all just one big room at this point, aside from the bathroom, which was operational thanks to a rain-filled cistern. A battery-operated generator provided electricity for the fridge and stove. That was it. Except for a card table, two folding chairs, and a bed with mosquito netting, there was no furniture. That's the way he liked it.

Of course, now he had a hope chest to add to his furnishings. And the midget-size plastic St. Jude statue sitting in the front yard, another of Tante Lulu's "gifts." St. Jude was the patron saint of hopeless causes. Tante Lulu was giving him a message with both her gifts.

"Auntie, there is something I need to say to you. My life is in shambles right now. I quit my job. I'm burned out totally. Don't even think of trying to set me up with some woman. I am *not* in the market for a wife."

René was no fool. He knew the purpose of his great aunt's hope chest and statue. Whenever she thought it was time for one of her nephews to bite the bullet, she started in on them. Embroidered pillow cases, bridal quilts, *doilies,* for chrissake. She was a one-woman Delta Force when she got a bee in her matchmaking bonnet.

Right now, he was the bee.

Tante Lulu ignored everything he said and continued on about the exercise guru. "Charmaine is gonna try to get us tickets to go see Richard—I likes to call him Richard, or Dickie—next time he comes to N'awlins."

Dickie? Mon dieu!

"Mebbe I'll even get picked fer one of his TV shows."

That was a hopeless wish if he ever heard one. He hoped. He thought a moment, then said silently, just in case, *St. Jude, you wouldn't! Would you?*

Charmaine was his half-sister and as much a bubblehead as Tante Lulu. The prospect of his great aunt doing jumping jacks on TV was downright scary. But then, Tante Lulu and Charmaine had entered a belly dancing contest not too long ago. So, it was not out of the realm of possibilities.

"Mebbe you could go to his show with us. Mebbe you could meet a girl there. Then I wouldn't have to fix you up."

"Don't you dare try fixing me up."

"And Charmaine's fixin' to get me the latest video of *Sweatin' to the Oldies* fer my birthday in September. You want she should get you one, too?"

"No, I don't want an exercise video. Besides, I thought Charmaine was planning a big birthday bash for your gift."

"Cain't a girl get two gifts? Jeesh!" She eyed him craftily and added, "Actually, I'm hopin' fer three gifts."

At first, he didn't understand. Then he raised both hands in protest. "No, no, no! I am not getting leg-shackled to some woman just to give you a birthday present. How about I take you to the race track again this year for a birthday gift, like I did last year?"

She shook her head. "Nope, this birthday is a biggie. I'm 'spectin' biggie gifts." She gave him another of her pointed looks.

"No!"

"Of course, I might be dead. Then you won't hafta give me anythin', I reckon."

He had to laugh at the sly old bird. She would try anything to get her own way.

"I'm only thirty-six years old. I got plenty of time."

"Thirty-six!" she exclaimed, as if it were an ancient age. "All yer juices is gonna dry up iffen ya wait too long."

"My juices are just fine, thank you very much." *Jeesh! Next, she'll be asking me if I can still get it up.*

"You can still do it, cain't you?"

He refused to answer.

"I want to rock one of yer *bébés* afore I die."

"No. No, no, no!"

"We'll see." Tante Lulu smiled and saluted the St. Jude statue. "Remember, sweetie, when the thunderbolt hits, there ain't no help fer it."

René had been hearing about the thunderbolt ever since he was a little boy and needed to hide out from his alcoholic father. He and his brothers Luc and Remy would hot-tail it for Tante Lulu's welcoming cottage. The thunderbolt pretty much represented love in the old lady's book.

He had news for her. This piece of land was all the love he needed. In truth, it was all the love—meaning trouble—he could handle at the moment. To say his life was in chaos was a world-class understatement.

He'd recently quit his job in Washington as an environmental lobbyist. Burned out after years of hitting his head against the brick wall, which was comprised of the oil industry, developers, and sport fishermen who were destroying the bayou he was so passionate about. For every battle he'd won in his fight to protect the Louisiana coastal wetlands, he'd lost the war.

Before he had become an environmental advocate, he'd been a shrimp fisherman, every type of blue-collar worker imaginable, and a musician (he played a mean accordion). Hell, if he ever finished his doctoral thesis, he could probably be a college professor, as well.

But there was no point to any of it. He was a failure in his most important work: the bayou. The fire in his belly had turned to cold ashes. For sure, the joie de vivre was gone from his life.

So he'd hung tail and come back to southern Louisiana and resumed work on this cabin in one of the most remote regions of Bayou Black. He loved this piece of property, which he'd purchased ten years ago. It included a wide section of the slow-moving stream at a point where it forked off in two directions, separated by a small island that was home to every imaginable bird in the world, including the wonderful stilt-legged egret. The only access to the land was by hydroplane or a three-day grueling pirogue ride from Houma. No Wal-Marts. No super highways. No look-alike housing developments. No wonder he'd been able to buy it for a song. No one else had wanted it. "I think I hear a plane." Tante Lulu interrupted his reverie. "Help me offa this thing. I'm stuck."

He went over and lifted her off the hammock and onto her feet. The top of her head barely reached his chest.

"It mus' be Remy," she said, peering upward.

His brother Remy was a pilot. He'd brought Tante Lulu here earlier that day for a visit, promising to return for her before evening.

But, no, it wasn't Remy, they soon discovered. It was his friends Joe Bob and Madeline Doucet. J.B. and Maddie could best be described as overage hippies. Both of them had long hair hanging down their backs, black with strands of gray. At fifty and childless, they were devoted to each other and the bayou where generations of both their families had lived and "farmed" for shrimp. They were quintessential tree huggers and they couldn't seem to accept that René had dropped out of the fight.

"Lordy-a-mercy! It's those wacky friends of yers," Tante Lulu said as they watched the couple climb out of the rusty old hydroplane and anchor it to the shore by tying ropes around a nearby oak tree.

Tante Lulu calling someone wacky was like the alligator calling the water snake wet. But they *were* eccentric. And not just in their often unpredictable behavior. Like, right now, J.B. wore his old Special Forces camouflage fatigues; the only thing missing was an ammunition belt and rifle. Maddie wore an orange jumpsuit that either had a former life with an airplane mechanic or a prisoner. Probably a prisoner. They had both served time on occasions when their participation in peaceful protests had become not-so-peaceful. J.B. had been a well-decorated soldier, then came home to emerge as a soldier for domestic causes.

"Holy crawfish! Where do those two shop? Goodwill or Army Surplus?" Tante Lulu whispered to him.

But he had no time to comment on that or warn his great aunt to be nice. Not that she would ever deliberately hurt anyone . . . unless she perceived them to be a threat to her family. She did have a tendency to be blunt, though.

"Hey, Joe Bob. Hey, Maddie. Whatchya doin' here?" Tante Lulu asked as they walked toward them.

Yep, blunt-is-us. He groaned inwardly but smiled. "J.B. Maddie. Good to see you again so soon." *Whatchya doin' here?*

They didn't smile back.

Uh-oh! The serious expressions on their faces gave René pause. Something was up.

"What's up?" he asked.

"Now, René, don't be gettin' mad till you've heard us out," Maddie urged.

The hairs on the back of his neck stood up on high alert. "Why would I get mad at you?" The last time he'd lost his temper with them was two years ago when they'd used their shrimp boat as a battering ram against a hundred thousand dollar sport fishing boat out on the Gulf. The sport fishermen's crime: they'd been hauling up near-extinct species of native fish as bycatch, which meant they just tossed them back into the water, dead. It had taken all of his brother Luc's legal expertise to extricate J.B. and Maddie from that mess.

"You got a lot of work done since we were here last week," J.B. remarked, ignoring both his wife's and René's words. The idiot was obviously making polite conversation to cover the fact that he was as nervous as a cat in a room full of rocking chairs.

I wonder why. "Forget the casual bullshit. What's going on?" René insisted.

"Remember how you said one time that what we need out here in the bayou is some celebrity to get behind our cause? Like Dan Rather or Diane Sawyer? TV reporters or somethin' who would spend a week or two here where they could see firsthand how the bayou is bein' destroyed. Put us on the news or make a documentary exposing the corruption." It was Maddie who put forth that fervent reminder. And, man oh man, he hated it when people quoted back to him stuff he didn't recall saying.

"Yeah," he said hesitantly. "So, did you bring Dan and Diane out here? Ha, ha, ha! Like that would ever happen!"

"Well, actually . . ." J.B. began.

René went stiff.

Tante Lulu whooped, "Hot diggity damn!"

It was then that René noticed how J.B. and Maddie kept casting surreptitious glances toward the plane.

"What's this all about? What's in the plane?"

"Jumpin' Jehoshaphat! They musta brought Dan Rather here," his great aunt said, slapping her knee with glee. "Great idea! I allus wanted to meet Dan Rather. Do ya think he'd give me an autograph?"

"It's not Dan Rather," Maddie said, her face flushing in the oddest way. Odd because nothing embarrassed Maddie. Nothing.

This must be really bad. "Spit it out, guys. If it's not Dan Rather"—he couldn't believe he actually said that— "then who is it?"

"Oh, *mon dieu*! It mus' be Diane Sawyer then. I allus

wanted her autograph, too. Betcha she could introduce me to Richard Simmons."

"What you be wantin' with that flake Richard Simmons?" J.B. asked.

Tante Lulu slapped J.B.'s upper arm. "Bite yer tongue, boy. He's a hottie."

"Are you nuts?" Maddie said.

"No more'n you," Tante Lulu shot back.

"Unbelievable!" René said, putting his face in his hands. After counting to ten, he turned on J.B. "Is there a human being on that plane?"

J.B. nodded.

There is! Son of a bitch! I sense a disaster here. A monumental disaster. And I thought I was escaping here to peace and tranquility. "Why is that human being not getting off the plane?" he asked very slowly, hoping desperately that his suspicions were unfounded.

"Because the human being is tied up." J.B. also spoke very slowly.

Tied up? They kidnapped someone and brought that someone here. Holy shit! Holy freakin' shit! I am getting the mother of all headaches. St. Jude, where are you? I could use a little help.

A voice in his head replied, *Not when you use bad language. Tsk, tsk, tsk!*

It was either St. Jude, or he was losing his mind. He was betting on the latter.

"A network TV anchor?" he finally asked, even though he was fairly certain they weren't that crazy. Best to make sure, though. "Did you kidnap a major network TV reporter?"

"Not quite," Maddie said.

Not the answer I want to hear. He addressed Maddie,

slicing her with his best icy glare. "What the hell does 'not quite,' mean?"

"Not from a major network." She glanced at her husband and said, "I told you René would get mad."

Mad doesn't begin to express how I'm feeling. "What the hell does 'not from a major network' mean?"

"She's a court TV reporter. And you don't have to yell."

You haven't heard yelling yet, Maddie girl. "*She?* You kidnapped a female celebrity?" His headache had turned into a sledgehammer, and it was doing the rumba against his brain.

He looked at Tante Lulu, and Tante Lulu looked at him. At the same time they swung around to the dingbat duo and exclaimed, "Valerie Breaux!"

"Yep," the dingbat duo said together.

"You kidnapped Valerie 'Ice' Breaux?" René choked out. "The Trial Television Network anchor? My sister-in-law Rachel's cousin?"

J.B. and Maddie beamed at him as if he'd just congratulated them, not raised a question in horror.

"Why her?" he asked through gritted teeth. Valerie Breaux was such a straight arrow she would probably turn her mother in for tasting the grapes in the supermarket.

J.B. shrugged. "She was available. She's from Louisiana. I heard she had a crush on you at one time."

"You heard wrong. Valerie Breaux can't stand my guts."

"Oops," Maddie said.

"Maybe you could charm her," J.B. advised. "You can be damn charming with the ladies when you wanna be."

"Charm that!" he said, giving J.B. the finger. Luckily, Tante Lulu didn't see him.

"She's the answer to our prayers," Maddie asserted.

"Oh, no! She cain't be the one," Tante Lulu wailed, now that the implications of their conversation sank in. "I won't let that snooty girl be the one. I remember the time she asked me iffen I ever looked in a mirror, jist cause I tol' her she could use a good girdle? She's not even Cajun. She's a Creole. Her blue blood's so blue she gives the sky a bad name. She looks down on us low-down Cajuns. Take her back. I doan want her to be the one fer René. St. Jude, do somethin' quick."

René's jaw dropped open. He wasn't sure which surprised him most: that his friends considered Valerie Breaux the answer to their prayers, the woman who'd called him a "crude Cajun asshole" more than once while they were growing up together in Houma, or that Tante Lulu feared this woman might be his soul mate. As if the Ice Princess would let him touch her with a ten-foot pole, let alone his own lesser-sized pole!

Could life get any worse?

Yep!

J.B. had waded out to his hydroplane and was now carrying the "answer to their prayers" over his shoulder. She was squirming wildly but unable to say anything because, of course, the goofballs had duct-taped her mouth shut. That was at least one felony count, plus who knew how many more for the restraints that bound her wrists behind her back and held her ankles together.

But that wasn't the worst thing of all . . . or best thing of all, depending on one's viewpoint. And René was taking in the view with wide-open eyes right now: Valerie Breaux's bare white behind.

She was going to kill them all for that indignity alone, after she'd filed every legal charge in the world against them.

The TV reporter was wearing what could probably be called a *Sex and the City* version of a power suit, which meant it had a very short skirt. A very short skirt that had ridden up with all her struggles, exposing her thong panties.

And thus the sun shone bright on Valerie Breaux's buttocks.

Very nice buttocks, by the way.

"Is she moonin' us?" Tante Lulu wanted to know.

"I never could figure out why women want to wear those thong thingees," Maddie mused. "Seems to me they'd be mighty uncomfortable, up in your crack and all."

"I like 'em," J.B. said.

Maddie probably would have hit her husband if he hadn't had his hands full of Valerie. Instead, she suggested, "You wear 'em then, honey." Honey was not said as an endearment.

René felt like pulling his hair out, one root at a time, over the irrelevance of this chitchat. Meanwhile, Valerie's tush was waving in the wind.

Then, J.B. turned slightly and René got a good look at Valerie's face. Her shoulder-length, wavy black hair hung loose all over the place, but still he was able to see her midnight blue eyes, which flashed angrily. Against the duct tape, she screamed something that sounded pretty much like, "Flngukkk yuuuaauu!" It probably wasn't a howdy greeting.

Grabbing a knife out of his toolbox, he walked over and lifted her off J.B.'s shoulder. She was unsteady on her high heels, but he managed to stand her against a tree and cut away the restraints. He saved the duct tape for last.

Once the tape was off, the first thing she did was shimmy down her skirt. Then she spun around to face him. "René LeDeux! I should've known you'd be behind these shenanigans."

"Hey, I had nothing to do with this."

"Save it for the judge, bozo."

THE EDITOR'S DIARY

Dear Reader,

Everyone has a few dusty skeletons in their closet. But what happens when your past collides right into your present? Brush off those cobwebs and jump into THE CAJUN COWBOY and MEANT TO BE, our two Warner Forever titles this June.

Romantic Times declared "humor and **Sandra Hill** are a winning team" and they couldn't be more right in her newest book, **THE CAJUN COWBOY**. So bust out your tissues—you'll laugh so hard you'll cry! Louisiana beauty salon owner Charmaine Le Deux isn't having a great day. She's got a loan shark on her tail and she just discovered that Raoul Lanier, the man she thought she divorced years ago, is still her husband! The only good news: they've inherited a cattle ranch together, giving her the perfect place to lie low. But living with this hunk is anything but easy, especially for a born-again virgin who can't stop tingling whenever he enters a room. So between the Dixie Mafia on hot pursuit, her belly-dancing great-aunt, and St. Jude, patron saint of lost causes, will Charmaine resist his charms? Or can this Cajun cowboy sweet-talk his way back into his wife's arms before she unties the knot for good?

Journeying from the hot Louisiana sun and even hotter southern nights to the beauty and peace of Pennsylvania's Laurel Mountains, we present **Edie Claire**. *The Road to Romance* honored her previous book with their *Road* *to Romance Reviewer's Choice Award*, calling it "emotionally gripping, suspenseful, and superb" and her latest, **MEANT TO BE**, is even better. With just a phone call, Meara O'Rourke's life changes. Her birth mother has died, leaving her half of an historic inn. Unfortunately, the inn also belongs to Fletcher Black. Furious that Meara is intruding into his family home and determined to protect the land that means everything to him, Fletcher doesn't want her there. But Meara can't let go of the sadness—and the passion—in his eyes. As lies unravel and stunning new truths come to light, Meara must risk everything to learn about her past and take the most frightening—and exhilarating—step of all: to claim a love that was meant to be.

To find out more about Warner Forever, these June titles, and the authors, visit us at www.warnerforever.com.

With warmest wishes,

Karen Kosztolnyik

Karen Kosztolnyik, Senior Editor

P.S. Independence Day is right around the corner so declare your freedom by indulging in our two reasons to celebrate—fireworks guaranteed: **Pamela Britton** pens a witty Regency tale about an earl who must live for a month without any help to earn his inheritance and the woman who offers him love instead in **SCANDAL**; and **Lori Wilde** delivers the wickedly funny and steamy story of an FBI agent who's hot on the trail of an art thief, and the woman who's following him in **CHARMED AND DANGEROUS**.